D0057380

In the late 1970s, Natalie Meg Evans ran away from art college in the Midlands for a career in London's fringe theatre. She spent five years acting, as well as writing her own plays and sketches before giving it up to work in PR. She now writes full time from her house in rural north Suffolk, where she lives with her husband, dogs and horses.

the Dress Thief

NATALIE MEG EVANS

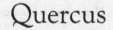

First published in the UK in 2014 by

Quercus
55 Baker Street
7th Floor, South Block
London W1U 8EW

Copyright © 2014 Natalie Meg Evans

The moral right of Natalie Meg Evans to be
identified as the author of this work has been
asserted in accordance with the Copyright,
Designs and Patents Act, 1988.

All rights reserved. No part of this publication
may be reproduced or transmitted in any form
or by any means, electronic or mechanical,
including photocopy, recording, or any
information storage and retrieval system,
without permission in writing from the publisher.

A CIP catalogue record for this book is available
from the British Library

PB ISBN 978 1 84866 588 0
Ebook ISBN 978 1 84866 590 3

This book is a work of fiction. Names, characters,
businesses, organizations, places and events are
either the product of the author's imagination
or are used fictitiously. Any resemblance to
actual persons, living or dead, events or
locales is entirely coincidental.

10 9 8 7 6 5 4 3 2

Printed and bound in Great Britain by Clays Ltd, St Ives plc

Typeset by Ellipsis Digital Limited, Glasgow

For Richard, whose presence has been the bedrock of my life.

Prologue

Alsace, Eastern France, 1903

The double crash that echoed through the timber-framed house killed one man and damned another. The first blow was metal against skull. The second was the crack of the victim's head against the corner of a stove.

Afterwards all was still but for whirling motes of dust and the sputtering of an oil lamp low on fuel. The young man dropped the iron bar he held. He wanted the victim at his feet to move, to make a sound, but Alfred Lutzman's eyes were frozen in their last emotion. The portrait on the easel would never be finished.

He wanted to get out. Why should he pay – perhaps with his life – for the madness of a moment? A muffled cry stopped him at the door. The artist's wife stood, immobile, beneath a skylight blanketed with snow. She seemed unaware of the blood trickling from her left temple, but aware of his desire to leave. She said something in Yiddish, her voice rising. He cut her off in the crisp German that was their common language. 'Frau Lutzman, listen to me. This tragedy –' he glanced at the body and nausea passed through him – 'was a terrible accident.'

She whispered, 'No accident. We must go to the police.'

'Absolutely not.' He spoke harshly, copying his late father's way of dealing with inferiors. 'They'd send us to trial. I wouldn't be afraid, but could you stand up to questioning? D'you know the penalty for murder? The guillotine. Then what would become of your child? So . . . we must think of something else. A story that removes suspicion from us both. I will deny I was here.'

'And throw me to the wolves?'

'We'll say your husband was shut away up here, finishing a painting. Which is true. You were . . . You were in your kitchen cooking dinner, with the door closed. You saw nobody, heard nobody. You will not mention my name, ever.'

Danielle Lutzman stared at him, repeating his words soundlessly. In the winter light, she looked younger than he'd originally thought, lithe under her ragged dress, her glossy black hair escaping from her headscarf. Was there understanding as well as desperation in her eyes? It seemed an age before she nodded. 'I heard nobody, saw nothing.'

'Keep to that, Frau Lutzman, and I will do the rest. Never tell the truth to a living soul. You swear?'

She nodded once and he saw his chance to leave. The smell of death and lamp oil was growing unbearable. But it seemed he'd underestimated his own shock – he could not take the first step. Then, from below, came the clash of a door. Their eyes locked in fear.

A voice piped – 'Mama! I'm home.'

Danielle Lutzman gasped, 'It's Mathilda. It's my daughter. Don't let her come up! She must not see – I beg you, stop her!'

He could not move.

'Mama, Papa, where are you?' Wooden soles clumped upstairs. 'I'm early. They closed school because of the snow. Papa, I've brought a drawing I did for you.'

'Stop her!' Danielle pleaded.

He found his will to move too late. The door burst open and a small figure, all hair ribbons and bouncing plaits, burst into the studio.

PART ONE

PART ONE

Chapter One

Paris, 1937

Mathilda's daughter emerged from the Continental Telephone Exchange wearing an ivy-green suit, the severity of which contrasted with her youth.

A tilted trilby and shoes of black glacé leather suggested a young lady of means, as did silk stockings accentuating slim calves and ankles. She carried a black handbag and wore matching gloves. As she went down Rue du Louvre at a fast clip, admiring looks met her – and more than one smile of invitation.

Alix Gower forced herself not to react. Eighteen months in this city had taught her that 'style never smiles back'. Ice-cool *Parisiennes* take admiration as their due. She was learning how to emulate such women, to avoid the gaffes that reveal too much of a person's roots. Hers were in London, where she'd lived for the first eighteen years of her life.

Her father had been a Londoner too, a working-class man who'd survived a war only to lose to tuberculosis. Her mother

7

had been Alsatian Jewish. Fought over for centuries by France and Germany, Alsace bred fatalistic people. It bred refugees. Though she'd never known her mother, Alix had inherited the fugitive's cunning. Right now, she was escaping a shift at the telephone-company switchboard. She was on an errand that could get her arrested, but was doing it with the panache of a debutante on her way to the Ritz bar.

On Rue St-Honoré, her pace slowed. She loved the exclusive 1st arrondissement and though it was already quarter to five and she had a distance to go, she stared into every window she passed. It wasn't just the clothes that drew her. She loved the hotel fronts with their uniformed doormen, the trees in pots, the flower displays. The patisseries with their glistening platters. She'd arrived in Paris eighteen months ago and it had set her senses ablaze.

There was one shop on St-Honoré she never could resist. Zollinger's was a heaven of handmade chocolates, pyramids of them topped with gold leaf and crystallised flowers. Her favourites were the violet creams, which had been her mother's favourite and that alone made them desirable.

Everything Alix knew of her mother had come second-hand and she hoarded details, not really caring if they were true or not. She *knew* that Mathilda had settled in London aged nine and left school at fourteen to work in a department store, because she had her mother's school attendance and leaving certificates. And she *knew* Mathilda had served as a nurse during the war. There was a photograph and a Nurses' Catechism to prove it. She *believed* Mathilda had possessed an eighteen-inch waist, because she'd inherited a fragile petticoat whose drawstring was knotted in that impossible circumference. The notes and faded flower labels Alix's grandmother kept in a box proved that dozens of people had attended Mathilda's funeral in 1916. And she had her parents' wedding photograph, a snapshot of frozen hope. The rest Alix invented. Her grandmother, who might have put flesh on the bones of the story, chose not to.

Counting the francs in her purse, Alix went into Zollinger's, coming out an absurdly long time later with a tiny package. She checked her watch. Five past five. St-Honoré was long and she had to get to the yet more exclusive Rue du Faubourg St-Honoré. An object of rare worth was on display there, and if she didn't hurry, it might be taken away. Or sold.

She'd paid dearly for this afternoon's freedom. 'Mémé – I mean, my grandmother – has sprained her ankle and has to go to the doctor's,' she'd told Mademoiselle Boussac, her supervisor. 'May I have leave of absence to take her?' Behind her back, tense fingers betrayed the lie but the supervisor saw only a modest, dark-haired girl with her eyes cast down. A girl who seemed younger than her twenty years, but who dressed like a model girl in a fashion house and did her work well. Who had a command of English the telephone company needed.

'I will understand if you say no . . .' Alix lifted sable eyes that must have contained true desperation because Mlle Boussac sighed and said, 'Very well' – Alix could leave her shift early, but she would not be paid for the time missed and such absence must not become a regular occurrence. 'The company cannot accommodate every family illness. If you become unreliable, your seat here can easily be filled.'

That sounded like a dream to Alix, to turn up for work and find her seat filled. Today's errand was part of a plan. A step towards a future which included a flat in a tree-lined boulevard and free expression of her ambitions. Those ambitions had flown ahead of her. They were waiting at No. 24, Rue du Faubourg St-Honoré.

'Oh, no!' Alix stamped her foot. She was at No. 24. At Hermès, the leather and silk craftsmen. The object for which she'd lied and forfeited precious wages was where she'd hoped it would be – in the window – but it was twisted through the straps of a handbag which in turn leaned against an exquisitely stitched saddle. She needed to see it flat.

'It' was a square of silk, the first scarf to come out of Hermès's new factory in Lyon. Well, from what she could see, it was predominantly white, the edges oversewn by hand. It had small trees printed on it, or perhaps they were bushes, and wheels and horses' heads and what seemed to be a man in a wig. She glanced down at herself. Did she dare go in, ask to see it?

Her suit was notches above anything her work colleagues

owned, but it was not Faubourg St-Honoré standard. What if the staff took one look at her and turned her out? Or guessed her mission?

They wouldn't, she persuaded herself. It was no crime, wanting to see something new and beautiful. *Marie Claire* magazine, brand new on the stands this month, insisted that 'confidence begins inside'.' But then, so did self-doubt and indigestion.

The purr of a car made her turn. A Rolls-Royce was pulling up, sand-gold panels gleaming. A chauffeur stepped out, straightening his leather gloves before opening the rear passenger door.

A woman decanted herself with the grace of a ballerina. Definitely not French, Alix judged. She was learning the codes of French society and knew that rich Frenchwomen tamed their hair for daytime. This woman's locks flowed in corn-yellow waves under a fox-fur hat. Her lips were crimson, her eyebrows pencil strokes. A film star? Whoever she was, the doors of Hermès opened before she was halfway across the pavement.

The chauffeur put a cigarette to his mouth, flicked a lighter and winked at Alix. 'Window shopping, sweetheart? You and me both.'

Alix returned a snooty look and followed the lady inside.

'Mademoiselle?' A young saleswoman, a vendeuse, blocked her path. Alix could feel the girl mentally pulling stitches out of her jacket, assessing its cut. Searching for the secret signs of wealth. Clearly she didn't find them, because she repeated in a sharper tone, 'Mademoiselle?'

'Gloves,' Alix replied wildly. 'I – I'd like a pair of gloves. And a scarf.' She glanced towards the window but didn't dare move that way.

'Gloves for the spring season?'

'Er – yes. Brown?'

Brown for spring? Tut-tut. The vendeuse gestured to a seat well away from the window. 'Mademoiselle will please follow.'

The lady from the Rolls-Royce was being attended by an older vendeuse and Alix heard her exclaim in American-accented English, 'Oh my! So this is Mr Hermès's new baby? Won't we all go wild for it! I suppose it has a name?'

Alix hesitated. They were talking about *that* scarf.

The vendeuse replied, 'Monsieur Hermès has named it, "*Jeu des omnibus et dames blanches*."'

'My blazing stars, you're going to have to translate that for me.'

'It refers, Madame, to the game of omnibus played in the eighteenth century and *dames blanches*, which are the horse-drawn carriages for the people in the towns, which are also called "omnibus". It is a little joke.'

'Well now, it's a joke beyond my comprehension,' said the lady, holding a square of silk up to the light, 'but I can't wait to have it around my neck. Am I allowed to own such a precious trifle?'

'We at Hermès are always honoured to serve Madame Kilpin.'

Alix inched closer. 'Madame Kilpin' wasn't a film star. Film stars always called themselves 'Miss'. Nor a diplomat's wife. *My blazing stars.* A flat box lay open on the counter and it struck Alix that there must be more of these scarves in stock. Of course there would be. The minute news of them spread, there'd be a run on them. All the more reason to absorb the design, the colours. Black, burnt orange, blue . . .

The motif of a horse-drawn omnibus was repeated in a double circle. Alix counted the images, noting their direction. The centre was a cartouche of ladies and gentlemen of the late-eighteenth century playing a game at a table. She counted the figures, noted their dress and hairstyles. A complex design.

'And who are you, Miss Wide-eyes?' The American twisted on her seat. 'You are staring at me.'

Alix backed away. 'I'm sorry, excuse me.' She fled out on to the street, though not before she heard –

'I dare say she's a journalist and will sell a story about me to the newspapers. What a bore. Still, six out of ten for effort.'

The light was fading as Alix crossed the River Seine at the Pont Marie and descended to the Quai d'Anjou. This was on Ile St-Louis, the smaller of the two islands that formed the ancient hub of Paris. St-Louis was an enclave of graceful streets and mossy wharfs and Alix had promised herself that, one day, *she'd* live in one of its crumbling mansions. She'd walked fast from Hermès, fuelled by humiliation. *Six out of ten . . .*

Her heels clicked on the cobbles as she came up alongside a rusty Dutch barge tied to an iron ring. The boat's name was '*Katrijn*', though from 'r' onward the name disappeared into the dent of some long-ago collision. It was home to her best friend. She called, 'Paul? It's me, Alix. Are you in?'

Identical fair heads poked through the wheelhouse door, then two little girls in cotton frocks scampered on to the stern. One of the girls held a scaled-down violin in one hand and its bow in the other.

Alix hailed the girls. 'Lala, Suzy, is your brother home? May I come aboard?'

Lala, the one with the violin, made a 'hush' motion of the lips. 'He's sleeping. He was at the market at four this morning.'

'Were you at school today?'

'Some of it. I had my violin lesson and Suzy went to her talking-lady.'

'You mean her speech therapist?' Alix laughed. 'Will you give me a glass of wine? I promise I won't wake Paul.' Her feet burned and she needed to sit down to record what was buzzing in her head. The girls threw down a gangplank – little more than a ridged board. Crossing it, Alix knew she shouldn't look down, but could never stop herself. Fate insisted that whenever she was halfway across, another vessel would chug past and the wash would make *Katrijn* buck and sway. She could take her shoes off, but stockings cost half a week's wages . . .

A chuckle made her look up. A broad hand was reaching down to help her, the arm above it tanned and bare. As was the torso beyond. 'Paul, you're naked!' she said.

'I can be,' said Paul le Gal, showing strong, uneven teeth. 'Have you come to make love to me?'

'Shush! The girls will hear.'

'No they won't. Listen.'

From the galley came a nightingale harmony – Suzy telling Lala to fetch a bottle of wine, Lala telling Suzy to find glasses. Though Suzy never spoke, she often sang. They'd lost their mother a year ago in harrowing circumstances and they reminded Alix of little ducklings, bobbing along in the wake of the tragedy. Swimming and swimming because the alternative was to drown.

Paul helped her scramble over the gunwale, caught her in his arms and kissed her as she brushed rust off her skirt. 'Don't,' she chided. 'I've come to work – I've got a copy, scorching hot, but I have to get it on paper.'

'I was asleep but heard you in my dream,' Paul said against her mouth. Twenty-two, he wasn't much older than her, but he seemed so because his work as a porter in the fruit market kept him muscular and smoking roughened his voice. Alix let him kiss her, knowing it wasn't fair to either of them. They were friends and business partners, and tonight was business.

She pushed him away firmly. 'I have to sit down, or I'll lose what's in my head.'

A circular table with four mismatched chairs filled the barge's prow. Paul pulled up a seat, lit a lantern and watched Alix take a sketchbook and crayons from her bag. Stillness came over him, lending him beauty despite the scars on his face and the bump of a broken nose. 'I'm always afraid you'll find a rich man and forget about me.'

'I saw a rich woman earlier,' Alix said as Suzy wobbled towards them, wine glasses and a carafe on a tin tray. 'She was drizzled in furs the same colour as her car.'

Suzy poured wine with the solemnity of a head waiter while Lala set two glasses of milk on the table, which was actually a cable drum with 'PTT' stamped on the top. Paul, Lala and Suzy sat in silence as Alix sketched, discarding page after page as she tried to reproduce the Hermès scarf. It was sharp as a photograph in her head, but her pencils wouldn't understand. Dusk fell. Lights came on in the Hôtel Lambert above them, casting golden playing cards on to the quay. On the far bank, Port des Célestins threw flares over the water. Her audience was fidgeting, but Alix didn't mind, because she knew they were rooting for her. They were all cut off the same cheese. All survivors. Lala protected Suzy and practised her violin so one day she could put a hat down and play to tourists. Suzy chopped vegetables for each night's supper, standing on a box, until she had a huge pile of equal-sized pieces. Paul worked all hours to feed them and school them. Alix understood their sadness as she'd lost her mother at birth. Losing the one you'd had all your life must be even worse.

'Nearly forgot –' she dug into her handbag for the Zollinger's package. 'One each, girls.' Lala and Suzy stared at the chocolates until Alix, laughing, gave them permission to unwrap them.

'Can I smell the paper?' Paul asked.

'I couldn't afford four. D'you know, the assistants wrap each chocolate in little pleats and twist it? It's mesmerising – except I was hopping from foot to foot with impatience—' Alix shushed Paul as he began an answer. 'Let me get on.'

The tip of her tongue poked through her teeth. Like the twins making luxurious inroads into violet cream, she slid into a far-off state. 'I will get this damn scarf and we will get paid. Six out of ten? One day, fox-fur ladies will come to my shop and beg to be allowed to buy my designs.'

Chapter Two

It was nearly nine o'clock when Alix finally closed her sketch-book, realised how long she'd been sitting and exclaimed, 'I'm late, I'll have to run.'

Paul saved her the trouble by taking her home on the crossbar of his bicycle. Alix lived on the Left Bank, on Rue St-Sulpice in the 6th arrondissement. Crossing the Seine at the Pont de Sully, they careered down Boulevard St-Germain in the middle of the road. Alix gasped as headlights streamed towards her. Just as her nerves were failing, Paul swerved off St-Germain and there were the table-leg spires of St-Sulpice, her home church.

'Paul, you can – ouch!' He skimmed a drain cover. 'I'll walk the rest.'

'Don't you want me to pedal you up your stairs?'

'Very funny. Mme Rey would come out and batter you with her mop.' The concierge of Alix's building was a put-upon soul who used her mop more in warfare than cleaning. 'I'd better go up, Mémé will be so worried.' She took a step back, knowing Paul would want to take her in his arms.

'Two minutes won't make any difference to your grand-mother.'

'You don't know my grandmother.'

He groaned. 'Why do I always have to say goodbye to a closed door?'

She pecked him on the cheek. 'You'll let me know about the Hermès sketch? You'll sell it?'

'I'll take it to my usual contact with my fingers crossed.' What he always told her. No names, no promises. 'Goodnight, then?'

'Goodnight. You'd better get back to the girls.'

She watched him wheel around a couple of parked cars and cycle away into the shadows of the great church.

The door to Alix's courtyard stood ajar. She closed it quietly, then sniffed. Urine. Getting worse.

New tenants had recently moved into some former wash-houses behind Alix's apartment building. She sometimes counted up the adults and felt there must be at least five families crammed in. Other residents complained about the newcomers' cooking smells and their plaintive singing. Alix was intrigued by them, but she'd never dare approach them. Moustached men looked at her with hooded fascination, their womenfolk staring between wings of black hair. Mme Rey called them 'foreign vermin' – 'Not a scrap of French among them, no effort to learn.'

Alix never joined in the condemnation. If she'd come to Paris with her own kind, she wouldn't have improved her schoolgirl French very far either. Being dropped in at the deep end, nobody standing by with a lifebelt, that's what made you fluent in a language. Her job at the telephone exchange demanded clear, correct French, and at some point, she couldn't pinpoint when, she'd stopped mumbling and begun speaking. Meeting Paul had helped because he'd corrected her errors without judgement, though he'd also taught her Parisian slang and numerous swear words.

'If you want to be mistress of a language, get a lover.' One of the first things he'd said to her, accompanied by that rogue of a grin.

Entering the lobby, Alix whispered a familiar incantation: 'Six flights of steps, blessed Providence, may our next apartment have a lift.' With luck, her grandmother wouldn't have realised how late it was. But when she reached the top landing, their door flew open and a voice rimmed with anxiety cried, '*Vey ist mir*, Aliki, you didn't notice the sun go down and the moon come out? I have to pull out my hair, thinking you've been killed or worse? Where have you been?'

'Sorry, Mémé. I lost grip of time.' They spoke English at home, or what Alix called 'Mémé's English'.

'Go to the table. Don't move. I'll get your food.' Danielle Lutzman let her granddaughter work out the contradictory commands before adding, 'You can tell me what kept you while you have your soup.'

Their apartment, hunkered in the mansard attic of a once

grand house, could never conceal its kitchen smells. Alix knew at once it was onion soup with thyme, cooked in beef-bone stock with a sprinkling of parmesan. Served with a crusty baguette . . . which would be stale by now; it needed to be eaten fresh from the oven.

She took off her jacket, substituting a thick cardigan. The flat was chilly. They paid for coal with their rent, and the heating was supposed to be on twice a day, but it was twice a month, if they were lucky. In winter, they were forced to use kerosene heaters which gave off fumes. When they complained about the cold, Mme Rey would explain that they'd used up their allowance of coal, or she'd claim the boiler was playing up. 'My son Fernand will poke it when he's here next,' she'd promise. Ah, the elusive Fernand. She cheated them, but a concierge had power. She was the eyes and ears of the landlord.

Alix looked about her as she waited for her soup, realising that just ten minutes inside Hermès had re-calibrated her ideas of elegance. Their serviceable sitting room now looked shockingly bleak. The linoleum was cracked, carpets worn in places to the warp. Stains on the walls told depressing tales of kerosene. The only charm was a small collection of paintings by the Impressionist painter Alfred Lutzman, landscapes and views of his home town of Kirchwiller in Alsace. Mémé had salvaged them from her pre-London life. Lutzman had been Mémé's husband, Alix's grandfather.

Alix longed to know more about her Alsace roots, but her grandmother was touchy about those days. She'd just mutter, 'It was a hard, harrowing time,' then change the subject or find Alix a job to do. It made Alix all the more determined to get a sense of who, and what, she was.

They'd arrived in Paris in September 1935, foreigners in a city wounded by riots and unemployment, nervous of German re-militarisation just over the border. Alix had lost count of the times she'd been challenged about her nationality. It was a question with only one right answer: 'French.'

She was English, of course. Germanic Alsatian. Jewish, though not in a religious way. She could technically claim French heritage as Alsace had been grabbed back by France in 1918. A mixture, in other words, and without a story to go with it. Paris had laid bare her ignorance and, weary of her grandmother's evasions, she'd reached out to someone to fill the gaps. She'd gone in search of Raphael Bonnet.

Raphael Bonnet was one of ten thousand painters living in Paris, but had the distinction – in Alix's eyes – of having been her grandfather's apprentice. Following Alfred Lutzman's sudden death, Bonnet had helped Mémé and her daughter Mathilda relocate to England, an episode her grandmother had described as being like 'amputation without opium'.' Alix could only imagine how essential Bonnet had been to someone as fearful as her grandmother. Mémé often spoke of him, a smile touching her lips, but during their eighteen months living in Paris, she'd never visited his studio in Montmartre . . . and Bonnet never came to the flat.

When asked why, Mémé would reply, 'He's busy! Always working on his next exhibition, which of course he never finishes. He should waste time with us?'

Yes, Alix thought, *he should*. If people liked each other, they met for lunch, went to museums, walked in the park. Her best guess was that Bonnet was a piece of Alsace that Mémé had taken to exile in England, cherishing the friendship because he represented a bridge between the home she'd left and that new place where she would always be a stranger. When Bonnet returned to France, letters and Christmas cards had kept the bond alive. And when London began to feel dangerous, Mémé's thoughts had leaped to Paris and her old friend. Having come here because of Bonnet, Mémé now stubbornly avoided him. Was it because years had gone by and each would be an old version of the person they remembered?

They still wrote to each other, though. His letters, which Mémé let her read, had whetted Alix's appetite to meet the man. He sounded irreverent, a little wicked, his word-sketches of the people in his world cruel as well as hilarious. He dropped tantalising references into his letters of his Alsace past, and only the river and a few arrondissements separated them. Paris was small compared to London . . . it would be foolish not to search him out . . . no?

So one afternoon Alix had crossed the river, striking north

along the grand boulevards, climbing ever-narrower streets to Paris's hilltop village: the Butte de Montmartre. Asking at a tobacconist's for 'M. Bonnet, the artist?' she had been directed to the Place du Tertre, to a café in the shade of an acacia tree. Her informer had grunted, 'Grey beard, paint on his waistcoat. Make your way to the bar. He'll be propping it up.'

When she located a stocky, bearded man who matched the description, and told him her name, he'd blinked for long seconds before engulfing her in a bear hug such as she'd not felt since her father was alive.

'Alix? Danielle's granddaughter? Mathilda's girl? *Mon dieu*, who else could you be? Mathilda come to life, and I see the old man in your eyes! Everybody –' Bonnet had invited first his intimate friends then the entire tavern to embrace Alix – 'Alfred Lutzman has come at last to his spiritual home in the person of this lovely girl. Let us drink to a miracle!'

A friend, a past, an identity in one shot: Raphael Bonnet told her more about Alsace and her family in an hour than Mémé had in her whole life. He'd introduced her to red wine too, and to a lusty crowd of artists' models, erotic dancers, musicians and those he termed, 'artistes of the jug'. Drinkers. Quite an awakening for a young woman whose experience of sex, alcohol and men could be written in the margins of a museum ticket.

Bonnet had wanted to visit them at the St-Sulpice flat, he confided, but Alix's grandmother had forbidden it. 'She thinks me an unsuitable acquaintance and she's right.' He'd gestured to a crowd of men and women clustered around a piano where an African man was banging out jazz. 'My tastes shock her, my friends would deafen her. Besides, I know too much. Your grandmother likes the past to stay in the past, so, alas . . . it is perhaps hello and goodbye.'

But Alix wanted the friendship, wanted more than one sip of this heady bohemian life. 'I shan't give you up now I've found you, M. Bonnet,' she told him. They still met at least once a month. Mémé never suspected; Alix made sure of that.

And the more Bonnet drank, the more he talked. Over a jug of Beaujolais, Alix learned the shocking fact that Alfred Lutzman had not died in his bed; he had been killed.

'How? Who did it?'

Bonnet had become uncharacteristically vague. An unprovoked attack, by thieves who broke into the house and were probably disturbed. 'Best ask no more – your grandmother wouldn't like it.'

No indeed, especially as Mémé had always claimed that Alfred had died of a heart seizure, in his sleep. Since that day, Alix had tried to wring more from Bonnet, but it was hard to make him concentrate. His anecdotes spun off into surreal realms and changed with every retelling. He'd hop over the decades, throwing out names like exploding chestnuts. He could be bawdy too.

'Remember fat Fiametta, the snake-dancer who comes in here with a big, covered basket? You know where she keeps her red-and-black asp?'

After a bottle or two, Bonnet would always try to borrow money from Alix. But she loved him all the same. He listened to her, really listened. He also agreed passionately with her that, had he lived, Alfred Lutzman would have been a leading artist of his generation. According to Bonnet, Lutzman had been the finest exponent of human flesh of the time. Of the paintings on Alix's walls, only one had a human subject, a smiling girl whose black plaits were crowned with a coif of stiff, Alsatian lace. The picture was titled *Mathilda* and was the most precious of all to Alix.

Knocking her out of her daydream, Mémé put a steaming bowl in front of Alix and pulled out a chair for herself. A ceiling light hung over the table, and in its glow Alix saw the traces of tears on her grandmother's cheeks. She almost put her spoon down, but stopped herself. With Mémé, you never cut straight to the most important question. She nodded at a nearby work-table strewn with gossamer silk and bobbins, and asked, 'Is that the Maison Javier embroidery? They keep giving you new commissions. You must be exhausted.'

'It's hard work but I never knew any other kind. Finish your soup. Sit nearer the table – you want that skirt ruined? How is the bread? Stale, I should think.'

'It's fine if I dip it in. Shadow work, isn't it, where you stitch on the reverse of the silk . . .' Alix laid down her spoon. 'Mémé?' A tear was slipping from her grandmother's eye. Mémé powdered her face each morning and evening, covering age spots

26

and blemishes, but the powder was smudged and the scar above her left eyebrow showed white. 'Were you so worried when I didn't come home?'

'I've been fretting all day.'

'About me?'

'I read in the paper how they treat Jews in Germany even worse now. I used to have cousins there. What will become of their families? And this civil war in Spain – how many must die before somebody puts an end to it? Then you didn't come home, all evening you didn't come home. Were you kept late?'

Alix was tempted to say, 'Mlle Boussac asked me to teach a new girl the ropes,' but she reminded herself she was twenty, too old for lies or prevarications. 'I went to see Paul le Gal. I had a glass of wine on his boat and forgot the time.'

'Le Gal, whose mother—?' Mémé bit off the rest. 'You were alone with that slaughterhouse boy?'

'His sisters were there. And Paul doesn't work at the slaughterhouses any more, Grandmère.' The affectionate term 'Mémé' had disappeared for the moment. 'He works at Les Halles, offloading the fruit and vegetables.'

'So. Alone with a porter whose mother made her living on the streets.'

'That's not true. Sylvie le Gal was never . . . what you're implying. Her business failed, that's all.' Alix would always be loyal to Sylvie, whose smile had cut through the uncertainty and stress of her first weeks in Paris.

She'd been going for a job interview in Boulevard Haussmann and had got her *Métro* lines mixed up, emerging miles away near Place de la Bastille. Close to tears – it was her sixth failed interview in a week – she'd struck up the nearest avenue, searching for a street name. She didn't see the pavement billboard until she crashed into it: 'Learn Tango in ten weeks'. A blonde head had poked out of an upper window, followed by a cheery, 'Since you fell over my sign, I'll give you the first lesson free.'

Like Bonnet, Sylvie had been an unfettered spirit. Her skirts were too tight, her tops too low, but she was that rare type who loved men and women equally. She never got cross if you muffed your steps either. Just slowed things down till you got it. But her school had closed, and with debts and two little girls to feed she'd taken to dancing at seedy *bal musettes* and in the night-clubs of Pigalle. According to Paul, she would dance with men and . . . whatever followed. What followed was a jump from a bridge, which confounded Alix because she couldn't match happy Sylvie with death in freezing black water. 'Paul's sisters wanted me to stay,' she told Mémé. 'They miss their mother.'

Danielle Lutzman wasn't ready to retreat. 'What will this Paul do when they're twelve years old and one of them doesn't speak? How will he teach that little girl about life if she won't speak?'

'Muddle through. People tell him to hand them over to the church orphanage. But then the river would have won.'

'You talk nonsense.' Mémé knotted her fingers. Because her speciality was fine needlework, she kept her hands soft with paraffin cream and from her slender earnings paid a local woman to do the rough work in the house. For all that, her knuckles seemed ready to break through the skin. 'I wouldn't take them to the nuns either,' she conceded. 'When I was young I went to Strasbourg to work in the lace mills. The nuns would visit, but they never asked about us Jews. Only the Catholic virgins mattered to them.' Mémé rapped on the tabletop. 'Eat. Finish your soup.'

Alix obeyed and Mémé said, 'You've a good job at the exchange, money every month. You might become a supervisor, catch a man who wears a suit to work, with a house in a nice suburb. Instead you want to get into trouble by a market boy?'

'Paul and I are just friends.'

'Pfah! Drinking wine in the dark, that's "just friends"? Not in my day.'

'Things are different now.'

'And some things never change. Men chase, girls get in the family way and lives are ruined. You are all I have, Aliki. I want you safe.'

Alix hovered on the brink of confessing her visit to Hermès. There was a speech ready in her head: *I don't want to spend my life in the telephone building – "I'll put you through, sir, please stand by." I don't want to marry a man in a dull suit. I want to learn the fashion trade and eventually open my own studio. Be the new Chanel, Vionnet, Jeanne Lanvin . . . open a shop in the 1st arrondissement.* A glance at the sewing table warned that rhapsodies would fall on stubborn ears. Out loud she said, 'I want to go into the couture business.'

'Work sixteen-hour days and get crab's claws?' Mémé held up fingers bent like river weed. 'Believe me, Aliki, go into that trade, you might as well put your life on a roulette wheel.'

Chapter Three

It was all very well for Mémé to tell her to stay safe, Alix mused a few days later as she crossed the Jardin du Luxembourg on her way to meet Paul, her hands deep in her pockets, her head bowed against a bitter wind. After all, there'd been no sign of caution the day Mémé announced they were moving to Paris.

July 1935, they'd been sitting at the kitchen table of their home in south London. The day was sticky and hot, an open window letting in the noise of tradesmen's traffic. It was also Alix's once-a-month afternoon off from Arding & Hobbs, the department store where she'd worked since leaving school. She'd intended to spend her free time on Clapham Common, making a sketch for her portfolio. Back then her unstated ambition was to go to art school, starting with evening classes, then full time if she could ever afford it . . . somehow progress from there to being a dress designer. An ambition not helped that day by Mémé's demand that she stay home and trim a bucket of runner beans a neighbour had given them.

31

As Alix de-stringed and Mémé sliced, her grandmother had announced, 'I want us to live in Paris.'

Alix had laughed without looking up.

'I mean it, Aliki. I'm sick of London.'

'Why Paris?'

Mémé waved her paring knife. 'The other day I took lace collars to a place in Portman Square. Hours I'd spent on them! The buyer – *dummkopf* slattern – picks them up as if they are a bunch of watercress.'

'What's that got to do with Paris?'

'In Paris, such girls are not given the job of buyer. In Paris, such girls sell watercress. I know I shall be happy in Paris.'

'You won't. You don't know anybody there.'

'My friend Bonnet is there.' Then Mémé had stopped, as if astonished by her own words. Before Alix could question her, however, she added quickly, 'He lives in a rough quarter and keeps strange hours, so we won't meet him. What I mean is, half of Alsace lives in Paris. I will see people who look like me and sound like me.'

'But I won't know a soul.'

'What will you miss? After all, I don't see any school friends calling.'

'Because they've all gone to finishing school in Switzerland.' She silently added, *I never had real school friends, none who would visit me here.* 'What about my job?' Alix continued. 'I got a good report last month and there's a vacancy coming up in the silks department that I'm certain to get.'

'In Paris, you'll have fifty silk departments to choose from.'

The truth eventually came out, though it took a few days. It was nothing to do with *dummkopf* buyers really: Mémé was frightened by the rise of anti-Jewish feeling in London. She told Alix, 'While you were tucked away at school in the country, Moseley's Blackshirts were taking lessons from Hitler. Jews are being attacked now in the East End. London is not safe.'

'Nobody round here supports them. Nobody with any sense.'

A neighbour, who was taking tea with them that afternoon, took Alix's side: 'They won't come over the river, Mrs Lutzman.' She'd winked at Alix. 'No Blackshirts in Wandsworth.'

'No?' Mémé's logic was offended. 'I was on the bus. I went to Spitalfields to buy silk thread and some boys got on and shouted at us old women. They knew we were Jewish. They were Blackshirts.'

'Spitalfields is east London, Mrs L.'

'And now they know which bus I get on, so they can find me.'

Nothing would dissuade Mémé. In her mind, London had become a nest of Nazism: of window breaking, of beatings and attacks. Always thin, by the time the August heat arrived she resembled a bundle of sticks. Alix caved in. She handed in her notice and spent August organising travel papers. She sold their furniture and acquired the addresses of accommodation agencies from the French embassy. By the time the leaves were falling, they were on the boat train heading for Dover, their household possessions packed for freighting on. Alix was coming to terms with a new future.

Once in Paris, Mémé got piecework from an embroidery atelier, but was paid less than in London. It was a shock, the low wages of Paris's luxuries industry. Yet another was having to pay six months' rent in advance for a tiny flat, six floors up, with no hot water. Alix wore out her shoes looking for work, but either she didn't have the right permit, or her French was inadequate, or she was at the back of a queue reserved for 'French citizens only'.

They were facing destitution when the job came up at the telephone exchange. That godsend followed fast on the heels of another – her meeting with Sylvie le Gal and through her, Paul. While Sylvie taught Alix to foxtrot, shimmy and tango, Paul gave her lessons in fashion piracy and corrected her French. Every accurate sketch Alix made of a couture outfit before its launch earned them two hundred black-market francs. She and Paul split the money – it kept the bailiffs from the door. That was another part of Alix's life Mémé knew nothing about.

Where was Paul this evening? He wasn't usually late. Alix took an illegal shortcut across an area of lawn, keeping a sharp lookout for the park-keeper who would blow his whistle if he saw her treading on the sacred grass. Paul always waited for her by the lion statue, bathing its proud underbelly in the smoke of his Gauloises cigarettes. Nearly a week had gone by since she'd been aboard the *Katrijn*, so it must have taken him longer than usual to sell the Hermès sketch. That worried her. Paris was full of copyists like herself, swarming around the collections each season. March was a quiet month, the spring–summer collections already history. There'd be a brief flurry in April with the mid-season launches, then nothing till the frenzy of the autumn–winter shows at the end of July. But even in quiet months, you couldn't slack. It had to be *your* sketch on the fast boat to New York if you wanted to make money.

A familiar figure in a mariner's jacket suddenly emerged from behind the lion's plinth. Alix ran forward. 'Paul, you were hiding.'

'Sheltering – I didn't realise you'd got here. You look like a cold princess,' he told her as they kissed cheeks. 'I like your coat.'

'Flea market,' she said, twirling so he could appreciate the generous fullness of the black cashmere skirts. 'Rue des Rosiers.' Not quite Schiaparelli, but almost – clearly copied from the Italian designer's spring offering. The coat had a belted waist and had originally been ankle-length, but Alix had shortened it and embroidered roses on the collar, so it was now an original Alix Gower. 'Shall we go for coffee?' Alix thought Paul looked tense. 'Tough day?'

'No more than usual.'

She didn't press. 'Who's looking after the girls?'

'Francine.' He meant the old barge-woman who moored

alongside him at Quai d'Anjou. 'I can't be long. She'll be half drunk by now and showing her bloomers to the men on passing coal barges.'

It was said without humour and Alix took his hand. 'Think on the bright side – maybe tonight she won't have her bloomers on.'

Paul gave a bark of laughter. 'That would clear the wharf! Come on, let's stroll like the lovers we aren't, eh? Good day at work?'

She answered in BBC English, '*I'm sorry, sir, I cannot place your call as there is washing on the line.*' Switching to French: 'Now what? You're glaring.'

'I can't understand that bloody language. You know that talking English to me is like throwing a ball too high for a dog.' Gem-green eyes glinted – Paul was fair like his sisters, rough-hewn, typical Frankish descent. But touchy as a cavalry officer.

'So I got an education, somebody paid for me,' she soothed. 'You respect learning, or you wouldn't break your back sending your sisters for extra lessons. When Lala's lead violin at the Paris Opéra or La Scala, it'll be because of you.'

They walked on, scattering pigeons. The park was almost empty, children and their nannies long gone. The writers, poets and students who haunted this Latin Quarter niche would be in the cafés on Boulevard St-Michel. Paul stopped once to light a cigarette, hunching around the flame until the tobacco lit. He drew heavily, his eyes lowered.

'Tell me before I burst,' Alix finally prompted. 'How much did you get for the Hermès?'

Paul blew out a stream of smoke. 'Nothing. My contact couldn't do anything with it. Not enough detail.'

'Not enough detail?' Along with bitter disappointment came fear. If this trickle of income dried up . . . she didn't want to think about it. 'Show me anyone else in Paris who remembers detail as I do, who can reproduce as perfectly—'

'Nobody doubts you, Alix. Well, I don't. But that's not the point. They need the real thing.'

'Half a day's pay down the plughole! What does he expect, your contact? If somebody gives me the money, I'll buy the scarf myself.'

'I expect somebody already has. It'll be zipping off to New York, to be turned into ten thousand fakes in a month. I'm sorry, Alix. For me too. I needed that commission.'

'They could have worked from my drawing.'

'She said not.'

'She? Your contact's a she?'

'Stop it.' He tried to smile, but squeezed out a frown instead. He kept her away from his 'contacts' and the backstreet bars where he did the deals. Paul had been involved in the black market since he was old enough to outrun the law, but reckoned Alix was too innocent for that world. 'You smile at policemen,' he'd tease her. 'First sign of madness.'

Now he shrugged. 'You win some, you lose some.' When she

stopped and stood in front of him, he misread her, pulling her close. 'I don't want you to waste your life stealing.'

Their lips came together in a leaf-soft kiss. Alix tipped her head back and replied, 'I don't steal.'

'All right, copying. Thanks to people like you, New York ladies get Paris originals the same time as Frenchwomen do. You offer a social service, right?'

'Right. Everyone gets what they want.'

'Except the designers who create the clothes. They'd like to string you up.'

'You got me into it,' she reminded him. 'We'd only known each other a week and you smuggled me into Longchamps races to see the rich women's outfits. You said you had a friend who sold fashion drawings to a New York magazine, a dollar a sketch, who was looking for artists with a quick hand. You seduced me.'

'I know. God, Alix, I wish I didn't need you so much.' Paul kissed her hungrily and Alix wriggled away, thinking he'd no right, that she disliked it . . . then realised that she didn't. In fact, she liked the pressure of his mouth, the feel of his evening-rough chin against her skin. Even the taste of Gauloises didn't alter the feeling.

She broke the kiss. 'Are you telling me there's no more work?'

'If we get caught, who'd care for my sisters and your grand-mother?' He sighed. 'Yes. No more. That's right.'

'There's another job, isn't there?' Paul never could lie.

He groaned. 'You'll fly at me, or snap my head off.'

She pulled his sleeve, kissed him briefly, then provocatively. 'Tell me, then I'll decide what I do.'

Paul told her.

Steal the spring–summer 1937 collection from Maison Javier, a couture house on Rue de la Trémoille, close to the Champs-Elysées. Steal from the house for which Mémé was currently working . . . Steal the *whole* collection?

Paul nodded. 'My contact wants every last ribbon and buckle.'

'Impossible.'

'That's what I said.' Paul raised her wrist, checking the time by her watch. They'd retired to a café, ordering the cheapest wine, both conscious of family waiting for them at home. 'People are wild for him in America, this Javier. It's to do with that American woman who slept with the English king.'

'Mrs Simpson wears Javier?' Alix thought a moment, then nodded. 'Maybe that's why she looks so tall in her photographs. Javier pulls women straight, like a stick of rock.'

Paul shrugged impatiently. 'All I know is, American women queue down the street for copies of his dresses. My contact wants somebody at his spring show, sketching every outfit.'

'Tell your contact she's too late.'

'But that's it.' Paul leaned forward, runkling the cloth. 'Javier's showing in April.'

'Nobody shows spring–summer collections in April.'

Paul opened his hands palm up. 'Javier is, this year. Don't ask me why.'

Alix's mind whirred. A whole collection, from one house? 'You'd have to be in the workrooms. You'd have to rob his atelier. Take everything: garments, sketches, samples . . . or kidnap Javier himself.'

'Can't you get into the salon and take notes? They have parades every day, don't they?'

'Not until the collection is launched. I get into couture shows by pretending to be a lady's maid. I follow a well-dressed woman inside. Or I pretend to be a titled English girl, desperate for her first Paris outfit. "What spiffing frocks! How do you people do it?" They fall for that. On a good day, I can memorise five or six designs. For a whole collection, I'd need three brains or a camera.'

Paul rubbed his nose, out of his depth. 'Thing is,' he said, 'my contact has wholesalers on standby. They have sweatshops in New York, full of what they call "table monkeys" – people who work all night at sewing machines to meet demand. American women want the fashion they see in the magazines. They want Javier. They want what Mrs . . .'

'Simpson.'

'– what she wears, and they want it yesterday.'

Alix was shaking her head. 'I've pushed my way into the collections too often as it is. The saleswomen circle like buzzards and drop on you if they see you making so much as a line with a pencil. Paul, you were correct when you said it was wrong. We should stop.'

Paul looked down at his fingers. The skin around the nails was snagged from rough work, from biting. 'Yes, I agree, but . . . you see, my contact, she knows an American speech therapist on Rue du Bac who's had incredible results, who could get Suzy talking again. But he's expensive.'

Alix sighed. 'Everyone is, except you and me. I'm sorry, Paul.'

Paul drained his glass. 'Don't look so wretched. I'll tell my contact the job's too big.'

'No. Paul . . . tell her I'll do it.'

'You will?'

She drank her wine. 'Just after I've learned to make myself invisible. How much was offered, by the way?'

'Oh . . .' Paul counted coins on to the table, and named a figure that made Alix's jaw drop. 'I know. Rather like putting a year's wages on a dark horse in the Prix de Diane and scooping the lot.'

Chapter Four

Seven hundred thousand francs. Enough, even split two ways, for Paul to refit the *Katrijn*, turn her into a home fit for small children and engage a dozen speech therapists. For Alix ... freedom from that swivel chair and the eternal clicking exchange.

She strode home, battling dreams and demons. She so wanted to help Paul. And she'd love to wake in the mornings free of financial worries. But ... the couture industry employed thousands of women like her grandmother. 'Steal a collection, you steal from people like Mémé.' But then again ... *seven hundred thousand francs*.

But what if they were caught? They warned each other of the danger all the time, even joked about it. But what if it really happened? What if she felt a hand on her shoulder as she was sketching? Or a stern voice stopping her outside a shop – *May I see inside your handbag, Mademoiselle?* Paul had been in police custody numerous times, and his descriptions made Alix squirm. You were put into a windowless cell stinking of the last occupant's sweat, or worse. They took your shoes and your top clothes and those came back with lice in them. They searched you, right down to your underwear. Women were meant to be searched by female personnel, but it didn't always happen.

In the lobby of her apartment building she walked past Mme Rey, too immersed in thought to see the woman.

'Ants in the pants?'

Alix whirled round. 'Sorry?'

'Been with your nice-looking boy?'

'No, I mean, yes.' Alix hurried up the first flight of stairs.

The concierge called after her: 'My boy Fernand's here tomorrow, delivery of coal. You'll leave a tip, *hein*? He gives his time for nothing and it's hard work, all those sacks.'

Outside the door of her flat, Alix caught her breath and ironed out her expression. Inside she found Mémé cooking potato pancakes on a skillet. The fleshless shoulders were hunched and Alix knew instantly that something was wrong.

As they sat down to eat, Mémé sighed. 'Old Misery Mop told me the landlord means to increase the rent.'

'What?' This couldn't be happening. Not with the copying work drying up, and coal to pay for as well. 'Why now?'

'The World's Fair is opening in June, drawing people from the four corners of the globe, so the newspapers tell us. Our landlord thinks they'll stay forever. He wants a thousand francs a month more from next quarter.'

'Next quarter starts 25th March . . .' Alix calculated. Just over two weeks away. She felt like the camel bracing itself for the last straw. She used a word learned from Paul that fortunately Mémé did not understand. 'Right, we'll find a flat near the canal or out at La Villette. We'll get somewhere for half what we pay here.'

'No, Aliki. I like a good address. Things like that matter when you're my age, and how would I make new friends by the canal? I'm too tired to move again.' Mémé gazed at her work-table. 'I could get another hour a day out of my fingers. Poor Brandel will have to go. Who are we with a charwoman anyway? Rockefellers?'

'I'll clean. And –' Alix pulled in a now-or-never breath, acting on a decision she was hardly aware of having made – 'I was thinking, I might apply for piecework with Maison Javier. You know, sewing I could bring home? I have the skills, and you could recommend me. Then in time –' she ignored the warning glint in her grandmother's eye – 'I could get a full-time job there. Javier promotes women, so I could work my way up to being a première. Premières are paid really, really well if they're good.' *Meanwhile, I would steal for Paul's contact and keep us all afloat. Maybe even hit the jackpot. Seven hundred thousand francs . . .*

Danielle Lutzman's mouth twitched in pain, then shock. Anger soon came. 'You hear me say I'll slave another seven hours a week, and you talk of throwing away your good job at the telephone company? A job I shamed myself to get you?'

'I'd stay until I was sure . . .' Alix caught up with Mémé's last comment. 'What d'you mean, "shamed"? I got *myself* the job at the telephone exchange.'

'Just when I need to feel safe, you talk of giving up the job that puts a roof over our heads?' Mémé beat her fist on the table so hard the crockery jumped. Alix seized the bony hands.

'Don't, please, Mémé! Whatever I said to frighten you, I didn't mean it. I'll stay at the telephone company. I'll work longer shifts.' She added silently, *I'll do whatever it takes to keep you safe*.

Yet, despite her protestations, she was to look back on this as the moment she stepped to the edge of the cliff, looked down into a pit crawling with deceit and danger . . . and jumped.

Chapter Five

NEWS MONITOR
10th March 1937

V. Haviland, Madrid correspondent,
reports from the heart of Spain's civil conflict.

A man lying in the gutter may comfort himself by looking up at the stars. For your man in a Madrid gutter, a layer of dust excludes the stars. He lies where he has thrown himself as fighter planes swoop over a street of cafés and shops. They fly in triangular formation, Heinkel fighter aircraft of the German Condor Legion, strafing the pavements with machine-gun fire, blowing out glass, raising chips the size of gaming dice from the road. The noise is past deafening and humans dart like terrified mice beneath raptor shadows.

The din becomes unbearable until, suddenly, they are gone. They don't come in plain day any more, thanks to the presence of fighter aircraft provided to Spain's left-wing government by its Soviet allies—

Jean-Yves, Comte de Charembourg, glanced up in irritation as a cough from the doorway broke into his reading. His secretary stood with a letter pinched between thumb and finger, his expression conveying its unsavoury nature.

'You will wish to see this at once, M. le Comte.'

Shaking his newspaper in half, Jean-Yves made a mental note to come back to that article later. Whoever 'V. Haviland' was, he'd obviously rolled in the dust of Spain. The *News Monitor* had been Jean-Yves's weekday reading when he'd lived in London and he'd been pleased to discover it could be bought in Paris from a vendor near the British embassy, if a day or two late. There was a French-language version, but it tended to pussyfoot around international sensitivities. Three decades spent in London had not made an Englishman of the Comte de Charembourg, but it had taught him the value of a press that colludes with its readers rather than with those in power. 'Second post, Ferryman?' he asked his secretary.

'It came by hand, Monsieur.' Jolyan Ferryman always addressed him as 'Mon-sewer.' The boy's French, though textbook correct, came with an excruciating English accent. To be in Ferryman's presence was to wince more than was comfortable or dignified.

'Just put it on my desk. Who's it from?'

'The personage declined to give his name and I felt it unseemly to ask. It was a working type of person.'

Jean-Yves got the subtext. His gentleman-secretary resented

performing tasks more fitted to a footman. Tough. This household couldn't run to footmen. In fact, if prices kept increasing, Jean-Yves doubted he would run even to a secretary much longer. Now, that would be a tricky conversation to have with his wife. When it came to their style of living, Rhona de Charembourg aspired to the grand ways of her English girlhood. Aisleby Park, with fifty indoor staff and an estate ten miles round, was Rhona's pattern of respectable living. Had she known she'd end up ruling a household of four domestics and a part-time gardener . . . undoubtedly she wouldn't have married him.

Jean-Yves dismissed Ferryman and tore open the letter, extracting a sheet that reeked of cigarette smoke. Without doubt, a worker's brand.

The click of the garden gate took him to the window in time to see his wife and daughters leaving the house. Each woman wore a suit of fine Prince of Wales check. His two daughters each held a dog lead with a white Pomeranian on the end of it. Rhona, Christine and Ninette with Tosca and Figaro, taking the air on Boulevard Racan. A charming ritual that wouldn't last much longer. Christine was marrying this June and the family circle would be cut by one.

Better read that letter. DE CHAREMBOURG was written across the top. He absorbed what followed and the blood faltered in his veins.

He sat down. Forced himself to breath evenly. He'd suffered

chest trauma in the Great War and, though only fifty-six, he sometimes rasped like a spent hackney horse. He reread the letter in silence:

On 21st December 1903, you slew Alfred Lutzman. Time to pay. There are witnesses living. Meet my terms or I will tell your dirty secrets.

I can hurt someone you love.

His gaze flew towards the boulevard where his wife and daughters strolled. In what way, hurt? When his telephone rang, he snatched it up. 'De Charembourg. Who is this?'

'You got my note, M. le Comte? You understand my meaning?' The voice was hoarse, the accent hard to place . . . something guttural mixed up in Parisian argot.

Jean-Yves answered in his crispest Academy French – an instinctive defence. 'Whoever you are, I imagine you are hoping for money. Prepare to be disappointed. Your accusations are as wild as they are offensive.'

A crackling pause. Then: 'You lead an interesting life, Monsieur. So many friends. So many *lady* friends . . . Can your wife count them on her fingers? I'm sure she tries.'

'How dare you speak of my wife?' How did this creature know anything of his life? Of his discreet liaisons? He was so careful.

The caller gave a thick laugh. 'You are an appreciator of female beauty, and what is wrong with that? Women and girls, ah . . . so tender and vulnerable, no? Is it not tragic when a young girl is hurt? You would not wish to cause the mutilation of a girl's face?'

'God, no. Of course not. What—'

The voice became businesslike. 'Five hundred thousand francs and nobody you love will know what a bastard you are – well, you *were*. I know what you did to Alfred Lutzman.' The line went dead.

Jean-Yves discovered his shirt was soaked. At last, after so many years, the horror of that winter's day in Kirchwiller had come back to haunt him. Five hundred thousand francs was equivalent to a year's untaxed income. How would he find such a sum?

In London he'd held a responsible position in the Banque d'Alsace, retiring with shares that bolstered his current, modest salary as a director of a textiles firm. Rhona had brought money to the marriage too, but what remained of that was invested for their daughters. And there was far less of it than she imagined. As Miss Aisleby, heiress to her grandfather's coal-mining fortune, she'd once been the richest girl in northern England. By the time she inherited, the Aisleby pits were exhausted and war had wiped out her invested fortune. Her grandfather's debts and death duties took much of the rest. Jean-Yves often tried to explain that it was mismanagement and socialism that had swallowed her wealth, not theft, but Rhona still believed her money existed somewhere. She certainly spent as if it did.

Bluntly, he wasn't up to the luxury of a blackmailer.

He realised the telephone receiver was slick with sweat, and wiped it quickly. Who did that malevolent voice belong to? And how could a stranger ever know about events that took place in Alsace thirty-five years ago? It had all been hushed up.

He could think of only one person who might tell him. He must break a taboo and ask her to meet him.

'Paul, I'll do it. I'll steal Javier's spring–summer collection so neither of us need worry about money ever again. I'll slip into his show in disguise with a sketchbook up my skirt. Just don't ever tell my grandmother.'

Having said her piece, Alix dug her fork into a mound of grated carrot doused in vinaigrette. She had radishes on her plate too – and cold green beans, boiled egg, onion and slices of Toulouse sausage. This café on Butte de Montmartre specialised in the cheap and the vibrant. It was Friday lunchtime, 12th March, and though the wind was still sharp, Place du Tertre was bright with sunshine, the trees squeezing into bud. Alix had just completed a night shift at the exchange and a further four hours to cover for a sick colleague. She felt light-headed. 'It's mad, stealing a whole collection. And impossible but . . .' She broke off.

Paul was making a dam of salt in a trickle of wine. When she asked, 'Am I dining alone?' he made a face and responded, 'I've something to tell you.'

Oh, no. Surely his contact hadn't approached somebody else

to steal the collection? Not after she'd spent sleepless nights working out how to do it without actually breaking into Maison Javier in the night and carrying away the clothes. She watched Paul trying to spear a radish only for it to bounce off his plate and on to the cobbles. 'If it's bad news, give it.'

Paul grimaced. 'I'm planning my words so you don't bite my head off.'

'I always bite your head off.' A closer look revealed the blur of sleeplessness in his eyes too. 'Midnight oil?'

'Nightmares. Every time I close my eyes, I see my mother's corpse.'

'Oh, don't, Paul.'

'And the police came to my boat.'

'Police?'

'Wanting to see my mooring permit.'

'You *do* have a permit?'

He gave her a look that said, *What d'you think?* 'Alix, you always say you want to be a couturier and open your own fashion house? Well, my contact has arranged a job interview for you.'

Her heart scudded to a halt. 'What?'

'At Maison Javier. Then you wouldn't have to sneak into his shows; you'd be at the heart of his organisation.'

'Oh.' That was it then. The chance she'd dreamed of. Only . . .

'Did I say something wrong?'

'No. Well, a bit.' Paul was enticing her to break her promise to Mémé, but offering her the chance to betray herself too. It was so hard to explain. She stared across the square, then waved her fork at an artist erecting his easel. 'See him, with the little fat legs? Bonnet – my artist friend who lives here on the square? –' she indicated a row of old houses behind her. 'He says that man has spent twenty years sketching tourists, smoothing out their chins and the bumps on their noses. When he goes home, there's a lake of charcoal dust on the cobbles with his footprints in it, a memento of where he's stood all day. For him, making a pretty picture and getting paid is what it's about.'

Paul grunted. 'From what you've told me about Bonnet's empty food cupboards, he could do with selling a picture now and again, rather than criticising those who do.'

She leaped to Bonnet's defence. 'He'd rather starve than paint to order! My grandfather felt the same. He believed that a finished picture had lost its soul.'

Paul tried to spear another radish. 'How d'you know?'

'Mémé says so. Grandpapa would paint the same scene over and over, trying for the perfect cast of light.' Paul's snort ignited her anger. 'If you'd ever read Zola's *l'Œuvre* you'd understand. In the book, Claude Lantier struggles against an establishment that only wants safe, traditional art. His whole life is dedicated to producing one great painting that fuses nature with authentic passion.'

'Only he runs out of paint and dies?'

'No, he hangs himself.'

'Oh.' Paul sent another radish careering into Alix's lap. 'Always a way out, isn't there?'

Alix was bitterly sorry for her tactlessness, but she wanted Paul to understand why she was so torn. She needed money, but the means being offered was dangerous and, more important, immoral. To her, couture was art. Copying a dress was like taking an apple from an orchard. Stealing a collection was like burning the orchard down. It was taking a man's genius, his soul.

Paul said, 'Do you want this interview or not? It seems a heaven-sent chance.'

It was an impossible choice. She'd have to give in her notice at the telephone exchange and withstand Mémé's distress. And what if she got taken on at Maison Javier only to discover she'd been mistaken about her talent? You could carry dreams around with you for years, like a cluster of balloons, only to discover they were all empty air. Gesturing towards the radishes, she told Paul, 'Use your fingers. Who's watching? I think, after all, I won't become a couturier. Bonnet asked me to pose for a painting. I'm off for a sitting after lunch.' She'd run into the artist at a second-hand clothes stall in Rue des Rosiers. She'd been selling a tweed skirt she no longer wanted.

He'd chuckled when she told him her rent was going up. 'That's fate telling you it's time to pose for me, *michou*. I can't pay much, but it'll give you something to throw at your bastard landlord.' He tapped his nose. 'Our secret.'

Paul poured wine for them both, the cheap kind that left a

red stain in the glass, and said gravely, 'Being an artist's model is fine when you're young, Alix, but do you want to live to see your wrinkles on a gallery wall? This interview is for the bottom rung at Javier, but it's a start in a career where women climb to the top.'

Her own argument, lobbed back at her. 'You only want me to do it so I can steal.'

'I want you to have your dreams too. But steal, yes, once. Just once. Alix, I'm desperate for money! I didn't tell you the end of my nightmare: my mother's corpse reaches up and grabs Lala and Suzy off me, down into the water. I can hear them screaming my name as they go.'

She drank her wine, feeling it rough on her tongue. 'This interview . . . when is it?'

Paul caught her hand. 'Tomorrow.'

So soon?

'I can tell my contact you'll go? Take the job, pirate the collection? I'll write down the details.'

She shushed him. In his excitement he'd forgotten to whisper. Slowly she responded, 'If I do, I'll never pretend stealing is right. You understand?' He was reaching for a pencil, so she said again, 'I'll never pretend it's right.'

'I'm not your judge.' Paul began writing on the back of a discarded bill. He formed his letters as circles, adding sticks top or bottom as appropriate, and marched his words to the edge of the page. Knowing he hated being watched, Alix turned away, following a troop of schoolgirls with her eyes. Pallid, uncooked girls – she must have looked like that once. An old man laid his beret on the cobbles and began to play a bourrée on elbow pipes.

Paul handed her a note which read, 'Javier, Rue de la Trémoille. Say Mme Shone sent you, ask for première Mme Frankel. 11.03.'

'Do you mean eleven thirty?' she asked.

'Yes. Change it.'

'Mme Shone . . . she's your contact?'

'Sort of. Tomorrow, remember. Alix? You won't be late?'

After they'd paid for their lunch and she'd kissed Paul on each cheek, she crossed to Bonnet's house. He rented two second-floor rooms overlooking the square. She searched in vain for a light switch inside the front door and eventually shouted up to him. No reply, so she climbed the creaking stairs and knocked at a door she was just able to make out in the gloom. At the invitation 'Come in unless you're the taxman!' she pushed.

Bonnet was in the middle of the room, brushing glue size on to a canvas. Assuming she was late, she apologised, but he said imperturbably, 'I thought I'd get on with a different job. Wish I hadn't. Go get yourself ready.'

As she undressed behind a screen, Alix became increasingly aware of a foul smell. She emerged wrapped in a robe, sniffing. Linseed, turpentine, spirits for cleaning and some for drinking

. . . the usual smells of an artist's garret, but also something more. 'Bonnet, is there a dead rat under the floor?'

Bonnet brandished his sticky paintbrush at her. He was no taller than Alix and his full beard gave the impression he had no neck. He wore serge overalls, and a collarless shirt covered by a moth-eaten sweater, and – with his face lined through years spent painting in the hills of Alsace and in the blistering fields of Provence – he looked the consummate peasant-turned-artist. On Montmartre his appearance gave him status; anywhere else he'd be moved on. 'It's dead rabbit,' he said morosely, 'I paid for best-quality rabbit size and it shouldn't smell, not if it's made properly. People tell me all the time my work stinks –' he shook his head at the glistening canvas – 'now it will forever. So. Nice long lunch with your boyfriend, *michou*?' His grin sent wrinkles speeding out of his beard.

'Paul's not my boyfriend. I'm sure I told you.' But she was smiling. Bonnet was balm to tumbled spirits. He brewed wonderful coffee, and when it got really cold he'd add a drop of Kirsch, the cherry liqueur of Alsace. 'You should take that size back, demand compensation, say it gave your model a fainting fit.'

'Don't faint,' Bonnet took up his stance at a second easel. 'If I have to wheel you home in a barrow, your grandmother will ask questions. She didn't bring you to Paris to fall among my sort, not after that expensive lady's education the Comte de Charembourg gave you.'

'How do you know about him?'

Bonnet gave a conspiratorial wink. 'I am a man who knows everything and everybody. One day I will tell you stories of the comte that will make your eyebrows fly off. *Allons*, let's work.'

Alix slipped off her wrap and settled into her pose. It was a modest one, as modest as a naked pose can be. She sat tall because tomorrow she'd have to enter one of the smartest buildings in Paris and not blush, stammer or run away.

'Tomorrow' – 13th March – came racing in like a riptide. After a night of troubled dreams, Alix was outside Maison Javier, a vast building filling the angle between Rue de la Trémoille and Rue du Boccador. The nearby Avenues Montaigne and Champs-Elysées provided background traffic noise, but Trémoille itself was empty but for a couple of taxis and a silver-blue saloon, chauffeur at the wheel. Alix was glad of it. The last thing she wanted right now was an audience.

She reread Paul's note, checking she was at the right location. Of course she was. A brass plate beside a double-height door announced 'Javier'. She was just reaching to open the door when the *jooshing* sound of a well-tuned engine made her turn. A Peugeot the colour of vintage wine pulled up on the opposite pavement. Its driver got out, a young man wearing a sharp jacket, wide-leg trousers and a Homburg hat with a deep gutter crown, set at a rakish angle. He flicked back his cuffs, pulled his hat an inch lower, unfolded a newspaper and leaned casually against his car bonnet. He looked in Alix's direction and she felt his practised appraisal — felt him taking in her hair, her figure and the battered wicker basket she carried. His glance intruded like a photographer's lens. Alix fumbled at the door of Maison Javier and, in doing so, dropped her basket. A pair of newspaper-wrapped fish flopped out, followed by the fruit and vegetables she'd bought that morning at the market. She rammed them back in the basket and a soft laugh added to her discomfort. She threw the Peugeot driver an angry glare. He wasn't much older than she was, she could see, but he acted as if he owned the world. Taking a breath, she entered Maison Javier and found herself staring into a paved court broad enough for a horse and carriage to have turned in former times. Crossing the court, she found another door. She pushed that and then she was stepping into opulence, into an interior finer than any she'd seen before.

Until forty minutes ago she'd fully intended to miss this interview. Tumbling out of bed that morning, she'd reached for a well-worn dress and headed to the market for the week-end's shopping. She'd been on Rue Mouffetard, buying those fish, when a church bell struck eleven. Paris was full of churches, full of bells, so why this one should sound like the voice of Providence she'd never know. But each knell told her she was throwing away her best chance to get what she wanted in life. Basket bumping, she'd hurtled to the nearest *Métro*.

Javier's vestibule smelled sweetly of orange-flower oil, but her basket was introducing a less pleasant note. The fish ought to be at home, on ice. She could have left the basket in the street, but if it got stolen . . . another thing to explain to Mémé.

At least it was Saturday. The ateliers – the workrooms – would be running white hot, dozens of sewing women bent over their work as they strove to complete orders for the coming Easter holidays. The wealthy ladies who would benefit from all that labour were most likely at home, feet up, or at their country properties. It explained the silence on this, the ground floor and why, as she climbed a stately staircase, the sounds of activity became clearer. She couldn't quite locate where they came from, though, which added to the feeling of unreality.

She reached an area carpeted in honey-gold, dominated by a desk of lacquered maple. Here she gave her name to a receptionist. 'I have an appointment.'

The receptionist extended a hand like a traffic policeman. 'You should not have come up these stairs.' She glared at Alix's bare legs, then at the basket. 'We have a separate entrance for trade.'

'My appointment is with the première, Mme Frankel.'

After a hostile stare, the girl opened a diary, flicked a page and muttered, 'Gow-ère.' She frowned and pointed to a seat in a corner. 'Wait there. I will fetch the directrice.'

'My appointment is with—'

The receptionist cut her short. 'The directrice meets everybody who comes through these doors.' Implying there was no more to discuss, she slid a panel aside in a silk-papered wall and left.

Alix sighed. If that conversation was anything to go by, she'd soon be shooed out with a stick. But if she did leave, she'd never find the courage to return. So she sat on her hands and tried to ignore the whiff of fish. To her right was an archway hung with near-transparent drapes. Beyond, she could make out gilt chairs and a lake of carpet. It must be the salon where the collections were shown every afternoon to the cream of Parisian society. To that elite band of women who bought ten-thousand-franc dresses with as much nonchalance as Alix bought carrots. The salon was the designer's domain, ruled over by a directrice who was queen of the sales ladies and also in charge of the girls who modelled the clothes. These model girls were called manne-quins because, once upon a time, clothes had been displayed on wooden dummies. Then Worth, the first grand couturier, had grown impatient of bodies that couldn't move and hired beau-tiful girls instead. But the name had stuck. Mannequins were a species apart, with their striking figures and perfect poise. They ranked among the most courted women in Paris and graced the pages of top magazines. They were paid 'in flowers and com-pliments', Mémé had once told her. 'And kept by their lovers.'

She could see people moving about behind the drapes. Heavens – they were coming this way. Before she could get off her seat, a woman pushed through the curtain. She wore an hourglass suit, the sort called a *tailleur* or 'tailor-made', her blonde hair rolled in a chignon. Seeing Alix, she gave a start of high-bred astonishment. She was followed by an older female encased in black velvet. This one shot Alix a rancid look, demanding, 'Who might you be?'

Alix stammered her name and heard the blonde lady give a quick intake of breath. No chance to dissect the meaning of that – both women had already proceeded down the stairs. The black-velvet female was back minutes later, however, pointing at Alix's basket and asking in scathing tones, 'What is *that*?'

As Alix blundered through an explanation, the receptionist returned, calling in relief. 'Mlle Lilliane! I was trying to find you. This young woman has an appointment –' She indicated Alix, biting her lip as her colleague enquired in a voice of disgust, 'You left her in full view because . . . ?'

'Because I went to find you. I thought you would wish to see her first.'

'I do not wish to see her at all. Need I inform you that the lady I escorted to her car just now was the wife of the most esteemed Comte de Charembourg? Mme la Comtesse does not expect to trip over riff-raff and their baskets.'

Alix had jolted at the name. The Comtesse de Charembourg – that was the lady in the flawless suit? Mémé had spoken of Rhona de Charembourg a few times, and with so little warmth Alix had imagined her to be one of those booming, upper-class Englishwomen who splashed you as they drove past in their cars. Rhona de Charembourg might well do that, but she was no tweedy frump. Actually she could have manifested fully formed from the pages of *Vogue*. But wait . . . for the comtesse to be here, her husband must also be in Paris, surely? How odd, to discover it so soon after Bonnet had mentioned the comte's name in passing. A strange coincidence.

Jean-Yves, Comte de Charembourg, had fought in the same regiment as Alix's father. On her father's death, he'd stepped forward and, as Bonnet had put it, paid for her to have a lady's education. Alix had never asked if the comte's wife was party to this generosity. Belatedly translating the woman's freezing demeanour, Alix answered the question – Rhona de Charembourg must have been as shocked as Alix herself at this meeting. If she knew of the arrangement that made Alix her husband's unofficial ward, she liked it not one bit.

Though really there was no cause for resentment. Alix loved the comte as she might a kindly uncle, but she'd seen relatively little of him over the years. He'd written to her each birthday, long, amusing letters, and visited her at school perhaps once a year. During holidays, when they were both in London, he'd occasionally picked her up in a nippy Morgan three-wheeler and taken her to dine in a place by the Thames. As a young girl, she'd fantasised that he might adopt her, but there'd always been Mémé to shrink fantasy to its proper proportion –

'He has daughters of his own to worry about. You think he wants you plucking at his sleeve, Aliki?' According to Mémé, the comte sprinkled crumbs from his table out of a combination of kindness and duty. 'Army officers take care of their men, and in your father's case, there was special reason for the comte to look after you. Your father saved his life when they were under fire. But that doesn't mean he thinks of you in any special way.'

Alix knew differently. The comte *did* care. He couldn't fake that smile, nor the twinkle in his eye. She missed his company and had feared that by coming to Paris she'd put herself outside his reach. What a miracle if he should be here! Though if they met, it would be another thing to hide from her grandmother.

The comte and Mémé both originated from Kirchwiller in Alsace and had known each other before the war and the battle that had given John Gower the chance to save his captain's life. But Mémé had come from the disagreeable-sounding Impasse Demi-Jour in the Jewish quarter, while de Charembourg had been born in the castle on the hill, so they hadn't met socially. Their other bond had been Alfred Lutzman – the comte had admired his work and had bought some of his canvasses.

Would he take her out to dine one evening in Paris then? It was unlikely the comtesse would mention seeing her, but Alix knew she could look up his telephone number at work. Would she dare call him to say hello?

Meanwhile, Mlle Lilliane was inspecting Alix's dress, white poplin dotted with pink roses, its skirt crumpled by *Métro* seats. Her gaze travelled downward to discover bare feet in rope-soled shoes. She shuddered. 'Get out.'

Alix pulled herself tall. The school the comte had selected

for her, where she'd remained until her eighteenth birthday, had taught her one abiding skill: dignity in the face of humiliation. Kingswood Place had catered to the daughters of the English upper-middle classes, the comte having put her there rather than hurl her into the highest ranks of society. He'd explained, 'Snobbery is a blood sport in England.'

He couldn't have realised that the most acute snobbery is found in the 'nearly' ranks. Alix, obscure, parentless, paid for, had been bait for the stockbrokers' daughters. At best a museum exhibit, her origins much discussed but never decoded.

Those Parents' Days, when Mémé would bring baskets of pretzels and almond biscuits for the friends she fondly imagined Alix had made and would invariably be mistaken for somebody's servant, would never fade from Alix's memory. When she got nervous, Mémé would revert to Yiddish, and the girls – and some parents – would laugh behind their hands.

Alix's voice shook as she told the directrice, 'I have an interview. I apologise for my basket and for the fish. They accompanied me here but we're not acquainted.'

'Who arranged this supposed interview?'

'Mme Shone.' This was shaky ground. She only had Paul's say-so regarding Mme Shone's identity. Or indeed her existence. Alix looked towards the salon to avoid the directrice's eye. 'She thinks I have what it takes to work here.'

Mlle Lilliane blared, 'What it takes? Have you any idea "what it takes" to wear the clothes M. Javier creates?'

Alix realised her glance had been misinterpreted. Good lord, she wasn't putting herself forward as a mannequin. She wanted to make clothes, not parade them. As she tried to explain, Mlle Lilliane launched into a tirade, pausing only when a dark-haired man emerged from the salon.

'Ah, Mademoiselle, I thought I heard your voice. Do I interrupt some difficulty?' The newcomer spoke with a foreign lilt. His skin was very brown above his white collar.

A tailor, Alix guessed, seeing the tape measure draped over the shoulder of his immaculate jacket. Trained in a men's establishment, employed to produce suits like the one the Comtesse de Charembourg was wearing. Late fifties, anything but handsome, but Alix warmed instantly to the gentleness of his eyes. Under his jacket he wore an ivory waistcoat embroidered with one perfect peacock eye.

'Was Mme la Comtesse unhappy with her fitting? I hope not, as her new gown is chief guest at her next dinner party.' The man coughed because Mlle Lilliane was still muttering in Alix's direction. 'Is this young person from Milady's household?'

Mlle Lilliane barked, 'She's nobody, except she imagines she has the makings of a mannequin. I have been striving to remove the notion. Join me in telling her that to be a house mannequin at Javier—'

The man politely gestured for silence. He turned to Alix. 'Are you Mlle Gower?'

Alix gulped. 'Yes, Monsieur.'

'Then I must offer explanation. My première has not forgotten you but she is embroiled elsewhere. She sends apologies –'

Disappointment flooded Alix. She was just beginning to believe that she might actually like working here.

'– and asked me to see you instead. It is Mme Shone who recommends you?'

'Yes, Mme Shone, that's right. And I don't want to be a mannequin. That's not why I came.'

'We will go to my room and untangle the knots,' he said, turning. When Alix made to follow him, he wagged a finger towards the floor by her feet. 'I think this fellow should come too.'

Her basket. Blushing, she grabbed the handle and followed the tailor through doors into a stairwell, cringing as Mlle Lilliane's voice rang out –

'On top of everything else, Monsieur, she smells.'

'Will you permit me to ask who you are, Monsieur? Are you really just a tailor?'

'Just a tailor?' He indicated she should take a seat at a cutting table – bare but for a bowl of lush pink roses the size of cabbages. 'To be a tailor is to be the *generalissimo* of couture. Take a minute, get your breath.'

They'd come briskly through a warren of corridors, then ridden a hydraulic lift to the top of the building. What he'd described as 'his room' turned out to be the whole top floor. From her seat, Alix could stare up into a lantern skylight and see clouds forming and massing. One side of the room overlooked Rue de la Trémoille, and on the courtyard side stood an army of figurines wearing 'toiles' of filmy muslin. Toiles were the early stages of couture clothes. Alix marvelled at bouffant sleeves, plunging necks and hems scrunched like rings of meringue. Evening gowns in the making.

Mlle Lilliane stormed in after them, planting herself between Alix and the figurines. 'Does it occur to you, Monsieur, that she might be a spy from another house?'

Shrugging, 'Monsieur' invited the directrice to stay if she wished – 'But no more crossness. Angry people give me pains here.' The tailor patted his stomach. 'Well, *petite*,' he invited, 'you wish to be an employee of Javier? What is your skill?'

'Um . . .' Alix had rehearsed a speech on the *Métro*, but suddenly couldn't remember it. 'I – I learned to sew at school and from Mémé – I mean, my grandmother. After I left school, I worked in the ladies' made-to-measure department of a London store, sometimes making alterations, sometimes as a fitter.'

'A fitter? What did that teach you, Mademoiselle?'

'That ladies whose waist measurement is thirty-six inches always think the fitter's tape measure is wrong.'

The man smacked his table in delight. 'Excellent. What else has life taught you?'

'Erm . . . I do fine stitching, every sort of seam and

buttonhole and every embroidery stitch. I've learned shadow work, open threadwork, smocking, quilting . . . um . . . I can make lace –' adding for truth's sake – 'but not very well. I can stitch broderie anglaise and blackwork.'

'Ah, blackwork is a good thing to say to me. Blackwork is a thing of joy for a Spaniard. Have you brought me samples?'

'No, I'm sorry.' She'd brought fish instead.

Mlle Lilliane crowed, 'How do we know she isn't lying?'

'Because Mme Shone sent her. *Petite*, show me your hands.'

Alix held them out. Mlle Lilliane shrieked, 'Look at her nails! Imagine those hands touching one of your gowns.'

Your gowns . . . ? A pulse began working behind Alix's ear.

The man opened a drawer and took out a marquetry box. 'This was my mother's sewing box. Take what you need.' He pulled a pristine silk handkerchief from his pocket. 'Create me something.'

Alix thought, *Paul, I'll kill you.*

Shaking, she threaded a needle with silk, stretched the handkerchief on to a hoop, then sewed grimly until she found her rhythm. At that point, the tailor retired to a side office, leaving the door ajar and Alix heard him talking first to himself in Spanish, then on the telephone in French. All this time, Mlle Lilliane remained at the table, eyes open like a snake's. It felt like an hour before the tailor came back into the room – though it was probably nearer twenty minutes. At last, Alix was able to hand over an image worked in satin stitch and French knots. The tailor took it from her, nodded, then commented, 'She smells, you say, Mlle Lilliane?' To Alix's horror, he raised her hand to his nose. 'Trout,' he said in a satisfied voice.

Alix's eyes flared. 'How did you know?'

'This nose –' he tapped it – 'blended Ersa from fifty different ingredients and achieved a miracle of balance.'

'Ersa?'

'My signature perfume. Can you not smell it . . . orange flower, sweet almond . . . ?'

She sniffed the air. 'And rose oil?'

'Perhaps. Ersa is complex. Only I know her secrets.'

'You are M. Javier, aren't you? Oh dear.'

'Oh dear,' he imitated, but he was smiling.

He passed Alix's embroidery to Mlle Lilliane, who snorted, 'Very poor taste.'

'*Au contraire*, Mademoiselle. It is the most beautifully worked fish I have seen in months. This young lady knows that to work in our business takes courage and a sense of humour.'

When Alix told her news that evening, Mémé slapped her face.

'A couturier's *midinette* – a skivvy – after everything I said? They'll pay you a pittance and want blood for it.'

Alix put her hand to her cheek. 'Javier pays his girls well and some of the richest women in Paris buy only from him. You should be proud he offered me work.'

'Alix, Alix, have you any idea what it took to get you that job

70

at the telephone company? I went cap in hand to the Comte de Charembourg, begged him to ring the director of the company to make space for you.'

'You saw the comte here, in Paris?' Alix was confused. 'Where did you see him? When?'

'At his house in the 16ᵗʰ. When I went to beg his help in getting you a job, Mme la Comtesse keeping me on the step like a vagrant. Bitter medicine, drunk for your good.'

'You should have told me he was here,' Alix said stubbornly. 'And I thought I got the job at the exchange on my own merits.' The bubble on which she'd floated home burst. 'You're always so harsh, so buttoned-up. Why punish me for making the best of a life I didn't ask for?'

When Mémé gave no answer, Alix's emotions rose. 'My father would have been proud of me even if you aren't. He always said I was an "original".'

Mémé sat down, throwing her hands wide. 'You were barely five years old when your father died. The longest talk you had with him was about which spoon to eat your porridge with.' She gestured at the portrait of Mathilda. 'They're all dead. You have only me.'

Something snapped in Alix. She flung out of the room, shouting, 'I bet my mother ran off to be a nurse to escape you.'

'Aliki!'

Ignoring the pain in that cry, Alix ran out of the flat. She'd spend the rest of the day with Bonnet. But, after puffing up the stairs of Abbesses, the *Métro* station of Butte Montmartre, she discovered her friend was otherwise engaged. He was in the square, part of a male group rolling knuckle jacks across a mat on the ground. A fold-out table was crammed with bottles and glasses.

'Boys' club,' she muttered. 'I'll go and see Paul.'

But at the Quai d'Anjou, she found the *Katrijn* away from her mooring. She stared at the empty patch of water, a formless sorrow coming over her. Paul was always here when she needed him.

The old barge-woman Francine grinned down from her deck. 'He'll be back. He's taken his sisters up the canal to visit his last living relation.'

'He doesn't have any relations, Francine.'

'Oh, he does. A great-aunt at Bobigny who washed her hands of Sylvie le Gal years ago. Didn't approve of naughty dancing.' Francine waggled her flanks. 'Paul's hoping his girls will melt her tough, old heart so he can hide them there when the authorities come to get them. I just hope the fuel's worth it; he had to borrow a can off me.' Laughing at Alix's glum expression, Francine beckoned. 'Step up, take a glass of pastis with me.'

Alix didn't really want to, but Francine's toothless smile urged her aboard. Once there, one pastis turned into several. Alix finally wobbled off Francine's boat as the light faded. Her cheek still smarted from Mémé's palm, but the intervening hours had refashioned her anger. Mémé was getting old in a world that handed out no fresh starts to a seamstress with bent fingers. Mémé was scared of the future, of Germans, of everything.

But by the time she was crossing the square in front of St-Sulpice, feeling the vibration of its famous organ in the slabs beneath her feet, Alix had reached a decision. She wouldn't take the job with Javier. Not even for Paul's sake, not even for Suzy's. It was too loaded with risk, with expectation.

She'd help Paul in other ways, she vowed. She'd slave at the telephone exchange, take every night shift going. Turn into Mlle Boussac and become a supervisor. That man in the dependable suit could sweep her off to a neat suburb – though he'd have to take Mémé too.

That was a good plan. *So why are you crying?* she demanded of herself. *Hope isn't dead. It just feels that way.*

Chapter Six

She stuck to her vow all the following week. Here she was, finishing another Saturday night on Rue du Louvre, another night shift. As Sunday's dawn edged through the blinds of the exchange building, Alix pulled off her headphones and thought longingly of coffee. Sweet, strong coffee. She checked her watch. Less than an hour to go. At least she'd been kept busy. Usually the night shift was quiet, but today the din of switches selecting and clicking drowned the murmurings of her colleagues as they processed calls.

'Bad weather over the channel. Sailings cancelled from all ports,' the night shift supervisor had reported. Caller after caller was being told they must wait over an hour to alert family and friends in Britain that they were stuck in France. Alix swivelled her seat from side to side. Ooh, her back! She must not think of strong, sweet coffee . . .

A light flashed in front of her and she plugged an answering cord into the jack and crammed on her headphones. 'Which destination, please?' When the answer came 'London' she prepared to inform another traveller that he would have to be patient. But there was no chance as the caller snapped, 'Get me Abbey 2310. I need a line right now!'

He spoke English, which annoyed her as it implied that her French was not perfect. In the starchiest English she could command, she said, 'I'm sorry, sir, lines to England are full. Waiting time is eight hours.'

The girl sitting beside her shot Alix a startled look and whispered, 'Eighty minutes, Mlle Dujardin said. Not eight hours, Alix.'

Alix pretended not to hear.

Her caller was less than impressed too. 'It'd be faster to swim.'

'Do you like fog?'

'Is that what I'm up against?'

'It's like mutton fat. Everything that moves is cancelled. The world needs to call London because Londoners love to discuss fog the way other people talk about vintage wine. There are infinite varieties.' Aware she was drifting towards insolence, she re-starched her voice. 'I will tell you when we can set up your call.'

'Are you English?'

'No.' He had a nice voice now he wasn't ordering her about. Sexy, even. But that didn't get him off the charge of rudeness. 'I'm half English.'

'May I say, the half that is speaks it very well.'

'That's why I am employed here.'

'Of course. Look, I'm a journalist, and it's vital I speak to my London editor before he wakes and leaves for the day.'

'Your name, please?' she asked.

'Verrian Haviland.' He spelled both names for her.

'And your party, sir?'

'Jack Haviland, Abbey 2310.'

'I thought you said "your editor".'

'Who happens to be my brother.'

'I see. Your present location?'

'Laurentin's hotel by Gare du Nord, in the passage behind the kitchen, unpleasantly close to the lavatory, shouting over clattering pans into a phone that smells of garlic and stale tobacco. Will you put me through?'

Alix choked back a giggle as much from shock as amusement. She shot a look behind her. The supervisor, Mlle Dujardin, sat a few feet away, writing up a report. Familiarity, especially giggling, was strictly forbidden. 'I have to send every request to another section or issue a "request and schedule" card. I can't influence the connecting switchboard.'

'But you could prioritise?' He had a graze in his voice as if he smoked too heavily, but he sounded cultured. Alix wondered what he was doing in that kitchen corridor. She knew the places near Gare du Nord station. They opened before dawn to feed railway porters, road sweepers and tired prostitutes.

She said, 'Not without appropriate authorisation.'

'And that would be too much to ask of a stiff-necked telephone operator?'

Her fingers hovered over the plug. One pull would terminate. But she surprised herself by answering sweetly, 'It would be. Fortunately for you, I'm not stiff-necked . . . Well, I am, but only because I've been working all night.'

A pause. Then, 'I'm truly sorry. I've had a hellish week and I really have to speak with my brother. He's in a position to save a man's life.'

She'd heard it all in her months on this switchboard, all the life-or-death reasons why one person's call should jump the queue. So why did she instinctively believe this man? Mlle Dujardin had closed her report book and was heading out the door. Alix whispered into her mouthpiece, 'Is this true – a man could die?'

'Yes. He's in prison in Spain, where I've just come from. He's in a desperate condition. My brother knows people in the British government who can pull strings. It's a shot in the dark, and every hour counts.'

Alix thought quickly. 'Give me a little time. I'll do my best, but I'll have to break the rules.' She heard a whisper of relief.

He asked, 'May I know your name?'

Her neighbour was listening avidly so Alix replied, 'I'm not at liberty to say.'

'Not allowed to fraternise? One last question: will you marry me?'

That giggle finally got out. 'Perhaps. But this time you really will have to go to the back of the queue.'

Alix slipped the earpiece off and muttered to her neighbour, 'I have to powder my nose.'

Ignoring her colleague's protest that surely she could hold on to the end of the shift, Alix ran along a corridor to a room where female operators sat at consoles either side of a gangway. Mlle Boussac was on duty in this section. She was at the end of an aisle, engrossed in some problem. Satisfied she'd chosen a good moment, Alix searched the rows for the destination sign 'London'.

She selected a girl the same age as herself and placed a priority request card in front of her. She'd filched it from Mlle Dujardin's desk and filled it in herself. 'It's been authorised,' she said, her stomach diving. She was risking her job for a stranger.

The girl looked unsure. 'Hadn't we better check?'

They looked to where Mlle Boussac was tapping the end of a connector cord. 'She looks busy,' Alix whispered.

At that moment, Mlle Boussac straightened up and looked straight at Alix. Then another operator summoned her to where a rapidly flashing light indicated an electrical fault.

'You're new, aren't you?' Alix asked the girl, and tapped the card. 'It's fine. It's from the ministry.'

'Which ministry?'

'*The* ministry. They always get priority.'

The following day, Monday, Alix was reported for breaking telephone company rules regarding the strict order of customers' calls. The girl who sat beside her had seen her take the request card and told the supervisor.

Alix was docked a day's pay and warned that no more infractions would be tolerated.

But the following day, Mémé called in at the exchange in great distress. Mlle Boussac sent a secretary to fetch Alix from the switchboard and to bring a glass of water.

Alix found her grandmother perched on a chair, trembling so hard her water was in danger of spilling. Alix took the glass away from her. 'Mémé, what is it?'

'The Germans are trying to break into the flat.'

'Germans, in St-Sulpice?'

'All morning I'm hearing *tap, tap, tap –*' The rest was lost as Mémé flowed away in Yiddish. Alix caught one name –

'Hitler was trying to break in at our door?' She exchanged a glance with Mlle Boussac, who looked as though she was sucking a bee.

'Not the door, the roof! He's lifting the slates to come in that way.'

'Why would he?' Alix asked. 'How would he get up there in the first place?'

'Perhaps he jumps from the building next door.' Mémé rocked forward.

Alix thought, *Is it delusions?* A new fear struck her – her grandmother failing in her mind, needing constant attendance. Then a bird flew past the office window and another possibility dawned. 'Mémé, d'you think you could have been hearing pigeons? They're nesting, fluttering about the chimney stacks. They woke me this morning.'

Mémé's brows furrowed. 'Pigeons? You are sure?'

'Spring's here and they're pairing. Don't they make a racket?' As her grandmother nodded slowly, Alix burst out, 'Oh, Mémé, you got upset over nothing, walked all this way and you'll have to go up those stairs again.'

'I am all right. It's my hands that hurt. I don't walk on my hands.'

Mlle Boussac glanced at Danielle's feet, her expression hardening. 'Alix has a point, Madame, considering you sprained your ankle so recently. What will your doctor say when he hears you walked across Paris to come here?'

Mémé, oblivious to danger signals, inspected her ankles carefully. 'Have I sprained my ankle? I don't think so. I'm stronger than I look.'

Mlle Boussac did not challenge Alix immediately. But after Mémé left, Alix was summoned before the head of department. While he looked on in stern silence, Mlle Boussac asked Alix if she had lied. 'On 4th March you claimed your grandmother needed to visit the doctor and requested time off.'

Alix admitted it.

'You wanted to see a young man, I suppose.' Anger flooded Mlle Boussac's cheeks.

Alix agreed. A young man, yes. It was simpler.

'It seems, Alix Gower, I have been mistaken in my estimation of your character. The company may tolerate one misstep but not two.'

The head of department was inclined to agree. Alix was invited to collect her coat and leave the premises.

On Rue du Louvre she stared around, her hand over her mouth. The air was thick with exhaust fumes. Outlines of buildings melted under her shocked gaze. She'd been sacked. What was she feeling . . . relief?

Maison Javier.

Out of one job, she had no choice but to take another. As she crossed the street, she wondered whether her English caller had reached his brother and saved his Spanish friend.

Chapter Seven

He often came to this church to hear its organ and view its famous Delacroix murals. 'Jacob Wrestling with the Angel' was his favourite. But today he couldn't face Jacob, a man abandoned to a combat he could not win. So he found a seat, bent his head and prayed she'd come. He wasn't sure she'd got his letter inviting her to meet him inside the church of St-Sulpice. He'd left the note with a concierge, who'd promised to 'find someone to take it upstairs' before pushing it into her grimy apron.

He wished someone was playing the organ today. Bach ideally, something complex and ear-filling. In its midweek silence, this monumental interior made him feel judged. And alone – though on the other side of the aisle a handful of women moved their lips in prayer.

She wouldn't come. He should never have suggested a church for a meeting. But he'd wanted somewhere they could speak in whispers without attracting notice.

'Whenever I'm here I marvel at the money you Catholics

spend providing a home for God. It says much for your confidence in his presence.'

He whipped round to see Danielle Lutzman settling behind him. His immediate thought was, *She's aged so much since she came to see me.* Was it a year ago that she'd called at Boulevard Racan to ask his help to get her granddaughter into some employment? That once-handsome face was now a wizened apple, dwarfed by a sombrous hat.

'I come sometimes to hear the organ,' she said, misreading his shock. 'A Jewess may hear a little Bach or Handel without taking anything that is not rightfully hers. It is the nearest I come to God, and my father would have shaken me, my husband too. Bolshevists to the bone. The only music my father liked was the clatter of falling monarchies.'

'What would he have made of this place?'

She stared upward. 'He'd have wanted it made into a grain store.' Fastening spectacles on her nose, she said, 'I received your note but I've been unwell. A little mad, I think. Would you believe, I thought a pigeon on my roof was that liver-worm Hitler coming for me? I read in the newspaper about his Gestapo police and cannot stop thinking of the day I was taken by the police from my home in Kirchwiller. I am so scared in Paris. I did not think I would be.'

'What made you leave London? You had a home and a life there.'

She shrugged. 'The eternal search for safety . . . for

atonement.' A nervous smile distorted her lips. 'Here, at least if the police come to fetch me I can call on you or on my friend Bonnet. Both of you helped me before, did you not?' She waited for his wordless acknowledgement before asking, 'What do you want of me?'

Her confession of fear had pushed him off track, and when he spoke he forgot to be cautious. 'I have become a victim of blackmail over your husband's death.' He saw her touch the scar at her temple. 'Yes, that day has finally returned. Madame, you swore to tell no living soul.'

'Yes, I swore it.'

'Somebody knows. Somebody telephoned me at home, minutes after I received this.' He passed her the grubby letter that had been delivered to his home on the twelfth. 'Tell me if you know the writing.'

She handed it back after a moment and her body was trembling. 'I don't recognise the hand. He threatens to expose the truth of Alfred's death. It is blackmail, Monsieur, but the writer is not sure of his ground.'

'Why d'you say that?'

'He threatens to hurt someone you love if you do not pay. Which shows that exposing the facts of poor Alfred's murder is not enough . . . because nobody cares any more.' She murmured in Yiddish. 'People thought *I* had killed my husband.'

'You were arrested on suspicion only, and released almost immediately.'

'Thanks to you. But to rescue me, you brought others into our secret. Perhaps one of those 'others' has crawled out from under a stone to threaten you.'

He agreed, adding, 'But who?'

'There was Kern.'

'The police inspector whom my mother bribed? He died a decade ago and had no reason to talk. After all, we made him rich. There is Célie Haupmann, of course, my mother's house-keeper . . . but she's frail now and her loyalty to my mother was always beyond question.'

'To your mother, but not to you. Was Haupmann the one who brought warm clothes to me in prison?' Danielle stroked her sleeves as he confirmed it. 'She did not like me. I don't think she liked you either. You say she is frail?'

'She is dying. I don't suspect her.'

'She has dependents though? A son or daughter who pokes her for money, who might benefit from a little windfall?'

'Haupmann has no children. She was always utterly depend-ent on my family and will be loyal to her last breath. Could *you* have revealed the facts of your husband's death accidentally? Perhaps to Raphael Bonnet?'

'We agreed on a story that would save us both, and I told nobody, not even my child! As for that –' she pointed at the letter – '*that* was written by a lout who smokes dung. My old friend Bonnet is a man of proven loyalty. Whatever he has learned of *my* failings – *mein gott*, I have many – he would not exploit them for money.' She clasped her hands, closing the subject. 'How much does your liver-worm blackmailer want?'

He found a smile. 'Rather a lot, and I'm struggling to raise it. According to his admirably detailed instructions, I'm to leave it behind a tobacco kiosk near Notre-Dame-d'Auteuil on Good Friday. That's the day after tomorrow—' He broke off as a woman walked by. She was slim, dark-eyed, and his thoughts jumped to Alix. 'How is our Aliki? I'd like to see her.'

Danielle scraped her chair as she rose. 'I must go.'

Jean-Yves followed her out of the church, catching her arm as she stumbled in the afternoon dazzle. 'At your request I haven't contacted Alix, but I hate pretending that I don't know she's in the same city. If she needs a friend here, money to study with, a letter of recommendation, anything, you will ask?'

Danielle swatted the offer away. 'You helped her to a position at the telephone exchange and that's enough. Save your wealth for your daughters. A wedding to pay for, no? Now you look as if I have said something vulgar. I read about it in the newspaper.'

He sighed. He had not wanted a public announcement, considering such fanfare to be indelicate. But Rhona had insisted.

Danielle unwittingly echoed Rhona's very argument. 'Why should you hide your great triumph from the world?' She reeled off, '"Marie Louise Alphonsine Rhona Christine, eldest daughter of the Comte de Charembourg, to marry Guy Philippe Antoine, Duc de Brioude, on 15th June at the family estate in

Kirchwiller." It's a stupendous match and I can understand this is a bad moment to have to pay a blackmailer. So, don't pay him. Tell him to piss in his own teeth.' When he hesitated, she raised a finger. 'Pay a blackmailer, keep a blackmailer.'

'You read those threats, but you didn't hear him, Madame. You didn't hear him gloating at the prospect of ruining . . .' he paused because he felt sick, 'ruining a sweet face. I don't know by what means. Burning, sulphur-acid, a knife . . . All I know is, I must pay.'

'Does the farmer's wife milk her cow only once?'

He had no answer to that and they made their goodbyes. He watched Danielle Lutzman hobble across the square having declined his offer to escort her home on the grounds that they shouldn't be seen together. 'People gossip, and it will upset that lady your wife.'

She was wise and he was a fool. But he was also a father, a proud and loving father. He was a husband, a guardian and – perhaps belatedly – a man of honour. So he must find the money. He had no choice.

Easter, 27th March

His daughter Ninette insisted she could always tell when a phone call was from Christine's fiancé. 'The ring goes all moist when Philippe calls. It wheezes with unexpressed poetry.'

'Don't mock your sister,' Jean-Yves reproved. 'Telephones, like all man-made technology, are reliably unimaginative.'

'No, no, Papa. They mirror our feelings.'

'Then allow your sister her private feelings and remember that a loving telephone will ring for you one day.'

When, three days after meeting Danielle in St-Sulpice, his telephone rang, Ninette's theory blew back at him. He knew before he picked up the receiver which voice he'd hear.

'Where were you yesterday. Not-so-Good Friday? You did not leave the money, broke our sacred deal. You are forcing me –' the catarrh was getting thicker – 'to give you one, final chance. I know where those you care about spend their days. I know where they walk, the young ladies, where they shop and take their lunch. Don't wait until my knife-hand is unbearably itchy.'

'I tried to pay, I swear. Listen, please—' A knock at his study door made Jean-Yves curse violently. He shouted, 'Go away!' but the door opened to reveal his secretary bearing a sheath of parchment. Jean-Yves dropped his arm behind his desk to hide the telephone receiver. 'Not now, Ferryman.'

'These are from the Duc de Brioude's attorney, Monsieur. Your signature is needed.'

'I said, later. I'm busy.'

Ferryman made an obsequious half-bow, but did not move. 'Permit me to suggest you sign them, Monsieur, so I can deliver them—'

'Just bloody well get out!'

The whole exchange took perhaps a quarter of a minute, but it was too long for the caller's patience: the line was dead. Jean-Yves replaced the receiver and waited for the man to ring back; waited like a cat ready to pounce. When that posture exhausted him, he got up and paced, never taking his eyes from the telephone. The instrument on the desk had gained the malevolent power of a devil's familiar. He swore never again to laugh at Ninette's flights of fancy.

When Ninette herself put her head round his door, asking if she might go to the Bois de Boulogne to ride with her friends, he snapped, 'No.'

She blinked at him. 'I only asked to be polite, Papa. You never say no.'

'Who else is going? Any young men in the party?'

'Well, yes, of course.' She named names, all young men of good family, one of them on leave from the cavalry school at Saumur. One couldn't ask for a better escort for a daughter. Even in his sweating panic, Jean-Yves knew he couldn't place his girls under house arrest. So he told Ninette she could go but on no account to leave her friends. And the chauffeur must drive her. Also, Ferryman must accompany her and wait at the livery stables for her.

'Ferryman?' Ninette's face stretched in horror. 'Papa, no! He bows like a waiter . . . people might think he's my boyfriend. Anything but Ferryman.'

He gave in to that too, because she was right without knowing it: life must continue as normal, even though he was unable to focus on anything but a blackmailer with a knife and an itchy hand.

He was adding up the value of his Banque d'Alsace shares – arriving at a different total each time – when there came a tap at his door. Expecting Ferryman, priming himself to apologise for his earlier ill temper, he was surprised to find his elder daughter, Christine. Her wedding trousseau consumed her at the moment and she was usually to be found in the morning room, embroidering linked de Charembourg and Brioude ciphers on to linen napkins.

She was dressed for lunch at home, and his first impression was that the copper-green bias-cut dress did not suit her. Christine was tall but not slender, and princess-line would have been better. He kissed her and sniffed. 'Schiaparelli's "Shocking"? Did an Easter gift arrive from Philippe, perchance?'

She giggled. 'You have a good nose for a man.'

'For a man? The best perfumers are men. I cite Ernest Beaux, who created Chanel's No. 5; André Fraysse who threw flowers into a pot to produce your mother's favourite, Arpège. The best couturiers are also men, and undoubtedly the best chefs.'

A frown bent Christine's brows and he presumed her feminine pride was touched, but all she said was, 'Philippe is dining with us tonight.'

'Good. I like your fiancé. In him, I have the joys of a clever son without having had the expense of educating him.'

Christine's frown deepened. She rarely understood his jokes. 'Philippe promised to call me to find out what flowers to bring for Maman. You know she likes men to bring flowers that compliment her evening clothes?'

'I am aware of that charming foible. Has he not called?'

'Oh, yes, but I told him gardenias because white is always safe. But then I remembered that Maman hates the smell.'

'So, ring him and tell him to bring roses.'

'He's gone out and won't be back all day, his man says. What shall I do?'

'How about, stop wasting energy on trivialities?' He instantly regretted his sharp tongue. Christine was in love; silly things mattered. Unlike Ninette, she hadn't the confidence to be playful or cheeky. With her heart-shaped face and negligible brows, Christine reminded him deeply of his mother. Like the late Marie-Christine de Charembourg, his daughter expressed her love in detailed care, in absolute loyalty, traits easily abused. So he continued gently, 'We can remedy the situation by going out and buying white roses. Ferryman can lurk in the hall with them behind his back. Philippe arrives . . . and a daring exchange is made without your mother suspecting a thing. *Voilà*.'

Finally she laughed. 'You are wonderful. Shall we go out for lunch?' Then, instead of letting him answer, she returned to that small, persistent detail; 'I suggested white flowers only because I have no idea what Maman will wear tonight. She's at Maison Javier, having the final fitting for her dress for dinner tomorrow.'

Ferryman knocked just then, entering sideways, as if by narrowing himself he might avoid a further telling-off. He brought a letter, hand-delivered moments before. Jean-Yves tore into it, preparing a nonchalant expression for the young people who watched him closely. He sagged in relief when he saw a familiar signature. 'It's from the chairman of FTM. I'm summoned to a meeting,' he said.

When Christine looked blank, he added drily, 'FTM . . . Fabrication Textile Mulhouse – the people who pay my salary?' He read the letter again. 'Well, now. There's a Swiss moneybags in town, interested in buying into the firm. Seems we're meeting today.'

'A business meeting on Holy Saturday?' Christine couldn't hide her disapproval. Another trait she shared with his late mother was religious devotion. 'Who is he, the moneybags?'

'Name of Maurice Ralsberg. A heathen, no doubt.'

'Ralsberg – oh, he came to a charity function Maman took me to.' Christine risked a smile. 'He was quite handsome when he took his glasses off. Very charming to Maman and me. He called her "comtesse" the whole time, which she likes.'

'Oho. A social climber. Shall I double the price of my shares? Tell you what,' he continued, 'we'll have that lunch. Come to Rue du Sentier with me first. You can sit in on the board meeting. It will be an education.'

'Me, come to a business meeting?'

'Absolutely. You can charm the moneybags, after which, since we'll be in the heart of the fabric quarter, you can choose some pretty cloth for your honeymoon—'

'Javier's making my trousseau,' she said quickly. 'Maman won't like me buying fabric without her there.'

'Shush. You can buy something Philippe will adore, and I'll have it made up. Then we'll have lunch somewhere quiet.'

Having sent her away and Ferryman with her, he checked there was nobody in the hall outside, then took a leather satchel from a locked drawer. He inspected the banded wads of notes. Five hundred thousand francs, all present and correct. Astonishing how little space so much money took up. He lifted the receiver, intending to call his broker and arrange the sale of half of his Banque d'Alsace shares. That would raise sufficient cash to make up for withdrawing so much from his bank account. But as he dialled the broker's number, he remembered that his man of business would be out of town for the Easter festival. The irony was, he had *tried* to pay the blackmailer. He'd gone to the drop-off behind the kiosk by Notre-Dame-d'Auteuil the previous day as instructed, and discovered there was no 'behind'. Just a pavement in full view of the world. The situation had felt too risky and – this was a strange choice of word – *amateur*. He'd walked on, clutching the satchel to him because he couldn't allow so much money to fall into the wrong hands.

PART TWO

PART TWO

Chapter Eight

On 31st March 1937, the German Condor Legion bombed the town of Durango in the Basque region of Spain. They chose market day, mid-afternoon.

Verrian Haviland wished to God he had been there, and not lying on a bed in a dingy Paris hotel, fighting off the remains of a fever. The newspaper that the maid had brought up with his morning coffee confirmed what he'd suspected during his last days in Madrid – the theatre of war was turning north. The Fascists had failed to take Madrid and were targeting Spain's industrial centres instead. But even so, striking little Durango made no sense.

Verrian had made that point in a dispatch from Madrid on 9th March. He'd typed up the copy in the aftermath of a raid and wired it, very late, for next morning's edition of the *News Monitor*. At some point during the night his editor – who was also his brother Jack – had got hold of the article and added his own creative touch.

Three days later, all hell had broken loose.

Verrian stretched out a tanned arm to see if his scars had faded. Not entirely, but they weren't painful any more. And he could clench a fist and count how many fingers he was wiggling. He knew from the fact that he was desperate for a cigarette that he must have thrown off the worst of his fever. He washed at the hotel sink and hunted for a clean shirt, remembering then that he only had the one he'd arrived in.

The thought brought back a slow-motion nightmare. He sank down on his bed, replaying the moment a Spanish Republican policeman had rammed a friend of his, Miguel Rojas Ibarra, against the wall of a room in a government office . . . taken Miguel's hand, raised it like a target . . . the sound that followed was engrained in Verrian's body as deeply as the shards of plaster blown from the wall. They'd dragged Miguel away and the police had come for Verrian. He'd fought his way out of the building, cut through backstreets and found refuge in a church crypt. Alone in the damp dark, he'd pieced events together. He'd filed his copy in all innocence, ensuring it would reach the *News Monitor*'s London office when his brother Jack was on night duty. Jack had run the piece having changed some vital wording to suit his own political prejudices. The Spanish authorities must have got wind of it around the 13th March, reacting with savage speed.

Verrian had stayed a week in the crypt, emerging into the bombed streets only to snatch the odd meal in a café, unable to risk returning to his hotel in case police patrols were looking for him. Being tall with blue eyes, he couldn't merge with a

Madrid crowd, and his blood-spattered shirt and jacket marked him out.

Eventually, fearing he'd die of exposure, and desperately anxious for Miguel, he'd thrown money at a taxi driver to take him to the nearest airport. He didn't remember much of the drive or the checkpoint stops. He must have talked his way through them. Using the last of his strength, he'd pounded across the concrete at Albacete aerodrome, reaching the side of an Avro Anson just as it taxied for take-off. The flight out . . . He'd never felt so sick. His forearms and the backs of his hands, which had shielded his face from the gun blast, were burned raw and he couldn't get one scene out of his head: Miguel bent double, shelves of white paper behind him drenched scarlet because they'd shot him in a stationery store room. Verrian remembered landing at Paris's Le Bourget airport and getting a taxi to this hotel. At some point he'd rung London, begging Jack to move heaven and earth to help Miguel because it had all been Jack's fault, that horror.

He'd tried to be calm. He'd begun well. 'That piece of mine you ran—'

'"Our man in the gutter: mice 'neath the raptor's shadow."' Jack's soft laugh had stripped the comment of any compliment. 'Were you aiming for the Robbie Burns Prize?'

Verrian bit down on an angry reply. There was no time to indulge Jack in game-playing. 'I wrote of the bombing raid I was caught in. My sign-off was; "If Madrid is getting it now, might not London, Oxford or Paris get it tomorrow?" You cut that out and substituted a lump of Fascist propaganda.'

'I did? You'll have to explain, old boy.'

'You added a sentence implying that the Spanish government plunders churches to buy arms from Soviet Russia.'

'As it does,' Jack came back smoothly. 'Spanish Republicans are Red to their bones. You can't swing a cat in Madrid without knocking over a Comrade. They should expect the opposition to retaliate with a few bombing raids.'

'And I suppose life on Fleet Street and weekends spent walking the dogs on the Sussex Downs makes you an expert in incendiary warfare?' Jack's emollient response of 'Now, now,' had the opposite effect to the one intended. The brakes came off Verrian's anger. 'I have spent ten months reporting from the Madrid front, striving to be neutral while being fired on and bombed, talking to the troops, eating with them, stepping over the dead. I was allowed on the battlefield because the Republicans trusted me. *Trusted.* By changing my report, adding that one line, you wrecked everything I built up! The government press department blamed their censorship people for those words, and one poor sod paid the price.'

The 'poor sod' being Miguel Rojas Ibarra, a middle-ranker in the censorship building whom Verrian had befriended through a shared love of jazz and the writings of Cervantes. Verrian described Miguel's punishment, ignoring Jack's pleas to spare him such ghastly details so early in the day. 'You will move heaven and earth to help him. *Heaven and earth*, Jack, or I'll go back to Madrid and raise hell. I won't let Miguel die of his injuries in jail.'

Jack accused Verrian of being a damn fool, too emotionally embroiled. But he agreed to do what he could, and also promised to wire Verrian his unclaimed expenses so he could get to a decent hotel. 'You'll need a shave and a bath if you've been a fugitive for a week. Stay awhile in Paris, re-civilise yourself, and I'll get back to you when, *if*, I have something to report. Now, there's something you can do for me . . .'

Verrian had a vague memory of agreeing to something, but he couldn't recall what. He'd left the telephone receiver dangling as nausea swept over him. He remembered dragging himself upstairs to his room, using the banister rail like a lifeline. He'd dropped on to his bed, his skin feeling as if it had been set alight. Had he then dreamed someone had placed cold flannels on his forehead? Made him drink bitter liquid?

He had no idea if Jack had tried to contact him while he lay sweating in bed, and if Miguel had been released. He must ring London and find out.

A freight train leaving Gare du Nord made his lampshade swing and he made another decision. New lodgings. Grateful as he was to Laurentin, the hotel owner, he'd rather spend his enforced holiday in Paris in a room that didn't shake. Unfortunately, it appeared he was trapped for the foreseeable future as he'd left his passport and press pass in Madrid. It would take time to renew them.

Laurentin just shrugged when Verrian explained his decision to leave. 'Try Butte de Montmartre, no trains there. Fancy a cognac while I write your bill? Lunch? Shall I lend you a shirt?'

Verrian answered yes to lunch and the shirt and asked for a cigarette and permission to make an international call. As he dialled, another memory swam back. A female telephone operator talking to him about fog and vintage wine. She'd swung between superiority and giggles, and he had a feeling that in his haze of fever he'd asked her to marry him.

It was an older female who connected him this time.

'Where the hell have you been?' were Jack's first words to him. 'You were expected at Rue Boccador days ago – a desk and office were made ready. The staff were all lined up, ready to shake your hand, and you didn't show!'

It took Verrian a few seconds to understand what his brother was telling him. The *News Monitor*'s French edition had its offices on Rue Boccador, not far from the Champs-Elysées. He must have agreed he'd write for the paper while he was in Paris in return for Jack's help with Miguel, because Jack never gave anything for free. 'Did you get my friend out of prison?'

'I did. Your gratitude is taken as read.'

Verrian slumped against the wall. *Thank God I got something right*. 'I am grateful. Is he still in Spain – Miguel?'

'Only if he has a death wish. He was given every opportunity to leave with his family. Now, let's talk about you and your promise to be my political reporter in Paris.'

'Listen, Jack—' The line broke into the whooping atmospherics that often took over international calls. Verrian resisted the temptation to shout 'Hello? Hello?' and whack the handset as it never did any good, except to divert frustration. 'Jack! Are you there?'

'Just about.'

'I'm going back to Spain, soon as I can. I'm a war reporter; I won't fit in here.'

Jack's laughter sounded metallic, like something from a fairground slot machine. 'You're our new man in Paris, Verrian. You gave your word in exchange for your chum Miguel's life—' A click indicated the line was lost.

Verrian studied the bill Laurentin put next to his ashtray, counting up the days since his arrival. Good God – he'd been ill for almost two weeks. The last time he'd been on his back so long was at school, with diphtheria. Laurentin confirmed it.

'You arrived in the early hours of 21st March. Lucky I stay open for the night-workers, *hein*? You had some breakfast, made a telephone call and fell down. I didn't know what to do with you – you had no papers.'

'I'm grateful you let me stay.'

Laurentin used a napkin to smack crumbs off the table. 'We had a conversation in French, but then suddenly you were talking Spanish. The local doctor speaks Spanish and said you were having a nightmare about burning to death. We decided it was malaria and gave you quinine. My waitress Marie mopped your brow.'

Laurentin wedged open his door and began setting up tables on the pavement for the early lunch crowd. Spotting a newspaper on Verrian's table, open at the report of the Durango bombing, he sighed. 'You need a vacation for the soul. Enjoy the possibilities of Paris.'

Friday, 2nd April

Christine's future mother-in-law, the Duchesse de Brioude, had arrived at Boulevard Racan after church on Easter Sunday and was to stay a little over a week. A pleasant woman, if rather overpowering, her coming had thrown Jean-Yves's world into chaos.

Rhona had hired extra staff for the occasion, who got under everyone's feet. She'd filled the house with flowers that made them all sneeze. Discovering the Duchesse disliked small dogs, she shut Tosca and Figaro in the music room, where they howled incessantly. This morning Jean-Yves had taken her aside and said, 'My dear, we have nothing much with which to impress the Duchesse, so how about we simply make her comfortable and welcome?'

Rhona took this as a criticism and punished him with icy formality. So he retreated to his study, a move that also allowed him to stay close to the telephone. At least he didn't have to keep sneaking to the front door in an attempt to intercept letters. Ferryman had taken on that job. Through necessity, Jean-Yves had confided something of the blackmail threat to his secretary, though by no means all. He'd explained that 'an unpleasant individual' was attempting to extract payment from him for a spurious bill. 'Repairs to a clock that I never owned.' It was a common fraud, he told Ferryman, to which men of his standing fell victim because petty criminals knew they'd pay to avoid embarrassment. 'I'm telling you in case you should encounter this scoundrel. Don't enter into conversation with him; just refer him to me. It goes without saying that the ladies must not be troubled with any unpleasantness.'

Had Ferryman swallowed the story? The boy had made that bow Ninette so despised and murmured, 'Very good, Monsieur.' There had been no more telephone calls, and no more soiled letters. Perhaps the blackmailer had given up? Such men were often cowards, or lazy. Perhaps he'd slunk off in search of easier prey. So, for the first time in many days, Jean-Yves felt able to write letters and read the newspaper without constantly glancing at the telephone or feeling the need to check who was walking along Boulevard Racan.

His light spirits lasted until a quarter to twelve that day, when Rhona entered his room and reminded him that they were all taking lunch together at home and surely he wasn't intending to sit down with the Duchesse in his lounging jacket?

In London, where they'd lived most of their married life, Rhona had been brittle and worldly – but charming too. She'd been capable of humour and the house had been alive with bustle, piano music and laughter. But a new obsession with appearances had descended within days of their arrival in Paris. As she'd stepped out of the car at Boulevard Racan, a sort of defensive snobbery had settled on her. He'd first put it down to homesickness – a loss of the familiar – but he could no longer deny that Rhona had changed fundamentally. No more laughter, no more music. Her life was now all about out-Frenching the French: couture suits and Reboux hats, sending out cards to the correct set of 'friends', eating in chichi places and admiring the right kind of art. Even the dogs wore coats in each new season's colour and went to a fashionable spa to be washed.

Rhona had also changed towards him. He supposed she wished he was riding alongside her, correctly attired, as she assaulted the citadel. But interestingly enough, it was he who had become the more *authentic* Parisian . . .

He had taken a mistress. Hélène was the wife of a Polish count who was absent most of the year, preferring Cannes to Paris. Hélène gave Jean-Yves all he needed sexually and intellectually, and left him alone in all other regards. They met three, four times a week.

Rising from his desk, he told Rhona that the Savile Row suit he was wearing was quite adequate for lunch *en famille* – 'But you look upset. What's troubling you, my dear?'

'There is a matter I've been trying to raise with you since last month. Don't deny it, Jean-Yves, the minute I catch your eye you come and lock yourself in here.'

He didn't deny it. 'You have me to yourself now. I'm listening.'

'It was a Saturday morning . . . I don't recall which Saturday, but I was at Maison Javier for a dress fitting and I saw somebody there – a scruffy girl with a basket.'

'Had she wandered up the wrong staircase?'

'I have no idea, Jean-Yves. One does not show curiosity about such people. My point is, I knew her. It was the creature you occasionally took out to dinner when we lived in London.'

'How do you know?' The words were out before he could stop them. He cleared his throat. 'What I mean is, I took many people out to dine when we lived in London.'

'Many young females . . . really?'

'Of course not. One or two perhaps, daughters of friends who were stuck in town, that sort of thing. What is your point, Rhona?'

'This creature – she's different. She had the most penetrating expression. An appealing quality, like a starving spaniel. Ordinarily I would not lower myself to mention it, but things are different now. Until Christine is safely married, Jean-Yves, this family's behaviour must remain above reproach. Who you meet, the places you are seen – they matter. People will make judgements about the family allying itself with the Duc de Brioude. Dalliances – or even dinners - with needy Jewesses simply will not do.'

She turned her face from him, presenting a smooth cheek – her way of communicating that she'd said her piece and there was nothing further to discuss. Trembling with an anger that threatened to overwhelm him, Jean-Yves counted ten, twenty heartbeats. When he'd mastered himself, he told Rhona he'd booked dinner at Maxim's for the Monday coming. 'Philippe prefers dinners at home, but we should take him and Mme la Duchesse out on her last night, don't you think? I'm giving you fair warning in case you need to have another dress made.'

'By Monday?' Realising he was being funny, she nodded. 'As you've booked, we must go. I will inform the Duchesse.'

As her heels snip-snapped away, Jean-Yves released a long breath. So, finally, Rhona had bumped into Alix. It must have been Alix – who else possessed eyes worthy of such a quarrel? But what could have brought Alix Gower to Maison Javier? And looking scruffy . . . though he doubted that. To Rhona, anything but couture that one's maid had pressed that morning was scruffy. How did she know it was Alix when they'd never met? For he'd made damn sure of that. This new mystery usurped everything, even his blackmailer. When the desk telephone shrilled, he jumped like a salmon before snatching up the receiver. 'Who is this?'

'Please may I speak to M. le Comte de Charembourg?' A young voice, shy.

'You are doing so.'

'Monsieur, it's me, Alix Gower.'

'Alix?' Was this a trick?

'I . . . I hope I'm not troubling you and I'm sorry to call you at home, I know I shouldn't, but I really want to speak to you. I – I have something to confess.'

Chapter Nine

On Saturday, 3rd April, carrying his worldly goods in a wooden vegetable box, Verrian Haviland rode the funicular up to the basilica of Sacré-Coeur on the Butte de Montmartre. Reading the directions supplied by the accommodation agency, he wandered into a square brimming with artists, tourists and those who must be locals, from the way they slouched on café chairs. He made an unhurried scan of the area: cobbles, peeling shutters, trees bouncing into leaf. Yes, Place du Tertre would do fine for now.

His prospective landlady was called Mme Konstantiva, and the girl at the agency had told him that 'long ago' she'd danced with the Ballets Russes. So when a majestic woman opened the door to him, he addressed her in his best Russian, a language he'd picked up during an unpaid apprenticeship on a Moscow newspaper. The woman stepped back with a graceful gesture and invited him in.

Verrian thanked her in Russian.

'English or French, ducks, else find an interpreter. I'm as

Russian as cod and chips. You can call me Rosa.' She eyed the crate Verrian carried on his shoulder, with its label declaring 'Quality Savoy cabbages'. 'What are you then, the Archduke of Austria? Where's your retinue?'

She spoke English, so he answered the same. 'Some way behind, carrying my robes of state.' Because she kept staring at the crate, he added, 'I'm not as poor as I look. Will a month's rent in advance be acceptable?'

'Whatever suits, ducks. Come on in. Watch the carpet – bit of a death trap. *C'*était la guerre. You're a good-looking boy, ain't you? Dark for an Englishman. What is it, Welsh?'

'Cornish, on my mother's side.'

She took him upstairs and opened a door, saying, 'You can have the double, since you'll fall off the end of a single. I only let two rooms, and this is the biggest.' The bedroom smelled faintly of cat and the last occupant's hair cream. 'View of the square at no extra charge and you can see Sacré-Coeur from the bathroom. You'll be staying long, Mr . . . um . . . ?'

'Haviland. A month, probably.'

'Writer, are you?'

'Of a kind.'

'Thought so. Illegal for writers to shave properly, ain't it?'

He grinned. 'No – merely discouraged.'

'I'll give you a gander at the facilities. Usual terms – you get your own key, you tiptoe inside after ten, twenty francs for a bath, no girls upstairs unless you can give me the names of all four grandparents. Fancy a cuppa?'

'I could murder one.'

At home in St-Sulpice, Alix sat on her bed, sliding silk stockings over her knees. What to wear though? She'd screwed up every ounce of courage to telephone the Comte de Charembourg the previous day, and he'd been so kind, inviting her to lunch today, but he hadn't said what style of place he was taking her to. Alix pushed open her window, testing the air. Warm, but not sunny. How very unhelpful.

She reviewed her choices. One could not call her clothes a 'wardrobe'; though this was supposed to be a furnished flat, the wardrobes had never arrived. Alix's garments hung from a broom handle balanced on ratchets.

She wished she had something in white linen, to be worn with a little cashmere cardigan, but reality was that same pink cotton dress, forever blighted by the memory of fish and Mlle Lilliane. Her amethyst? No, the amethyst dress was too sexy for a man who'd known her as a small girl.

She took down a shift dress of parchment-coloured crêpe and held it against herself. She'd sewn this in her last year at school, adapting it from a cover of *Vogue*. Miss Maguire, the needlework mistress, had doubted Alix could work without a pattern and was sniffy about French fashion, which she considered rather indecent. Alix had taken an entire term over the project, partly because Miss Maguire insisted, at a late stage, that sleeves be added. 'One never goes bare-armed except in the evening, Alice.' They called her Alice at school, finding 'Alix' too foreign.

'Sleeves will spoil the line, Miss Maguire.'

'Then make something else. I shall find you a Butterick pattern.'

So Alix had added short sleeves. The dress, based on a design by the couturier Madeleine Vionnet, had suffered a final insult when, ahead of the fashion show the needlework class traditionally gave at the end of summer term, the headmistress had insisted Alix iron it.

'It's *crêpe marocain*, Miss Peachman,' Alix protested, open-mouthed in the face of such philistine stupidity. 'It's meant to be crinkled. If I could show you Vionnet's original, you'd understand.'

'Press it, or it will be confiscated.'

Poor dress, but it was the safest choice. Alix slipped it over her head, buckled on ankle-strap sandals. Her hair had long grown out of its school bob, and her current style was to brush it straight across the left side of her head and pin it so that curls fell over her right ear. Since seeing the American woman in Hermès, she'd begun to pluck her brows thinner. Checking herself in her dressing mirror she decided she no longer looked twenty-going-on-fifteen – thanks to Paris, she was growing into her true age.

A dab of perfume, a straw hat, and just enough time to get clear of the flat before Mémé came back from the market.

In the hall, Alix hesitated by a console table dotted with family pictures. Among the framed portraits of Mémé's long-dead parents and brother was the one Alix treasured most: her parents' wedding photograph. She picked it up, smiling at the bride's arrow-straight dress, thinking, *That's not so different from what I'm wearing*. She kissed the cold glass. *Wish me luck, mother*.

Picking her up outside the Deux Magots café on Boulevard St-Germain, the comte handed her a posy of creamy narcissi tied with a blue ribbon.

'Lavin blue!' she exclaimed.

'The only blue that perfectly complements yellow.' As the comte opened the passenger door for her, Alix had a moment to appreciate the elegant cut of his grey suit. Studying him more closely as he got behind the wheel, she saw that his woven silk tie was charcoal flecked with yellow. She took that as a compliment; he'd once told her, 'A gentleman should always wear grey, you know, because then he will never upstage the lady he is with.'

'Unless she's a nun,' she'd retorted at the time, and he'd laughed and added, 'In which case, she'll forgive him.'

The comte drove fast, even faster in Paris than he had in London. They zipped across the Seine by the Pont de l'Alma, took Avenue Kléber and rocketed into the traffic swirling round

Place de l'Etoile, lane-hopping to the sound of klaxons. Alix felt she was holding her breath all the way to Boulevard Haussmann!

'My chauffeur Pépin used to drive a taxi,' the comte explained, mistaking her excitement for fear. 'He got me into bad habits, but I detest crawling in Paris traffic. Other motorists don't respect you if you look at all apologetic.'

She didn't feel remotely unsafe with this man, even when he went up on the pavements. 'Where's the Morgan?' she asked. 'I adored that car.'

'Ah, alas, we had to split up. She stayed in London.'

Their journey ended in Boulevard de Courcelles, a long road that divided the 8th and 17th arrondissements, flattening the top of Parc Monceau. Tossing his key to a porter, the comte led Alix into a small hotel where he was obviously well known. The dining room overlooked the park and Alix fancied she saw the sheen of water and the ruined columns of the *Naumachie* beyond. M. Javier had told her he lived on Courcelles in a hotel suite. It might even be this hotel.

'So . . .' her host smiled as they took their seats at a beautifully laid table, 'let's get this confession out of the way. What have you done, Alix?'

She told him about the telephone exchange, glossing over Mlle Boussac's contempt, embellishing her own noble act in putting through an unauthorised call. 'Booted out on the spot. I hope you aren't angry.'

'Did you enjoy working there?'

'I hated it.'

'Then all's well that ends well.'

'But you got me the job.'

'No, I suggested you to somebody I know, asked them to see you. You got yourself the job. What now?'

She told him about the offer from Javier, and meeting the great man himself.

The comte immediately invited the wine waiter to fill her glass, saying, 'Let us toast your future. Now, this is a Riesling grand cru that they keep in the cellar for me. You approve? We have a duty to drink the wines of . . . of Alsace, you know.'

At 'Alsace' he had checked. So faintly she could easily have missed it. Why did the name worry him? Or was it that he'd forgotten she was grown up and felt he shouldn't be encouraging her to drink? The Riesling was so fragrant, so perfectly chilled, she'd like to drink as much wine as Alsace could produce, and told him so.

'Leave some for me,' he laughed. 'To M. Javier, a toast to his excellent good sense.' After they'd clinked glasses, he flipped open a leather-bound menu. 'May I choose for you? If you'd rather I didn't, please say. But I know the chef and can find something that will please you. Is there anything you don't like?'

'No – well, I don't eat boiled hockey boots because at school they tasted like pig's liver and onion. I don't eat turnip unless I have to. Oh, and bright-yellow custard. Everything else I love. I'm greedy.'

He laughed with real pleasure. 'What perfection! A greedy girl with a hand-span waist. Well, Arnaud does the best Coquilles St-Jacques in Paris, so we'll start with that. How is your grandmother? No more nightmares about Herr Hitler, I trust?'

This time Alix gasped out loud. How could the comte know about Mémé's fears? Her grandmother was back to her scalpel-sharp self, but it had been a frightening episode, shared with nobody.

Alix was aware that the man now discussing the merits of duck breast over salt-marsh lamb with the head waiter was the only uninterrupted male presence in her life. He had educated her. His care, his notice, was the cornerstone of her self-belief. The visit he'd made to her school during her last term was a seminal moment of her existence – prior to her meetings with Bonnet and Javier, anyway. He'd come to watch her perform in a concert for which she had designed the costumes. As she made her bow at the end, his smile had told her that she was a credit. A success. That smile had made years of humiliation seem unimportant.

But did he also keep an eye on her and her grandmother here in Paris? Hire spies? She told herself not to be ridiculous. Why would he? If he kept an eye on Mémé, it was out of kindness.

Turning to her, the comte clearly realised he'd said something wrong. 'Alix?'

'You asked about my grandmother . . . you mentioned Hitler.'

He groaned. 'A name that falls off the tongue too readily

these days. I agree with you, one shouldn't speak lightly about such things. I simply want to know if Mme Lutzman is well.'

'She's well, thank you.'

And that was that. During their first course they talked fashion, and the comte told her what he knew about Javier. A lot, it seemed, and perhaps not gleaned just from his wife, but also from other women of his acquaintance.

'Javier began his career at the House of Worth, but was too radical. Then he went to Paul Poiret – clash of temperament. When he left there, the feeling was that he would fade. But he proved a sticker. Spanish and Jewish, he had to fight to be allowed to join the *Syndicat*.'

'You like him, Monsieur?'

'He makes women look adorable and he's one of the best tailors in the world.'

Alix recalled the tape measure over the shoulder and smiled. The 'best tailor in the world' had praised her skill. As they waited for their lamb, she asked, 'Monsieur, why have you been so kind to me all my life?'

The comte answered lightly. 'You know the story, how your father and I fought together. One day he walked into enemy fire to pull me away from certain death. One does not forget that. When he died leaving an orphaned child, I offered help. I paid for the sort of schooling I hoped would give you a chance in life. Your grandmother accepted very reluctantly – but she believed your parents would have wanted it.'

Alix nodded, lifting the glass that had refilled by magic. 'My mother would have chosen that sort of school for me, I know she would. "Mathilda was always halfway out of the door," people said. She wouldn't stick at her books, or be told what to do. But parents always want children to make up for their mistakes. Did you know, the moment war was declared, she enrolled as a nurse? Badgered the authorities until they took her.'

The comte smiled, but said nothing.

'She met my father feeding ducks in a London park . . . I'm not sure which one. She was in her nurse's uniform. He was in uniform too because he was waiting to be shipped off to fight. They fell in love instantly.' Unlike Mathilda, who was a creature of Alix's imagination, John Gower inhabited her real memory. Tall as a giant to her infant self, he'd smelled of engine oil, because after the war he worked for the railways. Alix remembered him coming home from work, his collar blackened, his face creased with exhaustion but always with a little present in his pocket for her.

She could still sing 'Guide me, O Thou Great Redeemer', which he'd taught her, and she had a clear picture of him singing it at the kitchen sink. No, not singing. Huffing it between coughing fits, the wheezing tap joining in so he sounded like one of the trains pulling out of Clapham Junction station. He'd tap his chest and say, 'Feathers in my lungs.'

What else . . . ? She remembered his watch on the draining

board next to a bar of green soap, and his braces hanging by his side as he washed. She remembered the excitement of him swinging her in the air, high as the lampshade. Once he'd accidentally cracked her head on the door frame. She could still hear her own squalling distress, his desperate soothing and Mémé's reproaches. Guilt marbled that memory. John Gower had come back from war whole and had died in 1921, when Alix was five, from a lung disease caught in a military hospital.

His early death had robbed them of a thousand conversations. He'd left nothing about himself – no letters, no diaries, just a few fuzzy photographs. Mémé said he was a Londoner, with roots elsewhere, maybe Ireland or Wales, and her tone was never warm when she spoke about him. She seemed to consider him more like her lodger than her son-in-law. And he was not Jewish; categorically not. He and Mathilda had married in the winter of 1915 at the Methodist chapel in South Norwood . . . or was it Streatham? Whichever, it was a gloomy place. End of story.

The comte could tell her about her father's war service, Alix knew, but she didn't know how to ask. Men who'd suffered the horrors of the trenches hated to speak of it. Well, except Bonnet. He told you even the things you didn't want to hear. So she asked a different question.

'Did you meet my mother, Monsieur?'

'Danielle's daughter . . .' Alix heard the hesitation in his voice. 'I sent a card of congratulation for the wedding but couldn't make the ceremony. Soon after, it was too late. What a sad subject, Alix. Finish your wine. We're having Pinot Gris with the lamb.'

'Did you ever meet my grandfather? I'm sorry, it's just I've a lifetime of questions stored up because Mémé can never remember things. You don't mind?'

'Of course you want to know about your family. Which grandfather – John Gower's father?'

'My Alsace one. Alfred Lutzman. I know you and he and Mémé lived in the same town and you were the most important person there.' She added the last bit in case he thought she was imagining they'd had picnics together.

'I don't know about the most important – the mayor and the chief of police would argue that one. Our paths didn't cross much though, of course, I was aware of Lutz – of your grandfather. A superb artist. The way he captured faces was breathtaking, and as a colourist I consider him without equal.' His eye rested on the flowers beside Alix's plate, tender yellow with their bold ribbon. 'My mother was an early collector of his paintings, some of which I inherited, and I was lucky enough to obtain one or two.'

'I knew you had some! How many? Oh, monsieur, when may I see them?'

'Some day. I've tried to acquire more down the years, without much success.'

Waiters circled, bearing silver domes that they lifted in a

choreographed flourish. As they were being served, Jean-Yves told Alix about Arnaud, the hotel's chef, who came from the Auvergne, a remote place where men were hunters. 'One day, we'll come here for the wild boar. Sauce for you? Tell me when.'

It dawned on Alix that the comte was trying to change the subject. Politeness told her she should let him, but she couldn't waste this rare opportunity. 'Monsieur, why did you fight for England during the war? Because really, you were German, were you not?'

Something stern came into her companion's face. 'I am a Frenchman. My mother was born in Paris and my father's lineage was French. The invasion by Germany of Alsace in the 1870s trapped us in a new nationality. My father chose German rule rather than abandon his estates, but I assure you it was always a technicality. I studied in England, took work there and when war broke out joined an English regiment. Not to fight 'for England'. To fight for freedom. But enough questions, my dear. Please understand, I have come to the age where my wife and daughters ignore me. To be face to face with a beautiful young woman who finds me interesting –' a smile crinkled his eyes – 'is a little overwhelming.'

Alix blushed.

'May I say something? It is not a criticism, but you have an intensity . . .'

'I stare?'

'Your eyes have the power to unsettle. Some men will be knocked off their feet. Use that power wisely.'

She really was blushing now.

He tapped the edge of her plate. 'Come on. I want to see proof of this greed of yours because I can't believe it. You're slender as a conductor's baton.'

'One more question. Just one? Please?' It had just revealed itself, this last need. She looked at him through her lashes. 'If my father could see me –' she pointed to herself – 'not clever, not always good, sacked from the telephone exchange, what would he think? You're the only person who really knew him. Mémé is always bad-tempered about the whole thing. I think she was cross that my mother . . . well, you know, *had* to marry him. If they'd left it any longer, she wouldn't have fitted into her wedding dress. Monsieur, do you think he would like me?'

Jean-Yves took her hand in his. 'I knew John Gower as a soldier, not as a father. But I'll try to answer. Looking at you, he would be rather shocked – you're so modern and self-sufficient. Remember, he was born when Queen Victoria ruled the globe and ladies wore corsets that made their waists smaller than the crowns of their husband's top hats. Your spirit would remind him of Mathilda—'

'So you did meet my mother?'

He squeezed her hand and continued. 'I'm sure your father would adore you.' He raised his glass. 'To your future at Javier.

May you burn a comet's trail. But leave some of us standing, wicked little Alix.'

Stopping beside St-Lazare *Métro* station, the comte opened the car door for her and waited for her to step out. 'Got your flowers?'

'Of course.' She'd cradled them in her lap so they wouldn't bruise.

'It's been a lovely afternoon, Alix. Thank you.' He presented her with a card. 'This is my office in Rue du Sentier. Contact me there any time you want. Are you sure you don't want me to take you to Montmartre? I can get the car most of the way there.'

She told him it was no trouble. She'd take the *Métro* to Abbesses. In truth, she didn't want the comte to see the Place du Tertre side of her life. She'd promised to pose this afternoon for Bonnet, but she wished she hadn't, because she was slightly drunk and also didn't fancy taking her crêpe dress into Bonnet's den. But then she couldn't let her friend down either. And as Bonnet only ever talked to himself when he painted, it would be a good opportunity to mull over everything the comte had told her.

Bonnet's shutters were closed. Alix paused, thinking that he was unlikely be sleeping on such a warm spring day. Perhaps he'd gone out to paint by the canal. Without much expectation of finding him, she climbed the stairs to his studio. There was just enough light in the stairwell for her to read the note pinned to his studio door:

'Bonnet absents himself' was written in messy capitals. He'd drawn a cartoon of a bearded buffoon asleep in a wine glass. How like him to forget their appointment. Bonnet never locked up, and his studio door opened with a push. Wrinkling her nose at the mess – empty bottles, the remnants of strong coffee and that vile rabbit glue – she scribbled a note, pinned it on his easel and was just closing the door behind her when she heard a creak from the stairs below. Then, a moment to realise that a figure was pounding up towards her before she was grabbed and pushed against the studio door – the air knocked out of her.

She tried to scream but nothing came out because whoever he was he was pressing the back of her neck with his forearm. She felt scratchy wool through the silk of her dress and smelled its oily heat. One of her hands was trapped between her ribcage and the door panel. It was the hand holding the flowers, their scent invading her nostrils. Something icy touched the side of her neck – a blade so sharp she could feel it splitting her skin without pressure.

A voice growled, 'Listen to me and no noise. Understood?'

She whispered, 'Yes,' into the door.

'I warned your stuck-up friend the comte that I'd hurt someone he loves if he didn't pay up, and I reckon he loves you, doesn't he?'

'I – I don't know.'

'Oh, he does. I was letting him off lightly, asking for only five hundred thousand francs. Well, the price has gone up: one million francs, because he cheated. He pays it, and you won't get hurt. Got it?'

'One million . . . and I won't get hurt.'

'He'll get a letter saying when to leave the cash. If he doesn't –' the knife blade moved to the flesh beneath her eye. 'Such a shame if my knife slipped. You understand?'

'Yes,' she cried, then felt a rough pressure on her scalp . . . he was cutting her hair.

It was over in an instant. 'Close your eyes and count to fifty,' he snarled. 'Don't look round or I'll make sure nobody will want to paint you again.'

When the pressure on her neck was eased, she collapsed on to her knees. She heard boots thumping downstairs and the front door slam shut. If she ran to the studio window she'd see her attacker in the square, but she didn't dare. Her lips moved in shocked bursts. 'One . . . two . . . three . . .' she kept counting even while she was sobbing. 'Twenty-seven, twenty-eight . . .'

On forty-nine she stumbled downstairs, opened the street door and ran . . . straight into a person walking past.

Somebody was reaching to help her up. 'Are you all right?'

A man. Anxious, curious – when all she wanted to do was

curl like a shrimp and be sick. 'Leave me alone. I have to find the comte,' she moaned.

'I see.' Though clearly he didn't. 'You're crying.'

'He made me count to fifty.'

'And you've blood on your face. Oh dear, your flowers. Mademoiselle, what happened?'

His concern made her cry harder and, perversely, hate him. What she could see of him, which at the moment was just boots and trouser hems. She raised a hand and he helped her to her feet. He was tall and intimidating in a tan fedora hat and trench coat, crumpled and unbuttoned. Her blurred vision told her he was older than Paul, younger than the comte, and a different species from Bonnet. He had a nice voice but she wished he'd go away.

'You have to find the comte, you say. Which comte?'

'I don't know . . . I mean, I don't know where he is. He went home, and I can't go there.'

'Ah. Then how about a taxi to your home? I don't have my own car here, I'm afraid.'

Her knees gave way, shock belatedly rolling in.

'Come and sit down.' The man supported her a few steps and unlocked the front door of the house adjoining Bonnet's. He took her into a hall and helped her to a chair, first removing a pile of musical scores from its seat. 'Your parents live where . . . ?'

'Nowhere. My grandmother . . . we live –' she paused blankly

– she couldn't remember where she lived. All she could call to mind was the brown door of their old house in Charlotte Road, Wandsworth. 'I've lost my memory.'

'Tell you what, we'll go into Mme Konstantiva's sitting room. Give me your weight.'

'About eight-and-a-half stone.'

'I meant, lean on me.'

This room was heavy with velour furnishings and dominated by an upright piano. Alix noticed dance figurines on the bookcase, and photographs of ballerinas with kohl around their eyes. She wasn't in any state to be curious, however. When the man helped her to an easy chair, she slumped down into it, then started in shock as a cat leaped on to her lap.

'I believe his name is Percy and my new landlady borrows this property from him. Here –' the man took a shawl from the back of the armchair – 'I'll put this between you and his wretched paws. Or you can chuck him off. He ruined my one pair of trousers in the time it took me to drink a cup of tea so I'm not his best friend, but he's a harmless fellow.' As the stranger tucked the shawl over her knees, Alix smelled his hair. Kitchen soap. Clearly he was poor. Probably a poet. Bonnet always said that if a painter ever wanted to feel sorry for somebody, he should go out drinking with a poet.

'I'm going to make tea for you. My landlady's out, so I'll have to search for tea leaves and work out how to light the stove.'

He left her and a moment later she heard a tap running and the striking of a match. He came back some minutes later with a tray holding a teapot with a knitted cosy, eyelid-thin china, milk jug and sugar bowl. He'd shed his coat, and even in her distress Alix couldn't help but make an audit of his clothes: very loose trousers belted around the middle, cat-claw damage apparent; dark-blue jersey rubbed thin at the elbows, a soft collar just visible above its crew neck. His boots had once been good quality – he'd walked or laboured recently, she decided, or maybe been in a fight. There were shadows around his eyes and fading grazes on his chin.

He laid out two cups. 'Milk in first?'

'I – I don't know.'

'And who cares? Sugar, lots, under the circumstances.'

When she took a teacup from him, it rattled and he quickly rescued it and drew up a side table for them both. 'Take your time.'

'You were going out,' she said, 'and I've stopped you.'

'I was going to work, but it'll keep.' He smiled and two things dawned on her: without realising it, they'd been speaking English from the outset, and she knew his voice.

Had they met? He had a strong face, a straight nose – dark hair, dark brows and eyes of ink blue. No, they hadn't met. She'd have remembered.

He reached for her teacup once more, minus saucer, and held

it out to her. 'Drink it down – England's secret weapon. Able to tell me what happened?'

She looked at her flowers, still clutched in her hand, necks broken. She ran her fingers through her hair. 'I was at Bonnet's – the artist?'

'Fellow next door? We had a conversation earlier. He called here, wanting to borrow fuel for his spirit stove.' He switched suddenly into French. 'From his breath, I did wonder if he'd drunk his own supply for breakfast. But I'm being unfair. Is he a relation?'

'No, I just sit for him sometimes. I thought we had a session today . . . but sometimes he forgets. I left him a note and a man came up behind me and rammed me against the door. Chopped off my hair.' She indicated the damage. 'He had a horrible voice, like a crackly radio.'

'Hmm . . . deliberately distorted, you mean? So perhaps he thought you'd know him?'

She stared. How could she know such a brute? 'He threatened to come back and hurt me.' She touched the flesh under her eye where the knife had rested. Tears ran over her fingers, into her teacup and on to Percy, his ginger coat readily absorbing them.

'Really you should call the police.'

But she was already shaking her head by the time he got to 'pol—'. 'Mémé is terrified of the police. Almost as terrified of them as she is of the National Socialists in Germany.'

'Well, she has a point. Mémé is . . . . ?'

'My grandmother.'

'Of course. You need to go home, and I'll take you.'

She protested. Even in shock, etiquette asserted itself. She would take the Métro. She knew how to get home even if she'd forgotten the address.

'There's no possibility of your going home alone. *News Monitor* policy.'

'*News Monitor*? Isn't that the English paper . . . you work for them?'

'Mmm. Paris office on Boccador. I'll go to the post office on Abesses where there's a telephone, and order you a car on the company account. Don't argue – it's an account that is abused daily. One more journey won't make an ounce of difference.'

He'd reverted to English, the transition unconscious. There'd been nothing halting in his French, though he spoke it with a Spanish overtone as if he'd learned it in the foothills of the Pyrenees. His English was clear and idiomatic, and upper class. This was no impoverished poet, Alix realised. The worn clothes must have some other explanation. 'Rue St-Sulpice,' she said suddenly.

'I beg your pardon?'

'I've just remembered, that's where I live.'

'Excellent. I won't be long. You wait here with Percy. Should Mme Konstantiva return, talk English. She looks Russian, but that's because she danced for Diaghilev for many years. These days she takes in passing strays – cats and lodgers, I mean. Be sure to tell her the names of all four of your grandparents.'

'My . . . what, all four? I don't know all four,' she stammered, but he was already out the door.

Chapter Ten

❧

A table at Maxim's on Rue Royale in the company of the Duchesse de Brioude and her son should be a special occasion, and Jean-Yves tried to play the genial host. But the Duchesse's visit had taken its toll. Rhona's constant patrolling of the house, snapping orders at the servants, had stretched everyone's nerves. But it wasn't all Rhona's fault; he'd not heard from his blackmailer and felt like a man on a bare hillside who knows a marksman has him in his sights. Every knock at the door, every movement outside his window, made his heart cramp up in fear. He prayed he'd get through this dinner without his self-control slipping.

But as they were being served their hors-d'oeuvres, a waiter bent close and whispered that a package had been left with the cloakroom attendant, for M. le Comte's urgent attention.

Fear, that sleepless dragon, sprang to life. Jean-Yves made his excuses and rose. The waiter, well trained in the arts of male conspiracy, led him to the men's room and brought him a brown packet. It contained a few lines of writing and a loop of glossy hair. Jean-Yves knew instantly whose writing, and whose hair.

As he returned to his table, several pairs of female eyes raked him for explanation. 'I dropped a cufflink at my club a week or so back,' he improvised shakily. 'Really, I could have collected it. They needn't have sent it.' Alix was in trouble. Should he drive to see her? The hair was hers, he was sure, but how had it been taken? He should have checked it for blood. No chance now.

'I didn't know you'd lost a cufflink.' Rhona drummed on the cloth. 'Which one?'

'Er, one of my college ones – sentimental value only.' Knowing there was a chance Rhona would ask to see it, Jean-Yves turned to his future son-in-law. 'I'm starting a collection of single cufflinks, Philippe, donated by the gentlemen of France to send to those men who lost an arm in the war. Good idea, do you think?'

Philippe de Brioude, who was rather in awe of him, consulted wordlessly with Christine, then stammered, 'I'm . . . I'm not sure.'

Jean-Yves turned to his younger daughter, who could usually be counted on to appreciate his dark humour. 'Good idea, Ninette?'

'It would be less work to make a collection for the men who'd lost both arms, Papa,' she answered, fluttering her eyelashes at him over the rim of her wine glass. Eighteen, discovering the power of her blonde beauty, Ninette used 'Papa' as a practice target. He looked away, unable to stop himself comparing her to Alix, whose effortless charisma cut to the sinew. Over lunch two days ago he'd told Alix, 'Some men will be knocked off their feet,' while adding the silent warning, *And some women will do anything to bring you down.*

Conversation had died at the table. The Duchesse stepped into the gap, saying, 'If I listed the young men I knew who lost limbs at Verdun alone, I would be counting until the cheese arrived. Of course Ninette was born after the war's horror, so for her it is history.'

Rhona made a 'do something' face across the table, which Jean-Yves ignored. Typical, expecting him to rescue a conversation she'd sent off the rails. This was Rhona's way. His mother had warned him: 'Your Rhona will never distinguish your drawing room because she sees the world through a slit – a fault of character that will never mend. But if beauty is enough . . .'

He'd thought it was. Rhona shone still, even in Maxim's, which was a magnet for the rich and pampered. This evening she surpassed her daughters in a red moire evening gown with a high waist that elongated her shape. The focal point of her ensemble, now she was seated, was a choker of pearls with a ruby medallion. Stunning, but all that red made Jean-Yves long for a walk in the woods. He wished Alix had a telephone so he could assure himself she was all right. He'd send a note as soon as they got home. The chauffeur could take it to St-Sulpice.

*

Once at home, the comte made to slip into his study, but Rhona caught him at the door. 'Why didn't you say something when the duchesse started reciting the blasted casualty list at Verdun?' she snapped. 'Christine wanted to discuss her honeymoon this evening. She's keen for Philippe to take her to Italy or Switzerland – are you listening?'

He had a glass of Calvados in his hand. His other hand was in his pocket, that curl of hair between his fingers. 'Heavens, Alix, no more talk tonight, please. I'm exhausted.'

Deathly silence. Then, 'What did you call me?'

He turned to the woman, his wife, whose dress made him think of hellfire, and said, 'Your pardon. I am a little drunk, for which I humbly apologise.' And, in order to spare himself further unpleasantness, he returned with her to the salon.

It was two in the morning by the time everyone was in bed, too late for sending notes. So he skipped family breakfast the next morning, shutting himself in the music room. He'd had his mother's Bechstein grand brought here on her death, supposedly for his daughters' benefit, but it was he who played most. Using the piano as a desk, he dashed off a few words to Alix, then sent his chauffeur to St-Sulpice with the instruction to wait for a reply and bring it straight back.

A Brahms intermezzo calmed him slightly, and he played solidly until Pépin returned. Alix's reply quelled his worst fears, though it was the writing of a frightened child:

I am well, Monsieur, but how did you know what happened? A man wants a million francs from you and I should have told you but didn't know how. He says he will <u>really</u> hurt me if you don't pay. Please don't tell Mémé because she'll be scared stiff and will try to stop me leaving the flat. I said I fell getting out of a train.

Yrs, AG

The telephone rang in the hall. He moved so quickly to reach it, for the first few seconds on the line he couldn't speak.

That gritty voice again: 'Enjoy Maxim's? I called to see you and some hired dunce of a footman said where to find you. Did you get my little offering?' A chuckle, then a chopped-up finish. 'One million francs, used notes. Same cigarette kiosk, five past six tomorrow evening. Plain bag. Leave it and walk—'

'Listen, you damn fool, if I leave it there some passer-by will have it. I'll put it in the church, at the foot of the right-hand column nearest the altar. A million is impossible, totally impossible. Take five hundred thousand and be damned. And swear never to go near Alix again. Swear it.'

'I scared her a bit, that's all.'

'Swear it, or you'll get nothing.'

'All right. Five hundred thousand and I'll never hurt the girl again.'

'Because if you do,' Jean-Yves snarled into the mouthpiece, 'I will find you and kill you. The well-being of Alix Gower is a sacred trust to me. Harm her, and I will send you in pieces to plead your case with the Almighty.'

A sound made him look up. Rhona was regarding him from across the marble hall. He thought at first it was fury that twisted her mouth so, but when she spoke he heard something far deeper than simple rage.

'A sacred trust? You are indeed a saint! How many years is it since you said anything like that to me, Jean-Yves? In fact, did you *ever* say such words, or even think them?' She strode over to him and hurled into his face, 'Why does that girl get what I have never had?'

Then, before he could answer, she ran away up the stairs, sobs breaking from her.

Chapter Eleven

When Alix began at Maison Javier at the start of April, she found controlled chaos. Javier had launched his delayed spring–summer collection two weeks earlier and orders were starting to flow in.

According to the bespectacled Mlle Lefoine, the supervisor of the workroom where Alix was to start her apprenticeship, Javier had returned from the Christmas holidays in an unfathomable mood. In February, when his collection should have launched, he'd instead left Paris to visit his sisters – 'On an island somewhere off Spain. He had planned to bring them to France but he came back alone and locked himself in his studio. Not to work, to listen to sad songs on his gramophone. We didn't think he'd do a spring–summer collection at all and I wish we hadn't. Everything's rushed – three months' work to do in one. It's why he engaged you on the strength of one interview,' she added, inspecting Alix without enthusiasm. 'Generally we give new girls a week's trial before they get seen by the première, let alone Javier.'

That first day, Alix toured the production side of the business. There were twelve ateliers, each with long tables and huge windows. There were also cutting rooms and storerooms crammed with cloth. Pressing rooms, finishing rooms . . . She was shown the button room and the thread room and the storage room, where finished garments hung awaiting delivery. To Alix these resembled a seminary of ghostly nuns – each garment protected by a white tunic bearing the name of a customer, store buyer or export agency.

One silent room contained four sewing machines. Her guide, a young première's assistant called Marcy Stein, told her, 'They're only ever used for curtains and table covers. M. Javier believes machines cannot achieve a flat and invisible seam, such as this house is famous for. Here everything is done by hand.' Marcy looked askance at Alix's green suit and ventured, 'You'll prefer to wear something looser for working.'

'I'm not a factory girl,' Alix retorted. 'I like to be smart.'

'It's your choice.'

Day two brought a dose of reality. She heard one of her new colleagues mutter to another, 'Who's she trying to impress?'

The friend snickered back, 'I shall like to see her climbing over the bench. And she'll rip those stockings by the end of today.'

Alix blushed as she hitched her skirt to make the awkward step into her place at the work-table. Some couturiers made their seamstresses work in low light, but at Maison Javier sunshine poured in. Alix sweated. Tight elbows made her first task – hemming swathes of voile curtain for the salon – uncomfortable. Her supervisor leaned over her and tutted. 'I heard you boasting you were a quick-stitch. Faster than a snail, I grant you.'

To cap a miserable day, when Alix went to collect her almost-Schiaparelli coat she found somebody had been careless with a box of dressmaker's chalk. Blue powder was embedded in the roses she'd embroidered on the collar.

The next day she wore a skirt left over from school days, a cotton blouse, comfortable underwear and cotton stockings. Mlle Lefoine handed her two tobacco-brown smocks, telling her she must embroider her name on the pocket, keep them surgically clean and wear one every day. Quietly taking her place, Alix prayed she'd passed the ordeal of the newcomer. Surely today somebody would offer a comment that wasn't snide or pitched over her head. Surely somebody would smile or invite her for lunch . . .

But the whispering continued. It was like school again. '*Who is she?*' '*Gower.*' '*That's not French. Mlle Lilliane thinks she could be German . . . foreign, anyway.*' It was a relief when Mlle Lefoine sent her on errands.

And when it wasn't errands, it was menial tasks. 'Alix, fetch a broom, there's thread-waste on the floor.' Or, 'Alix, why aren't you picking up pins? I can see a dozen from where I'm sitting. And don't use a magnet like one stupid girl did. She didn't last.'

Alix accepted that humble work was the price of learning this trade. Couture was as much a state of mind as a job. Work was done fast but never hurried, and nothing was skimped because women who had the money and leisure to buy made-to-measure from houses such as Chanel, Boulanger, Patou, Lanvin and Javier had eagle eyes for perfection. Or if they didn't, their husbands, lovers or lady's maids did. And, she would remind herself, the greatest couturiers had started at the bottom. The female ones, anyway.

And what of that other trade – theft? When could she start pirating the spring–summer collection for Paul's contact? Alix still dreamed of those promised riches. But, as she warned Paul later that week as they shared a glass of wine in a stupidly expensive café on the Champs-Elysées, she hardly ever saw a finished garment.

'The directrice would rather see a weasel climbing the curtains than a seamstress in the salon.'

Paul removed an olive stone from his mouth. Olives came free here, six in the bowl and they took three each. 'You must see the clothes sometimes, or at least the patterns.'

'It's not a big dressing-up box.' It was late, and she was tired. The shock of being attacked in Bonnet's stairway had not yet worn off and she was shaken by the hostility of her colleagues who, she had come to realise, thought she was some kind of spy 'placed' by Javier. 'This is how it works, Paul. Madame so-and-so orders model number twenty from the collection. Call it an azure-blue day dress. She chooses a slightly heavier fabric in peacock and, with the advice of a première and a fitter, has alterations made to flatter her shape. Her vendeuse persuades her to buy two more in different fabrics, with a little jacket maybe . . . *voilà*, she is dressed by Javier but is also unique. And private,' Alix stressed, 'until she wears that dress in public.' Daintily she ejected an olive stone. 'Javier never gives one seamstress a dress to work on from start to finish, for security reasons. One garment might be shared between three workrooms.'

Paul still had that stubborn expression on his face and she sighed. 'Imagine you're a trainee chef, and you've never seen a raspberry millefeuille in your life. The head chef hands you a list of ingredients and tells you to make a perfect one, right now. That's what you're asking me to do.'

'You want me to tell my contact the job's off?'

'Tell her to be patient.'

On the Friday afternoon of that first, shattering week, Alix was again ordered to put down her sewing in order to pick up pins. 'And don't miss any. I don't know why you imagine a pin under the table should be a lost pin.'

Because when I go underneath, Janice and Séverine bloody well kick me, Alix fumed as she reached under the bench. Pretty with their upswept hair and red lipstick, Janice and Séverine were best friends and ringleaders in the conspiracy to isolate Alix. She could hear them now, whispering. But whatever they were planning, they weren't able to carry it out as the workroom door opened and somebody came in. Someone whose rank caused everyone to stand. Janice still managed to tread on Alix's ankle.

'Be seated, all.'

It was Mme Frankel, the première of Maison Javier. 'Première' meant what it sounded like: after Javier, Pauline Frankel was first in consequence here. Her kingdom was these workrooms, where she oversaw the detailed making-up of garments, but she was just as often at Javier's side as he designed, advising him on the capabilities of the cloth, turning his nebulous ideas into something wearable. Her world was less glamorous than Mlle Lilliane's salon, the fitting rooms or the world of the mannequins, but without Mme Frankel, there would be no seasons, no collections . . . no Maison Javier. Her near-holy status showed itself in the way Mlle Lefoine scuttled forward to inspect the item she'd brought in to show them.

'A skirt, Madame,' Mlle Lefoine said breathlessly.

'Indeed, and required for Monday afternoon . . . Yes, I know you're busy, but M. Javier has given his word it will be finished.'

Alix emerged from under the table, pins in her mouth.

Seeing her, Mme Frankel gasped. '*Mon Dieu, petite!* Never, never put pins in your mouth. Imagine if you were to hit your head. We would be pulling pins out of your tongue.' She turned to the supervisor. 'Can you find no better work for Alix than this? M. Javier did not intend for her to be a floor sweeper. He won't be pleased, I can tell you. Can she not take this skirt?'

The supervisor dashed a resentful look at Alix. 'I heard you say it was important, Madame.'

'So it is,' Mme Frankel answered in a polite voice of steel. 'And if Alix is being underused, your problem is solved.'

The sewing tables were covered with baize cloth, which stopped silky fabrics slipping to the floor – its olive colour kind to the eyes. Replaced every single day, expensive cloth could be laid on it without fear of grease. Mme Frankel opened out the sections of skirt in front of Alix. She'd asked the girls either side to move, oblivious to the mutinous muttering this produced. 'This skirt is a commission from a highly valued client, Alix. Show me your needles, please.'

Alix fumbled at her needle pouch. She'd given up on being liked, but please, *please* let her not fail this test. Her fingers felt like sausages and in the end, Mme Frankel untied the pouch for her. Alix noticed that she had smooth, short nails and no wedding ring.

'Good, plenty of choice,' the première murmured as she revealed the miniature armoury Alix had collected during her time at Arding & Hobbs. 'Which will you use to tack the seams? Yes, you may touch the cloth. Tell me your thoughts.'

The skirt fabric was woven silk, and as Alix ran her fingers over the grain the visits she'd made with Mémé to the warehouses of London's East End came to her aid. 'Is it a Lyon silk?'

'Correct.'

The colour was ripe wheat with a trellis pattern in a deeper shade. The skirt was cut narrow, but not on the bias. 'Bias cut', the defining technique of the decade, meant cutting fabric diagonally across the grain, which gave fluidity to the finished garment. Bias-cutting ate up metres of cloth and was a challenge to sew. This skirt, by contrast, would be straightforward. 'I don't fear these seams stretching,' Alix said, 'so I'll tack using a long sharp, and a between for the stitching itself.'

'Show me that one.'

Alix took out a needle with a narrow point and a short shank.

Mme Frankel nodded. 'Short enough for fine work, able to carry the weight of the cloth. You'll use silk thread? Good.' She gave Alix a sample of the trellis silk. 'That must not leave the premises. When you've tacked, go to the thread room and Mme Albert will supply you. Be sure to stand in natural light. What kind of seam will you sew?'

'A . . . a flat seam, pressed open, raw edges turned and over-stitched. The silk is thick enough not to need *couture anglaise*, but there's a small chance of fraying.'

Mme Frankel smiled. 'Many girls can sew but have no instinct for fabric. Mlle Lefoine has found no actual fault with your work?' This last comment was directed at the supervisor, whose grunt made Alix's colour rise. A word of praise, surely, after she'd hemmed enough curtain to cover the street outside?

As Mme Frankel's steps echoed away, somebody mimicked

her deep voice; 'Many girls can sew, but *Alix* has an instinct for fabric.'

'Well, we know that. Remember the lovely coat she wore on her first day? *Achoo!* Oh dear, I've got powder in my nose.'

Mlle Lefoine shushed them. 'Get on with your work, all of you. Alix, why are you staring at Janice like that? You look like a fish.'

'A trout,' somebody added, and the room convulsed in giggles.

In the thread room, Alix shifted from foot to foot as a woman in a white pinafore inspected a length of Petersham ribbon and gave forth on the iniquities of dyers who couldn't tell one green from another. A girl in brown culottes stood by, nodding impatiently. She was a 'matcher', to judge from her lithe shape. On any working day, the Sentier – the 2nd arrondissement district of Paris – swarmed with matchers dashing between the ribbon, button, tape and buckle makers' shops and the fashion houses. A day's production often depended on a matcher's speed and judgement. Get it wrong and – by the sound of it – you endured a sermon, at the very least. Though at Maison Javier, it seemed, not a harsh one –

'A cabbage is not the same colour as an apple, Suzanne, and never has been.'

'No, Mme Albert.'

'Insult my eye a second time, I will probably have to get annoyed.'

'I tremble in fear, Mme Albert. It won't happen again.'

'Madame?' Alix called as the girl hurried off with the offending ribbon. 'A client expects a garment by close of Monday. I need thread.'

'Give.' The woman held out her hand for the sample and waddled to a chest twenty drawers deep. She pulled one open and Alix saw compartments full of silk bobbins, beginning with off-white, ripening to corn, maize, saffron, then sable. Yellows and in-between hues. There would be a red drawer, a blue drawer . . . what a lovely job to have.

Mme Albert selected four corn colours and went to the window.

'I think the lightest one, Madame?' Alix had seen at a glance which would be best, but still the woman turned each bobbin over slowly. Aware that her patience was wearing thin, Alix followed her to the window and discovered it was raining. Damn, she'd only worn a thin jacket. She'd be soaked by the time she got home. It took her some moments to realise that this side of the building looked out on Rue Boccador, and that the grey building diagonally opposite was the *News Monitor* office. She'd walked past it on her way to lunch, pausing to read the brass plaque, which said 'Calford Press'. The man from the Place du Tertre worked there, the one who'd taken her home the other day.

She tried to bring him to mind. Tall, with arresting eyes. Well-bred but rough-looking. What had they talked about? She remembered he'd used the word 'trauma' to describe her state. A new word, but a good one. She shuddered . . . Her attacker had sent her hair to the Comte de Charembourg. It was like something out of a penny dreadful. The comte's note to her, by contrast, had been so warm.

A car was drawing up at the kerb. A common-or-garden Peugeot, though this one was the shade of Rhône wine. Her gaze sharpened . . . hadn't that car drawn up just as she was plucking up the courage to enter Maison Javier for the first time? No surprise, then, to see the same young man in the wide-lapelled suit climb out. His hat was lodged under his arm and Alix was struck by the gleam of his hair as it caught the rain. Its colour would have belonged on the lightest side of Mme Albert's bobbin drawer. He put on the hat and, as if he sensed her staring down, glanced up and touched his brim in salute. Had he recognised her? Not at this distance. Not after one encounter. Habitual good manners? Or just a flirt . . .

'The lightest colour will not do.'

Alix jumped. Mme Albert was holding out a bobbin. 'One must always use a darker thread than the fabric itself. Right?' She prodded Alix to secure her attention. 'Silk thread catches the light, raising it by two, even three shades. You will think I'm wrong until you sew the garment, but next time you'll say, "Oh, Mme Albert, thank you for saving me the trouble of having to unpick!" *Bien?*' The woman smiled, displaying buck teeth. It was the kindest expression Alix had seen all week.

Mme Albert looked down at the man lounging against the Peugeot's wing. 'There he is, hanging around until the parade is over. Wouldn't you like to be so beautiful a man like that waits for you in the rain?'

'Who is he, Madame?'

'He's called Martel, I believe. Unless I have my facts tangled, he runs some kind of dive.'

'Dive?'

'Nightclub. Squeeze . . . Speakeasy. Don't you watch American films? It's in Pigalle, which is the sort of place your mother wouldn't let you go to.'

Alix nodded, not bothering to mention that she had no mother. Dive. Speakeasy. Squeeze. More new words. They stood in silence, arrested by the muscular Adonis whose suit was growing darker with rain by the minute.

'He's Solange Antonin's latest,' Mme Albert added. 'You know, the dark-haired mannequin with the long neck, the one Javier always puts in white or black? I don't go for light-haired men myself, except Leslie Howard. Did you see *The Scarlet Pimpernel*? My favourite film ever.' Mme Albert sighed, then glanced at the clock. 'You'd better trot along or your supervisor will be on your tail.'

Mlle Lefoine was out of the room so Alix managed to avoid a scolding. She settled on to her bench and picked up her work.

At just after six, the supervisor returned and Alix asked if she might take the skirt to the pressing room.

'You've finished?' She replied with a sceptical frown.

'As far as I can without having it pressed.'

'Let me see.' Mlle Lefoine held the skirt up to the light. She gave Alix a strange look, then pulled in a breath. 'You stupid girl, you completely stupid girl! I cannot believe what I'm seeing.'

Alix stammered, 'Surely there's nothing wrong? I took so much care.'

'You've sewn it inside out,' Mlle Lefoine hurled. 'It will have to be unpicked and if you've damaged the material, you'll pay for it.'

Alix began a denial, even as she realised her supervisor was correct. The 'right' and 'wrong' sides of the silk were almost identical, but not completely. How had it happened? She'd double-checked before she went for her thread. Then she noticed Janice and Séverine snickering behind their hands. So – while she'd been in the thread room, sly fingers had undone her tacking and re-sewn the pieces the wrong way.

Alix wanted to cry, but she drew on her ability to ride out the humiliation and said in a voice pitched between meek and defiant, 'I'll start again and stay until I've done the work correctly.'

'Indeed you will,' the supervisor snapped. 'In fact, everyone will work an extra hour because, thanks to you, this has been one of the least productive days I can remember. And, Alix, when you have finished sewing, you will sweep the floors.'

She sewed as the building emptied, as dusk fell and the floors creaked with the outflow of feet. She sewed until the skirt was ready for its first pressing. Keening with exhaustion, she draped it in tissue paper and hung it in the storeroom. Then she swept the floor. Her knuckles were swollen, her neck muscles burning. *Mémé's right*, she confessed to herself, *it's hard*. When she was finished, she headed to the door. And found it locked.

In the building opposite, Verrian Haviland sat on the corner of his desk, telephone receiver in hand. An hour ago he'd received a wire from his brother with further news of Miguel and now he was about to say words he'd never imagined would pass his lips. 'Thank you from my heart, Jack.'

'Good God. Well, thanks accepted.'

'Which South American country is he on his way to?'

'Venezuela to begin with. After that, it's up to him. Reports say he and his family are F&D.'

'F&D' was Jack's shorthand for 'fine and dandy.' Verrian doubted Miguel could be either, considering his maiming and subsequent handling, but the important thing was that he was out of Spain. Jack had actually delivered.

Jack said, 'On your chum's behalf I took a stratospherically dull Foreign Office fellow out to dinner and stood him a round of golf. You are truly in my debt and it's time to start showing it. Paris desk says you pop in and out at whim. When I ask your hotel to pass on a message, I get some halfwit who laughs at me.'

'That'll be Laurentin. He finds the English side-splitting. Actually I've moved. To Montmartre, a house without a telephone.'

His brother swore. 'I told you to check into a proper hotel. I wasn't suggesting the Ritz, but you're not too bloody proletarian for the Polonaise?'

Verrian released a slow breath. Jack might be the elder by two years, but he often pushed the privilege. 'I can't face duck down and silk wallpaper. I'm sorry, Jack, I know I'm going back on my word, I'll never be able to explain what Spain means to me . . .' What it had cost. 'I'm going back.'

'Not on our ticket!' Jack exploded. 'The Foreign Office says the Spanish police will arrest you if you put so much as a foot over the border. Damn it, you pushed one of their officers down some steps.'

'He was trying to put handcuffs on me.'

'I daresay he thought it was his job. We're sending another chap to Madrid, somebody a little less emotionally embroiled.'

'I'll go as a freelancer then, with the Agence Espagne.'

'No passport, remember? No accreditation. Thanks to that mix-up with the censors, you're on every blacklist going. Now listen –' Jack's tone warmed – 'guess who's coming to Paris? Mother and Lucy. Father wants you to squire them about.'

'I'm not in good shape for family. Why are they coming?'

'Why does any woman go to Paris? To shop, dear boy. It'll be your sister's first visit to the City of Light, so of course you'll want to show her the sights. I'll wire you their time of arrival.'

Alix rattled the door. Banged, shouted until her voice cracked. Had the caretaker locked her in by accident? Or was it deliberate? Surely her colleagues wouldn't imprison her all night? She stood on the sewing table and bumped the broom handle against the ceiling. Flakes of paint sprinkled her but nobody thumped a reply. It was after nine on a Friday night. Everyone had somewhere else to be – family suppers, dinner with friends, parties. Mme Frankel would be at home in the upmarket suburb of Bois de Boulogne. Javier was probably changing into evening dress in his suite overlooking Parc Monceau.

Mémé would panic as the night progressed, would set out to look for her. Alix opened a window and leaned out into the dark. It was still raining, the street below as glossy as a sea lion. She needed one sympathetic person. A policeman, if necessary.

Only the police hardly ever patrolled this smart district and it was hard to make eye contact with anybody, staring down over the tops of umbrellas and rain hats. Everyone was hurrying. 'Excuse me!' she called at a man and woman crossing the road directly in front of her. 'Will you help?' They looked side to side in confusion. 'I'm up here!'

The man tucked his hand under his companion's arm and they sped away.

'I hope this happens to you one day,' Alix yelled after them.

She caught the attention of a young man in an overcoat and cap. Desperation had set in and she shouted loud enough to stop him in his tracks. 'I'm locked in. I need somebody to fetch a policeman or find the caretaker to let me out.'

'Anything for you, darling,' the young man grinned, wiping rain off his face. 'You stay right there.'

Her relief lasted half an hour, the time it took to realise that her white knight had given up or never intended to help. Maybe she'd have to jump. She leaned over the window ledge and was hit by a wave of nausea. Jump? 'I hate this place,' she bawled into the darkness. 'I hate couture. I hate Paris.'

'That's a shame, Mademoiselle.'

Alix squinted through slanting rain lit by headlights. A black car had pulled up below. A rear door was open and a man stood looking up at her. He was wearing a trench coat and hat and his arms were folded.

'I made my taxi stop, Mademoiselle. I thought you were about fall out.'

'I wasn't.' She knew him from the fedora hat and from the hint of Spanish in his French and she cringed. Did he always have to see her at her worst? 'I was seeing how far it is to the ground, but I'm afraid of heights and felt sick.'

He came directly beneath her. In the darkness, with a glare

behind him, he cut a jagged shape. 'Pardon my curiosity, but are there no stairs? No lift? Just a question.'

'Of course there are stairs!' A day's misery spurted up, finding expression in her tone. 'Hasn't it occurred to you that I'm locked in? Or did you imagine I like jumping out of windows?'

'You haven't jumped,' he pointed out. 'And I think it's too far actually. You'd break an ankle or land on someone and break his neck. Isn't there a better way?'

'Of course there is. Find the person who holds the keys to this damn building –' Alix stopped, realising she was spitting fury at the one person available to help. She swallowed and said, 'Would you kindly fetch the caretaker?'

'Of course. Tell me who he is and where he's to be found.'

She sank to her knees, her head on the sill. All week, since she'd stepped over the threshold, she'd been drinking in facts about Maison Javier, but hadn't thought to ask how the place was locked up at night or opened in the morning.

A cough from below. 'I'm still willing to help, but I don't want to stand here getting soaked. I could try to find a ladder.'

'No. I don't mind being on a ladder, but I would never be able to climb out and step on to one. I can't. It terrifies me.'

'Right. Then it'll have to be the fire brigade.'

'No!' Return on Monday as the girl who brought the *pompiers* to Maison Javier? Clanging bells and blazing lights? 'I'll climb over the sill and drop down. It's not far. If you would stand by and make sure I'm all right?'

'Scrape you up if you crack your skull? Right.' This sounded more decisive. 'Stay there, Mademoiselle.'

He walked back to his taxi, and Alix expected him to get in and leave her, but he went to the driver's window and indicated the man should wind down the glass. She thought it was odd that he hadn't recognised her.

He returned. 'Are you brave enough to drop into my arms?'

'What? I would kill you. I'm quite tall, you know.'

'I don't mean from the second floor. No man can actually catch a woman falling from that height, except in the movies. And besides –' whatever he added was lost as the taxi driver lined up with the building, getting as close under her window as he could without damaging the bodywork. Was she supposed to drop on to the car roof without leaving a dent? Parisian taxi drivers were not known for their forgiving temperaments.

Her rescuer took off his coat and spread it on top of the car. Then he stepped up on to the running board, wheel arch, bonnet, finally the roof. He was lithe for a big man, something cat-like in his movements. The coat, she realised, was to stop him slipping.

'You must wriggle out backwards, then drop. I'll break your fall. Only a few feet between us, so remember to bend your knees. Aim for the car, not the gap.'

She moaned, 'I don't think I can.'

'Well, that's fine. You'll have to stay overnight. Is there anyone you'd like me to inform?'

Alix tried to imagine this man trying to stop Mémé wringing her hands long enough to explain that she should retire to bed, leaving Alix incarcerated in the centre of Paris. 'That's not possible either. Oh, heavens.'

'Quite so. By the way, we're attracting a crowd. Soon somebody will call the police and then it will be the fire brigade.'

'All right. I can do it.'

'Remember, flex on landing, and trust me.'

She only half heard, because having made up her mind to go, she couldn't hesitate. She leaned over the sill, wriggling until her legs were outside. There she balanced, aware of her stockings and the clear view upward should her rescuer be ungentlemanly enough to look. Then, crying, 'Are you ready?' and receiving an assurance, she dug her toes against the wall, pushed back, yowled in fright and plummeted.

About six feet. She landed with a thud and a scream. She heard the rip of fabric, felt arms close around her as her legs went from under her. She coasted on her backside on the slick roof, thought she was going over the edge but came to a stop with her feet dangling. Relief brought hysterical laughter. Then she heard cheers and clapping and struggled to sit up.

'Bravo, Monsieur,' a woman shouted. 'Will you do it for me if I jump?'

'Stay still –' this was spoken into her ear. 'I'll get down first.' A moment later, he was holding out his arms and Alix slithered into them, her knees crumpling as she met solid ground. She leaned against him.

'Come on, girl, aren't you going to kiss him?' demanded the same woman. 'He's saved your life and ruined a good coat!' A straggle of cheers made Alix hide her face against the man's waistcoat. The sky finally rescued her. Rain suddenly pelted down so hard the onlookers dashed away. Alix was aware of being kept in a very wet embrace. Her rescuer wore no jacket. White cotton plastered itself to his arms, revealing a wiry strength. His face glinted under the sodden halo of his hat as he waited for her to speak – to thank him, which she should.

But she didn't know what to say, conscious that her blouse was pasted to her body and her hair was running rivers. So she just looked upward, noticing that his collar was torn – her fault – that his throat was muscular. And then, without really knowing how, they were kissing. A kiss that tasted of rain and which felt completely right. Her lips parted and the kiss caught fire. Hands knitting into her hair told her that her response had ignited something in him. Never mind that they were on a public street, a torrent of water gurgling along the gutters beside them in search of a drain.

Four blasts of a car horn broke them apart.

'How did you persuade the driver to let us use his car?' she asked.

'I promised to pay him and told him any damage would be

reimbursed. I doubt there was any. Your fall had the grace of thistledown.'

She bunched her lips. 'That's a polite lie.'

'At least you didn't go through the roof.' He sounded different tonight. A bit impatient. 'Mademoiselle . . . do you spend your life getting into tight spots?'

'You recognise me from the other day?'

'Course, but I thought I should get you down before mentioning it. Have you recovered from being attacked?'

'Mostly.'

'And tonight's calamity?'

'I got locked in.'

'You should be more careful. It's Javier, isn't it, this place?' He looked up at the façade. 'You told me you worked here. In the car, when I took you home. Are you one of his models?'

'Me? No, I'm just . . . just a seamstress. A *midinette*.' A skivvy. A table monkey.

'You're shivering. Come on.' He opened the taxi door.

'Your coat's still on the roof.'

He laughed. 'Wetter than I am. Get in.' When she was inside he said, 'Fancy dinner, or is it St-Sulpice?'

'St-Sulpice,' she answered with regret. Was he going to get in beside her?

He wasn't. He leaned in at the window, saying, 'We live on different sides of the river. I shall bid you goodnight and walk.'

Alix heard him giving the driver directions. She saw money

being handed over, large denomination notes and called out, 'Monsieur, that's too much!'

He came back to her window. 'For allowing his cab to be used as a trampoline? Cheap, I'd say.'

'You're sure your employer will reimburse you?' She picked up the ghost of a smile and wished she'd kept her mouth shut. Her next try was even worse. 'I'd better see you again . . .'

'Yes?'

'I mean, since we . . .'

'Since we . . . ?' He tilted his head.

'I mean – since you helped me twice and I owe you two taxi fares.'

He passed her a white card. 'My business number. Call me next time you get locked in.' He stepped back and gave the roof a couple of smacks. Alix sat back, recognising a classic brush-off.

Silence would be the most dignified state. But she'd suddenly realised where she'd first heard his voice. There was just time to slide across the seat and shout out the window, 'Did that poor friend of yours survive or did he die in prison?'

As the taxi pulled away she thought she heard, 'Deux Magots, tomorrow teatime, and I'll tell you!'

Chapter Twelve

It was while travelling on Métro line eight the following day that Verrian realised he'd found a reason to stay in Paris. A sweet, husky voice which, though it had taken him time to realise it, had haunted him from first hearing. Alix Gower had been the disembodied voice of the telephone exchange. How extraordinary that they kept meeting. Some people would call it fate. There were so many fascinating ingredients to Alix Gower. Like oil and water in a jar, a vigorous shake would emulsify into a rather perplexing girl.

As the train rumbled into Bonne Nouvelle station, sucked in more passengers and closed its doors, he weighed up his feelings. He was physically attracted to Alix, but she sounded – and had felt – quite young. Kissing her last night had been an irresistible impulse, but not the act of a responsible grown man. Had he not been stirred up from his conversation with Jack, he wouldn't have done it. He hoped not, anyway.

Why was he so drawn to her? The first time he'd met her,

she'd been slathered in tears. Last night she'd been soaked to the skin. But . . . the voice and hair and near-black eyes.

Or was he seeing another face? Was he reaching for Alix because he longed for somebody lost to him?

'Penny for them?'

'Scrap – I'm sorry.' He'd temporarily forgotten the two women opposite him in the first-class carriage. Studying them again, Verrian felt the same jolt he'd experienced when he'd first greeted them off their train half an hour ago. While he'd been in Spain, his sister – ten years his junior and known as 'Scrap' – had evolved from a tomboy in jodhpurs into a young woman with professionally waved hair and a grown-up suit.

His mother had altered too. Somebody had taken the confident woman he'd kissed goodbye a year-and-a-half ago and replaced her with a nervous matron. Both now rocked with the motion of the train, handbags clasped in tweed laps. Jack's wire had arrived first thing that morning. Not at Verrian's lodgings, at the *News Monitor* building. '*Ma and Lucy on way Paris, meet Gare du Nord, elevenish.*'

Luckily the *Monitor*'s editorial secretary was so devoted to her duties she came in on Saturdays. She'd shot a boy-messenger to Place du Tertre and Verrian had woken to the realisation that his squiring duties began in three hours.

Bloody Jack must have known last night that the women were already on the boat train. Verrian wondered how he was going to juggle his mother and Lucy and still manage to meet Alix that afternoon.

Lucy was a good face-reader. As the train stopped at Rue Montmartre, she said, 'We've been sprung on you, but don't worry – Ma and I will spend hours in Printemps and then we'll collapse into bed. Just so long as you have dinner with us and take us somewhere nice, we'll be fine. We've missed you.'

'Is the old girl all right?' he asked Lucy in a whisper. Their mother was staring into the blackness of the train window, locked in thought.

'That depends on you. What you drop in her lap this time.'

The doors closed, wheels rolled. Explanation was impossible.

He took them to Printemps, the famous department store on Boulevard Haussmann, and bought them lunch in the café under the cupola. Watching his mother poke doubtfully at her pink beef, turning a slice over to see if it was better done on the other side, he reflected that you could take the English landed classes out their country, but you could not take the country out of them. His mother's philosophy was utterly simple: everything she'd learned during her Edwardian childhood represented Truth in all its forms. Whether the topic was food, politics or marriage, there was a right choice and a wrong choice. And if one came from a good family, one simply knew what the right choice was.

Lucy, catching Verrian's expression, imitated the Haviland

family cook: 'Don't you let them Frenchies palm you off with raw meat, Madam!'

Their mother glanced up, gravely surprised at the comment. 'Underdone meat is dangerous, as you'd know if you were Chairlady of the Sussex School Visitors' Trust. Half the malnutrition we see in rural children comes from intestinal parasites.'

'Mummy, honestly,' Lucy reproved.

'Continentals don't get them,' Verrian said, rolling a slice of beef around oiled lettuce. 'Get school dinner ladies to add garlic to everything, problem solved.'

'They'd be more inclined to add brimstone.' His mother was cutting the darker meat away, pushing circles of pink to the side of her plate.

Verrian couldn't abide waste. His mother's malnourished Sussex brats would look peachy compared to those he'd seen in Spain. In Madrid, a rumour had spread in that jittery, bombarded city that local con-men were catching cats and selling the meat as rabbit. It had made those plates of *olla podrida* his hotel had served, a stew of stringy meats cooked with red cabbage, seem a culinary lottery.

'What's your plan for today?' he asked.

'Anything but grey,' Lucy said. 'I need a couple of suits for my secretarial course and something glam for –' She broke off so abruptly she might have sketched an exclamation mark in the air.

'For?'

'. . . Um, parties and things. And this one –' she pinched her mother's arm, 'her wardrobe is a coffin of old tweed. The poor girl's still wearing dropped waists.'

'Only for gardening. Dear –' Verrian's mother patted his hand – 'you might like to visit the men's department?'

She'd been eyeing his jacket and tie-less neck since the ticket barrier. 'I bought three shirts the other day and a suit and tie,' he told her.

'But you are not wearing them.'

'True.' He'd put on the clothes he'd left on his chair the night before, the priority having been to shave before meeting his mother. 'Some women like the flung-on look.' An African lady, walking towards them in that undulating way of people used to the Tropics, threw him a smile on cue. He responded and she returned a twinkle. 'See?'

Lucy giggled. 'That's the third woman you've flirted with since we sat down.'

'You're counting?'

'You are a flirt though. And such an egalitarian. That poor old fright, begging on the station concourse? She had her skirt tucked into her bloomers but you still called her "Madame".'

'It's how they're wearing bloomers in Paris this year.'

'Enough,' said their mother. 'Not a subject for airing at lunch. Lucy, you should be glad your brother has manners. Verrian, take care you don't become too foreign.'

Verrian surreptitiously checked his watch. Skip cheese and coffee, and he'd have time to go home and change before meeting Alix for tea. If she meant to turn up, of course.

At the Deux Magots, he took an inside table because the spitting wind outside ruffled his newspaper. Might as well find out what the French press were saying about developments in Spain following the Durango bombing. Four o'clock and no sign of Alix. He was betting she wouldn't come.

Shame. She'd miss the debut of his new suit, unique for being the first he'd ever bought off the rail. It was stone-coloured linen, a size too large because the Spanish heat had given him a horror of anything tight-fitting. Under the jacket he wore his shirt open, a breezy Left Bank style that in his hometown of Heronhurst would bring cars to a halt and probably cause bicycle tyres to spontaneously deflate. In Heronhurst, gentlemen buttoned their coats and wore their collars starched even on the hottest summer day.

He ordered coffee, folded the newspaper into a comfortable shape and tried to read. But his attention refused to fix, so he studied the crowd instead. The Deux Magots was a writers' den. Smoke hazed every straight line. Leather banquettes were occupied by men and women whose pencils worked furiously over notepads held down by their cups. Here one could write all day over one cup of coffee without being moved on or charged for air. *The French let culture breathe*, he thought, looking up at the wooden statues attached to a corner pier. Those were the *magots*, the Mandarin wise men that gave the café its name.

'Maggots?' Lucy had echoed when he'd announced where he was going. 'You're meeting someone at "two maggots"? Can we come?'

No, Scrap, you can't. The waiter brought him his coffee, but after a sip or two he decided it was making his heart race. It couldn't be nerves he was feeling. He was only meeting a dowdy and unsophisticated girl about his sister's age. They were palpitations of embarrassment, he told himself, because what had seemed right yesterday in the dark now felt hideously ill-judged.

A man and woman entered. The man wore a sloping beret, a cigarette between his lips. He was talking fast with big, self-reverential gestures. The man's companion, a tall girl way out of his league, was ignoring him. Verrian watched, amused, until he realised who she was. Then he stood up so clumsily he knocked his newspaper to the floor. A waiter picked it up, standing in his way long enough for him to master his confusion and say her name.

This was not the girl who'd scrambled out of a window into his arms. Nor the one he'd rescued in Place du Tertre. In a purple dress whose nipped-in middle gave her an hourglass figure, this was a fantasy he might have created out of the raw fabric of Alix Gower. Her hair was a cloud of curls under a devastatingly chic hat. She wasn't seventeen or eighteen, he realised. She was about twenty, and that made him feel a lot better.

She reached to shake his hand with a grace that drew stares. The man in the beret gave a Latin shrug and plodded back to his outdoor table. She asked, 'I hope I haven't kept you waiting?'

You have, and I expect you meant to. 'Teatime is fluid in Paris. Thank you for coming. I'd told myself you wouldn't. Please sit down.'

She sipped water while she waited for her coffee. He discussed the weather, the April showers, the tourists crowding the métro. 'You're looking beautiful today. May I say that?'

'You mean, I looked a ragbag yesterday.' A smile softened the reproach. 'They were my work clothes. This is something I bought because I liked the colour.' She gestured towards the dress – its neckline was nun-like, but black, Indian-file buttons insisted the eye follow the contours of her body down to her midriff.

Verrian gulped water. 'I'm one up on you then, having bought something entirely new to impress you.'

'I noticed.' She gave his lapels and shoulder line a tilted inspection. 'It's a good suit and I hope you keep Mme Konstantiva's cat away from it.' Two fresh coffees arrived. He noticed that she stirred a lot of sugar into hers. Kept stirring longer than necessary.

'How are you,' he asked, 'after your ordeal?'

'Leaping out of a window? I was very angry with my colleagues this morning because I know they locked me in. I should have risen above it, but I put pins on their chairs instead.'

'Sharp side up?'

'Of course. Only one each,' she added when he raised an eyebrow.

'Actually, I meant your ordeal on Place du Tertre. You never really told me who hurt you that day or why.'

She shrugged. 'I don't remember what I said to you – I expect I burbled a lot of nonsense. I'm all right now, except where he cut my hair –' she indicated a curl over her left ear. 'It wants to stick out like a turnip top.'

Verrian was glad she could laugh at herself, a rare commodity in attractive women, but he didn't believe that shrug or her claim of forgetfulness. 'In the car you said your attacker had demanded a lot of money. Doesn't that mean he'll come back?'

'I don't know. No, I don't think so. Everything's sorted.'

'You mentioned needing to "find the comte". May I ask who that is? Your father?'

'No, just a family friend. Well, a sort of neighbour. Well, a kind of guardian. In Alsace, long ago, the Comte de Charembourg and my grandmother . . .'

He leaned forward. 'This is gripping.'

She laughed. 'They lived in the same town. The comte owned the castle and all the land.'

Now he saw the fellow as a music-hall villain, complete with black cloak and curling moustache. 'How is the mysterious Comte de Charembourg connected with your being scalped in Place du Tertre?'

She frowned slightly and he supposed he'd pushed too far. It was early to be demanding the identities of other men, but he'd had a flash of jealousy at the first mention of the name. 'I'm a journalist,' he explained. 'I live in a sea of questions, and if they're not quickly answered, I get a twitch. I want to know why a young woman, apparently sober and well-bred, should be threatened by a thug on a Montmartre staircase. I've no right to know,' he added, taking her hand because she'd begun stirring her coffee needlessly, 'but I'm good at discretion. I'm also quite good at thumping people, if I think they need it. What I'm saying, Mademoiselle, is if you want to confide in someone, I'm a good bet.'

'Call me Alix.'

'Well, Alix, I'm willing to help or just listen. I owe you a favour.'

'Do you? But I owe you . . . for rescuing me twice?'

'You broke the rules to get me a line to London. It was important, that call. Hang on . . . you're working for Javier. Does that mean you're no longer employed at the telephone exchange?'

'We parted company.'

'I hope it wasn't my fault.'

She made a 'maybe' grimace. 'What happened to your friend?'

'Miguel? On his way to a safe Latin American country and I may never hear from him again. War does that to people. It creates and erases friendships. I'll find out more when I return to Spain.' Studying her hand, he thought what an exquisite colour her skin was, emerging from an amethyst cuff. Then he looked up to find her expression that of a child who's seen the cake taken off the table. Did she mind that he was leaving? 'I'll be around for a while still,' he added, and thought, *Is that true? Have I just changed my plans for this woman?*

'Were you in Spain covering the fighting or doing the fighting? Your boots were like a soldier's.'

'Covering it. I am – was – the *Monitor*'s Madrid correspondent.'

'That's very impressive.'

'Not really. I washed up there. Eighteen months ago I was in Abyssinia when the Italians invaded. I was the nearest man when Franco's Fascists landed in Spain from North Africa some months later. I signed on with the Republican Party as an accredited correspondent.' He was telling her what side he was on – raising his colours over the table – and she was staring back, impassive. Was he speaking of things that were over her head? Almost certainly. Catalans, Basques and Castilians argued endlessly about the causes of their country's conflict and he often lost the thread too. Why should she understand?

Anyone who approaches this civil war believing in black and white, right and wrong, hasn't seen enough. His own words. Driving to the front every day from Madrid – until the front came so close he could sit at a café table on the Paseo del Pintor Rosales and watch it – he'd seen men reaped like summer corn. Spanish Fascists, Italians and North African mercenaries had behaved like

172

medieval bandits. Of course, the Republican side had committed its atrocities too. The war he'd quitted was not good versus evil, it was an *olla podrida* of human depravity.

He told her, 'I was in my hotel room in Madrid, and a note came inviting me to meet with one of the government's propaganda men. I thought I was getting a scoop.' He was hoping she'd yawn so he could stop, but she looked at him, waiting. 'Instead I was marched to a room at the back of a windowless building where a man called Miguel was shot in front of me.' He felt her shock at that. 'Not killed. A punishment maiming, because his bosses thought he'd turned a blind eye to a piece I'd written. Actually I hadn't written the bit they objected to, but that came later. Two fingers were shot from his hand and he was dragged away half-conscious. I was arrested but got away.'

'How?'

'I stamped on a policeman's foot, on the top, where it hurts most, rolled him down a short stairwell and ran. I eventually made it to Albacete aerodrome, where a friend of mine was taking off for Paris. He flew me out, but I couldn't stop thinking about Miguel. That's why your help meant so much.'

'And you want to go back to Spain? I wouldn't.'

'I feel that by leaving, I betrayed a cause.'

'I don't often read newspapers,' she said, 'so I hadn't heard of you.'

He traced a little circle between her thumb and index finger and raised her hand to his lips. 'I'm rather glad of that.' He was about to discover if her skin tasted of the almond cream it resembled when a sharp, 'Verrian, really!' made him jerk back.

It was Lucy who apologised. 'Bother, now I'm being a gooseberry. I really didn't . . . honestly, I just assumed . . .'

That I was meeting a male friend, he filled in silently. Disengaging his hand, he stood and said, 'Lucy, allow me to introduce you to Mlle Gower. Alix, this is my sister, Lucinda Haviland.'

Alix extended her hand. Lucy, over-anticipating the gesture, grabbed air then managed to get hold of Alix's wrist. 'Gosh, sorry.' Then her handbag fell down her arm with a clunk that broke the handshake. 'Oh Lord.'

'Coffee?' Verrian pulled out a chair, reckoning they'd all be safer seated.

'Righto, though I need a dram. Shopping in Paris is murder. The saleswomen are without mercy. Honestly, as soon as I entered the changing room I remembered the state of my underwear.' Lucy's eyes strayed to Alix, to the moulded dress, and she sighed. 'My unmentionables only just pass in the ladies' department of Grindle & Whiteleather. That's our shop in Heronhurst,' she explained to Alix. 'Everybody buys their clothes there.'

Alix said, 'Vendeuses see fifty sets of undergarments a day. Don't take it to heart.'

'Are you wearing a corset?'

'Lucy,' Verrian shot back, 'three minutes' acquaintance doesn't allow that.'

'Sorry,' Lucy mumbled.

'I am not,' Alix replied, unperturbed. 'I also find vendeuses terrifying, and they mean us to.'

'Your English is terribly good,' Lucy told her.

'I am English . . . mostly . . . I was at school in Hampshire.'

'Which school? Was it Roman Catholic? I know a few RC girls.'

'Lucy.' Verrian meant, *Shut up.*

'No,' Alix said simply.

'C of E?'

'How was your shopping?' Verrian interrupted, meaning, *One more gaffe and I'll put you on the pavement.* 'I don't see any bandboxes.'

'Mummy took them to the hotel in a taxi. She needed a lie-down, having bought a black evening dress with lace sleeves identical to the one she bought last year. I got two suits – one grey, one grey with a grey stripe. Heartbreaking. There was a check I loved, but mother thought it looked like bus-seat upholstery and the saleswoman conspired.'

'Grey will suit your colouring,' Alix said. 'In my view, grey is the only colour that goes perfectly in spring and autumn.'

Alix's voice had changed, Verrian noticed. It was more reflective.

'But I wore grey every day at school.'

'Then add a neck scarf.'

'I could . . . red maybe, or your colour, mauve.'

'Mmm.' Alix studied Lucy's face. She did it without staring, just let her focus soften. 'I would choose spice colours: ginger, burnt orange, perhaps with some slate blue. If you have time to go to Hermès, they have something there that would suit you.' Reaching for her handbag, she took out a wand of coloured pencils and a small sketchbook. Verrian watched her fast strokes, saw how she changed colours, feeding her vision from the pile of pencils. She ripped out the page and handed it to Lucy who said, 'Gosh, are you an artist? Carrying crayons in your bag feels jolly professional.'

'I don't consider myself an artist, but my grandfather was.'

'Oh, will we have heard of him?'

'I don't know. His name was Lutzman. He died before he created his best work.'

'How can you know that?'

Alix's silence told Verrian that Lucy had finally offended. 'By studying the progress of his art, Lucy,' he said, 'and making a judgement.'

'Yes, but we still don't know who he was.'

'His name was Alfred Lutzman,' Alix repeated.

'Isn't that a Ger—' Lucy felt her brother's eyes on her face and blushed. She scanned Alix's drawing, then handed it to Verrian.

The stylised fashion sketch captured the lower part of Lucy's face, continuing down to the hip, slimming her considerably. Alix had drawn an elegant town suit and captured the shape of Lucy's jaw perfectly. To the side she'd scribbled a chart of colours she presumably thought would complement Lucy's complexion. Rather over Verrian's head, but he wouldn't argue with her choices.

'Frightfully clever,' Lucy breathed.

'You're welcome, and perhaps Grindle & Whiteleather will search out accessories in those colours for you.' As she spoke, Alix bundled up her crayons and held out her hand to Verrian. 'Thank you for the coffee, but I must go now.'

He felt absurdly robbed. And so irritated with Lucy that the angry pulse came back. 'Must you?' She must, it seemed. 'I'll get you a taxi.'

'No, no. I'm so close to home, I'll walk. Goodbye, Miss Haviland.'

'Lucy, please.'

Verrian followed her out, knowing from the way she walked that she wanted to get away. He caught up with her. 'I have an idea we've upset you. I'm sorry.'

'On my mother's side, I'm Jewish,' she said.

He blinked. Where had that come from?

'Your sister was fishing. Tell her that "Lutzman" is Jewish. I think she minds about that sort of thing – as did many of the girls I went to school with. I'd imagined, in Paris, I could stop explaining myself.'

'Don't walk off. If you do, we won't know how to see each

other again.' He held out his hand until she gave him hers. 'And you don't ever have to explain yourself to me.'

That evening Verrian joined his mother and Lucy in the restaurant of the Hôtel Polonaise on Place Vendôme where they were staying. His anger towards Lucy had cooled but his mother poked the embers by saying, 'Lucy tells me she interrupted your tête-à-tête with a Jewish girl.'

'Her name is Alix Gower. She's Anglo-Jewish, if that matters.'

'Of course it matters. Where did you pick her up?'

'That is insulting and unworthy.'

Lucy touched his arm. 'This is all my fault.'

'At what point, Lucy, were you taught to interrogate people on their religion?' He kept his eye on his mother because he knew perfectly well where Lucy derived her bulldog chauvinism. 'You've not met Alix, Mother, but are still prepared to speak disparagingly of her, doubtless because she isn't a Grosvenor Square debutante. Are you turning into Father?'

'Really!' Peggy Haviland fluttered her napkin about her mouth. 'Below the belt. I didn't mean to attack your friend, Verrian, but when Lucy said she'd interrupted you canoodling, when you'd led us to believe you were meeting work colleagues—'

'I said no such thing. You heard what you wanted to hear.'

'Another girl we know nothing about, so soon after rumours of the last one.'

'What rumours?' From his tone, both women realised they'd begun something dangerous.

'Simply –' Peggy Haviland dabbed her lips again – 'that you had a "fling" with a Spanish girl. We worried you might bring her home.'

'Inflict a Papist on Heronhurst? How would you explain that to the Rowley and Heronbridge Women's Institute?'

'Don't mock me, Verrian.'

'Then don't be a bloody prig.'

'Please don't swear.'

He counted silently. 'I apologise. Let me assure you,' he said, as evenly as he could, 'there's not the slightest chance of any Spanish girl coming to England with me. That's all I will say.'

'I am relieved, dear. I feel as if I've lost you to a world I don't understand.' His mother fumbled in her quilted evening purse and Verrian feared she was looking for a handkerchief. But she took out her reading glasses and picked up her menu. 'I swear, the spaces between words get smaller every day.'

A well-worn joke, but Verrian laid his hand over hers and the flag of truce flew.

Their mother was ready for bed by ten. Lucy wasn't, so Verrian whisked her off to a cabaret near Place du Tertre, one recommended as suitable for one's sister. In a corner niche, cognac in front of him, crème de menthe in front of her, he said, 'Scrap – one of us has to tell Mother that I won't turn into the man who takes the morning train to Waterloo.'

Lucy tasted her drink, making a face. 'It's like cough medicine but rather intriguing. Actually, I should have asked for sherry. No, don't wave to the waiter, I'll soldier on. You're going back to Spain? But Jack says the Republicans will shoot you.'

'Dear Jack. Always the silver lining.'

'He says that if the Republicans don't, the Fascists will think you're a spy, and if they capture you, they'll torture and shoot you.' She stared at him through fair lashes that were suspiciously wet as if a tear had sprung. 'I'm sorry I was rude about Alix, but please don't go to Spain just to get away from me. I know I'm tiresome.'

'Don't, Scrap.'

'Coming to Paris went to my head. I cycled to Grindle & Whiteleather specially to buy a new outfit. I thought I looked swish, but when I saw her . . .'

'Alix has been born with a spectacular set of bones and that's her luck.'

'I suppose she's really very nice?'

'I don't know much about her.'

'Golly –' Lucy dropped her voice – 'is that a tramp?'

A man was shambling past and Verrian's attention sharpened as he recognised the bearded profile. No tramp. It was Bonnet, who lived next door to him. Verrian watched the man go to the cashier's window and pull a roll of notes from his pocket, exchanging it for a bag of gambling chips, then walk unsteadily to a roulette table where a croupier was inviting bets. He pushed a stack of chips on to a single number. The wheel spun, the ball clacked like a loose nut. Raphael Bonnet clasped his hands and Verrian had the impression of a man praying to an unlucky god.

'You aren't listening,' Lucy chided. 'I said – tell her I shall take her sketch to Whiteleather's.'

'Good.'

'And Mrs Whiteleather will open the ladies' scarf drawer and say, "That's all we have, dear. Have a rummage." Oh, I'm going to have to say it . . . Jack and Moira are engaged.' She blurted it out, as if it had been stuck on her tongue all day.

He didn't answer at once. He had to ask himself if he was shocked. If he minded. Back in the summer of 1935, Verrian and Moira Durslop, daughter of Sir Chester Durslop MP, his parents' Sussex neighbour, had become engaged. Neither of their families had rejoiced. As far as Moira's parents were concerned, a younger son who worked as a journalist was far beneath their daughter's deserts. His own father, who didn't think much of him, declared he wasn't ready for marriage. His mother, whose opinion, in Verrian's view, was tinted by maternal blindness, thought Moira too silly and vain for *her boy*.

To some degree, both his parents had been right. It had been a flimsy affection, tested to breaking point when, in October 1935, Verrian went to Abyssinia to cover the Italian invasion.

Moira's love for him died when, instead of coming home for the Season of '36, he'd gone from Abyssinia to Spain to report on the Fascist invasion. She'd written telling him that if he wanted his engagement ring back, he'd find it at the bottom of her father's fishing lake. She considered herself free to find a husband who wasn't addicted to other people's wars.

'She and Jack will do very well,' he said slowly. 'They're suited. I just wish he'd told me himself.'

'Jack's terrified you'll come home and thump him. That's why he's so desperate for you to stay in Paris. Doesn't want a big black eye. Sir Chester wants him to take his parliamentary seat when he retires next year.'

'Jack, an MP?' He thought about it. 'Why not? He was born for the role.'

'And getting worse. He stands with his thumbs tucked into his waistcoat and gives speeches to his wardrobe. They don't want you to return to Spain either. When Moira heard you had a Spanish girlfriend, she started saying the most awful things about "foreign floozies". She's jealous,' Lucy said sagely, 'and scared that if you bring such a person home, everyone will say, "Poor Verrian, on the rebound because Moira threw him over to get her claws into the elder son."'

'I'd say she has.'

'I wish you could hear Father ranting at Mother every time you go somewhere dangerous, or have a fling. It's why she's lost weight. She's sensitive, you know, under that galvanised exterior. So please don't get too keen on your Alix – I mean, if you were drifting that way. Can you imagine how Father would react?'

He took Lucy back to the Hôtel Polonaise, keeping the taxi, and went on to Laurentin's place, where he ordered a triple cognac at the bar. He took a photograph from his wallet and propped it against his drink. It had been taken in a bomb-damaged square in Madrid. A dark-haired girl squinted at the camera, one side of her face shadowed by a beret. Not a fashionable beret, a military one. It was the only picture he had of Maria-Pilar. The only reminder of their cruelly brief union. Lucy was right – it would be insane to grow fond of anyone new. He must put a halt to it. He must leave Paris.

Chapter Thirteen

When Alix had handed her first Javier wage packet to Mémé,
her grandmother had counted the money and reminded her that
the telephone company had paid her a third as much again. The
one she presented on 16th April received the same response.

'And if the job is so wonderful, Aliki, why are you moping?'

'I'm tired.'

'You call this tired? You wait till you've hemmed your way
around the coast of France, then you'll know tired.'

The job was tough, but Alix's low spirits had other origins.
Verrian Haviland had not called since they had shaken hands
outside the Deux Magots nearly a week ago.

She worked on Saturday, but on Sunday, her day off, she went to
see Bonnet. Her first visit to his studio since she'd been attacked.
She'd written to him about that incident, promising to sit for
him again when she felt ready and he'd replied with a short note:
'*My door is always open.*'

She walked fast from the métro, on the watch for anyone

shadowing her. She allowed herself a moment in front of Ver-rian's lodgings to wonder if the room top front with the green shutters was his. Outside the Deux Magots he'd seemed so eager to see her again. She'd waited. And waited. Turning her back on the green shutters, she thrust open Bonnet's door and clattered upstairs shouting his name.

Bonnet was at work and spun round, spattering paint. Seeing her distress, he opened his arms. 'Bear hug awaits. Explanations can follow.'

'Haviland . . .' Bonnet studied Verrian's card. She'd asked his advice. Should she swallow her pride, go next door and ask to see Verrian? Or put him from her mind?

'Not the family that manufactures the aeroplanes, wrong spelling. Should you chase after him? Newspaperman . . . hmm. Inky fingers and lunchtime drinking.'

'You should talk, Bonnet.' Alix took the business card back and discovered a blue thumbprint on it.

'How old is he?'

'I don't know precisely,' she confessed. 'Twenty-eight . . . thirty . . . He's very gentlemanly.'

'As a gentleman, he'll realise you're only seventeen. Hmm?'

'Bonnet, I'm nearly twenty-one. How many times?'

'*Pardon*. Your innocence misleads. But has he called? Sent a note? Flowers?'

When Alix shook her head, Bonnet slung an arm round her.

'My first – and only – wife told me, if a man calls you next day, he's too eager. If he leaves it more than three, forget him. How many days?'

She counted on her fingers. 'Eight, if you include Sundays.'

'Sundays are included, I think.'

'Bonnet . . .' though the weather was mild, the studio was freezing, 'must we work today?'

'Course not. By the way, if you came hoping to be paid for last time, I'm a bit short.'

'That's all right.'

'A fellow was going to buy my views over St-Martin canal, supposed to come yesterday.' Bonnet pointed to twin impressions of reflected trees and a bow-shaped bridge, then finished his story in one sigh. 'Next week I'll be better placed. Fancy a drink?'

'I've only got the coins in my pocket.'

'We'll go to Mother Richelieu's. She puts it on a slate for me.'

Over a glass of wine, Alix asked Bonnet a question that had been troubling her since the day of her attack. 'That thug . . . do you think he followed me across Paris?'

'It's possible. Or perhaps he saw a pretty girl go into a shuttered house and decided . . . you know? On a whim.'

'No, he knew me, and why I was there. And he knows the Comte de Charembourg, and that the comte cares for me. It's why he picked on me, as a way of making the comte pay him.

It makes me ill, thinking that some revolting stranger knows about my life. Secret things. Who could it be?'

Bonnet shrugged. He'd downed his first glass of wine in one and was trying to attract a refill. 'Mother Richelieu, *attention*, empty glass over here!' He watched the *patronne* pour him more wine. 'To the top, Madame, I don't pay you for empty air.'

'You don't pay me at all, Bonnet.'

He laughed delightedly, smacking the woman's bottom, then said to Alix, 'You'd better hope nobody ever comes after you to pay my bills.'

'That isn't funny. Bonnet, how did you get tangled up with my family? I know you were my grandfather's apprentice, but after his death why didn't you find another master to learn from and move on? Why have you kept in touch with my grandmother all these years? You're such a mismatched pair.'

He pinched her cheek. 'Mismatches are often the best. But the truth? After your grandfather died, somebody had to get Danielle and Mathilda out of Kirchwiller. The place had become a graveyard for your grandmother. She couldn't sleep, eat . . . there were those who blamed her for your grandfather's death.'

'Why? You told me that thieves killed him.'

Bonnet brushed the question aside. 'It was felt she should leave Alsace, get right away, to another country. I suggested London because Alfred had studied there in his youth. Somebody contacted his former tutor in London – the old Comtesse de Charembourg wrote the letter, I think. A reply came, offering Danielle and Mathilda a home. Money was raised for their journey, of which at least half came from the comte and his mother.'

'Why so generous?'

'They were the big fish in Kirchwiller. Back then, they owned streets of houses, including the one your grandparents lived in. I expect they felt a sense of noblesse oblige. The only question remained, how would Danielle and Mathilda make that long trip? They couldn't go alone, so I volunteered to take them. Or was volunteered, I'm not sure which. Have I answered your question?'

'A bit. I know where the story starts, and where it ends. Here in Paris. But what about the bit in the middle? I know the comte and my father joined the same regiment when war broke out, but why was the comte living in London? And how was it he never met my mother?'

Bonnet stopped his glass halfway to his mouth. 'What d'you mean, never met your mother?'

'He never knew her. He told me.'

Bonnet made a rude noise. 'Then he's being discreet, or forgetful. I escorted your grandmother and mother to London in the winter of 1904, right? I meant to settle them in with their new friends and go back to Alsace, but I discovered I liked England. I was invited to remain, given a room and studio and stayed for many months, long enough to be there when the Comte de Charembourg came to Oxford, which is not very far from London.'

Alix nodded. 'He studied at Oxford University. I remember him telling me.'

'Now, you see, Danielle had been taken in by the painter Martin Fressenden and his wife, Magdalen. They ran an art school from their home by the River Thames. Danielle arrived exhausted, but after she recovered she planted herself in the kitchen as cook-housekeeper. She was happier there. She felt awkward in the drawing room, all those merry people shouting at each other in English. Not so little Mathilda, who learned the language in a month and became everyone's pet. De Charembourg would visit from Oxford once a month or so, and grew very fond of her. He'd bring her presents: dolls, chocolates, a kitten once. He was like a big brother and she adored him. A big brother . . . until she grew up and met him in his uniform. Then you can be sure she looked upon him differently.'

'They met . . .'

'At the front in the early months of the war, I believe. He a captain, she a nurse.'

'So . . .' Alix's lips felt stiff, afraid to form the question, 'why would he pretend not to know her?'

'God knows. Perhaps he's wiped the past from his mind. We all do to some extent—' Bonnet broke off as two men sauntered in. 'Didiot, Ambrose, hey! Come drink with us. My pretty friend and I are talking about life and other sad events.'

Knowing he would soon have a noisy coterie around him, Alix put a question to him that she'd struggled to ask for months.

'Bonnet, will you tell me more about how my grandfather died? What did those thieves do to him?'

She got the story of Alfred's death, but it was the same one as before, and this time peppered with so many asides and interruptions even Bonnet lost the thread. And by the time he'd emptied several jugs of wine, the tears were falling. When he started calling for cognac, Alix gave up. Heading home, she got off the train a few stops early, walking to clear her head and review what Bonnet had told her.

So the Comte de Charembourg and her mother had met. First as brother-figure and little girl, then in the midst of war when Mathilda was just a little older than Alix was now. Had they strayed into forbidden love? When war broke out 1914 the comte had been married and – Alix drew on her limited knowledge of his domestic circumstances – father of at least one daughter. Was that what everyone was avoiding telling her? It would explain so much . . .

Alix was crossing Place St-Sulpice, head bowed in thought, when she heard her name being called. A bicycle pulled up in a screech of brakes.

'Paul –' In the sunshine, he seemed almost brutally solid. And he was scowling. 'What are you doing here?'

'I've been waiting ages. It's Suzy, she's ill. Your fat concierge-woman told me you were out. Have you been drinking?'

'I've been with Bonnet – what d'you think?' It came out sharply and she immediately put out her hand. What she'd thought was a scowl was fatigue. 'What's the matter with Suzy?'

'Croup. She was so bad yesterday, seizing for breath, I took her to a doctor. He pretty much told me our living conditions were to blame, and if she didn't get better soon, he'd intervene. He means an orphanage.'

'We've got honey at home. Shall I get it? Or I could come and sit with Suzy to give you a break?'

'Not with drink on your breath.' Paul added a half-apologetic shrug. 'Somebody already gave me some honey, and Suzy's too unwell to leave with anybody. Alix, I need money. My great-aunt will help with the girls — if I pay her, and I need to refit the boat this summer. Are you doing what you promised? Mme Shone is like a cat on hot bricks and I keep making excuses. I said you needed time to settle into Javier before giving us the copies, but it'll be the end of April before we know it. She says New York's on the telephone every day. Have you thrown us over?'

'Course not.' In some ways, Paul was right. Alix needed money too, but for all her new job was hard, her colleagues spiteful, she'd fallen in love with Maison Javier. She didn't want to be a thief, even though she knew it was only a matter of time. 'Let's go to a café, talk it over.'

But Paul had to go. 'Come and see me soon, Alix. Promise.'

She promised.

A further surprise awaited in her courtyard: Mme Rey swabbing the flagstones with a wide-headed broom, steam rising from a canister of hot water.

The concierge stopped mid-stroke. 'See how I look after you people? The stink of piss was making me ill. And they –' she jerked her head at the laundry house – 'wouldn't know which end of a mop is which. One of your boyfriends called earlier.'

'Paul. I met him.'

'And a parcel came. Hand-delivered.' The concierge dug inside her bib pocket and drew out a small box. 'Not your birthday, is it?'

'Not till June. Thank you, Madame.' Alix went upstairs, tearing the wrapping as she went. She found a pale-blue box containing a pair of silver embroidery scissors and a note:

My dear Alix, please accept this in token of my affection and admiration. I hope they will help you in your new profession as they are the finest Sheffield steel, very sharp!
From one who prays – and knows – that you will now sleep easy,

Jean-Yves de Charembourg

'Sleep easy' – he was telling her that he'd paid her attacker and she need not fear any more. But why not state plainly what he meant? Everybody bamboozled her with half-facts, or gave her a truth so diluted it wasn't worth having. Or disappeared, like Verrian. Only Bonnet treated her as an adult with a brain. Crossly she dug into her handbag for her door-key. It wasn't there. She tipped the bag's contents on to the floor and felt the lining. Definitely not there. She'd put her bag down at Mother

Richelieu's, which one should never do as Montmartre was notorious for bag-snatchers. Her purse was there, so maybe the key had just fallen out. She knocked and Mémé let her in, giving her granddaughter a disgruntled look, telling her to sit down while she made black coffee.

It was much later when Alix got round to writing the comte a short thank-you, which she addressed to Rue du Sentier. She signed it 'Mathilda', a gesture she knew was both provocative and childish.

Monday arrived and, with still no word from Verrian, Alix accepted that Bonnet was right. Verrian Haviland was an experienced man for whom a kiss in the rain meant nothing. But when, eleven days after their parting outside the Deux Magots, Pauline Frankel came to her workbench and said, 'Alix, take off your smock and come to the salon, somebody wishes to speak with you,' her heart still bucked like a spring lamb. It could only be Verrian.

Why hadn't he warned her? Disaster! She was wearing her dowdiest skirt and *ugh!* flat shoes. Mme Frankel showed her into one of the trying-on rooms off the salon, telling her to wait. 'You may not appear in the salon itself, you understand?'

Alix perched on a sofa, bubbles popping inside her. Would Verrian bring flowers? Use that sexy, amused voice? Would he want to kiss her? On balance she'd rather he didn't, not while she was wearing these clothes. She'd rather be kissed in a cabaret, wearing her favourite evening gown. Well, her only evening gown.

The door opened and Alix leaped up. It wasn't Verrian who entered, but a woman whose hourglass shape came wrapped in a beige suit. A white cone hat was pinned to her blonde hair. Pale fur swathed one shoulder. Good God – it was the American from Hermès, the one who'd given her six out of ten. Alix sagged. No sexy smile, no flowers. But something was about to happen. A telling-off, maybe?

Mme Frankel made introductions. 'Mme Kilpin, this is Alix Gower. Alix, Mme Kilpin called into my office the other day, expressing a desire to meet the girl who sews so neatly and fast. I was delighted to agree as it's always the salesgirls and the fitters who get the praise when an order is delivered on time. Seamstresses are the poor cousins. I should know; I was one once. Mme Kilpin, do please sit. Ah, good, tea has arrived. You will take refreshment?'

As Alix tried to make sense of the woman arranging herself on a sofa of cream damask, a junior saleswoman laid out fine china and slices of lemon on a salver. Mme Frankel poured. Mme Kilpin stared at Alix.

'Recognise the skirt, kiddo?'

'The trellis silk, Madame. I sewed it for you.'

'It arrived two hours before my husband did, and I wore it to meet him at the airport. He didn't notice. I might have been wearing a grain sack to him, but the point is, I was wearing an ensemble I'd put together in my mind, so I was happy. I like my plans to work.' Mme Kilpin's French was riddled with errors and her accent was a crime, but Alix guessed she didn't care. Why should she? 'Madame' had no need to please anybody. But still, Alix couldn't fathom this meeting – no lady ever thanked her dressmaker.

'I'm glad I put my mark on you, Mlle Gower.'

'Mark, Madame?'

'Oh, shoot, she hasn't guessed. Put her in the picture, Mme Frankel.' The American raised her teacup to her lips.

'Mme Kilpin goes by a different name occasionally, to amuse herself. Not so?' Pauline Frankel threw the visitor a quizzical look.

'Sure. I give myself a laugh three times a day.'

'She calls herself sometimes . . . Mme Shone.'

'Shone – oh.' Blood hammered into Alix's cheeks. It was 'Mme Shone' who worked with Paul. Who wanted Javier's collection dropped in her lap. Not the same 'Shone', please no.

'Before her marriage, Mme Kilpin designed clothes in New York. She had her own business.' Mme Frankel's smile was so bland it was impossible to tell what her opinion might be.

'Pretty successful, tell her that. I called myself "Shone" as in *Schön*, German for "beautiful" – "Fashion Modes by Mme Beautiful". I always say, if you don't clang your own bell, nobody's going to do it for you.'

'No, Madame,' Alix muttered.

Mme Frankel frowned. 'Alix, Mme Kilpin is not only a leader in fashion, she is respected for her knowledge of couture. When she approached me in March, asking me to interview a young protégée who wished to work here, I agreed immediately. Why do you think, when I was detained, that you were interviewed by Javier? D'you think every girl who walks in here is treated with such distinction?'

'I suppose not,' was the best Alix could offer. From the sound of it, Mme Kilpin had as good as *placed* her here. She must really want something in return.

'I do love tea.' The American drained her cup. 'I'm not the greatest Anglophile – and I know you're half Brit, Alix, so pardon me – but I admire them for their tea. I used only to – oh, I nearly forgot –' She turned to the première. 'My vendeuse–' she pronounced it 'ven-doose' – 'mentioned that Javier has created a Scottish tartan for his autumn–winter season and some of it is in my colour? Would you fetch me a sample, dear Mme Frankel? Mr Kilpin is taking me to Scotland in the fall and I want some sporty little suits. Alix will entertain me while you're gone, won't you, dear?'

'If you wish, Madame.'

The moment Pauline Frankel was out of the room, Mme Kilpin leaned forward, saying in English, 'We've got five minutes. Let's get this hog roped and tied.'

'Hog, Madame?'

'Don't piffle with me, Alix. I know you and you know me. Here –' She dug into a suede handbag and a moment later was flourishing silk at Alix. 'Take it. As a gift.'

It was the Hermès scarf. The genuine article. Alix shook her head.

'Sure you can.'

Alix sat back, her whole body saying no.

Mme Kilpin sighed. 'Pride rarely earns a buck, but all right. I'm going to say a few things very fast. One, Paul le Gal is a doll. He's worth ten of any man you are likely to meet in the next decade and if you don't know that . . . oh, look at your face. Your funeral, but the boy's in love with you. Two, the boat he lives on is a floating disgrace.'

Alix nodded. That she could not refute.

'Those dear little girls. What'll get them first, dysentery or the nuns? Three, he needs money, I need money –' a knowing glance at Alix's brown stockings and shoes, 'I guess we all need money.'

'You need money, Madame? I don't believe it.'

'Well, believe it. Four –' her voice fell soft as snowflakes – 'you're unable to steal Javier's spring–summer line. Paul's explanation involved raspberry desserts and an angry head chef, from which I gather you couldn't get enough detail to make proper sketches. I hate waving goodbye to money, but I accept that you were finding your feet. I want the mid-season stuff that's coming out next month. I'll want Javier's autumn–winter collection, which he'll show end of July, start of August. And he's sending a dress to the Expo—'

'Expo?'

'The World's Fair, the Exposition of Arts and Technology that's to open at the end of next month, if they finish building the pavilions in time. I want that dress.'

Alix shook her head. 'I can't.'

'Honey, you can because thousands already do. You think your little seamstress friends don't copy the muslin *toiles* they sew? Think they don't drop the odd one out the window so a friend can catch it? You imagine the fitters and cutters don't sketch on the sly? Think the saleswomen aren't on the take? Think the mannequins go home and forget about the clothes they've worn all day?'

'Perhaps—'

Mme Kilpin ploughed on. 'You imagine customers don't "lend" the models they buy, so that copyists can make more of the same, cheaper? Hell, honey, some women *rent* their new clothes to counterfeiters. Just long enough for patterns to be cut, fabric to be sampled, embroidery to be copied. It's dog-eat-dog-eat-cat out there. I have the contacts, but I've always needed a smart girl right inside a couture house. That girl is you, and if you hold your nerve, we'll make a tidy living. You, me, Paul – we'll be the Three Musketeers, all for one and one for . . .' She'd taken off a crochet glove to drink her tea and withdrew a card from inside it. 'Call me.'

Alix took the card reluctantly.

'Ring first, speak to my maid. She'll tell you when to come and see me.'

Mme Frankel returned, sample in hand. She said to their visitor, 'I'm afraid I cannot let this cloth leave the room. It is a special commission.'

Mme Kilpin held the tartan to the light. 'Very pretty. Based upon Black Watch. Undercheck of . . . sand, auburn, saffron, auburn, sand. You listening, Alix? Auburn tramlines run single, double, single, double-double, single, which makes it look complicated. Yet it's woven from just three colours.'

'I am amazed,' Pauline Frankel said.

'That I can read a tartan? My husband's a Scotsman – thought it would be a blast for us to spend our honeymoon in a weaving shed. He's a Campbell on his mother's side and I was a Miss McBride, so he had a plaid designed for us. I watched the threads being counted on to the loom.' Mme Kilpin frowned, patting the back of her head. 'What did that wind outside do to my hair?' She took a mirror from her handbag, then unpinned her hat. 'Mme Frankel, I hate to ask, but would you tidy me at the back? I have a comb, here.'

Alix smothered a gasp. As Mme Frankel obligingly combed the blonde locks, the American used her hatpin to separate threads in the tartan cloth. With a deftness that suggested regular practice, she liberated a strand of each colour, dropping them into her bag. All without the première suspecting a thing.

'All done?' The smile turned on Pauline Frankel held no shame. 'Was I hideous?'

'Not at all, Madame.'

'Well now, I'm away to be bullied by my vendeuse. Do allow the young lady to finish her tea.' Mme Kilpin smiled at Alix as she re-pinned her hat. 'She needs to keep her strength up.'

The day after that meeting, Alix was leaving through the side door at Javier. It was twelve o'clock lunchtime, *midi*, the hour that gave 'midinettes' their name, because that was when they could be found bolting down their lunch in cheap cafés. Alix heard a shout.

'You – wait!'

She turned, thinking, *What now?* But it was Solange Antonin, the swan-necked mannequin Mme Albert had spoken of, hobbling towards her in a tight skirt. Alix and Solange had spent the morning together. Javier was creating the dress he intended to show in the Pavillon d'Elégance at the forthcoming Paris Expo. Now that Alix understood what the fair entailed, she could appreciate the excitement and secrecy around the project. Thousands of visitors would come to the fair and there was global interest in the gowns the top Paris couturiers would create. Javier was making his exhibit directly on to Solange, and Alix – freshly gilded by Mme Kilpin's praise – had been called from her workroom to sew the *toile* as he draped it. He was on his third attempt. All morning he'd torn length after length of muslin cloth, cotton sparks flying from his fingers as he struggled to translate the design in his head into reality. Mme Frankel was working alongside, advising on the fabric's strengths and limitations, and the atmosphere had run hot. Solange had borne it without emotion and her expression was no warmer now as she thrust a stiff white card towards Alix.

Alix took it and read:

The proprietors of the Rose Noire cabaret
request the pleasure of

<u>MLLE GOWER and ESCORT</u>

at our gala opening on 29th April 1937. Dress formal.
Frazer Hoskins and his Smooth Envoys will play.
Lenice Leflore to sing.

'What's the Rose Noire?' Alix asked.

'It's my boyfriend's club and he said you were to come.'

Alix looked at the card with new eyes. Solange's boyfriend . . . the man who drove the wine-red Peugeot. Who waited in the rain.

A few days ago, Alix had bumped into him again as she left work for the day. She'd dropped her bag and he'd picked it up, holding it above her reach, the way prefects used to do at school. 'You can have it back if you come for a drink with me,' he'd laughed.

She'd reminded him that he was waiting for his girlfriend.

'So I am.' He'd handed her the bag, his eyes never leaving her. 'Wave a wand and you might be the prettiest girl in Paris.'

She hadn't liked that, the implication that she needed a wand. She didn't like *him*. Thickset, that pale hair combed back over a broad brow. His eyes were the lightest she'd ever seen, like gin on ice. Straw-coloured lashes completed an unnerving stare. Everything about him looked expensive – his suit, his watch, his car – but his shoulders were too padded, the jacket waist too waspy, for her taste. She put him down as a mobster or, more likely, a working-class boy swaggering the flash.

She'd stalked away and his mocking laugh had followed her. She couldn't imagine why he wanted her at his nightclub.

Solange clearly thought the same. 'It says "formal", and that *means* formal. You won't have anything to wear and you'd have to bring a man who's presentable and he'd have to wear black tie and know which glass to drink from. You won't know any men like that.'

'I might,' Alix flung back. She suddenly wanted very much to go to this gala opening. *Rose Noire* – Black Rose. It sounded edgy and exciting. A dive? A squeeze? And she'd never heard a top-flight American jazz band. She checked the date . . . the 29th was one week away. 'Where is it, this club?'

Solange bathed her in contempt. 'If you have to ask, you shouldn't be there.'

*

That evening Paul enlightened her. 'It's in Pigalle.' He turned the invitation over. 'Boulevard de Clichy, the worst end. "Rose Noire" – for God's sake, sounds like the pox. It was closed down by the police for stolen liquor and I've heard bad stuff about the new owner.'

'He's obviously no cheapskate.' Alix snatched the invitation back. 'It's hand-printed. It's classy.'

They'd met by arrangement at their usual café near the Jardin du Luxembourg. The one where the owner called them 'lovebirds' and always brought them a brimming carafe. Paul said, 'I'm glad you talked to Una.'

'Who?'

'Mme Shone. Well, Kilpin.' Paul drew on his cigarette. 'She lets me call her by her first name when we're alone.'

'How well do you know her?'

'No interrogation, not today.' He'd been up all last night with Suzy on his lap to help her breathe, he told her. She was better today. Well enough for Francine to be trusted to look after her for an hour or two. So far Lala hadn't succumbed to the croup. 'We'll get through this one, but next winter . . .' Seeing Alix studying her invitation again, he added angrily, 'Shall I tell you what I know about the Rose Noire's owner?'

'If you must.'

'When he gets into fights, he doesn't use a knife.'

'That's good.'

'He uses his teeth. Anyway, who'll take you? It says, "and escort". You can't go alone.'

'You?' she asked hopefully.

'Not the best time, Alix. Are you sure they're not shipping in free girls? You know, dollar-a-dance? You could spend all night being groped in exchange for a glass of bad champagne.' When Alix pushed out her lip, he said, 'Don't try that. Anyway, I haven't got a suit.'

'But, Paul, wouldn't you like to dance again on a proper floor. With me?'

Sorrow seeped into his eyes. 'Course. Till I drop. But when I hear music, I see my mother. She'd been dancing for money the night she killed herself. The official report called her a prostitute.'

'Well, it was wrong.'

'Maybe. Some bastard roughed her up and took her money. Maybe she thought a plunge off a bridge would wash it away.'

Alix didn't want to imagine Sylvie le Gal fished out of the river a week after she'd drowned. She let Paul light her a cigarette and blew a smoke ring. 'Your mother was the first person in Paris to treat me as a friend. She didn't mock me because I could only fumble a waltz. She'd hold my hands and let me follow her feet till I was perfect.'

Paul blew his own ring that floated over hers. 'She could teach an elephant to tango in ten lessons.'

'Hey, I took eleven.'

He smiled, though sadly. 'I used to walk up Boulevard de Clichy some nights, looking for her. So I know what goes on in places like the Rose Noire, the people who hang around, what they're selling. They whisper into your ear, then bite it off.' Paul then brought the conversation back to its usual sticking place – her promise to steal.

Not a promise, she objected. 'Your Mme Kilpin – "Mme Shone", for pity's sake – she's got more nerve than a cat burglar. Taking samples under the première's nose.'

'She wanted to give you a shock,' Paul said, 'and remind you why we got you the job. You *did* promise. On Place du Tertre you said you'd get the collections so long as nobody asked you to pretend it was moral. Nobody is asking. But the money's waiting and I need it. Stop holding out on me, Alix.'

The day after that conversation, Alix left Maison Javier thinking, *This morning I was innocent. Now I'm a criminal.*

She'd arrived at work at first light to find Javier and Mme Frankel working on the dress for the World's Fair. From their rumpled appearances, they must have been there all night. The day before Javier had said, 'I cannot keep wasting muslin. How long – two weeks? – until I present this dress to the committee of the Pavillon d'Elégance? Mme Frankel, let us make our decision and lose no more time.'

Walking into the vast studio, Alix stopped dead, her mouth round. A wooden mannequin was decked in a ball dress of gold dupion silk. More gold than Alix had ever seen in her life. A night shift must have been sewing while she slept. She walked slowly around the figurine, assessing the gown's tight waist, the voluptuous skirt that fell in graded flounces. It had a neckline out of a Renaissance painting, which would leave the arms bare. Javier's dream was that this dress 'should move like waves of molten gold'.

One look at Javier's face this morning, Mme Frankel's too, told Alix that the dream had got stuck.

They'd tried underwiring the flounces, but that made the skirt stand out like a tent. Stiffening-cloth had allowed movement in one direction at a time, like a tolling bell. 'So your job today, Alix, is to unpick all these flounces and line them with starched tulle. If that doesn't work,' the première said, 'I'll wrench out my hair and use that.'

Javier said, 'The dress is called "Gold" in Spanish: "*Oro*".'

'*Burro*,' Mme Frankel said. 'Mule.'

Javier laughed and shouted for his personal maid. 'Ana-Sofia, fresh coffee!'

As Alix got to work, Javier, Mme Frankel and assistants turned their attention to other works-in-progress. Having scrapped all the evening wear in his spring–summer collection because there'd been no time to complete it, the late-running mid-season line was to be just ball gowns. A break from tradition and a commercial risk because of the cost and labour involved. But Javier relished breaking rules. Tradition was for dowagers and courtiers, he said.

Towards midday Mme Frankel straightened up and said, 'Javier, I wish you'd plough your whims into your work, not into the schedules. Fourteen ball dresses will kill me.'

Javier looked up from inspecting a bolt of cloth that had just been delivered. 'Whims are the butterfly wings of creativity.'

Pauline Frankel snorted. 'Then somebody hand me the fly swat.'

'Madame needs more coffee,' Javier announced to the room. 'Everyone, ten minutes rest, come back inspired.'

This is it, Alix decided. The moment excuses run out. Smothering every qualm, she ran downstairs to the lavatories. Locking a door behind her, she took off her shoe and retrieved some folded paper from the toe. This morning, she'd rolled a pencil to the back of the cistern. It was still there. Sitting on the lavatory seat, she sketched the dress she'd watched Mme Frankel working on all morning. It was easy enough. She'd already seen the working drawings – the front and back views – and she'd handled the fabric. Later, if she got the chance, she'd snip off a sliver.

Next she sketched Oro, ears straining for footsteps. Nobody would have questioned her swift exit. After all, she'd been working without a break for five hours. But that didn't stop her imagining the word 'thief' flashing over the lavatory door. Only the memory of Paul's distress, his fears for Suzy, made her carry on.

When they broke for lunch at two – Javier's days were always off kilter – Alix dashed to her usual café for her staple of onion soup and bread. She bought *jetons* for the telephone and rang the number on Mme Kilpin's card. A woman answered, announcing herself as Mme Kilpin's maid. Alix hesitantly explained her business. The maid said she'd been expecting her call.

'Mme Kilpin hopes you will come here to her home on Avenue Foch, this evening, so you can discuss plans in detail.' The maid gave the directions. 'Come at seven. A taxi will take you away at eight as Madame has an engagement. Do not mention Madame's name to anybody at your place of work, or at home.'

'What about a fake beard and a big hat?' Alix muttered as she hung up. It was starting, the theft. She felt sick.

Chapter Fourteen

It was 29th April and tonight was the gala opening of the Rose Noire and she still hadn't found a date. She did, however, have a dress, a breathtaking creation she ached to dance in.

As ordered, she'd gone to Avenue Foch after work the previous Friday. The black maid had spirited her up a backstairs into a small office that clearly doubled as Mme Kilpin's shoe room, as racks of blonde-coloured suede, kid and glacé leather lined the walls. Their meeting had been brisk, Una Kilpin doing most of the talking. Alix was to accumulate a portfolio of stolen designs, to be presented to an American associate of Mme Kilpin's who would oversee their mass production. Alix must note every detail, as detail was key. 'Get going and don't get caught.' Mme Kilpin then rang for the maid to escort Alix down to a waiting taxi. And that was it. Faster than having a tooth pulled and, actually, less painful.

Before she left, though, there'd been an unforgettable moment. When Alix had casually mentioned the Rose Noire – her lack of anything suitable to wear to its opening night – Mme

Kilpin had chuckled, 'Poor Cinderella.' Then, 'Come with me.'

She'd taken Alix into her private suite, opening a door in what Alix had presumed to be a mirrored wall, revealing . . .

The eighth wonder of the world. Mme Kilpin's evening-gown collection. Her hostess had then uttered the most magical words Alix had ever heard; 'See if anything grabs your fancy, kiddo, but be quick. I have to go out.'

It had taken days for Alix's heart to stop thumping. She'd been on tenterhooks all today, desperate to leave work and have one last stab at persuading Paul to be her escort. Because without a male escort, going to the Rose Noire was out of the question. The ticking-away of the hours had been agonising. Then, having dropped her scissors for the fifth time, she'd been told to go home. She looked feverish, Mme Frankel said.

Alix hadn't needed telling twice. A brilliant idea had hit her: she would hire Paul an evening suit and pay Brandel, Mémé's former charwoman, to mind Lala and Suzy for the night. Paul would have no excuse to say no. If he still objected, she'd shame him by saying that if she was thieving, he could at least take her dancing. Leaving the métro at Pont Marie, she ran to the Quai d'Anjou.

Only to find the *Katrijn* gone. Alix sank down on a bench. This couldn't be happening. Dancing to a jazz band in a rakish club had become an obsession. Which meant she had about five hours in which to find a man . . .

★

At the *News Monitor* offices on Rue Boccador, she learned that 'Mr Haviland' was on a working trip to Germany. Expected back tomorrow night at the earliest, the receptionist conceded when pressed. Alix was invited to leave a note. She wrote a few lines, feeling utterly dispirited. Was it one shovel-full of pride she'd swallowed, or two, coming here to ask Verrian to be her date? Nothing for it now but to head back to the Quai d'Anjou, a journey that took two hours because of some unexplained train failure at Châtelet. Close to crying, she stumped over the Pont Marie and down the wharf stairs . . . and there, in her mooring, was the *Katrijn*! Alix ran forward shouting, 'Paul!' so eagerly a fisherman on the wharf shushed her. So she threw a pebble at the cabin window.

She saw the flick of a curtain. 'Paul, hurry up,' she giggled. Francine was on her boat, watering her seedlings and grinning, all gums. 'Give him a chance. He's hauling on his trousers.'

Did that mean Paul was between shifts, and she'd woken him from the depths of sleep? She'd go on board, Alix decided, and wait for him to stumble into the light. The gangplank was in place. A new gangplank, with batons for grip. Her terror of the old one must finally have got through to Paul. She'd thank him for it, even kiss him perhaps. But only after he'd agreed to take her to the Rose Noire. She thought guiltily of the letter she'd left for Verrian. Maybe he wouldn't get it in time – or at all. The girl on the reception desk had taken it very snottily.

She stepped down into a windowless galley kitchen lit by

an oil lamp, noticing that the draining board was strewn with the remains of lunch. Cheese rind, torn bread, olives. Perhaps Paul had taken the girls down the river for a picnic. But where were the girls?

'Paul?'

She heard whispering. Then the cabin door opened and Paul was there, naked to the hips, buckling the belt at his waist. She thought he blushed. She certainly did.

'Alix – what are you doing here?'

She searched for the smile he always had for her, that always replaced fatigue. No smile. 'I came earlier but you were away,' she said, fear making her sharp. 'Where were you?'

Before he could answer, a voice came from behind the cabin door. 'Honey, who is it?' Then Alix saw hair the colour of wood shavings and a determined chin, which came to rest on Paul's shoulder. A possessive hand curled round the muscular stomach. 'Well met by oil light,' said the apparition.

Alix gripped the front of her dress, bunching the fabric like a confused child. 'Paul? Say something.'

Paul stared at the floor.

Mme Kilpin ducked under his arm. She was wrapped in a bed cover, dishevelled and sated. Embarrassment was nowhere. 'Alix, this boat is too small for catfights, if your thoughts were tending that way.'

'What . . . what . . . ?'

'Am I doing here? Not painting the ceiling, nor watering the begonias. How about, I've come to inaugurate the first formal meeting of the Committee of the Three Musketeers.' Mme Kilpin hooked the lamp off its nail. 'Let's go sit out on deck. Two is a love affair, so three had better be a party. Poulbot, honey –'

Poulbot, Alix flared. She has little names for him?

'– fetch the wine. God knows, this occasion calls for alcohol.'

Dusk spread over the river. The two women regarded each other across the cable-drum table, the lamp attracting moths and midges. Madame still wore her bed wrap but had pulled a fisherman's sweater over the top. One of Paul's. That was *her* privilege, Alix fumed, to wear Paul's jerseys when it was cold.

Paul stepped forward from the prow rail to light a cigarette, only to retreat. *Struggling into his trousers*, Alix thought. *Ha. Old Francine knew what I was going to find*. The wine was good though. A ruby Burgundy, way out of Paul's league.

'You can call me Una here.' Mme Kilpin spread her hands around her wine glass. A square diamond glittered on her forefinger. 'All friends, all equals.' Getting no response, she sighed. 'Paul, you did nothing any red-blooded young man would not. Alix, d'you begrudge me the thing you didn't want yourself?'

This was too much. 'You're a married woman and older than Paul. Far, far older.'

'Ouch. You gonna tell Mr Kilpin?'

'I could.' Alix glowered at Paul, then back at Una. 'No – I don't know him. I don't care about him.'

'I'll drink to that,' Una said. 'By the by, I'm not old enough to be Paul's mother, not by any stretch. I'm glad you stumbled on us, because I like things in the open.'

'Yes – the old witch next door knew what was going on.'

Una threw back her head. 'Y'know she used to dance at the Folies Bergère in a skirt made of corks on threads? Paul, sugar, I could use a cigarette and Alix could too, if only to keep these damn flies off.'

Paul pushed two Gauloises into his mouth and lit them simultaneously. He handed them to the women, lit another for himself, knocked back a glass of wine and said, 'I'm tired of being tired.'

Alix heard the strain in his voice. Meanwhile, Una descended to the cabin and returned with a piece of splintered wood, which she laid in front of Alix. 'If you need an incentive to get our enterprise on the road, this is it.'

It was the neck of a half-size violin. 'Heavens, what happened?' Alix asked.

'The other day Paul came back off the night shift. Twenty-four hours straight. Nights at Les Halles, then a day job at the World's Fair building site, hired muscle, shoving up walls for a gangmaster who isn't fussy about union membership. Lady Francine –' Una jerked her thumb towards the stern of the boat – 'was in charge of the girls. Frankly I'd rather employ an amiable dog. Paul got home to find the old cow dancing the hula dance that briefly made her the craze of Pigalle, Lala's violin stuck on one foot, the girls weeping hysterically.'

'Where are the girls?' Alix put her hand on Paul's shoulder and felt his muscles spasm.

'With my great-aunt, Gilberte. We took them there this afternoon and she's agreed to keep them until I can do something about the damp in this boat.'

Una relit her cigarette in the candle. 'I've made Paul a loan to pay their keep, but they can't stay with Tante Gilberte indefinitely.' A cynical smile danced. 'Alix dear, watching you is like a dose of Pathé News. It's all on your face, all at once. Yes, *loaned*. I have to have it back because, believe me, I'm as broke as you are. Mr Kilpin checks every item of my expenditure, and if he doesn't like it, hell breaks loose. Lesson for you; rich men may keep their wives poor. Hubby has an accountant, a bean-counter called Pusey, who goes over my spending line by line, down to my underwear. Even I blush when Pusey intones, "Oyster silk camiknickers, twenty-two dollars fifty."'

'You should divorce,' Paul said bitterly.

'I cannot. My business in New York went down owing an infinity of dollars. My husband keeps the debt collectors away from my family in Texas. In return, I look pretty and do as I'm told. Alix, you're just ol'-fashioned poor, but you can still join our club.' Una topped up their wine. 'Let's hear it for the

Three Musketeers, who will battle their way to wealth, health and happiness. Hey, what's that?'

Alix had taken out her invitation to the Rose Noire and was holding it in the lantern flame, meaning to burn it. Una snatched it from her, blew it out and read it.

'Gala opening, what a hoot. Why don't we pile in there tonight, the three of us, and celebrate? We'll take Mr Kilpin — somebody has to pay for the drinks. Are we on?' She kept her glass high until the others wearily raised theirs.

Chapter Fifteen

At the precise same moment, at the *News Monitor*, Verrian closed the doors of the second-floor lift and listened to the noise of a single, clacking typewriter. He followed the sound and put his head around the door of a glass-walled office. 'Evening, Beryl.'

A middle-aged woman stopped typing, but instead of the smile he was used to, he got 'You're back early! Since you're here, you'd best go straight to the boardroom. Oh, dear, I'm glad I'm not you!'

'That puts rare heart into me, Beryl. What's happening in the boardroom?'

Beryl Theakston, the unwaveringly loyal editorial secretary of the *News Monitor*, stared at him. Verrian guessed that even as she pondered his dangerous ignorance, she was marking his lack of tie.

'Surely you knew? Mr Chelsey informed you before you left for Germany?'

'Derek Chelsey tells me nothing. It's a policy of editors – never tell humble journalists anything that could be useful or flattering. What's going on, Beryl?'

'Lord Calford has arrived. He got here an hour ago in a bad temper. Well, actually –' her voice dropped – 'a monumentally dreadful temper. You didn't know Lord Calford was in Paris?'

'No, or I wouldn't have come back. Is Sturridge up in the picture studio?'

'It's daylight, Mr Haviland, and as far as I know there isn't a hurricane blowing. So, yes, our picture editor is in his studio.'

It was unusual for Beryl to be wrong about anything in the building, but Verrian found the picture studio deserted, dark rooms ajar. He took several canisters of film from his pockets. Driving from the French city of Mulhouse across the border to Köln, he'd found the German roads clogged with military transport. Streams of them, heading west. It had opened his eyes to the extent of German military build-up. Returning his hired car to Mulhouse, he'd caught the fastest train back to Paris. He had an article drafted and he wanted his pictures by tomorrow morning. Calling Sturridge's name and getting no reply, he resigned himself to waiting, eyeing the shelves that lined the studio.

Photography was Sturridge's passion, but French painting was the man's obsession. Sturridge was compiling an encyclopaedia to be titled *Light Upon the Impressionists* and clearly using this place to house his research material. Verrian lifted down a file marked 'M' which contained handwritten notes, cuttings, postcards and photographs of the painter Monet. After flicking through, he replaced it and reversed back along the row looking for the letter 'L'. He found another 'M' and 'K', but no 'L'. *Good*, he thought. He didn't want to spend the afternoon reading about Alfred Lutzman. Then he heard a muffled cough.

'Sturridge? That you?'

The next moment, a wiry man in khaki shorts and shirt emerged from a side room carrying a metal contraption. Heavy, from his grunting.

Verrian grabbed its base and helped hump it on to a table. 'What the hell is this?'

'Technical name is "loupe", old bean, but to you and me it's a magnifier.' Sturridge rubbed the creases out of his hand and shook Verrian's. 'It helps me with the fuzzy bits of photographs. I snapped a respectable French politician the other day viewing the World's Fair building site with his lady. Only I wasn't sure if it was his lady or somebody else's. Best to know. The *Monitor* doesn't like scandal. Too much flack from the embassy and the FO.'

'Of course.' Verrian had used hand loupes in the past, but never anything this big.

'Ten times magnification,' Sturridge told him proudly. 'You can pick out faces from the murkiest crowd. Enemy of the adulterer, the loupe. If you like, we can count the whorls on your fingerprints.'

Verrian indicated his rolls of film. 'I'd rather you processed those for me. I'll owe you dinner.'

'Pleasure. Been to Germany, I heard. Fun?'

'No, it was . . .' Verrian stopped, his eye falling on a black binder on a nearby table. He went to it, consulted its spine. 'L'. He opened it and raised his eyebrows at Sturridge. Could this perpetual Boy Scout and all-round good egg also be a mind-reader? 'The artist Lutzman – you know about him?'

Sturridge joined Verrian at the table. 'Ah, the last of the "L's". Not much in his file, unfortunately. When I've done him, I'll be halfway through the first draft of my book. Did I tell you I'm compiling an encyclopaedia?'

'You did. Tell me about Lutzman.'

'Painter from Alsace.' Sturridge turned a page to a sepia photograph of a bearded man aged forty-five, fifty. Hard to tell. The gaze was myopic, but obsidian eyes told Verrian he was looking at Alix's grandfather. Had she ever seen this picture?

'These are typical of his later work.' Sturridge showed him a set of colour postcards, reproductions of landscapes typical of the French Impressionist movement. Or what Verrian asso-ciated with Impressionism, which, he calculated, would have come into vogue during Lutzman's early manhood.

'Did he study in France?'

'Not a chance,' Sturridge replied. 'By the time he was out of short trousers, the dear Bosch had invaded his homeland. Many natives of Alsace fled to France, but Lutzman's lot stayed put. Painting trips over the border weren't on the cards. Germany in the 1870s had little time for radical art, and Impressionism was radical when it started. Lutzman was kept an eye on. He was Jewish and his family had Bolshevik sympathies.'

Verrian nodded. 'What's his story?'

'Son of humble tobacco-pipe makers. Went into the family business. But by the age of twenty he was living in Deptford, in a sprawling mansion by the Thames, under the aegis of English Impressionist Martin Fressenden.'

London. Things were edging into place. 'Fressenden?'

Fetching down another binder, Sturridge gently exposed Verrian's ignorance. 'A fashionable painter of the late-Victorian period, able to indulge his passions thanks to a private art school run mainly by his wife. Lutzman studied there.'

In the prints of Fressenden's work, Verrian detected a similarity between master and pupil. To his eye, the pupil was more interesting, particularly in his use of colour. He thought of Alix giving his sister a palate of hues Lucy wouldn't have put together in a hundred years. 'I confess, I'd not heard of either of them.'

'You're not alone. Good artists both, but fashion moves on. Fressenden was one of those men, in my view, who had more charm and determination than talent, but stretched that talent a long way. Lutzman ... Lutzman had talent by the bucket but was blighted by his own character. Tricky customer – reclusive, reluctant to finish his work. Why the interest?'

'A friend mentioned him. She said his career failed to blossom.' On Boulevard St-Germain he'd told Alix, *You don't have to explain yourself to me.* So why was he scratching through her life, looking for clues?

'Course,' Sturridge said, 'most records disappeared when Germany handed Alsace back to France after the war. Archives were lost – Lutzman's paintings seem to have gone the same way. Most of what I know is thanks to his former pupil, Raphael Bonnet, who is a painter of no small talent himself.'

'I know him,' said Verrian. 'He lives next door to me.'

'Good Lord. Then you'll know why Bonnet's genius will never flower.' Sturridge mimed a man knocking back a glass of wine. 'Do him a favour, lock up his corkscrew.'

'Lutzman also failed to flower through drink?'

'Nothing so dull, Haviland. Lutzman was murdered by—'

'Mr Haviland?' Beryl Theakston whispered round the open door. 'He knows you're here – Lord Calford. Please come down before he explodes.'

Lord Calford was chairman and majority shareholder of the *Monitor*, both London and Paris editions. A large man with a high colour, when angry he could reduce adult men to jelly. His first words to Verrian were, 'What time d'you call this?' followed by, 'Chelsey's out, you're taking over as editor.'

Sitting down at the boardroom table, Verrian said, 'As you wish, Father. Good to see you, by the way.'

And that was it, meeting over. Verrian managed a word with a furious Derek Chelsey and learned that today's ruction was over an article in which the editor had described the British pavilion at the World's Fair as, "Featureless as the inside of an Aspirin bottle." It had gone on to state, "While other nations strike postures on peace and war, Britannia will show the world tennis rackets and country-house tea sets."

'I stand by every word,' Chelsey thundered.

'Good for you,' Verrian answered. 'See you here tomorrow.'

Beryl Theakston tapped his arm as he flagged down a taxi. 'Mr Haviland, a letter came for you earlier. Somebody left it at reception.'

Verrian shoved it into his pocket without looking at it. His father was getting into the taxi with him.

'Chelsey can stand by every word,' Lord Calford roared, having instructed the driver to ignore whatever direction he'd just been given and go to Place Vendôme, to the Hôtel Polonaise. 'I came to Paris to raise a hurrah for Britain's exhibitors and I find the man sneering in my name. Damn swine.' Lord Calford pulled out a cigar box and extracted a fat Havana, which he jabbed at Verrian. 'What the hell were you doing in Hun country? Who said you could go? When did you last have your hair cut? Why must you look like a Spanish anarchist?'

Verrian ignored the questions. 'Chelsey wasn't "sneering in your name",' he told his father. 'You own half the paper's shares but it isn't yours. The minute it becomes so, it's dead. That's why you have men like Chelsey.'

'I haven't got Chelsey, have I?' Lord Calford wrenched a gold cutter from his pocket and docked his cigar. He pierced the end with inquisitorial relish. 'You're Paris editor now.'

'I won't regurgitate your opinions either, so you're no better off.' Verrian laid his head against the back of the seat as his father ignited the Havana. 'Drop me off at the next Métro station. I've had a long day.'

'Your mother wants to see you — she's at the Polonaise. I promised to bring you.'

'Mother's here? What's she doing back so soon?'

'Wasn't happy with the outfit she got the other week, needs something distinct and only Paris will do.'

'Something to wear to Jack and Moira's wedding, perhaps?'

Lord Calford narrowed his eyes at his son. 'Glad you know about that. Damn Chelsey and his Aspirin bottle — frankly unpatriotic.'

Somebody had once observed that, physically, the Havilands were 'split down party lines'. Lord Calford, Jack and Lucy had seaside colouring, grey eyes and freckles. The sandy Havilands went pink when they drank or grew angry, and scorched at the first ray. Verrian shared his mother's dark hair, Aegean eyes and skin that tanned. He'd often wondered if his failure to win his father's love came down to pigmentation.

At the Hôtel Polonaise, where Lord Calford kept two suites, Verrian's mother pressed him to stay for dinner. He declined on the grounds that he had nothing to wear . . . only to discover that his mother had brought a trunk of his clothes with her.

'Including your evening wear, dear.'

'So that's why you came back.' He hugged her. 'You shouldn't have bothered.'

'Until you have a wife, I shall bother.'

By eight that evening he'd rediscovered the glory of a huge bath and inexhaustible hot water. He was in evening dress, in a lounge under pearly light, listening to a pianist play Chopin. The person he'd most like to share it with was not there.

His mother came in and he stood to greet her. He knew her evening dress by heart – one of the designer Molyneux's, green satin with a layer of beaded gauze. About seven years old. Since their last meeting, however, her hair had been brought up to date, cut and set in finger waves. He complimented her and she complimented him back.

'Very handsome, dear. I'm sure you'll get your hair cut soon.'

'I'm sure I will, Mother.'

'Yes, well. Lucy sends her love and says "apologies for her ghastly gob". Where she gets such phrases . . .'

Verrian ordered cocktails and let his mother talk. She told him of the Women's Institute summer pageant, currently in rehearsal, the cook's lumbago and a late frost that had nipped the buds on the apricots. He raised a hand.

'Do not tell me about the Mother's Union bring-and-buy sale. I don't care and I don't think you do.'

'I shall when I'm back at Heronhurst. Your father tells me he appointed you Paris editor.' She watched his face.

'By tomorrow I won't be.'

'I wish you had more ambition,' she said. 'You, not Jack, are the true heir of Quentin Thomas Verrian.' She always referred to her father by his full name, enunciating each syllable. 'He founded the *Monitor* as a voice for liberal opinion, and only you grasp that. Even Jack says you're one of the few writers who can explain socialism to Middle England without scaring the pants off them. I still own half my father's shares and as I intend to leave them to you—'

'Jack and I won't work in harness,' he interrupted. 'He thinks I'm wrong about the right things, and I think the same of him. Nor will I work alongside the brother who swiped my fiancée while I was out of the country.'

'I can see that. I'm afraid I was rather poisonous to Moira when they told me. But there . . . you're not heartbroken?'

'My heart is like a jobbing violinist's tailcoat, worn to a thread and badly mended, but it'll see me out.'

'And your lodgings? Are you still on Montmartre, with that . . .' Lady Calford cleared her throat, 'Russian dancer?'

'Who's as gorblimey as a pearly queen.' He explained, 'Dancers adopt Russian names. It's a creative tradition. She's Connie Marshall from Bethnal Green, east London. Her mother did the laundry for a dancing establishment and took her into work one day. Mme Batavsky, a real Russian, took one look at her and cried, "Mary Mother of God, angel's arms and legs like pipe cleaners!" and enrolled her in the baby class.'

'Heavens. Does she still dance, this – er – Connie?'

'She's fifty-eight, Mother. These days she lives on her annuity and lets a couple of rooms.'

Lady Calford looked profoundly relieved. Then, spotting Lord Calford coming through the entrance arch, she leaped to her feet. 'Clarence, dear, where will you sit? Verrian, move up a little, your father doesn't like sitting with his back to the door.'

Nor should he, thought Verrian, since there were at least six former *News Monitor* editors who'd like to stab Lord Calford between the shoulder blades. Drawing on patience he hoped would sustain him through three courses, Verrian rose.

His mother retired after they had finished eating. Verrian also tried to make his excuses, but Lord Calford told him that he could jolly well spare his father an hour of his precious time, and ordered cognac. They recessed to the gentlemen's lounge, his father smoking as he talked – about politics, the forthcoming World's Fair, now ruined for Britain by bloody Chelsey; about the imminent marriage in France of the Duke of Windsor, formerly King Edward VIII; about editors, weasels all, with the exception of Jack, of course. Jack had the Haviland mettle.

Verrian resigned himself to a very late night. Conversation with his father was like being rolled up in heavy carpet and left out in the sun. Struggling only made things worse.

'Now – how much scandal did the *Monitor* print concerning

that American adventuress Mrs Simpson and her appropriation of our king?' Lord Calford demanded.

When Verrian replied, 'None that I know of,' his father grunted triumphantly.

'Exactly! And we handled the abdication crisis with un-equalled discretion. Did your mother say – I received a letter from the prime minister, commending my patriotic restraint?' Lord Calford sucked on his cigar. 'We're the Absolute Ticket, we Havilands, trustable with privy information. I wouldn't rule out a viscountcy. Viscount Calford. Sound all right?'

'As a younger son, I can hardly get excited.' At some point in his life, Verrian had discovered a way of beating Lord Calford in a quarrel. Not sarcasm, not humour. A caressing brutality. 'Here's one for you, Father,' he said. 'Should I go to my usual café for breakfast tomorrow or make an early show in the ed-itorial office with mop and bucket? It'll be carnage without Derek Chelsey.'

His father boiled up on cue. 'Why can you never ask a damn simple question?' He relit his cigar, having growled at it for going out. 'I don't understand you, never did. I offer you a suite here at the Polonaise and you trot back to some dormi-tory with bedbugs.'

'There are no bugs chez Rosa and there were none at my last place. The patron there used to take a blowtorch to the bedsprings once a month. I only moved to get a quieter night's sleep. Montmartre suits me.'

'Crawling with artists and lefties,' Lord Calford grunted. 'I suppose you would feel at home. When you were twenty-two I offered you a prime job at the *Monitor* and you went off to Russia to scribble for a Bolshevist rag. People said you were a communist then and they say you're one now.'

Verrian picked up his glass, and cognac fumes warned of throbbing temples and persistent memories. 'If we're to understand the communist world, we have to see it from the inside, otherwise we're just guessing.'

His father swallowed smoke, blew it out. 'Well, you've lost your chance of ever editing a decent British newspaper. Just as you lost your chance with Moira. Warned you not to neglect her.'

Verrian shrugged. 'She could have waited or joined me.'

'Sir Chester Durslop's daughter, hacking about Spain under fire?'

'She'd have been in brave company. But it's as well she didn't because I fell in love with someone else. Enduring love, not the English drawing-room variety.' Verrian gave his father a frank gaze and, when nothing came back, downed the rest of the fiery brandy. 'I'll send them a pair of china poodles and stay away from the wedding so they don't have to blush. Now, excuse me, Father, I'm going home.'

Lord Calford followed him into the hotel foyer. 'I won't stand for family rifts, d'you hear? And I won't stand for you bringing a foreign tart home. Lucy saw you with some Jewess shop girl.

Foist a gold-jangling Jezebel on us, I'll bar every door against you.' A cloud of smoke brought Lord Calford's outrage straight into Verrian's face.

Verrian walked out.

Back at his lodging, throwing off his outdoor clothes, he saw a white corner protruding from the pocket of the jacket he'd slung over the shoulders of his evening wear. It was the letter Beryl had given him.

> *Dear Mr Haviland, I have been sent an invitation to a new night-club on April 29th, the Rose Noire, and wonder if you would like to attend as my escort? I hope you will not think this forward, but I know so few men in Paris. If you cannot or do not wish to, it doesn't matter. Yours –*

'Oh, Alix,' he groaned. Tonight was the twenty-ninth. He shouldn't go. One, he was in his customary post-Calford mood. Two – he'd resolved to break off the friendship for both their sakes. And three, four, five and six. On the other hand –

It was only midnight. His watch told him he had time to find the Rose Noire, and since he'd just spent an afternoon learning about her grandfather, seeing Alix was arguably duty, not pleasure.

Chapter Sixteen

The jazzmen swung their instruments, slicing through sound

The jazzmen swung their instruments, slicing through sound and light. Frazer Hoskins and his Smooth Envoys. Alix stroked her bare arm and thought, *I want to dance.* She looked at her three companions, all absorbed in the music. *Won't somebody ask me to dance?*

She'd thought getting here was all that mattered and was discovering it wasn't. Having got Paul, she'd got Una too. And Gregory Kilpin, who hadn't smiled once.

Paul, what a transformation! The labourer had disappeared beneath a white tuxedo and black tie that Una had borrowed from her husband's wardrobe, and Paul's straw-coloured mop was greased to a dark honey. He'd been friendly to Alix in the taxi coming here, but that sense of being special, of being the single object of his gaze had gone.

Please, Alix silently begged as she saw Paul lean over to light Una's cigarette, *somebody ask me to dance.*

'Frazer Hoskins should run an iron over his Smooth Envoys.' Una's hair rippled in the light as she blew smoke across the table.

A silk-jersey Lucien Lelong dress was poured over her contours. Alix had assumed it was a Lelong original, until Una disabused her: 'A copy, and so good even I forget it's not the real thing.' Una said now, her eyes on Paul, 'I never heard swing played with violin and guitar.'

'This is Paris.' Paul touched Una's wrist and Alix flinched at the intimacy. Had they forgotten Gregory Kilpin, sitting inches away? 'In America they play the music of the soul.' He pitched his voice over 'Limehouse Blues'. 'Here we have hot jazz played by gypsies. Every city finds its pulse.'

'The bandleader's from New Orleans, I'll buy that.' Una slanted her cigarette holder towards a sweating black trumpet player. 'Maybe the horn section too, but the rest jumped ship at Toulouse, bet you a hundred.'

'I hope that's a joke, Una, or I'll be reviewing your allowance.'

Alix checked to see if Gregory Kilpin was joking. His mouth suggested not. Una's husband had small darting eyes and rather unformed features, as if he'd melted a little. According to Una, he'd been born in a Glasgow slum – 'A year ago he had a brick taken from that very slum and plated with gold,' she'd confided.

A waiter brought them champagne, slipping the bill into a leather folder at Kilpin's elbow. 'I suppose I'm paying for you pretty people tonight?' Kilpin grunted.

'Naturally,' Una answered, 'as you're the only one here who owns a shipping line. Oh, listen, they're playing "Autumn in

New York".' She extended a hand and Paul escorted her on to the dance floor, Alix following with her eyes. Una danced languidly, and Paul led her with his usual ease.

Gregory Kilpin bent towards Alix so his words reached her undiluted. 'I know you're something to do with this dress-exporting business. Just don't think you're going to scramble all over her like ivy.'

Alix felt like saying, *It's the other way round*, but Kilpin's presence had a damping effect on her and she couldn't bring herself to respond. Picking up her champagne, she let her focus melt. The band had upped their tempo to a faster swing, the horn section rising to play the eight-bar bridge. When they finished, they sat down behind their inlaid mother-of-pearl music stands and the drummer took up the rhythm. A guitarist joined in, then the clarinettist rose to his feet, eyes closed for an improvisation. Frazer Hoskins and his Smooth Envoys sounded wonderful to Alix.

Looking about, she saw none of the dollar-a-dance girls Paul had feared. Nothing to suggest the Rose Noire was the haunt of anything but attractive, sophisticated people. Did Solange Antonin's boyfriend really own this place? People often made things up . . . they gilded themselves, like Gregory Kilpin and his brick.

Alix stroked the skirts of her dress. Her choice from Una's wardrobe was another Lelong copy, this one a dark caramel. It left one shoulder bare, showing very little but revealing a great deal and she loved its feel. She could develop a taste for silk jersey, and for Lanson champagne, she decided.

At a neighbouring table, six or more Javier mannequins sat with their escorts. One of them bent to pick up an evening bag and Alix saw Solange Antonin's dark head resting on the shoulder of a man in a white tux. A moment later, they all stood up to dance. At the close of each season, most couture houses allowed their mannequins to keep one of the dresses they'd modelled, and Javier was no exception. Alix knew she'd have taken the one Solange wore tonight, with its glove-tight bodice and skirt made of a thousand tags of black organza, each with a single sequin. She watched Solange glide on to the dance floor, her partner leading. They slid into a foxtrot and Alix's throat tightened with envy.

Face it, she told herself, this evening was a misery. All she could see was other people enjoying themselves. She glanced up to see a tall man coming down the stairs and her heart stuttered. Verrian? He'd got her letter! She half rose as he walked towards a cocktail bar lit with coloured bulbs . . . then realised he was somebody else.

A singer came to the microphone. 'Can't they find a white girl to sing?' Kilpin muttered.

Lenice Leflore was Creole, her black hair in a chignon fixed with a lily. When she sang 'These Foolish Things' with a slight catch, Alix's pain intensified. 'I need fresh air,' she gasped, getting up without any idea where she was going. To the ladies' room if she could find it. Then a hand fell on her arm and curled around her elbow. A teasing voice said, 'Told you you'd end up the prettiest girl in Paris. Let's dance.'

She blinked at the white tuxedo, a dark-red rose in the button-hole. At a pair of smiling lips and light eyes that contained no fear of rebuff.

'I can't dance with you. You're Solange's –' she tripped on the word *lover* – 'friend.'

'If you say so.' His accent was difficult to place. A bit of Paris, a bit American. She looked around for Paul but saw Solange instead, the girl's fists bunched. This was serious. Solange might have a hatpin in her evening bag. 'I don't pinch other girls' men,' Alix said firmly.

'You can't refuse. Order of the club's owner.'

She deliberately misunderstood him. 'I don't care what the owner says. I don't like people telling me what to do.'

He put his hands on her arms, a prelude to pulling her into his. 'I'm Serge Martel. I own the Rose Noire. I did own it together with my father, but he passed away a few weeks ago.'

'I'm so sorry.'

'It's hard . . . have you still got a father?'

'No. He died years and years ago.'

'Then you know how it feels. Dancing helps, *hein*? Music washes away sadness. Not everyone understands.' With each word, he drew her nearer to the floor where couples were dancing to 'My Blue Heaven'. She could feel Solange's fury, but Serge Martel had suddenly become more human. Maybe his eyes weren't cold; maybe it was grief.

'I don't believe you own this place. You're too young.' He couldn't be more than twenty-five.

'Lying, am I?' He dropped his arms and stalked away across the dance floor. Jumped onstage and tapped the bandleader's shoulder. The man lowered his trumpet. A moment later the music slid to a stop, leaving the singer holding an unaccompanied note.

Serge came back through the crowd like a breeze through corn. He took Alix into his arms and the bandleader counted, 'One, two, three, four.' The drummer gave the intro, the leader played a lick and 'My Blue Heaven' was on its way again.

'I hate starting a dance halfway through. Relax, baby, you might as well stop fighting. In the end, we're going to be lovers.'

Verrian spotted Alix as he came down the stairs. When he saw blunt fingers stroking her spine, he understood how murders happen.

Chapter Seventeen

Lenice Leflore was scatting to 'The Very Thought of You'.

Verrian went to the bar, attempting to park his darker feelings. He had a serious motive for being here, remember? He'd seen a picture of Alix's grandfather, learned something of the man's early life – and the abrupt manner of his end. If Alix didn't know about that last bit, she needed to. Taking a cigarette case from his pocket he pulled out a Navy Cut. Not that it was exactly small talk for the dance floor.

As the singer reached the tender climax of her song, the lights went off. Shock gave way to cheers as a single spotlight turned the stage into a shining lagoon. Verrian moved towards the centre of the floor, at last finding Alix by touch. He felt her recoil, ask 'Who are you?'

'Verrian Haviland and I'm taking you out of here.' He led her off the floor, using beads of light from the bar as his guide.

She resisted. 'I have to stay.'

'Why?'

'My evening bag – my door key's in it. I don't want to lose another one.'

'We'll fetch your bag.'

'No.' The lights were flicking back on, one at a time. 'I can't just leave without a word.'

'I don't see why not.' Something hit him lightly on the shoulder and, for an instant, Verrian thought bats had been let loose in the club or the ceiling was coming down. Then he realised, rose petals. Red petals were falling on to the heads of those below. In the middle of the floor, the man in the white tuxedo who'd been dancing with Alix was making a slow scan of the tables.

They found Alix's table, where Verrian scooped up her bag and evening jacket, then guided her up the stairs, saying, 'I'm taking you somewhere more authentic, assuming you like jazz.' Out on the kerb, a taxi was pulling up and Verrian helped Alix into the back. Getting in beside her, he drew her against him and said to the driver, 'Rue Pigalle, chez Bricktop, but take us the long way round.'

Her resistance held as the taxi crossed Place Pigalle, passing the Moulin Rouge. It held as far as the junction with Rochechouart where she leaned into him with a sigh. Her hair smelled of lemon and almond and he felt a physical surprise at how fawn-like she was without the packaging of day clothes. It made him want to protect her eternally from bigots like his father, and predators like the fair-haired man in the white tux. As they sped east down Rochechouart, then south on to Boulevard Magenta, Verrian thought of hotel rooms and the span of a double bed, of silk sheets and time. He and Alix needed time. Her breath feathered his cheek.

'I think we've made Serge Martel very angry.'

'Do you care?'

She hesitated. 'He knows where I work.'

'If he bothers you, let me know. You're not officially his girlfriend?'

'Oh no. That's Solange. She's a mannequin and very lovely, but I don't think he cares much for her.'

'I expect she has other ideas. She'll slap his face for the way he acted tonight, call him a no-good lying cheat, and then they'll spend all tomorrow in bed.'

'I hope not. She has to take part in the collection at three o'clock.'

'He'll have forgotten it all by then anyway.'

Alix said nothing as the driver turned on to Rue La Fayette, taking them through a series of lesser streets. As the taxi slowed, she said, 'Do men forget humiliation so fast?'

The answer was no, so he tightened his arm around her. She was looking up at him, her eyes reflecting the carnal lights of Rue Pigalle. He was about to kiss her when the taxi drew up at an entrance door and the driver shouted, 'Bricktop!'

The Dress Thief

In this club, a quintet played hot gypsy jazz with a sweating intensity that made Frazer Hoskins's band seem like a chamber orchestra. Verrian had to speak right into Alix's ear. 'Drink or dance?'

'Dance.'

On the floor they were shoved up like sardines. Alix had never been in such a crowd but still felt that she and Verrian were alone in the world. For the first time, it was just the two of them. No dramas, no audience.

She looped her arms over his shoulders and he put his hands into the curve of her waist. When their lips touched it was with the same unforced ardour as when he'd kissed her in the downpour. She opened her lips and he responded, pulling her so hard against him she felt every sinew of his body. His cologne contained lemon and bergamot; she smelled it on the curve of his jaw, under the rim of his collar as they stayed locked for ten, twenty heartbeats before pulling apart. They danced, one tune sliding into another. Then they kissed all the way through the Bricktop version of 'My Blue Heaven'. Eventually Verrian said, 'Would you like a drink now?'

'No. Well, coffee, please.'

He'd purchased them a table and they eventually found it. They sat, hands locked, until the coffee came. They both drank it one-handed, spare hands still linked.

'Why were you dancing with that Martel earlier?'

'He asked . . . Nobody else would dance with me.'

'You were supposed to wait for me.'

'You didn't answer my letter.'

'I only read it three hours ago. You should have faith, Alix.'

'Why?'

He laughed and she felt his energy pass through her. She said, 'On Boulevard St-Germain you ran after me to make sure we didn't part on bad terms, then nothing. No word.'

'Not "nothing". I went to do some research on German re-militarisation, and while I was there I thought of little else but you. I needed time away because I know I'm falling for you and you deserve somebody better.'

His intensity disturbed her. So did the fragments of pain in his eyes. 'Somebody better?' She tilted her head. 'Yes, I probably do.'

It was nearly three in the morning. They were waiting for a taxi and Verrian had given her his jacket to wear over her own insubstantial one. She leaned into his embrace, a tide of night-clubbers passing behind them. The whole night felt unreal. She yawned, almost dislocating her jaw. That felt real.

Verrian said softly, 'I suppose I'm going to take you home.'

'Yes.' Was that the precise moment she fell in love? She looked up at Verrian, but he'd spotted a black Peugeot taxi and was hailing it.

At her building, Verrian had the driver wait. He got out, holding the door so Alix could slide across. 'Give me your key.' He unlocked the street door and followed her into the courtyard, waiting while she unlocked the door to the building. 'I'll see you up.'

'We don't have a lift.'

'I like stairs in Paris. I dislike them in London, but they feel different here.'

'You make no sense,' she laughed.

Reaching the door of her flat, he told her he knew how she kept so slim. She gave him back his jacket and Verrian kissed her, not on the lips but in the centre of her forehead. Since they had to part here, there was no point in prolonging things. 'Good night.'

Which of them weakened? Somehow she was in his arms again and he heard himself saying, 'I have to see you tomorrow. What time do you finish work?'

'Seven, but then I have to go somewhere else.' Earlier, Una had extracted a promise – *Musketeering begins tomorrow, no backing out now, Alix.*

'Where?'

'Nowhere important.'

'Sweet Alix, tell a newspaperman to mind his own business, you might as well issue a downright invitation. I'll be waiting outside my office door at seven tomorrow evening. Walk past me if you choose.'

Chapter Eighteen

The next morning, Alix flew down the stairs, the Lelong dress, in its cover, over her arm. A handbag stuffed with the day's necessities bumped the wall as she jumped the last four steps. She'd overslept.

'Late night?' Mme Rey dragged her mop bucket into Alix's path, using the mop as the steering mechanism. 'Heard you come in well after witching hour.'

Alix kept her eye on the exit. 'Sorry if I woke you.'

'No. I don't sleep well, always half awake. New man with you, was it?'

Alix gave a clenched smile. 'Yes.'

'Bit older than you I'd say, from the sound of his voice. Nice voice though.'

'He has a very nice voice. Sorry, I have to—'

'Took you right upstairs, did he? That's the sign of a gentleman. My mother used to tell me, if a man doesn't see you to your door, forget him.'

'Very wise, Madame. I really have to—'

243

'Hang on, dear, I've got newspapers for your grandmother. I'll just fetch them.'

Alix bent forward. Her period was due to start in a day or two and it felt as if somebody were twisting her innards on a stick. When Mme Rey eventually returned with copies of *Le Petit Parisien*, Alix said, 'I'll leave them on the bottom step and take them up when I come home.'

'That won't do, dear. Those oiks across the way will have them. I caught a couple of the little toerags in here yesterday, though they scooted fast enough when they saw me. Anyhow, I'm sure Mme Lutzman would like to read them with her breakfast, but I can't manage all those stairs more than once in a day.'

Cursing roundly, though still under her breath, Alix hurtled upstairs. *He's got a nice voice* . . . How close had that grimy old ear been to the door last night?

Reliving the feel of Verrian's arms around her made her stomach flip. So much to dream over when she wasn't in a hurry.

'Alix, are you feverish again?'

'No, Mme Frankel.'

'Only you were late, and now you keep staring the way Javier does when he's getting one of his migraines.'

Alix reassured the première, who replied, 'Good, because it's every hand to the pump and I still don't know how we're going to get the mid-season ball gowns finished for showing in two weeks' time. We've just thrown away yesterday's work on Oro too. I wish I could start this year again.'

'She says that every time,' Alix's companion Marcy whispered later. They'd been sent down to help one of the assistant designers, a solid young man called Simon Norbert who had spent twenty minutes ignoring them. They could hear him in his office, voice rising as he complained to some caller – 'Only eight of the fourteen complete, the mid-season show fixed for 12th May. And all Monsieur does is lament in Spanish. As for that bitch Oro, I said from the start that underpinning was never going to work. There's only so much you can ask of a length of tulle. Wire! I said it would have to be wire, though I warned Monsieur, "It'll look like a lampshade, you'll never get it to float like feathers."'

Alix, in love with Oro even in its unfinished state, had complete faith in Javier and Mme Frankel. She was shocked by this show of disloyalty. Without thinking, she shouted, 'Just because you're a dumpling does not make Oro one. She will float!'

Marcy shushed her. Simon Norbert stood in the doorway of his office. 'Dirty little cockroach,' he yelled. 'When I want you, I'll send for you.'

'Norbert has a point, you know,' Marcy said as they crept away. 'M. Javier conceives a look and asks Mme Frankel to devise the technique. Norbert's people get caught in the middle and Javier can be hard on them if they don't interpret him perfectly. We'd better go back to Mme Frankel.'

Alix and Marcy were working together in a capacity that had no name. If they were called anything, Alix reflected, it would be 'donkeys'. They fetched fabrics from storerooms and liaised with the workrooms, withstanding the howls of harried supervisors who couldn't see how shaving another hair's breadth off a seam could improve anything. They also handed offcuts to the matchers, which gave Alix the chance to trim off slivers of cloth. She had a treasury of samples, along with five detailed drawings from the mid-season line which tonight she'd hand over to Una Kilpin and the New York businesswoman who was Una's associate. Those two would turn stolen sketches into real-life copies.

'You like busy?' Mme Albert asked when Alix was sent to the thread room to pick up a box of white bobbins.

She did like busy. She was learning a trade she loved. And in Marcy Stein, a gentle girl from the suburb of Batignolles, she'd found her first friend at Javier. But tonight, when all she wanted was to meet Verrian and hold hands over a table, she had to take one step deeper into a world she already regretted entering.

'Alix? You've been ten minutes fetching those. I said I needed them at once.' Anger showed for the first time in Pauline Frankel's face. 'If you don't want this chance, go back to your sewing bench.'

'I'm sorry, Madame. It's –' she looked around to check that none of the male staff were near – 'my time of the month. I feel dreadful.'

Pauline Frankel's features evened out. 'Ah. I understand that well enough. If you want to lie down –'

'I'd rather work, take my mind off things.'

'Very well. Go and see if Javier needs you, but, please, no tragic faces. All that tulle you sewed under Oro's skirt? He's had someone unpick the lot and I only just stopped him from throwing the dress out the window. We cannot afford theatricals. We need finished clothes. We need cash and custom.'

In the top-floor studio, Solange Antonin held a pose in a gown destined to be No. 14 of the mid-season collection. '*Lune de Minuit*' – Midnight Moon. It had a body of black velvet with alternate flounces of ivory and black lace. During his trip to Spain, Javier had watched Flamenco dancers and this mid-season collection reflected it. Arms and shoulders were bare. Bodices were boned like basques, skirts flared in fishtails. It was, thought Alix, enchanting. But . . . again, as with Oro, something about this dress felt not quite right.

Poor rejected Oro looked like a burst balloon with her underpinning removed. And Simon Norbert had a point, Alix mused, wire would be wrong. What it needed was something strong as wire yet light as silk. Something with movement. Something alive . . . She stared until the dress melted into flame and cried, 'I know!'

An assistant shushed her, nodding towards Javier, who stood cupping his chin. Simon Norbert mirrored his pose, his pot belly pushing in and out as he strove to contain his anxiety. Up on the pedestal, Solange bore the signs of a late night. Noticing Alix, she jerked as if an electric current had hit her.

'Keep still,' Javier snapped. 'How can I judge a dress if you squirm?'

Solange flung a look of hatred at Alix, and Javier said wearily, 'I can see you too, *petite*. What do you want?'

'Mme Frankel sent me to see if I could be of any use.'

Simon Norbert sniffed. 'Hardly likely.'

Javier opened his arms. 'Wave the magician's staff, make me love my collection.' His hands danced. 'I who could once make a poem out of a bundle of sheeting have lost my gift. We might as well shut down. I am a spent force.'

'Monsieur, I've an idea about Oro, how to make it float.'

Simon Norbert snorted.

'That mule of a dress.' Javier shuddered. 'She has defeated me. I have given up. Now I am instead in anguish over Minuit. It is the couturier's fate, Alix, to be speared through the heart by those you love.'

Alix could see that beneath the melodrama lurked desperation. She walked towards Solange, then took five steps back, narrowing her gaze. Any other day she'd have kept her mouth shut, but this was not any day. Last night in the Rose Noire, Serge Martel had told her 'We're going to be lovers.' Minutes later, another man had snatched her away. A man whose touch made her feel dizzy and abandoned.

She said, 'There's nothing wrong with any of your gowns. Your collection is a triumph of grace.'

'Shame yours is the least important opinion in the building,' Norbert muttered.

'Dummies, M. Javier.' Alix pointed at the wooden mannequins that kept silent witness against a far wall. 'You're seeing your clothes on dummies. It's all wrong.'

Norbert blustered, 'You've no right to a point of view.'

'You are saying . . .' Javier engaged her in visual combat, 'my designs are for wooden dolls, not women?'

Like a roulette player hurling everything on black seventeen Alix dared to continue. 'Have you a gramophone?'

Javier blinked. 'I have.'

'Have M. Norbert fetch it and some records. Romantic ones. Do you have anything by Hildegarde or Lucienne Boyer?' She turned to Norbert. 'Would you bring them?'

'I will not, cheeky little article.'

Javier formalised the instruction and Norbert strutted away.

'I know what you're about, *petite*, and I am indulging you. Make a fool of me, I might throw you and the gramophone out of the window.'

'All the mannequins are here by two o'clock? With your permission, I'll have Mlle Lilliane send them up. They should be prepared to wear one gown each. I'd like a taxi to fetch a friend of mine. And I'd like to send a matcher to my home.'

'Why?'

'May I tell you later?'

She drew curtains, had candles brought and, with Marcy's help, moved the furniture to the wall. Javier watched, going along with it all because he was in a hole and as a man in a hole will accept the hand of a passing madman, he was accepting hers. Each time the door opened, Alix looked for the one person she wanted to see. But it was usually somebody sent up by Mlle Lilliane to enquire if the design studio was 'still intent on wrecking the smooth schedule of the afternoon'.

Alix wound the gramophone and chose a disc. The first of the mannequins arrived, asking, 'Are we having a special showing? Who's coming?' Followed by two more who laughed like children given a break from lessons. A couple more sauntered in, blankly incurious. Each girl carried shoes and evening gloves and was followed by a dresser carrying a calico bag like a gigantic puffball.

'The salon showing starts promptly at three and the girls will have to get downstairs and change.' Javier consulted his pocket watch. 'Ten past two. Alix, tell us what we're to do.'

The matcher came back and gave Alix a package, along with a message: 'Your grandmother says, this was weeks of work when her fingers were nimble and she still feels the pain each morning when she wakes.'

Thank you, Mémé, Alix transmitted silently.

Nearly ready to begin, Alix reflected that she had gambled on one other person, and it looked as if she'd overstretched her luck . . . until Marcy rushed into the studio followed by a man. Alix ran forward. 'Paul, you came. Oh . . .' He was wearing an old shirt and building-site trousers. 'Didn't you get my message? Black-tie evening suit. Like last night.'

'You know it wasn't my suit.' Paul looked about in resentful wonder. One of the mannequins giggled and his mouth turned stubborn. 'You had me woken, Alix. What do you want?'

'Your services, for an hour. But you have to be properly dressed.' She looked at Javier who raised an eyebrow.

'No good asking me. My evening clothes would not fit him. We are wide in completely different places.'

She turned to Norbert, silently begging. He pretended not to notice, then finally huffed and told her, 'I don't keep evening clothes here.'

'You do, M. Norbert,' Marcy said. 'You always keep a suit in your room. You've asked me to sponge your jacket and press your shirt on numerous occasions. Shall I fetch it?'

'As you please.' Norbert didn't quite stamp a foot, but still raised it and put it down with a decided snap.

The suit was very 'just' on Paul. A belt had to be found, and the jacket was so tight he looked like a scarecrow with a broom handle through both sleeves. The mannequins, who had changed

The Dress Thief

into their gowns, tried to help. Laughter bubbled up all around, but it was not malicious.

'I can't wear this jacket,' Paul told Alix, 'so stop trying to shove me into it. I'll dance in shirt and waistcoat.'

That brought an appreciative 'Ooh' from the girls. Only Solange remained untouched by the fun. She sat at a remove, her eyes rarely leaving Alix.

The waistcoat buttoned over a white ruffled shirt and – with the addition of a sash and some breathing in – the effect was as Javier said, 'The " *morillo*",' which, he explained, was a term for the neck and shoulder muscles of a fighting bull. He took out his pocket watch and swung it in front of Alix. 'Time, he ticks.'

'Heloïse?' Alix beckoned a Titian-haired girl whose luminous beauty had inspired a gown of ivory velvet with an overskirt of chiffon, 'here is your dance partner. Paul, the watchword is smooth, fluid and romantic.'

'That's three words.'

'Just dance.' She set the gramophone going and Lucienne Boyer's 'Parlez-moi d'amour' spilled into the room.

Whatever he was by day, on the dance floor Paul was a fish returned to water, and Heloïse began to dance like a woman in love. Her dress shaped to her, the skirt flicking, the overskirt fanning, making sense of the dress's Spanish name: Seguidilla – That Which Follows. Shadow-work appliqué – Mémé's work, Alix was sure – winked in the light. They danced again, and then

252

it was Marie-Josèphe's turn, then Arlette's, then Claudette's, then Nelly's, then Zinaida's. Alix hoped Javier was seeing what she was seeing, that his designs gorged on light and came to life with movement.

The clock said five minutes to three. The dresses were snatched away, the mannequins sent downstairs. All the gowns had been danced – except one.

'Solange?' Javier clapped his hands. 'You aren't ready.' Solange had taken off Lune de Minuit and donned a robe. She said, 'I have a bad head. I can't dance.'

'Then you must take a taxi home. Why did you not say?' A little hardness crept into Javier's tone. Solange walked out.

'Where is Minuit?' Javier demanded. 'Zinaida,' Javier beckoned at the slender Greek girl. 'I must see Lune de Minuit dancing.'

'I'm too short,' Zinaida protested. 'I'll put my foot in the hem.'

'*Mais oui*, I keep forgetting you are *petite, ma petite*. Who is as tall as Solange? Bah, such a temperamental girl. I am the temperamental one and there is not room for two. Send Nelly back.' A dresser went, but returned to say that Nelly was dressing for the afternoon show, already in her tailor-made and having her hat pinned on.

Alix was whispering with Paul when she felt a hand grip her arm. 'You,' said Javier. 'Put on the dress. Can you dance?'

Paul answered for her, 'I taught her. Of course she can.'

Before she could invent an excuse, Alix was whisked away behind a screen by a dresser. The girl chivvied her out of her top clothes, saying, 'If Minuit isn't ready to show in the salon in fifteen minutes, Mlle Lilliane will cut off your ears.'

Alix shivered. Not from the cold, but because she'd witnessed the mousseline glory of the mannequins' lingerie and was now exposed in her work-a-day brassière and knickers. The dresser held the gown open and Alix stepped into it.

'Marcy, do up the hooks. Heaven bless me,' the dresser tutted, 'You're wearing tennis shoes – and you should be wearing a strapless brassière.'

'Alix wears tennis shoes because she runs all day,' Marcy said. 'And I'll push the brassière straps under the shoulders. Look . . . gone. She can borrow my shoes.' Marcy stepped out of her low-heeled court shoes.

'*Sockettes de fille!*' the dresser exclaimed in disbelief at Alix's ankle socks.

'Slip them off, Alix,' Marcy ordered. 'Bare legs won't matter under the dress.' She patted Alix on the hip. 'You have a smaller waist than Solange.'

'Don't say that too loudly,' the dresser muttered. 'That cow takes everything as an insult. She's always getting us into trouble. Right, Alix, go and dance. Damage that dress and I'll have your hide for a handbag.'

As she melted into Paul's arms, it occurred to Alix that in the last two hours she'd been threatened with being thrown out of a window, ear-loss and flaying. If her audacity fell flat, at the very least she'd have to resign. Which might be no bad thing, though how she'd break the news to Paul . . .

'Loosen up,' Paul muttered. 'It's like dancing with a suitcase. I suppose this is all to show off the dress? So let the dress show. Close your eyes and let me lead.'

Lucienne Boyer sang 'Si petite' and Alix tried to imagine she was at Sylvie le Gal's school of modern dancing and they were exhibiting to an audience of rapt younger pupils. 'Did you notice I left the Rose Noire early?' she whispered.

'Did I notice? When he found you'd gone, Serge Martel stood under the heaps of red rose petals and slowly turned the same colour.'

'That's not making me relax.'

'In the end, he laughed it off. Came over and treated us to champagne, introduced me to Solange's friends because they wanted to dance with me.'

'You wouldn't dance with me. Why didn't you ask me?'

A pause. 'I think I waited long enough for you, Alix.'

'I'm sorry.' It was the only thing she could think to say. 'This is Javier's favourite dress, so please help me not to dance like a suitcase.'

'Then imagine you're in love with me, that we're under the

stars, the moon a milky sickle. I've brought you away on my ocean-going yacht to . . . to . . .'

'Where?'

'I can't think. Whenever I think of water, I see the Seine or the St-Martin canal.'

The music finished and somebody – perhaps Simon Norbert, hoping to catch her out – switched to a record of Carlos Gardel singing 'Mi Buenos Aires Querido'. Alix and Paul veered into a tango. Alix forgot she was wearing thousands of francs' worth of couture miracle and followed Paul in a sequence of sinuous turns, dips, kicks and flicks. She leaned backwards in his arms until she felt the velvet sheath pinch her waist. Rolled back up, spun, and heard the soft crack of fabric around her calves. Opening her eyes, she found Paul gazing down at her, such fire in his gaze that the snap of their heads away from each other was a relief. The song slowed. They ended with a dip, Alix's head thrown back, yielding throat and bosom. Paul righted her, still locked in an embrace, and asked, 'Do I get paid for this?'

'Course you do. Oh, Paul, listen.'

'To what?'

'The silence.'

It was then that Simon Norbert chose to lift the gramophone arm with an unpleasant scrape. Marcy hustled Alix off behind the screen. 'We need to get this dress off you five minutes ago.'

Paul was waiting for Alix in the studio, back in his baggy trousers and mariner's jacket. 'I've got a shift at the building site later, and if I don't get some sleep first, I'll die.'

Telling him to wait in the corridor, she approached Javier, who stood at the window, so lost in thought it was half a minute before he noticed Alix or the package she was holding.

He took it. 'And this is . . . ?'

'Horsehair lace, Monsieur. My grandmother made it. The ladies of Alsace used to decorate their heads with it. This morning I had to go back up to our apartment and I found my grandmother staring at a picture we have of a girl with lace butterfly wings on her head.'

Javier drew the weave through his fingers. 'This is sometimes used in ball gowns and in the theatre . . . you are thinking . . .'

'Oro. Feel how light it is. Yet stiff enough to bear weight. A glimpse of it beneath Oro's flounces would be beautiful.'

'And where would I get forty metres? And at what cost?'

Her heart dived. 'From Alsace, I suppose.' Then a thought raced in. 'From Fabrication Textile Mulhouse in Rue du Sentier. M. le Comte de Charembourg is a director of the firm, and he comes from Alsace. He'll understand what you need.'

'Ah, the comtesse's husband. Well, well. I will send four horsemen galloping to the Sentier. Meanwhile, your young man is hopping from foot to foot.'

Alix hurried Paul out to the street where she said, 'I'll see

Mme Frankel later about money. What d'you think? Were they impressed?'

'Alix, I don't know these people. The older man – is he Javier? – enjoyed himself, but the younger—'

'Simon Norbert. He's nobody.'

'He certainly isn't your friend.'

'Who cares?'

Paul put his hands on Alix's arms. 'You can't afford enemies. Who took you home last night?'

'Just a man I know. I wanted to go anyway.'

Paul said, 'Listen, about me and Una . . . it just happened. She called one night, all done up in her furs. She walked on to the *Katrijn* like a Russian queen, bringing one bottle of chilled gin and one of martini.'

'Always helps.'

'I'm her fun. A way of punishing her husband. But I like her,' he said defensively. 'And she's lent me more money. She sold some jewels and it means I can keep the girls at Aunt Gilberte's.'

'So Una can call when she pleases. No kids cluttering the ship.'

'That's not fair. Una's a good person and, like she said, you didn't want me, so why should it matter to you? And soon we'll all be making money. How's the musketeering?'

'Shush, not here. Go home and get some sleep.'

As Paul strode away, a wine-red Peugeot pulled up. The driver got out, slamming his door in a yawning stretch. On cue, Solange emerged. Her hair hung loose and she was wearing one of the fitter's smocks. Actually she did look unwell, pale and hollow-eyed. Alix didn't want to be seen by her or by Serge. Not after the way she'd shown him up in his club. She was sidling towards the trade door when her name was shouted.

It was Paul, sprinting back towards her. 'I forgot to change my shirt,' he gasped, indicating the frill at his neck.

Alix groaned. 'How could you not notice?' Solange and Serge were staring in her direction. 'Simon Norbert will yell at me again.'

'Nothing to what will happen to me if I go to a building site in a frilly shirt.'

'Come on.' They entered the trade entrance of Maison Javier. Serge tipped his hat as she went by. Nothing to hint that he was angry, but the length of his look suggested a game in its early stages. He wasn't done with her.

Mme Frankel was searching for Alix, having given her the task of dismantling all of Oro's flounces again so they could be lined with horsehair lace. Javier had telephoned FTM and been told of a supplier in Mulhouse. Within half an hour, an order had been placed which would be sent to Paris by train. 'When you've unpicked,' Mme Frankel said, 'take the flounces to the pressing room with a fabric sample, so the women can test their irons first. And Alix?'

'Madame?'

'If you need a tablet for your monthly pains, go to the sanatorium. If anybody challenges your presence there, say you have my permission.'

After an hour spent unpicking gold dupion, Alix took Mme Frankel's advice. The sanatorium was off the salon, being as much for the benefit of clients as staff. It wasn't unusual for ladies to faint after several hours' fitting. The resident nurse insisted Alix sit on the edge of a bed while she checked her pulse and temperature and asked penetrating questions about boyfriends and 'romance'. Alix realised the woman was probing to see if she was pregnant and answered that she was fine.

'That's good, dear,' the nurse replied. 'You'd be surprised how many girlies aren't, and I'm often the first person they can tell.' She watched Alix down a glass of fizzing analgesic then said, 'Early to bed with a cup of hot milk, what I advise during ladies' week.'

Alix felt a giggle boiling up. She was still giggling as she came into the reception area where she'd waited with her basket the day of her interview. A man sat there alone. A newspaper shielded his face but he must have heard her, because he lowered the sheet when she came near. It was the Comte de Charembourg. He stood, held out his hand and raised an eyebrow at her brown smock. 'Why do they make you dress like a penitent?'

His palm felt dry and over-warm.

'It protects the dresses . . .' Then she threw politeness away. 'Monsieur, you look ill.'

'Old ailments.' He touched his lapel, near his heart, then kissed her cheek. 'You, on the other hand . . .' He trailed off and it dawned on Alix that he was nervous. Some reserve was understandable, considering what had happened to her after their last happy lunch date back in March, but he seemed almost afraid of her. Clearly, signing her name 'Mathilda' had struck home.

'Thank you for my scissors,' she said abruptly. They were hanging around her neck on a ribbon.

'I hope I chose right. I guessed what kind would be most useful. They're not too delicate?'

'These are perfect. Monsieur—' She said it just as he blurted out, 'Alix—'

She indicated he should go first.

'I'm so sorry you were frightened that awful day.' He reached out to touch her hair. 'It was a misunderstanding. A bill got lost—'

'Monsieur, you were being blackmailed. The man told me.'

'I see.' He put his palm to his forehead, as if to quell a pain there. 'Alix, I'm trying to protect you. It's all I've ever tried to do, protect you and . . . and my daughters from harm. If I could tell you more, I would.'

Would you? she wondered. 'Did you pay up, Monsieur? Did you pay that disgusting man a million francs?'

'Not that much, heavens, no.' He cleared his throat and turned his neck uncomfortably. Alix held his gaze until he said, 'I only paid half that. Whoever my blackmailer is, he has a practical streak. He believed me when I said I couldn't raise one million, so we struck a deal. I can only pray that I've done enough. Now, forgive me, I must go and do my duty. Madame la Comtesse and my elder daughter are in there somewhere.'

'In the salon?'

'In a fitting room. Javier is making Christine's wedding gown.'

So Alix had heard. The comte's wife had been a nightmare, reducing both the fitters and her daughter to tears. 'Will your daughter welcome your opinion?'

'Hmm. I think young ladies have a very particular use for their fathers. More to do with our wallets than our fashion sense. Don't you think?' Seeing her reaction, he made a quick gesture. 'I'm sorry. That was supremely tactless.'

She asked slowly, because she was suddenly afraid she would cry, 'How could you of all people forget that I have no father?'

'Alix, I meant . . . Forgive me.'

'He saved your life.'

The comte made to leave, but she snatched his arm. Their eyes locked and both felt the impact. 'That's not true either then, that story of my father walking between you and the guns?'

'Would anybody lie about such a thing?'

'They might, if they were trying to hide a shameful secret. What about my mother? When was the final time you saw her?'

He jerked. 'Not here, Alix, please.'

She checked that they were still alone. 'I know you met Mathilda many times. Bonnet said you were like a big brother to her and that you met later during the war, when she was a young woman. And she fell . . . Bonnet hinted that she had feelings for you. Did you love her? Did you educate her, as you did me? No, actually don't answer,' she said, noting his ashen face. 'Better silence than lies.'

'Alix, I wish things were different. Believe me, falsehood is not my way.'

'One last question.' It came unbidden. 'Do you know where my father is buried?'

No answer. The man she'd looked up to as friend and mentor was squirming. It was clear that the Comte de Charembourg had no idea where to find his 'friend' John Gower's last resting place.

'Monsieur, when you look at me, what do you see?'

'You have no concept of "last question", have you, Alix?' He touched her shoulder in contrition. 'What do I see when I look at you? When you smile, I see a clean page. So, please, always smile for me.'

Chapter Nineteen

Alix left work, her back aching. Her heart too. What else had the Comte de Charembourg lied to her about? His affection for her? His compliments on her looks and her talent? Did that mean she had none after all?

On Rue Boccador, Verrian stepped out in front of her with the greeting, 'Is this you ignoring me?'

'I can't stop, I'm late.'

'For?' He matched her pace.

'My other job. I'm starting work in a sort of fashion house, helping out.'

'After a full day at Javier? And what about after that?'

'Home. My grandmother has a meal waiting for me.'

At the junction with Montaigne, Alix stopped, too tired to make the crossing.

Verrian took her arm. 'How will you get home?'

'Métro or bus.'

He said, 'I'll pick you up and will do so every night – buy you a glass of wine, a bit of conversation, then drive you home.'

'You don't have a car.'

'True, but I'll get one.'

She sniffed like a girl who's heard that one before. 'Go to Billancourt and buy a small Renault.'

'That's a thought. So, it's a deal?' They crossed the road together. 'We meet every day and I see you home?'

'I've never seen anybody every day, except my grandmother. We might argue.'

'I should think we will but—' He stopped. 'Alix, you're limping. Is there something in your shoe?'

'No.' It came out too quickly.

'Well, you're a different person entirely today. Are you trying to tell me something?'

She denied it, adding, 'Only that you'll get bored with me, find me frivolous.'

'Your frivolity has depths. Nothing will stop me admiring you except –'

'There's always "except".'

'War or death. How's that? What time do you finish this extra job?'

'About nine.'

'Where shall I wait?'

'The Champs-Elysées, the Concorde end. I'll find you,' she finally conceded. After all, Verrian had proved his feelings could last a whole night and day this time.

It took Alix a while to find the discreet green door beside the tailoring shop on the Champs-Elysées that was Una's associate's place of business. As she raised a hand to knock, a familiar voice hailed her.

'My, you look like you spent a day up the rigging. Couldn't you kill a rose macaroon? No time, more's the pity.' Una Kilpin waved her driver off, watching the Rolls-Royce nose into the traffic. 'Is that my Lelong dress?' She indicated the garment bag over Alix's arm. 'You left in a rush last night. Anyone I know?'

Alix muttered something unintelligible while Una gave three short raps on the door followed by a heavy one. 'One day I'll summon up the ghost of Beethoven. Now listen, Alix, the lady you're meeting upstairs knows every New York apparel manufacturer worth knowing. We go back a long time, but I warn you, she's hard on the ears.' A female voice behind the green door demanded identification. Una called, 'The talent, honey.'

Letting them in, the receptionist asked for the code word. Alix wasn't sure she'd ever been told it. Una said, 'Mariette. Twice – in case we forget next time.' They climbed the stairs to a door with a spy grille where the words 'Maison Godnosc' were displayed on a brass plate. The receptionist unlocked that door and Alix wondered how many times a day the girl went through this procedure.

The girl melted away into a side office as Alix followed Una into a large room with drawn blinds. From the far side, a woman scurried towards them with a cry of, 'Is this her?' She was wish-bone thin, of indeterminate age, with hair dyed the colour of a burning bush.

Una made introductions. 'Alix, this is my business partner, Mabel Godnosc, and these offices are by writ and custom American soil. In other words, we shake paws, no kissing.'

Mabel Godnosc demonstrated, pumping Alix's hand. Because she wore five bracelets per wrist, she clanked. 'What sort of day have I had?' she said, though nobody had asked. 'Three Lanvins ordered and a Patou "maybe". Every customer without appointment, so we dragged out the house models till we saw the colour of their money. Does this kid understand me?' Mrs Godnosc demanded of Una. 'Did you tell her? No French spoken, English only.'

'I understand perfectly,' Alix replied and thought 'No French' was probably the reason this woman wasn't in jail – Mabel Godnosc's dress and jacket were a bullseye copy of a Chanel. By 'house models', Alix presumed Mabel meant the dresses she whisked out in emergencies to give the front of being a legitimate fashion house. Seeing Alix's interest, Mabel did a twirl.

'Forty-five dollars, including washing instructions and fancy wrapping. Whaddya say, petal?'

Alix was to learn that Maison Godnosc worked everything in dollars.

While the older women bantered, Alix began the work she'd

come to do. Sooner finished, sooner out. All she wanted was to be with Verrian again.

Sitting down at a table, she took off her shoe and retrieved the folded paper hidden inside. It resembled a mad professor's jotter. Mabel peered over her shoulder.

'These squiggles are clothes?'

'Please understand, Madame, I have to memorise the dresses and draw them quickly. I'm going to translate the squiggles for you now.'

Mabel turned to Una. 'Have I offended her?'

'You have not offended me, Madame.' Alix was itching to get started. 'Will you bring me paper and coloured pencils?'

'You've not brought your own?'

'I cannot go to work with drawing materials sticking out of my bag. Of course you must supply them.' Alix's patience was cracking. Una nodded to Mabel, and Mabel dashed out, haring back into the room with an artist's box and block.

'So, petal, how many today?'

'Five models, Mme Godnosc.'

'Only five?'

Una cut in. 'Mabel, we're not canning peas. Five, but five accurate to the last thread. Could your girl mix me a Gin Alexander? Alix will have tea.'

'The girl can't make tea; don't ask her. Anything with gin.'

'Alix will have milk.'

Five copies, accurate to the last thread . . . While Una and

Mabel clinked glasses, Alix sketched Oro, then evening gowns one to four from the mid-season collection. Unlike the Spanish-inspired gowns that would crown the show, dresses one through four were intended for evenings in Cannes or Cap d'Antibes. For watching the sun go down from the rails of an ocean liner, cocktail glass in hand. They were a silk-linen blend with a pattern of Moorish fretwork and orange blossom. A Lyon manufacturer had made the fabric for Javier as an eleventh-hour favour and it was unmatched anywhere in the world. Alix had taken samples in the stockroom, cutting absolutely straight so the next person handling the cloth would notice nothing. She reckoned she'd lost a pound in weight from fear.

She drew front, back and side views, adding vignettes of the detail – a self-fabric belt with a buckle in the shape of orange leaves; a puffed sleeve with a squared-off top; a wide collar showing a plain revere. Tomorrow she'd give them Lune de Minuit and Seguidilla. She'd give these women the whole collection, hem by hem, sleeve by sleeve. And when she'd earned her payout, she would never do it again.

Mabel Godnosc hovered over her. 'How d'you manage it? Did you sneak a look at Javier's sketchbook?'

'Never. Only the designers and premiers are allowed in the studios alone, and only they see the full collection before it's shown.'

'Alix has the eye,' Una chipped in. She was perched on a desk, displaying a slender calf and knee. 'Knew it first time I saw her.

Most women look at clothes and imagine them on themselves, and most men look straight through them. Alix soaks them in. She has the savvy to know why a garment is put together the way it is.'

Mabel Godnosc made a thoughtful noise. 'If Javier's mid-season kicks off middle of May, our factories need sketches and samples by last week. They need to be on to it now.'

Una and Mabel begin to fling dates and schedules at each other. Alix listened impatiently before cutting in with, 'Wait! Nothing must be released until after Thursday 12th May, which is the day the collection is previewed. You understand?' She put down her pencil to show she was serious. 'These drawings must not travel until Javier has shown the originals in Paris.'

Una shrugged 'sure' and looked at Mabel, who said, 'Don't fret, petal. We keep schtum at Maison Godnosc. Any sign of you-know-who coming in to order?'

Wearily Alix picked up her pencil. 'Who, Madame?'

'Mrs Simpson. The future queen.'

'The king abdicated. She won't be queen.'

'Future duchess who oughta be queen. Don't those English know how hard the lady works to look like that? Hips that slim, they'd save a fortune on thrones.'

'She bought a few pieces from Javier,' Alix murmured, not looking up, 'but she likes Mainbocher best.'

'Maybe she comes up the side stairs when nobody's looking.'

Una said, 'Mabel, let Alix work.'

'Sure, but listen,' Mabel persisted. 'If Javier made her wedding dress and we got it two weeks early, we might as well be printing dollars. If she wore Javier to marry the king—'

'She isn't marrying the king,' Alix snapped. 'She's marrying the ex-king.'

'Una, is she always so grouchy?'

'Always, Mabel, and it's why you'll get your collection. Leave her be.'

Not the whole collection, Alix decided on an irritable whim. They weren't having Seguidilla, because she wasn't handing over Mémé's shadow work, nor would they get Midnight Moon, in which she'd danced the tango with Paul. She shaded in the last detail . . . now she could go and find Verrian.

But Mabel had other ideas. She gripped Alix's arm. 'Why don't you knock out a little original for me?' When Alix echoed her question, she nodded hard. 'We have to keep up the front of being a legit house and I'm no hand at designing. My niece was doing it, but she's gone back to New York and I've tried to recruit, but getting the right person . . .'

'Go to it, Alix,' Una urged. She was on her third gin. 'You want to be a couturier and here's Mabel giving you the go. She'll give you a commission on any frock of yours she sells, won't you, Mabel?'

The Godnosc eyebrows contracted over the Godnosc nose. 'Sure, why not? Make it a day dress, an easy-wear, million-seller. Just one. One little one.'

The Dress Thief

Vey ist mir. Woe is me. Alix studied the blank sheet in front of her, then the clock on the wall. Verrian Haviland had better like waiting.

When Alix looked within for that million-seller frock, all that appeared was an uninspiring tube. She gave it a crossover front. Ugh, that was what Mme Rey wore because it accommodated her bosom. She added buttons. Now it reminded her of school domestic science. New page, start again. Bold, puff sleeves à la Javier, a stand-up collar with a vivid lining. A diamond shape under the bust, defining the stomach, skirt falling from the natural waist. Now, that felt different. For years, fashion had made a smooth curve of the waist. The 1930s had given women back their figures after the drop waists of the previous decade, but the prevailing look had been willow-wand, the emphasis on the shoulders. The diamond midriff she'd just drawn was out of step. Too radical? Probably, but it was already twenty past nine.

Fabric . . . safe black crêpe. Reveres and cuffs picked out in patterned crêpe, crimson perhaps, hand-printed with a black motif. A flower . . . a Pugin-style rose like those she'd embroidered on her poor 'Schiaparelli' coat. There, done. She drew a back view and four small vignettes of the dress's detail, scribbled in the fabric notes and said to Mme Godnosc, 'I must go.'

Una picked up the drawing. 'You have to do your floor exercises to get away with that look. Not that you have to care, Alix. I'll be your first taker, but change the colours.'

272

'The dress is the colours,' Alix said.

'Not when I'm the client. Dog black and blood red? You've been reading the papers again. What are you going to call it?'

'I don't know.' It was half past nine. 'Wait, call it "Rose Noire".'

Chapter Twenty

It took Alix only a few minutes to find Verrian, but one look at his face told her he very much disliked waiting. She took the seat he pulled out for her. He'd chosen an outside table near the junction of the Champs-Elysées and Place de la Concorde. She'd have walked right by had he not hailed her, because the avenue was hidden in the conflicting glare of café and car lights and two women had been standing right in front of him.

As Alix approached, they'd sashayed away, casting glances over their shoulders. *Only a streetwalker would wear a suit two sizes too small unbuttoned to the bosom*, Alix thought. 'Friends of yours?'

'No – as you perfectly well know.' Verrian had a glass of beer in front of him, which was propping up a broadsheet newspaper. 'Would you like one?' he asked, tapping the rim.

'Wine, please, red.' She added, 'I tilt my hats, but I don't stick them to the side of my head like a custard pie. Why do those girls do it?'

'A discreet form of advertising. Simpler than carrying a banner. You're late, Miss Gower.'

'I couldn't get away.'

'I was happy to wait.'

'Your expression says otherwise.'

He nodded. 'It's not your fault. I picked up this newspaper. Three days old – I've been having a rest from the news and I missed something calamitous. Another town was bombed in northern Spain. Guernica, in the Basque country. I have – had – friends there.'

'I hate newspapers,' Alix said fiercely. 'They make me feel the world is a horrible place.'

'It is, sometimes.' He put his hand over hers. 'But why should you care about people utterly unconnected to you?'

Alix sensed his darkening mood. On impulse, she told him about meeting the Comte de Charembourg earlier. 'He said the same thing you said the other day.'

'Which was?'

'That I was a clean page. Only you said "clean sheet". Is that what I am? Blank paper, for people to write their opinions on?'

'Maybe.' He tossed the newspaper, which was *The Times*, on to an empty chair. 'I suspect it's because your indomitable spirit reminds us that anything is possible, if we're prepared to work at it. Not so bad when you put it that way, is it?'

Her wine arrived and the waiter put down bread and a bowl of olives. She dived on them, saying, 'Sorry – my work makes me ravenous.' *Never tell me clothes don't matter*, she thought. That time in the Deux Magots, and last night in Una's Lucien Lelong, she'd felt the sophisticated equal of this man, but this evening, in her work clothes, she felt like one of the sparrows that hopped between boulevard table legs. Verrian dwarfed her, with his big-shouldered coat slung loosely about him.

'Alix, the other day you spoke to me of your grandfather . . .'

Her hand stopped halfway to her mouth. 'So?'

'It seems he keeps popping up. As do you.'

'I live here,' she retorted. 'It's you who pop up.'

'You're right.' A smile softened his eyes. 'My sister Lucy, who owns every book written by the palm reader Cheiro, would say it was written into our life paths to entangle. So, having got tangled, I did something that's none of my business. Yesterday I asked a friend about Alfred Lutzman.'

'But I saw you last night. Why didn't you say something?' Alix asked through a mouthful of bread.

'Because there were more pressing thoughts in my head than your grandfather. But I want to talk about him now. You said he died before his talent could flower . . .'

Watching him select an olive, Alix burst out, 'You don't have to pussyfoot. I know some bad things about my grandfather.'

'Tell me.'

'He left home and went to England to study, leaving his father to manage his business alone. He didn't write to his family until he was in London, and they thought he'd been taken away by the authorities. It made his mother ill. He broke promises. And he was mean.'

'With money?'

'There wasn't much of that, but yes. He promised Mémé – that's my grandmother – that he'd buy her a wedding dress, so she had one made. But then he wouldn't go to the bank, so she had to pay for it week by week herself. She took in mending to make ends meet, and after that he expected her to keep doing it. Sometimes he'd let his daughter go hungry rather than sell his work. When she speaks of him, I hear Mémé crying inside. But that doesn't mean he wasn't a great painter.'

'Was the Comte de Charembourg your grandfather's patron?'

'I don't think so. He bought some paintings but he was very young then. Young men don't collect art, they chase girls,' she finished imperiously.

He squeezed her hand, not gently. 'There's another thing. I want to understand how you and M. le Comte know each other. How it is he sees you as a sweet, blank page.'

'Because of Alsace, because of the war. My father fought alongside him. At the outbreak of war they both joined the London Rifle Brigade. During a battle – near Arras, I think – the comte was thrown into the air by shell blast and my father ran forward to rescue him.' She faltered because, after her conversation with the comte in Javier, she could no longer picture that heroic scene with any clarity. 'When he heard both my parents had died, the comte helped grandmother financially.'

'Alsace . . . art . . . London . . . war . . . so many things link you.'

She snatched her hand away. 'Is it the Comte de Charembourg you're interested in?'

'I'm interested in you.' He pushed their chairs together so they fused at the leg. She shivered and he flung his coat around her.

She'd have liked to cuddle up but his probing questions had made things complex again. 'Because of your job, you can't help prising out people's secrets?'

'Guilty.'

'Let me save you some time. The comte isn't my father, in case you're wondering. People always think it, because he's been generous to me.' She picked up her wine, meaning to knock it back, but instead choked and grabbed a napkin. 'They said it at school when they wanted to be mean. I asked Mémé, when she'd had a little to drink, and she said I must never think it. She said I looked very like my true father and nobody who's seen a photograph of John Gower would ever doubt it. Now see what you've made me do.'

He spread a napkin over the wine stain on the tablecloth and called for a refill. 'As I said before, you don't have to explain yourself to me.'

'You're trying to explain me to myself!'

'I'm sorry.' He touched the curls at her temple. 'Nobody's stolen more of your hair, I hope?'

He was trying to sooth away the storm, but she felt idiotic because she had wine dripping into her shoe. People walking by would think she was his younger sister. 'I'm going to have my hair cut short,' she said, reaching for a subject she knew often touched a nerve with men. 'Really short, once Bonnet's finished with me.'

'Bonnet now?'

'Finished painting me. I told you I was sitting for him. Light falling on my hair is the most important part of the composition, he says. He says, if he wanted me to be all neck and shoulders, he'd have asked me to put my hair up.' Ah, a reaction. Like a spark from a locomotive wheel as it grates the track. She pursued it. 'Bonnet was my grandfather's pupil. Did you find that out too? That's why he's a master of female flesh, like my grandfather. He paints slowly and has to be cajoled into completing his work. I get very cold sitting for him.' There.

'Alix, have you any idea what the image of you sitting naked for another man does to my self-control? If we were together in a hotel room, I would enjoy this conversation very much. It would have a very different texture and very different possibilities.'

She looked away. Unable to say anything clever or remotely seductive in return, she snapped, 'I told you we would argue.'

'You did.'

She turned back to see him reaching for *The Times*, his expression closed. Obviously the bombing of a faraway town meant more to him than she did. Of course it did. Her ignorance would bore any intelligent man. She suspected that under Verrian's light manner lay a very serious character. To get his attention, she raised her glass in a toast. 'Your health.'

He nodded. 'Yours too. Though you should stop sitting around in the buff in Montmartre attics if you want to keep it.' He folded up the newspaper and stood. 'Time I took you home.'

She wouldn't let him come into her building. 'Our concierge snoops.'

'Will I see a light go on, so I know you're safe?'

She promised to hold the apartment door open and switch on the hall light. Their stairwell bulbs had been replaced recently, after months of darkness, but they were blown again already. 'You'll see a glow right up there.' She pointed to the mansard roof.

'I'll wait. I'm afraid I have to work over this weekend, but I'll see you Monday. Same café?'

'All right.'

He waited for Alix to reach the top of the stairs and was rewarded with a wink of light. *The Times* wedged under his arm, he turned, sighing deeply. This was turning into a long, long day, but he didn't feel ready for his bed. He was doing everything wrong. Problem was, there were so many versions of Alix he wasn't ever sure which one he'd meet. He felt frustrated. The woman who had mesmerised him in the Deux Magots was not the minx whose ears he'd wanted to pull tonight.

In a narrow street off St-Germain he entered L'Arancia, a

restaurant in the vaults of an ancient building, favoured by Sorbonne University students and the staff of the *News Monitor*. He needed company. He didn't exactly *want* company, but knew he ought not to be alone. He nodded to the chef-patron, an Italian called Visconti whose wife, Basque-born Arantxa, looked harrowed under the candle sconces. Verrian guessed Arantxa knew already of the bombing of Guernica.

Derek Chelsey sat at his usual corner table, editorial secretary Beryl Theakston beside him in a velvet hat. Three male journalists made the rest of the party.

'Haviland, wail-fellow-hell-met!' Chelsey bawled over the chatter of diners. 'You've blown it with the langoustine tails, but we're having beef stew.'

As predicted, Chelsey had been quickly reinstated as editor of the French language *News Monitor*. Lord Calford had very soon tired of Verrian's sardonic style and put Chelsey back in his post.

'Arantxa my angel, get this man a chair. Hand that over – no desk work over dinner.' Chelsey held out his hand for Verrian's newspaper, snorting as he recognised the typeface. 'Reading the opposition? Suppose you can be forgiven this once. We were talking about it, "The Tragedy of Guernica". None of these bright sparks knew where Guernica was.' Chelsey damned his colleagues with a broad wave. 'They do now it's bombed to buggery. Just when we needed you in Spain, hey, Haviland?'

'It's awful, this war.' The braid shook on Beryl's hat. 'German pilots machine-gunning people as they run away. Beastly, wicked – pitting bombers against little children.'

'Not bombers,' Verrian corrected, 'fighter planes.' According to *The Times*' special correspondent who had witnessed the smoking aftermath, bombers had begun the attack on the Basque town, dropping high explosives on its centre. Market-place, churches, even a hospital hit. Fighter planes had come in after, flying low to pick off the terrified survivors with machine-gun fire. He added, 'It's not war, Beryl, it's murder. They even bombed farmsteads outside the town.'

The Times article had revived memories Verrian had thought were locked away forever. His mind kept filling with one persist-ent image: a vehicle opened like a tin can, the boil of amber as a fuel tank exploded. Being with Alix had briefly quelled those memories – he needed her. There, he'd admitted it. Without her, the only pacifier left was alcohol.

'Damn good copy though. Whose work?' Chelsey filled a fresh glass with wine from a jug.

'Steer, I'd say.'

'Don't like the *Monitor* getting scooped. The good stories are all in Spain.'

'And plenty of them. It's become brutally easy, opening hatches over towns. It happened yesterday when we were having tea.'

'Oh, don't, Mr Haviland.' Beryl shuddered.

Derek Chelsey charged everyone's glass. 'It's war, Haviland,' he slurred. 'If you feel you know so much about it, why are you here?'

Before finally falling into bed, Verrian wrote a letter to a friend in London who worked for the War Office. Alix's comments about the Comte de Charembourg's war service had piqued his curiosity. Had they really been comrades in arms, an aristocrat and her father? Even Alix seemed to have her doubts, and call it professional cynicism, but to Verrian it also felt unlikely. 'Both men apparently served in the London Rifles,' he wrote. 'All I can say of John Gower, to make him easier to trace, is that he married a foreign-born woman and had one child, a girl.' He sealed the letter, wrote a Whitehall, London, address on it and threw it aside for posting next day.

Then he lay on his bed and pondered Chelsey's parting shot. Why was he lingering in Paris and not sharing the suffering in Spain?

It was the end of an equally shattering day for Jean-Yves de Charembourg, who had just read about the fate of Guernica in his mistress's bedroom on Avenue Montaigne. Hearing a bathroom cabinet click shut, he put the newspaper aside, because politics was forbidden between himself and Hélène after dark. He'd acquitted himself poorly this evening, and though Hélène was philosophical, generous even, he felt diminished. The mind was a great rationaliser, while the body was an ungovernable child, unable to camouflage its needs and failings. After bumping into Alix – had it really been only that afternoon? It felt like a week – he'd emerged from Maison Javier emotionally skinned. She'd stood before him in her penitent's smock, accusing him of betraying her. *You lied.* If only he and Danielle Lutzman had told her the truth from the outset! If Danielle had allowed him to speak of his love for Mathilda, and the circumstances of their first meeting, a lifetime of fiction could have been avoided. But . . . to be fair, when Alix was small, lying had felt comfortable and right. Nobody had guessed she'd grow up with questions in her blood. She blamed him unfairly, but she could hardly turn on her grandmother. Old Danielle was all she had.

And his blackmailer had been in contact again. Ninette had taken the call that afternoon, writing down a garbled message. She'd brought the note to him as he walked through the door of his home, bewilderment in her face. Another five hundred thousand francs was to be placed behind the column in Notre-Dame-d'Auteuil.

'Papa?' she'd asked. 'Is it true you owe somebody all this money? He was talking about a murder in Kirchwiller . . . he said he knows who did it. He made me write down names of others who know.' She showed him. 'You and somebody called Lutzman, oh, and poor Mme Haupmann. What could Grandmother's old housekeeper know about anything? She's ancient! He said Grandmother knew all about it too, which is ridiculous. And then he said something that made my skin creep

– "Somebody pretty will get hurt" if you don't pay up . . . Not me, Papa?'

Thank God, he'd managed to convince Ninette it was a prank. The pig, his blackmailer, wanted the money by the end of the week.

Pay a blackmailer, keep a blackmailer. How, though? He was cleaned out and couldn't sell the rest of his bank shares without alerting the financial community to his cash problems. One had to be so careful of one's credit. He'd have to sell something physical. His car, the Panhard? But by the end of the week?

Hélène came into the bedroom bathed in a miasma of Chanel No. 5. 'Are you awake, Jeannot?' she whispered.

He pretended to be asleep.

Chapter Twenty-One

'Alix, Monsieur wants you in his studio, at once.'

Alix took the lift and, when she emerged, found herself following the aroma of coffee. It was early Monday morning and she'd left home without breakfast, eager not to repeat last week's crime of being late. The weekend had dragged because Verrian had been too busy to meet her. Or had he been holding himself aloof? She stopped a few feet from Javier's studio door, biting her lip. Why did Javier want her? Could she have been tailed to Godnosc's? Had someone seen her taking fabric samples? Or looked inside her shoe . . . Now she was being ridiculous. She knocked at the door.

Javier wasn't alone. His elderly Spanish maid was pouring coffee so strong it overpowered the house perfume, Ersa, which was sprayed in the room every morning. The maid indicated to Javier that his cup was full.

'*Si, si,*' he replied, not looking at it. Dozens of sample books were spread across his desk. Filled with sketches, fabric and embroidery samples, they were the working drawings of a professional lifetime. Javier's archive. 'Sit down,' he told Alix. 'Coffee?'

'Yes, please.' Alix sat, ramrod straight.

'Ana-Sofia —' Javier made a request in bullet-fast Spanish and the maid fetched another cup and a jug from which she poured hot frothy milk followed by coffee black as engine oil.

'When I was a boy,' Javier picked up his cup, 'my mother ran our island's laundry and my father made his living driving a cart down to the port. He would meet the boats, and bring the passengers up. A taxi service before there were motorcars. In the mornings, everybody was rushing and my elder sister, Abigaíl, would make coffee you could cut with a knife. It would be left on the side, but the milk was always boiling hot. I cannot change my habit, though the French shudder at it. Habit is the last to die.'

He slid a brown-paper parcel towards Alix. 'Open it.'

She used her scissors to cut the string. Paper fell open to reveal a tight coil of blond horsehair lace. 'Goodness, there must be ten miles of it.'

Javier smiled. 'I tried your lace on Oro — you will allow me to pay your grandmother for the sample — and you have solved the problem. Alix, I salute your instincts.'

'I suppose this was expensive?'

'Beyond expensive, but that hardly matters — there is something very particular I want you to do for me.' Javier opened a drawer and brought out a newspaper. 'My sisters Abigaíl and

Carmen are the only family I have now and they will not leave our island though I tried to bring them away. Nobody knows what will be the fate of Spanish Jews if the Fascists win this war, but my sisters will not come to France.' He put a cube of sugar into his coffee, gently so it wouldn't splash the precious books beside him. 'What would you say to them, Alix, if they were your sisters?'

'Um . . .' She'd known about the civil war in Spain, even before meeting Verrian, but had assumed the politics were too complex to attempt to understand. 'Do . . . um, do Spanish Jews have reason to be fearful?'

Javier blinked and she amended, 'I mean, are they in the same position as German Jews? My grandmother reads about their plight in *l'Humanité* and it upsets her.' She hoped Javier would extricate her, but he seemed content to wait while she unravelled her logic. 'Grandmother is terrified of Nazis . . . they're the German National Socialists—'

'I do know that, Alix.'

'Yes, sorry. She's afraid she'll wake up one day and find them in France. I don't like to think about it. You'll think me very stupid, but I always supposed politics stopped at a country's border, like language or signposts. It was that way in England.'

Javier nodded, growing serious. '*Petite*, you were seen wearing a very beautiful Lelong dress a few nights back. Is it one you bought yourself?'

A blush scorched her cheeks. She stammered that she'd

borrowed it from Mme Kilpin. No point in lying. Una Kilpin's presence at the Rose Noire gala opening would have been as obvious as their dresses. 'She invited me to call and opened her wardrobes for me.'

'How marvellous. Did you see many fake couture gowns among her hoard?'

'I – I don't know. But her boudoir has white carpet, thick as bearskin, and walls polished to such a sheen you can almost see your reflection in them. Her wardrobe doors are mirrors too. When she opened them . . .' Alix was sure Javier had used the word 'fake' to shock her. The last thing she wanted was to seem familiar with piracy – or, worse, end up confessing her involvement. 'I've never seen so much pale gold and biscuit in my life. You know, she buys clothes in other colours too, but never wears them?'

'Extraordinary. Who understands the very wealthy? The truth—' The maid returned with fresh coffee and Javier snapped at her to leave.

Alix eyed him in dismay. She'd never known him to be rude before. This was it. He was going to confront her about her stealing. She steadied herself, praying she'd come through it with dignity. 'The truth, Monsieur?'

'. . . is,' he continued, 'they're afraid of leaving their cats and the grave of our parents.'

'I beg your pardon?'

'Abigaíl and Carmen. They said they would come with me,

packed their trunks, gave away their food stores. The cart came, we loaded it, but at the last, they would not climb on board. I helped them put everything back inside and I left. I came home and drew sketches of dresses. My shows must go on, no?'

Alix nodded. 'Of course.'

'You spent your childhood in England, I believe?'

'I was born and went to school there.'

'Your father was English?'

'A Londoner, a railway engineer.'

'Ah,' Javier wagged a finger. 'You have inherited his wisdom. You can judge the load-bearing capacity of lace.'

As she laughed in relief, Javier pushed his newspaper towards her. *The Times*, dated 28th April, the one Verrian had been reading. 'Please, read me the column that describes a town destroyed by an air attack, I have not had the courage to read it yet myself. Say it quietly – I do not want Ana-Sofia to hear.'

As Alix read the eyewitness account of the destruction of a Basque town, she was conscious of breaking terrible news. Javier must have heard about the attacks but not the detail. '. . . *at 4.30 p.m. the church bell rang . . . and the population sought refuge in cellars . . . Five minutes later, a single German bomber circled over the town at low altitude, then dropped six heavy bombs . . . thenceforward the bombing grew in intensity, ceasing only with the approach of dusk.*' She glanced up. Javier was looking fixedly at a spot behind her head. '*The whole town . . . slowly and systematically pounded to pieces* . . . I'm sorry, Monsieur. So sorry.'

He thrust his hand towards her and she assumed he wanted her out and, courteous to the last, was trying to shake her hand. But what he wanted was the newspaper. He took it to a waste-paper basket and dropped it in. There he stood while Alix struggled for something to say. When he returned to his desk, a sheen on his brow betrayed his emotion but everything else was under rigid control. 'Thank you. Now, please return to the atelier.'

'To the workroom?' she gasped. 'You're sending me back there?'

He nodded. 'Last week you showed me how beautiful my gowns are when danced in candlelight. You breathed life into models from which all the vitality had been wrung. You and your charming friend danced a little magic.'

'You're angry?'

'You held up to me a mirror. But it has just become clear to me that this mid-season line cannot go ahead.'

'Not go ahead?' She got messily to her feet, her chair landing upside down on the floor.

'At this time of pain, of mourning, I cannot launch ball dresses. Not while Spain writhes and the free world looks the other way. It is all over.'

'Cancelled the whole mid-season collection? All those ball gowns? Just . . . cancelled?'

Alix slumped in her chair. Una's fury was making a bad

headache into an unbearable one. She whispered, 'He sent me back to the sewing bench.'

'Javier did?' Una snarled. 'What's got into the man? Nobody cancels a collection they've nearly completed unless they're dead or certified insane.'

'Mme Frankel is beyond words,' Alix said, kneading her temples. 'She thinks they'll go bankrupt. Mid-season sales tide a business over to the summer. All the drawings I've done for you –' she turned to Mabel Godnosc, who sat oozing shock, 'you'd better burn them.'

'Burn them?' Una paused inches from Alix. 'Chuck away money because your boss has mislaid his brain and you've mislaid your nerve? We're going to sell those damn dresses because we don't get paid otherwise.'

Mabel wailed, 'I've got half the Seventh Avenue wholesalers ready to supply Javier modes by the third week of May. They serve some of the classiest shops on Fifth and Sixth Avenue. Press agents are writing articles for the fashion pages. Clients are telephoning orders without seeing a thread. Hundreds of garments, sold on spec.'

'Then sail home and un-sell them,' Alix groaned.

'Sail? Shoot me from a cannon straight to Cape Cod, I'd be too late. Every sketch you've given me is either in production or waiting for the fabric to come off the looms.'

'What?' Suddenly afraid, Alix strode over to Mabel. A new scenario was presenting itself – that of Javier reading the New

York fashion pages, seeing his clothes on sale even though they'd never been outside his own studio. 'We agreed, nothing to be made until after the launch. You promised!' She'd assumed Javier's collection would seep into New York's Fifth Avenue stores towards the end of May, along with the stolen designs of every other major Parisian couturier. 'He'll know there's a thief . . . he'll call the police.'

'It's called risk and reward, sweetie,' Una said. 'It's why you're being paid.'

'I'm not being paid! And what danger is there for you?' Alix grasped Una's sleeve, ignoring the woman's yelp of protest. 'What's going to happen to you if we're found out? You'll still have your apartment, your car, your chauffeur, your thousand dresses and your maid. You can be brave because you've nothing to lose.'

Una wriggled free, furiously smoothing her sleeve.

'You haven't got manufacturers to sue you, like Mme Godnosc.' Alix continued, 'You don't work all day for a pittance. You don't have an arthritic grandmother sitting in a cold flat, or little sisters catching croup!'

Una opened her mouth to reply, but Alix beat her to it. 'You don't have children, you don't even have a cat. You're a spoiled, greedy, stupid woman who steals the work of a genius because she failed in the same business. It's not money for you, it's . . .' if there was a word that fitted Una Kilpin's motives Alix couldn't find it so she substituted, 'prostitution.'

'Prostitution?'

'And it's not my fault the Germans bombed Javier's country!'

Una attempted a scathing laugh, but something harsher came out. 'I could say a few fine words to you on the subject of being a tease, Alix Gower, but I won't. Just this: you are not alone in having dreams, nor wants and needs.'

'Hush, ladies,' Mabel pleaded, 'or you'll bring them up from downstairs.'

Una replied icily, 'Let's decide – at a modest volume – how we pull something out of the wreckage Alix has sprung on us.'

'We call it off,' Alix said. 'Everything copied from Javier, everything in production in New York, must be destroyed.' She spoke with all the calm authority she could muster. 'Javier has already written to the press, announcing the cancellation. If we go ahead with a copied collection – well, we might as well print "Wanted" posters with our faces on them and stick them up all over Paris.'

'Cut and run?' Una had regained the better part of her composure, though crossed arms diminished the full effect. 'Impossible. What about medicines for your poor grandmother? What about Paul, sinking deeper by the day? You should instead be asking what will get the ladies of New York queuing ten blocks for our Javier copies.'

'How about, "Because nobody else will get them now"?' Mabel suggested. 'Exclusivity.'

Alix stamped her foot. It was that or scream. 'The game's

up! If I get found out, I'll be sacked at the very least. For you, Mabel, it'll be worse. The police will come.' Alix was desperate to finish this and get away, see if Verrian was waiting or if her impulsive words about sitting naked for Bonnet had killed his interest. But she couldn't go until she'd got these women to understand the danger they were all in.

Una had been tossing a pencil in the air and it dropped with a clatter. 'Alix, take us through your meeting with Javier again. He may just be having a creative tantrum and tomorrow the collection will be on again.'

Alix closed her eyes. 'He's isn't having a tantrum; he's grieving. He asked me to read him an article from *The Times*.' She related the details of the bombing of Guernica and Mabel Godnosc said, 'Dear God,' and even Una looked at the ground. 'His homeland is dying and he feels he should be fighting, not making clothes.' She described how, the previous week, she'd sought to dispel his growing depression. 'I made him see his dresses move with dance and music.'

Una's head lifted. 'You danced for him?'

'I had the mannequins brought up and they all danced, one by one, with Paul—'

'You danced with Paul? My Paul?'

'The tango.' Alix met the tempest in Una's eyes and thought, *You think you own everyone. Well, you don't. Paul will never look into your eyes the way he looked into mine.* 'We danced to "Mi Buenos Aires Querido", our bodies fused in candlelight.'

'Spare me the gush.'

'How did Javier react?' Mabel Godnosc sat forward.

'He told me I had revealed to him the allure of his clothes as nobody else had ever done before.'

'And was so impressed,' Una came back, 'he smacked you on the tush and sent you back to buttonhole duties. Honey, you served up your sex appeal to the wrong guy.'

Mrs Godnosc let out a banshee shriek. 'That's it! Oh, shut up,' she snapped as Alix began a riposte. 'That's the angle; that's what will sell Javier. It's delicious. It's, pardon me, orgasmic. I need to ring my press agent.'

'What? No!' Alix shrilled. 'I told you, that collection mustn't get into the shops. If you want to stay out of jail, it mustn't get into the shops.'

'Sure, sure, whatever you say.' Mrs Godnosc scuttled to the door. 'Go home, both of you. I've had enough.'

Verrian waved from his regular table at the café, white shirt-sleeves glowing orange in the sodium light. 'You're dragging a leg, Alix. Long day?'

She hid her joy at seeing him, offering him a reserved smile instead.

'You look worn out. Shall I take you home?' he asked. Some kind of klaxon battle was going on behind him at the junction with Place de la Concorde. 'If I ruled Paris, I'd make car horns illegal.'

'Then how would pedestrians know they were about to be hit?' she replied, sitting down beside him.

'Good point.' He looked at his watch. 'Shall we go somewhere less exposed?'

'Please. I don't have to be home early because it's Mémé's cards night. She takes a cake to a café across the road and all the old ladies play till eleven or so.'

'I'll take you to dinner. And you look fine,' noticing her quick downward glance.

As Alix got up from her café chair on the Champs-Elysées, Jean-Yves sat down in the apartment in St-Sulpice. Danielle had answered his knock, inviting him into the living room, but he'd indicated a chair by a hall table. His heart objected to six flights and he needed to get his breath back. Anyway, it was clear that Danielle was about to go out. She was wearing short boots and a black hat like a cottage loaf trimmed with netting. There was a basket by the door with a cake tin and spectacle case. 'I won't keep you,' he began.

'Only going over the street. How can I help?'

He took a steadying breath. 'On Friday, one of my daughters took a telephone call from my blackmailer demanding more money. Yes, yes, I know what you told me. I should have listened to your advice. But . . .' a deep breath, 'he knows for certain what happened in Kirchwiller. He knows details that only you and I should know. He had my daughter write down names including that of my mother and her old housekeeper, Célie Haupmann. Madame, who but you or I could know such intimate facts about your husband's death?'

She leaned against the wall, not answering.

He waited, thinking silence might jog her memory, occupying himself by picking up a framed photograph from the table. A wedding picture, which he could date precisely. John and Mathilda, married 18th December 1915. The groom's hair was cropped and he wore khaki uniform. The bride wore a dress narrow to the ankle, showing a glimpse of white stocking and T-bar shoes. Her toes must have been icy because there was snow on the ground. Snow on the chapel roof behind them. The bride's condition would explain the large spray of artificial flowers held over her stomach. And perhaps the groom's tense smile.

'They married before John sailed for France,' Danielle said, looking over his shoulder to see what held his attention. 'I was furious, my daughter in the family way, her nursing career cut short. My shame spoiled their day. He did his best, John Gower. Did the right thing. If I had known my poor girl would be dead so soon . . .'

A smaller picture had been knocked on to its face. Jean-Yves picked it up and emotion rammed him – Mathilda in the uniform of a VAD, Voluntary Aid Detachment nurse. Her face under her white cap was solemn, but nothing could dim that roguish twinkle in her eye. Her starched pinafore bore a cross and it took him back to his own weeks in a casualty clearing station in France. 1915, summer. He'd been stunned by shell-fire, lungs punctured, and had no idea how long he'd lain on the ground, or how much time he'd spent in the field hospital. But he remembered the nurses. 'We loved those girls,' he said. 'You'd lie in bed, waiting for one to walk past. If she stopped and brought you water or puffed up your pillow, you felt the luckiest man alive. A strange place for love to blossom.' He tried to put the small photograph back, but his fingers were shaking.

Danielle said, 'The little thing at the back . . . what's it called? Hinge. It's broken.' She took the picture from him. 'I think now I must go.'

'I spoke to Alix at Maison Javier the other day.'

'I begged her not to work there.'

'She asked questions about her father, her mother, how well I knew them. Other times she's wanted to know all about her grandfather. She's a grown woman, Madame, and it's time to tell her the truth.'

'Never!' Danielle rasped. 'Her mother died, but he –' she pointed at John Gower in his uniform – 'lived long enough to fill her head with fantasies. He would tell her she was his princess. Princess, indeed! I would tell him, it's no kindness spinning dreams to a girl born in the gutter.'

Jean-Yves flared at the oblique accusation. 'Why should Alix have been born in the gutter? Damn you, Danielle Lutzman, I followed you to London to take care of you. You could have had anything you wanted, including a decent home and an obstetrician for your daughter. Mathilda didn't have to die in childbirth.'

'Enough.'

'I sent you cheques which you ripped up.'

'I had no bank account.'

'Bone-headed false pride. You let your loved ones die rather than take help from me.'

Her furious gaze expanded behind her demi-veil. 'I did what you asked. Told lies to the police in Kirchwiller, left my home for a strange country, a new language. I lost my only child. You blame me? You, who took everything I loved from me? You think I will come to you for money? Only when I have no choice, and then with disgust at myself.'

She hobbled to the door, forgetting her basket. He picked it up and followed her, pulling the door behind him. Though fury hung in the air between them, he took her arm. Plunge down these stairs and she'd break every bone. They descended in rhythm, as bound together now as ever. On the ground floor, a savoury smell met them.

'Hare in red wine,' he said.

'The concierge is having dinner with her son. She'll have used our coal to cook it.'

Jean-Yves took the olive branch. They could not risk parting as enemies. 'You'll keep your door locked, Madame?'

'Always. Will you pay that scum who threatens you?'

'I have to. I can't risk –' he nearly said, *Alix being hurt again*, remembering at the last moment that Danielle knew nothing of the indignity her granddaughter had suffered in Montmartre.

'I love her, Madame. I've only ever wanted her to be happy.'

'Then don't speak of her grandfather's death, or your wartime romance with my daughter. Why make Alix witness to shameful events that will fade?'

'Fade?' he sighed. 'When you and I die – is that what you mean?'

'And when old Célie Haupmann goes too. Isn't she even older than I am? She must be one of the last witnesses of that time. After all, she was your mother's go-between, taking messages between your castle and me in the prison.' Danielle laughed without humour. 'How she resented being put to work to help one such as me. She made sure everyone knew she was only doing it to oblige her mistress in an act of charity.'

'We'll all go in the end, and our sorry sins will go with us.'

Danielle made a 'tsk' sound. 'Life is never so tidy. But let us stay quiet so Alix can live her life free of our mistakes.'

'I don't think I've ever eaten so much. Arantxa is a wonderful cook.' Good food and Verrian's company had charmed away Alix's headache.

'It's her husband in the kitchen.'

'Lucky woman.'

They were drinking coffee, between them a plate of irresistible *oreillettes*, vanilla fritters sprinkled with sugar. They were seated in a corner niche of L'Arancia, their seclusion lit only by a red candle that was sinking into waxy tendrils. Verrian reached across and stole a fresh one from the table next to them, lighting it in the stammering flame. 'Alix, I'm not sure there's a good time to say this, but I have to tell you what I know about your grandfather –'

'You're going to tell me he was murdered.' She took an *oreillette* and bit off the lobe.

He made a noise in his throat. 'Any reason you didn't mention that before?'

'Would *you* shout about it?' She sent an enquiring look at him through the candlelight, not wanting to be accused again of game playing. 'Bonnet told me that grandpapa was hit over the head, in his studio.'

'Bonnet knew who did it?'

'They were never caught.'

'They?'

'Pedlars, vagabonds, whatever you call them. They would work in twos, a boy and a woman. The woman would have strings of kitchenware around her neck to give her an excuse to knock on doors. While she showed her wares to the mistress of the house, the boy would slip upstairs to steal valuables. Afterwards they'd melt into the forest. Kirchwiller's forest is crossed by paths only hunters and tinkers know about.'

Verrian frowned. 'That's what the authorities thought? Passing thieves?'

'It's what Bonnet says. He was there.' Verrian's gaze jumped to hers. 'Nearby,' she amended, 'in his lodgings. Mémé ran to fetch him after she found grandfather's body. Bonnet was with her when she was taken away by the police.' Seeing Verrian's eyes widen, she added hastily, 'It was a dreadful mix-up, some slow-witted policeman got suspicious because Mémé had blood on her.'

'Your grandfather's blood?'

'She'd tried to revive him and staunch the wound. When my grandmother's hysterical, she doesn't make much sense and she was led away. The authorities wouldn't let Bonnet see her, so he went to the comte for help. Mme de Charembourg, the comte's mother, came to the jail in her furs and demanded to see the chief inspector. Back then, local aristocrats had power.'

'She sounds like a good woman.'

'She saw a miscarriage of justice. She made sure Mémé had food and warm clothes and had her freed after a few days. Nobody ever really thought she was guilty. Except her. Sometimes I hear her murmuring that it was her fault.'

'And the vagabonds . . . you said, "Never caught."'

'No.' Stories about her life always fizzled out, Alix reflected.

'So a boy killed your grandfather. One hard-bitten lad.' Verrian took her hands and lifted them into the candle's aura. She gasped as something caught her eye, driving thoughts of murder and vagabonds from her mind.

Verrian's skin glowed in the flame, the hairs on his wrists bronze from exposure to the sun. Faded scars flecked the backs of his hands and the third finger of his left hand bore the ghost of a ring. He had removed a wedding ring for Paris.

He must have noticed her sudden distance, her shock, because he called for the bill. They walked the short distance to St-Sulpice. Outside her building, Verrian cupped her face and she felt an energy moving through him. He groaned softly, bending his head towards her. A chaste touch until she reached up and stroked his neck, finding the islets of bone under the tapering ends of his hair. 'Verrian, are you married?'

His response was there beneath her fingertips. A flinch. 'I was, briefly.'

'What is her name?'

'No, Alix.' And then his mouth was on hers, demanding and hard. She tasted wine and coffee and felt textures that were becoming familiar – chin and jaw with its evening roughness, the lock of hair that fell over his brow and tickled the bridge of her nose. The tang of cologne and tobacco and recently washed cotton. All this, and another ingredient. As she opened her lips and let him deepen the kiss, she felt something break inside him. He'd done this before, caught fire, but this time he was demanding something back. Flirting was over, his body told her.

'If your grandmother were not waiting, would you come to a hotel with me?'

Would she? She hesitated. She knew Mémé would be

horrified by Verrian's question and Alix's slowness to answer. 'I don't know.'

'I do. I'll see you inside.'

'You're angry. I'm sorry . . . I'll go in by myself.'

'Don't be ridiculous.' He caught her hand, but there was no caress, no tenderness any more. *He despises my inexperience*, she thought. *He mixes with society women, female journalists and photographers who'd laugh at me because I've never been with a man. And he's been married.*

The door to the lobby was on the latch. The concierge was growing careless, she thought, or Mémé had forgotten to close the door behind her. 'Don't come up,' she said. 'My grandmother may be in her dressing gown and I'd rather introduce you to her in daylight, properly.' *If you want to see me again*, she tagged on silently.

'I'll wait outside until I see the light,' said Verrian.

By the time Alix reached her level she was in darkness, the landing lights having failed again. One day of light, then black again. *Rather like life*, she thought to herself. She had her apartment key ready, but as she nudged it against the lock, the door creaked open. The hallway of her flat was dark.

'Mémé?' she called softly. She sniffed. An acrid smell. Burnt milk. Mémé often made herself hot cinnamon milk at bedtime. Maybe she'd left the pan on, tired from her card game. Tipsy, even. Alix reached for the light switch, feeling for the place where the wallpaper was smooth through rubbing. The click of an interior door made her pause. 'Mémé? I sorry I'm late, I—'

Hurried footsteps were the only reply. And harsh breathing.

She thought, *That's not Mémé*. A scream stuck in her throat as a body rammed into her, knocking her down. Before she could snatch a breath, a hand pressed down on her mouth. It tasted of sweat, grime. Whoever he was, he stank of garlic and tobacco and something else. Something putrid. And he had a woollen jumper on, a rough one which seemed to engulf his face. Then detail dissolved – he was pushing a slimy rag into her mouth while holding her nose.

Chapter Twenty-Two

She used her only weapon.

Her scissors, on their ribbon. Pulled them free and jabbed. She must have hit a belt buckle or something because they bounced away. He grunted, called her a filthy bitch. But she'd forced a gap between them, space enough to bring up her knee, hard. Her attacker pulled a sharp inbreath. She had another go with the scissors, but he caught them, pulling the ribbon tight and twisting it until she was choking. That was when she felt a knife against her neck. The blade bit and a hot trickle rolled towards her shoulder. Same blade, same smell, same attacker as at Bonnet's studio. Dragging the rag from her mouth, she screamed.

The apartment door crashed open and she heard her name shouted. The pressure on her neck was released. She curled into a ball, because whoever was shouting had run into her, and was treading on her hair, her shoulder. Alix rolled tight as a struggle took place above her head. She tried to shout, 'Knife!' but a boot glanced off her jaw. Men swore and grunted. She heard the squeak of soles on lino then an agonised, 'Bloody hell.'

He switched on the light and his heart missed a beat as he saw Alix sprawled, a chair on top of her and her head underneath a side table. Framed photographs lay shattered on the lino. The apartment door was open. Verrian could hear the attacker's frantic escape – two flights down by now. Too risky to chase, he might have an accomplice. Alix tried to lever herself up. One side of her skirt was hiked up and she tugged at it fiercely.

Verrian reached out a hand. 'You're cut on the neck. Let me see.'

'It's not deep. I must go find Mémé – God, Verrian, you've got blood on your shirt . . . it's everywhere.'

'He slashed my hand.' Between the middle and index fingers of his left hand, to be precise. He was wearing a fetching glove of crimson which, he realised now the initial shock had worn off, was exquisitely painful.

Alix took his wrist. 'We need to staunch that. There's bandage in the kitchen cupboard. Where *is* Mémé? I wonder if she's still at her card party.'

They didn't bother turning on the living-room lights because the kitchen door was open and a halo of gas flame lit the way. In the kitchen they found chaos. And Mémé.

*

She was crumpled on the floor and at first Verrian thought the scarlet beneath her head was a scarf. Then reality reached him. Her scalp was split open, her clothes awry as if she'd put up a struggle. The floor was strewn with broken crockery. A pan containing scorched milk explained the stench. He turned off the gas flame as Alix sank down with a keening sound that went straight to his soul.

'She's dead.'

Crouching by her, he pressed fingers to the thin skin beneath the old woman's ear. A faint pulse. 'She's alive. Is there a telephone in the building?' Alix shook her head. Shock was speeding through her like a drug and he wasn't surprised when she grabbed him to keep herself from collapsing. 'Alix – nearest restaurant with a telephone.'

'Chez . . . Chez Jacques,' she stammered, 'opposite, down a little towards . . . I can't remember.'

'I'll find it. Can you stay here alone?'

The question became redundant as neighbours from other floors appeared all at once, competing to describe the shouts and thumps they'd heard earlier. At first Verrian wanted to ask what the hell had stopped them coming upstairs, but they were all elderly females, he realised. A couple of them stared suspiciously at his bloody hand, until a cry from behind caught their attention.

'*Mon Dieu*, look at this room. Ransacked!'

The living-room light revealed chairs pushed over, drawers

pulled out, Mémé's sewing box upended. Paintings were piled in the middle of the floor. Verrian turned the top one over, a portrait of a smiling girl. It seemed undamaged.

He heard a neighbour sputter, 'We don't have to look far to know who did it. Those vermin across the courtyard – stands to reason. Madame,' the woman said to the concierge, 'you should send your son to call the police.'

Instead Verrian sent the concierge to Chez Jacques to telephone for an ambulance. He sent a couple of the others for towels and warm water and told the remaining gaggle to go. Alix pulled herself out of her stupor and put a folded towel under Danielle's head. After checking her pulse again and placing his coat over the old lady, Verrian allowed Alix to bandage his hand.

'They'll take her to the Lariboisière hospital,' he said. 'She's not bleeding any more, which is a good sign.' But neither was she moving, or responsive.

'It was the same man who attacked me before. He must have been waiting for me,' Alix whispered. 'Why wasn't I here?'

As the answer to that was obvious, Verrian answered a different question. 'Sometimes robberies turn violent, if the perpetrator is disturbed. Your grandmother may not have realised he was in the flat. Did you see anything of the man?'

'It was pitch dark. But I felt him. He had big boots . . . He could be a fisherman or a hunter.'

'Go on.'

'His sweater was the sort men wear outdoors to protect them from the rain. I know it was the same man as before; I knew that sweater. Pulled up over his face.' She started crying again. 'I should never have left her so late. It's my fault.'

An ambulance came and Mémé was stretchered away. One of the ambulance men commented on the whiff of alcohol on the old lady's breath. 'Overbalanced, maybe?'

'She had a night out, playing cards,' Alix told them. 'She wasn't drunk, if that's what you're saying.'

Police arrived and Mme Rey came in their wake, her son Fernand with her. The son eyed Mémé's workbox and the oil paintings with beady interest. Seeing it, Verrian made a show of counting the paintings in front of the policemen. Turning around, he saw Mme Rey go into the kitchen, and was too late to stop her washing the black iron skillet he'd mentally labelled as the likely weapon.

'I'm wondering if Mme Lutzman didn't trip and fall,' the concierge said as Verrian filled the doorway. 'This lino's up all over the place. I've already caught my heel in it.'

Verrian answered, 'Then a word to the landlord would be in order. Madame, would your son fit a new lightbulb in the stairwell? The ambulance men had to find their way in the pitch dark.'

'Fernand put a bulb in this morning,' Mme Rey insisted.

'Well, it's blown or blown away.'

The policemen glanced around each room. One of them

311

asked about Verrian's bloodstained hand while looking covertly at Alix, who was sobbing as she rehung the paintings. *They're putting it down as a domestic squabble*, Verrian realised. *They think it's a madhouse and we're all drunk.*

One of the policemen secured a taxi and Verrian sat with Alix in the back. At the hospital, a nurse cleaned and re-bound his hand, tutting about lovers' tiffs.

Later he took Alix to his own lodgings, giving Rosa Konstantiva the bare bones of the drama. Rosa, who'd been on the point of retiring, immediately offered to fetch blankets and make up a bed.

'She won't mind kipping down on the sofa?'

Alix could have his room, he said. He'd find a bed elsewhere. He had no qualms about passing Alix into Rosa's care. Rosa's bedrock was kindness and she came from a background which absorbed stray people and orphaned kittens without fuss.

He went next door to Bonnet's and found the front door ajar. Climbing the stairs in darkness, he entered a studio and saw a man blocking shapes on to a canvas with feverish strokes. Bonnet – working by the light of a pair of hurricane lamps. Unaware of interruption, the artist worked on, whistling harshly through his beard. Verrian tapped on the wall and said, 'Good evening.'

Bonnet's arm froze mid-movement.

Verrian let the door whine shut. 'I'm Haviland, your neighbour and Alix's friend. There's something you need to know.'

He left Bonnet's at 2 a.m. Montmartre was still busy, still lit, cabaret customers oozing out of open doors. *No wonder this quarter looks jaded*, Verrian thought. *It never gets any rest*. He hailed a taxi and told the driver, 'Boccador, corner of Trémoille.' He could have gone to the Polonaise and slept in a bed the size of Wales, or gone back to Laurentin's and asked for his old room, but he couldn't face servility or bonhomie. He leaned against the taxi's headrest and let the pulse of his injured hand fill his brain.

He'd given Bonnet the news of Danielle Lutzman and watched the man stagger. Verrian had steered him to an armchair, removing an empty tobacco tin full of cigarette butts first. The butts looked as if they'd been salvaged from bars – some had lipstick on. Bonnet must really be down on his luck.

The man had groaned, 'I have to finish tonight.'

Realising Bonnet meant his canvas, Verrian wondered, *You can think of painting after what I've told you?* 'Is it a commission?'

'It's money, my friend. Money I need. Danielle, is she dying?'

'I'm not a doctor. It was a hard blow . . . two actually.'

'Two blows. How hard?'

'Alix can tell you tomorrow. She's going to the hospital first thing, to talk with the surgeon.'

'Poor, poor Alix. How is she?'

'Appalled, distressed. Feels it's her fault.'

'No.' Bonnet's lips drew back. 'It's your fault. Where the hell were you when this happened?'

313

'At ground level, waiting to see a light go on. Thank God I was.'

Bonnet continued peppering him with questions. Might Danielle describe her attacker? Was she, you know . . . humiliated in any way? He finished with, 'The man who did it, did he leave footprints?'

'Not that I saw. By the time fifteen people had piled in and out, traces were gone.'

Bonnet hunched over, muttering about the world's evil. '*Ma pauvre chou*, I will look after her. As I did for Danielle and Mathilda, yes, I will go to the hospital and sit with her. Yes, Bonnet will do that. It was those vagabonds in the courtyard. Filthy fungus, seeping through the cracks.'

Verrian felt surprise. Alix's neighbours had spooned out similar bigotry, but Bonnet? He'd always assumed artists took a broader view of the world. 'I shall take Alix to the hospital tomorrow,' he said as Bonnet went to a bench and rootled among the jars.

'Leave Alix to me.' Bonnet brought a decanter and poured two measures of amber spirit, handing one to Verrian. 'Truth is,' he continued after a mouthful, 'I'm the only male in Alix's life who won't break her heart.' He beckoned Verrian to a corner of the studio and uncovered a large painting. It was done with a flourish, perhaps to stop the sailcloth cover catching the paintwork underneath. Verrian's insides jerked.

Alix, naked. This was the picture she'd teased him about and thoughts of it had kept him awake much of the weekend. His first impression was that Bonnet was indeed a master of flesh. His second impression was that he'd lost two nights' sleep for no reason.

Paris would not feast its eyes on Alix Gower's unveiled sensuality. Bonnet seemed as much interested in the articulation of her joints as he was in goblet-shaped breasts, long thighs, the hint of shadow between. Her hair hung across her face, framing a gaze that seemed locked on some faraway world.

Behind him Bonnet murmured, 'Her heart was broken at birth. Broken again when her father died before she was old enough to understand what "death" was. Then I daresay it was broken at school by the first nasty girl to call her a Hun or a Jew. Broken by that bastard de Charembourg who picks her up and puts her down again like a salt pot. Now there's Javier who, if one is to believe Alix, makes angels' robes with scissors of gold . . . he'll break her. Danielle beaten – dear God. But I will care for Alix. Who else is there? You left her too, Haviland. Gave her your card like an insurance salesman and walked away. If you have a thread of decency, you'll do that again. Back off.'

Verrian let himself into Calford Press. Three tries at getting his key into the lock because he was rocking on his feet with blood loss. On the first floor he used a second key to open Lord Calford's private office. He filled a long glass from a soda siphon, his throat parched from Bonnet's cognac.

Turning on the reading lamp, he collapsed into a leather chair and thought, *I hate that bastard because he's right. If Alix is heartbroken, I'm hardly the man to mend her.* He took the same photograph he always kept in his wallet and said to the girl in the Basque beret, 'I failed you too, Maria-Pilar. My poor wife. I let you go into danger and couldn't pull you out of it.'

He woke with a start to the sound of a telephone ringing. Once he'd worked out where he was, he followed the noise down to the reception desk, squinting at his watch as he went. It was six in the morning. What day was it . . . Monday? No, Tuesday. 'Hello? *News Monitor*?'

A babble of Spanish made his heart leap and he said, unthinking, 'Maria-Pilar?'

'*Maria no soy. Escucheme*—' A woman, speaking so fast he couldn't make out a word.

'Señora, whoa, please. Your name, slowly.' She gave it and he repeated, 'García . . .' Señora García y Rojas was his friend Miguel's wife. 'Where are you calling from? Where is Miguel?'

'No Miguel!' she shouted. She was in France, she said. In Marseille on the coast, penniless, alone but for her little son who cried from hunger. No one to turn to except Verrian. He must help her, if he had a heart, and if he did not she would throw herself and her son into the docks to drown.

*

316

Arriving at Le Bourget aerodrome in the sharp light of early morning, Verrian found his friend Ron Phipps drinking coffee and stuffing down a croque-monsieur in the pilots' mess. It was Phipps who'd rescued him at Albacete after his escape from the Madrid police. Phipps made a precarious living flying between London and the Spanish war zone, picking up rolls of film from journalists who had no way of developing their pictures themselves.

'You want me to take you to Marseille?' Phipps scratched his head once Verrian had explained his dilemma. '*Can* be done, but I won't be taking off for several hours and I prefer to get over the bumps –' his name for the Pyrenean mountains – 'at night, while the buggers with anti-aircraft guns are asleep. Don't want to run into any Luftwaffe either. We always take a line over Pamplona. We know the landmarks, d'you see?'

By 'we', Verrian presumed Phipps meant himself and his beloved six-seater Avro Anson, currently waiting to be refuelled for the six-hundred-miles to Madrid. But, promised another refuel, his good nature firmly leaned on, Phipps finally agreed to land Verrian at Marseille and fly on over Andorra. They talked of Spanish adventures for a while, but with a long day and night in prospect, they stretched out on the mess chairs and slept.

They touched down at Marseille-Marignane at sunset that same day, Tuesday, 4th May. Verrian gave Phipps most of the French francs in his wallet on the understanding his friend would come back in two days to pick up four passengers.

'Four?'

'A woman, a boy, the woman's husband – God willing – and myself. You can tip me out in Paris, then take the others to Croydon and put them in a cab to London.' Where Jack could emerge from his ivory tower and sort them out with visas. Now all he had to do was find a Spanish refugee and child in the chaos of the Marseille docks.

It took him six hours. From her doorway in a malodorous tenement, Celestia García y Rojas stared at Verrian before bursting into tears. Her cotton frock was a rag, a fitting companion to the draggled cardigan over her shoulders. Legs and feet were bare, her hair tied in a lank ponytail. At first he thought he'd got the wrong woman. Was this really the sophisticate he'd met two or three times in Madrid back in the days when couples still entertained? He asked tentatively, 'Where's Miguel?'

'Not here.' She used her cardigan sleeve to stifle her sobs until a child's wail of misery behind her claimed her attention.

Verrian followed her into a filthy room furnished with a mattress and two crates. No food, so he went out again foraging and found a café willing to fill a box with brioche and bread and lend a jug of coffee. They ate in silence at first, then Celestia began to talk. She told him that after his punishment shooting, Miguel had been taken to a prison on the outskirts of Madrid. The authorities had allowed no contact. Then, a couple of weeks later he'd been as abruptly released. All three of them had been given safe-conduct passes into France and some money so they could take a South America-bound ship here at Marseille. Crossing into France was easier than getting through a war zone to one of Spain's Atlantic ports, they'd been advised.

Thus far, Verrian thought, Jack had delivered.

Though Miguel was feverish from his wounds, he'd begun the journey in good spirits. Then, fifty miles from the border, he refused to go further, saying he would not leave Spain as a coward. He would go to his mother's native Basque country and fight there for the People's Army – fight for an independent Pais Vasco. Celestia and the child should go to Marseille, he said, and use their tickets. He would join them later.

'I knew we'd never see him again if we went to South America,' Celestia explained in her quick Castilian Spanish. So, agreeing to stay together, they'd found an abandoned truck which Celestia drove north on bomb-pitted roads, knowing every corner might conceal an ambush, every cloud a fighter plane. Miguel had lain in the back, dosed with aspirin, sweating and moaning. At the border with the Basque country, the truck's engine blew up. 'We begged lifts in farmers' trucks and in a few days arrived at the place where Miguel was born.'

Guernica.

By this time Miguel's fever was raging and he was admitted into the town's hospital. Celestia spent her last pesetas on a cheap hotel room. The next afternoon, the Condor Legion came.

They finished their breakfast. Celestia, who'd watched Verrian struggle with his injured hand, helped him take off the stiff bandage. The little boy, Pepe, watched silently, flinching neither at the sight of the bloody dressing nor the jagged fissure beneath.

'You're injured in the same place as Miguel,' Celestia told Verrian. 'They shot off two fingers of his left hand. The hand that held the censor's stamp. They said he approved journalists' lies.'

'I was there, Señora.'

She flung a strand of hair off her face, then fetched a road-stained bag and extracted a handkerchief, which she tore into strips for fresh bandage. 'This is a sign, I think. You, same place, same hand.'

'Except I'm right-handed.'

She brushed this aside and moved on, to another thought – 'The girls downstairs gave me food and this.' She tugged at the limp cardigan. 'Strange, I need to come to a slum to find kindness. When I ran to the hospital in Guernica to search for Miguel, the planes were low overhead. I had left Pepe alone in the hotel. One plane swooped so low over my head I could see the . . .' She waved a hand, trying to summon the words.

'The rivets? The panels?'

'Guns, spitting white fire into the street. Everyone was dying – old ladies, a nun, even the dogs. They were shooting everything. *Infierno*.' Hell. 'The noise . . .' She clapped her hands to her ears, either to show him or because she was reliving it. 'I couldn't go forward, I couldn't get back to Pepe. Everything was smoke and fire, people dying on the ground . . . in cellars, in the shelters. And the hospital. I howled for my husband because I knew he was dead. I turned my back to it and went to find my child.'

She sobbed for several long minutes. Verrian stared at his hand, knowing how it felt to close your eyes and re-experience a cinematic show of your worst nightmares. He couldn't enter hers, but his was a khaki-green vehicle engulfed in a ball of heat no human could penetrate. And from its heart, screaming.

He asked how she'd reached Marseille, a journey of more than three hundred miles. She'd got a lift to Pamplona with a truckload of freedom fighters, she said. Then somebody flagged down a French lorry heading for Marseille. She'd been determined to get on that boat for Venezuela. Only, presenting herself at the docks, she'd learned that the boat had sailed.

'I prayed to Our Lady – please help. I met a woman downstairs who works in a big house some mornings. She goes at dawn to do the laundry and she let me in when her mistress was still in bed. I was allowed one telephone call. I prayed as I dialled that you would still be in Paris, that you would come.'

He nodded. 'Señora, do you have Miguel's papers? His travel permits, his passport?'

Her eyes flashed as she understood. 'You love Spain that much, Señor?'

'I don't think I do. Not now. But I loved . . .' He cleared his throat. 'There's a song we used to sing, "Lady of Spain". I loved a lady of Spain.'

'What was her name?'

'Mrs Haviland, briefly.'

On the evening of 6th May, he settled Celestia and Pepe in the Avro Anson's cabin. Pepe wore a new corduroy suit and jersey. Verrian had bought Celestia a coat, hat, gloves and decent shoes. It wasn't charity; it was polishing them up because he felt a refugee must be able to look a new country squarely in the eye. She'd refused to go to London. 'I speak English so badly, and England is heathen, no?' She would stay in Paris. Paris had Catholic churches. Paris felt closer to Spain.

Ron Phipps, sheepskin jacket hanging loose, grinned under his flying helmet and said in a side whisper, 'Nice-looking lass. Sad story?'

'Awful. Phipps, stay with them at Le Bourget until they're safely in a taxi.' He handed his friend a letter. It was for Laurentin, the hotel owner who'd seen Verrian through his fever, and it contained the last high-denomination note from Verrian's wallet. The money would cover a couple of weeks' stay for Celestia and Pepe. The letter asked Laurentin to apply to 'Mme Theakston at the *News Monitor*' for further funds to cover their accommodation until he returned. If he returned. Verrian handed over a second letter. 'Give this to Beryl Theakston in person,' he told Phipps. 'She must take this one to Maison Javier, the fashion house. It's for Alix Gower – tall, dark-haired, slim. Got it?'

Phipps squinted at the letters, then at Verrian. 'You're coming back to Paris with me, aren't you?'

'No.'

Then Phipps really looked at him, taking note of the trench coat Verrian had slung on top of his suitcase. Then at Verrian's growth of beard. 'What's occurring, old chap?'

'I'm going back.'

'To Paris? Absolutely.'

'Into Spain.'

'Hang on.' Phipps glanced up at the Avro's cabin, where a small face peered out. 'You got chucked out, remember? Re-entry strictly denied. Blotted the old copybook.'

'I'm not going back as a journalist. I'm joining the International Brigades. I'm going to fight.'

Phipps's good-natured face sagged. 'Listen, the French won't let you across. They're sending all deluded do-gooders back at the border, won't have their country used as a military recruiting office. Bloody hell, Verrian, get on board.'

'I won't get stopped.' Verrian took a passport from his pocket, flipping it open at the bearer's photograph. The face was part-obscured by the official stamp of Pais Vasco, Basque region, and showed a man maybe five years older than Verrian. Sculpted cheeks and a beard gave the air of a scholar.

Phipps groaned in comprehension. 'You're going to fight as Miguel Rojas Ibarra? Why?'

'Seems only fair.' Sensing Phipps needed more, he added, 'Someone I cared for in Spain burned. Nothing to be done, but I must pay the debt because until I do I'm not free to offer myself to anyone else.'

'I hope you have something worth surviving for.'

Verrian answered, 'If I do, she's in Paris.'

Chapter Twenty-Three

Alsace, Eastern France. Saturday, 22nd May

Jean-Yves gazed out at the countryside. They'd travelled almost an hour through beech forest speared by sunlight. It was hypnotic. The Panhard-Levassor's suspension coasted over potholes and swallowed hairpin corners with ease. They'd just crossed the river that would accompany them all the way to Kirchwiller.

He was going home. To prepare for Christine's wedding, to ensure his castle was ready for a duc and duchesse. And to talk with his land manager about selling off a parcel of the land that had once been his family's hunting estate.

Most difficult of all, he was going home to face a dying woman. His steward had written warning him that his mother's former housekeeper might not make it through the week. Jean-Yves knew that if he didn't ask Célie Haupmann a certain question on this visit, it would be too late.

The road grew steeper and soon they were carving through orchards, sunshine flickering on slipper-satin bark. In a week or so, these trees would be blizzards of crimson, the slopes crammed with workers and baskets. Fragrant cherries would dominate the markets all June and July, the spare sent off to produce the regional speciality, Kirsch liquor. The air would taste bittersweet for the whole season.

In spite of the beauty around him, Jean-Yves hadn't enjoyed the drive from Paris. His mistake had been to bring Ninette and Jolyan Ferryman. His daughter, chattering away beside him on the rear seat, and his secretary's obsequious attentions, intruded on his thoughts. Ferryman sat up front beside the chauffeur and Jean-Yves was sick of the sight of the back of his head. The boy used so much hair oil, you could see the tracks of his comb and the scalp beneath.

They reached the point where the river plunged into a gorge thick with spruce and mountain ash. Rising from a dark forest was the plateau of Kirchwiller, his castle crowning it. The Panhard's windows filled with a panorama of treetops and wheeling hawks. Thinking out loud, Jean-Yves said, 'The windows of my castle look into France, the arrow slits towards Germany.' Then, to Ninette, who had stopped talking in order to sulk because he'd refused to let her take Pépin's place at the wheel and show off her nascent driving skills, 'Imagine your medieval ancestors riding this final league and seeing their stronghold before them.'

It was Ferryman who answered. 'You're proud of the place, Monsieur?'

'To love the lands and forests of Kirchwiller is a birthright. My father changed national allegiance for it. I fought a war to get it back.' Jean-Yves added silently, *And, if I don't find the answers I'm searching for soon, a blackmailer will take it from me.*

That evening, leaving Ferryman and Ninette playing chess in the drawing room, Jean-Yves went to pay the call that mustn't be delayed.

Célie Haupmann had been at Kirchwiller all his life and most of her own. She'd arrived as the kitchen dogsbody, rising to become his late mother's most trusted assistant. On Marie-Christine de Charembourg's death three years ago, an apartment had been made for Célie in one of the gatehouses. These days she retained the title 'housekeeper', but it was a courtesy.

Jean-Yves knocked at her apartment door and was let in by a nurse, who, from her grey tunic and white coif, had been recruited from a nearby convent. The nurse informed him that Mme Haupmann was expecting him, though she may have nodded off, and that a maid had been in to lay out refreshments. She ushered him to a sitting room and withdrew.

Jean-Yves took a moment to inspect his surroundings and was glad to see that his steward had provided comfortable accommodation for the old servant. Clearly, Haupmann liked her knick-knacks. His eye fell on candlesticks, clocks, china animals – some he recognised as having belonged to his mother. All very pretty and neat . . . unlike Haupmann herself.

Once she'd been full-lipped and comely, her face ringed by butter-blonde plaits. Now she filled her armchair like bloated dough, a yellowed complexion hinting at failing organs. When he coughed politely, she opened her eyes and muttered in her native Alsatian.

Jean-Yves greeted her in French and waited for a gruff reply. She'd liked him as a child but had grown cold as he grew taller and lost his chubby appeal. He suspected she'd never forgiven him for 'joining the enemy' – that is, becoming a man. Or perhaps she'd been jealous of the intensity of his mother's love for him. Their infrequent meetings were always a bit of a tap dance.

No gruff response today, but a weak attempt at a handshake. She invited him to sit and indicated the refreshment table, the slices of Kugelhopf, a speciality of the region, and a decanter of Kirsch. Would he kindly pour? Was dear Christine here, had she come?

No, the future duchesse was in Paris with her mother, where her dress and trousseau were being finished.

But of course. What was the wedding dress like?

'I've not been allowed to see, Madame.'

Was the bridegroom handsome? Where was his property . . . the Haute-Loire? Goodness. She'd never been so far in her life.

Jean-Yves poured Kirsch and answered her questions. If she wanted gossip, she could have it. He doubted she got much company. Only when a cuckoo popped out on its springs to brandish the hour did he finally ask his question. 'Madame, has anybody contacted you in recent months probing the death of the artist Alfred Lutzman?'

Colour flooded Célie Haupmann's cheeks. The old hostility returned. 'Why dig that up? It's not decent.'

'While my mother was alive I never referred to it, but you and I can be open. Have you spoken to anybody? Answered a letter? Passed on details of that time?'

Contempt thickened her expression. 'So much fuss over one stupid Jew. Who cares if there's one less in Kirchwiller? They take our trade, make themselves rich and never spend their money here. It sits in banks in Germany while we go hungry.'

Never had anyone looked less hungry. 'You were my mother's confidante,' Jean-Yves continued patiently. 'She told you things she otherwise kept for her father-confessor. If you revealed the events of that December day in 1903,' he moved his chair nearer in a gesture of intimacy, 'be assured I am not angry, but I must know.'

Célie lifted her Kirsch glass unsteadily. 'She talked of you all the time, your mother, how she missed you. Her only child – who abandoned her.'

'So you say every time we meet, though it was she who insisted I leave here. My mother was only at peace when I was out of the country. She feared my past might catch up with me if I stayed.'

'Bah! She had no peace. Her marriage was misery. I saw new bruises every morning when I went to her for my orders.'

He stood, turning his back, counting down to quell his sudden anger. Célie was referring to the 'marital battery' inflicted on his mother, which had only stopped with his father's death in 1902. Jean-Yves had been victim of his father's violence too, but he'd learned very young that it was never to be mentioned. He and his mother had shared their experience through glances alone – a touch here, a quick hug there. 'You forget your place,' he said coldly to Célie.

'I'm dying. It gives me the right. Your father was a brute. His greatest pleasure was beating your mother. I hope you are not the same.'

'Good God, Madame!' He couldn't help adding, 'You speak as if I should have stopped him. I was a child.'

'You were not always a child, but it's over now. She is at peace and he is . . . roasting in hell, I hope. Pray your daughters marry good men, mm?' Célie tilted her head, forcing a last familiarity between them. 'As for your big question, I told nobody what you did to that Jew. Why should I? We should get rid of them all.'

Chapter Twenty-Four

❧

Paris, 28th May

Flower-figured chiffon over silk satin, six sunray darts from neckline to bust, medieval-style sleeves. Alix tallied the myriad details that made Christine de Charembourg's wedding gown unique. Yesterday – or the day before; the weary hours were merging – she'd sewn hundreds of lead pellets into the hem so that if the wedding day turned breezy, Christine's dress wouldn't end up over her head.

They were in Javier's salon, Christine on a low, wooden stage, Alix on her knees arranging the Chantilly cream skirts over the steps. This was the dress's first public appearance. After today, it would be carefully packed and taken to Alsace for the wedding day scheduled for just over two weeks' time. A tear slipped from Alix's eye and she dashed it away, angry with herself for being silly. The feel of wedding chiffon in her hands brought back Verrian's voice: *'I'm falling for you . . .'* At some point in his descent, he'd obviously had second thoughts, because he'd disappeared. He'd been gone for more than three weeks, and this time even his newspaper office didn't know where he was. Rosa, in whose home Alix was now a permanent lodger, insisted he'd be back. 'I know men, ducks, and he isn't the runaway type.'

Alix wished she could share Rosa's certainties.

'More of a curve, Alix.' Pauline Frankel stood a distance away, studying the line of the wedding dress. 'Fan it out a little. The train must look as if it's painted on to the steps.'

Soon a photographer would arrive to take the traditional picture of the bride-to-be with her mother and father. The session had already been put back once because the comte had stayed longer than expected in Alsace. He was unwell, it was whispered. A heart complaint.

Alix wished Christine de Charembourg would stand straighter. She seemed locked in a flinch. Worried about her father? Or was it because her mother oppressed her? The comtesse was prowling around the room like a plantation overseer, searching for reasons to poke and complain. She'd insisted on a dozen changes to the dress already. A square neckline had been designed to show off the family pearls, but a week ago the comtesse had demanded a redesign. 'Christine will not be wearing the pearls after all.'

This last dictum had pushed Javier towards an emotional earthquake. He was not a corner-dressmaker, he had shouted.

The girl would look like a camel in a high neck, and he, Javier, had not yet sunk to dressing camels.

Mme Frankel had soothed him. 'It's not the girl's fault that the family pearls have been lost, or discovered to be paste or whatever. You will think your way round this new shape and it will be triumphant.'

And so it was, Javier creating a bodice that slimmed Christine's shape and drew the eye away from her square jaw. Alix had been drafted in to help fit and sew after a previous assistant fell foul of the comtesse's temper. Her escape route from the workbench, and she'd seized it. Worried to the bone about Mémé, who was still unconscious in hospital, heartsick over Verrian and missing the flat at St-Sulpice that she was too scared to return to, she needed to be mindlessly busy. She could have done without the bride's mother treading on her fingers though.

Many highbred ladies were sharp, even downright rude. But it turned out that the mere sight of Alix goaded Rhona de Charembourg to fresh heights of malice. Only this morning she'd swung her hand so that her ruby ring caught Alix's lip. At the sight of the blood, Rhona had shrieked, 'Get away from my daughter's train! Get away or my daughter will not wear this dress!'

Pauline Frankel had sent Alix down to the sanatorium. As she left, Alix heard Christine de Charembourg say, 'Maman, you hit the girl. I saw you.'

*

At eleven prompt, the photographer arrived, but the Comte de Charembourg did not. The session was rebooked for the following day. As she left, Rhona de Charembourg informed Mme Frankel that she did not want to see 'the dark girl, Gower' in the salon again. She would not have a Jewess working on her daughter's bridal clothes.

Mme Frankel answered, 'As that also excludes me, I hope Madame la Comtesse can find another technician.'

The comtesse was momentarily shaken. Then, all smiles, she explained that she had not meant to offend. Indeed, she trusted that her daughter's trousseau would be finished by the date agreed, in time for the family to travel to Alsace.

'The trousseau will be finished as long as you demand no more changes, Madame. And that includes changes to my workforce.'

'Javier says that woman's face is branded in acid on his heart,' Pauline Frankel remarked later in an undertone to Alix. 'I don't know about that, but she's keeping me from the autumn–winter collection. I'm marking off the days until the end of July and there aren't that many left. It was hard enough persuading Javier to put last month's cancelled mid-season collection behind him and start designing again.'

Alix nodded. The fashion press had savaged Javier's caprice in cancelling a collection, having already launched the previous one late. Some suggested he was not quite enough of a genius to get away with offending the fashion world twice in one year. A right-wing magazine had gone further, with a caricature implying that Maison Javier was built on Jewish money, not talent. Alix knew what Mme Frankel was implying – the comtesse's rants might be the thing to tip Javier back into melancholy, and none of them could afford that. She said, 'At least Oro is finished.'

The next day, as the photographer assembled his equipment and a minion gave the stage a final polish, Alix prayed they'd seen the last of Christine's wedding dress, the comtesse and her tantrums. 'Tears in the car,' a fitter whispered to Alix as Rhona arrived, clad in a suit of lilac silk, her younger daughter and the bride-to-be trailing behind. 'Poor girl – we should have made her dress out of blotting paper.'

Then the comte arrived, giving them all a lesson in gracious sincerity. 'I have tested your patience, Mesdames. I was taken unwell in Alsace. The doctors there kept me under observation longer than I needed or wanted.'

Alix was determined not to meet his eye, but as they waited for Christine to be dressed he approached, asking in a low murmur, 'How is your grandmother?'

'They call it a coma.' She spoke brusquely. 'She blinks but I don't think she hears anything.'

'I'm so sorry. Thank you for informing me and for sending the letter to my business offices.'

'I thought you'd want to know.'

'I visited your flat the moment I got your letter, but you'd left St-Sulpice and nobody seemed to know where you'd gone.'

'I couldn't stay there. Not after what happened.'

'Of course. Let me know where you're living now, and if there's any help I—' he broke off.

Alix followed his glance. It led to Rhona de Charembourg who was staring hard at them. 'I don't want your help,' Alix hissed. 'I don't want anything from a family that hates Jews.'

He recoiled. 'My wife's opinions are not mine. I'm not even sure they're hers – she mixes with people who think it fashionable to admire Hitler. It's a fashion that a dose of reality will soon change.'

She saw the lines about his mouth, the threads of white in the grey hair, and felt a wrenching sense of loss. She kept hoping they could restore their old trust and intimacy, but perhaps there was no going back. 'Ever since I can remember, Monsieur, you've been in and out of my life and I've been wracking my brain to understand why. I keep coming back to my grandfather and a picture I keep in my head of him in his attic, in a muffler and fingerless gloves, striving for that one defining work of genius. Never achieving it—'

'Alix, may we speak of this another time?'

The old Alix might have stopped there, but she was so exhausted, so raw, the boundaries of propriety had dissolved. Rosa, who had looked after her like a mother since Mémé's accident, said she was still in shock from seeing her grandmother in a pool of blood. While shock had you in its grip, you felt as if you were seeing the world through a pane of glass, but what Rosa hadn't known was that shock could also make some things clearer.

'After my grandmother and mother went to live with the Fressendens in London, you followed and became a part of their circle. Eventually, Mémé moved further into London and you took a house in a nearby borough. You kept an eye on her.'

'In as much as your grandmother would let me.'

'But was it for Mémé's sake? I asked you once what you see when you look at me. You said, "a clean page". Do you draw a face on the page, Monsieur? Do you see Mathilda?'

'I see you, Alix.'

'Not the child that killed Mathilda? You know, I was born two weeks overdue? If I'd arrived on time, my mother might have survived and you wouldn't have been obliged to avoid her funeral.'

'My precious girl, enough.' He gripped her arm. 'Don't acquire the habit of cruelty.' Another glance for his wife.

An aggrieved voice interrupted them. 'Why is everything to do with marriage so slow? I'll definitely elope when it's my turn.' Jean-Yves jumped as his younger daughter tucked her hand under his arm. 'Papa, why are you talking to this girl?'

'Go back to your mother, Ninette.'

Rhona de Charembourg made that unnecessary by striding towards them, confrontation in every muscle. Alix was saved by

Mme Frankel, who called after Rhona that the bride was about to emerge from the fitting room.

Alix was again spreading Christine's silken train over the steps to the exact pattern they'd rehearsed, when a shrill command made her rock back on her heels.

'Don't you dare touch my daughter's hem. Do so and Christine will not wear this dress and I will ensure the whole of Paris understands why. Mme Frankel —' the comtesse's voice travelled the length of the salon — 'send that girl out!'

'Go to Javier,' the première said, taking Alix's arm. 'A press photographer has come to take pictures of Oro before it goes off to the Expo, and Solange hasn't come in. Do something with your hair and put those words out of your head. Oh damn, the bride is crying again.'

Javier lifted an eyebrow as Alix halted in the doorway. 'You will not make a mannequin if you cannot walk forward with confidence.'

I don't want to be a mannequin, Alix thought. *I want to see Mémé sitting up in bed. I want to know why Verrian left. I want Rhona de Charembourg to fall down a drain.*

Javier sent her to the changing room. 'Freshen up, get rid of that not-so-charming smock, then put on Oro.' He sent Marcy to the stores for stockings and told Alix to borrow shoes and a girdle from the mannequins' supplies.

'Your waist measurement?' he asked Alix when she returned, washed and clad in a silk robe.

'Twenty-one inches.'

'You have lost weight. So has Solange. What is it with you girls? Boyfriends?'

'I don't have a boyfriend, Monsieur.'

He tutted. 'No boyfriend, just misery. Well, misery is good for the figure. And only misery can teach you what happiness is. As you're to model my Expo dress, you will receive a brassière and other underwear, including a girdle which will take two inches off your waist. Be very careful from now on about eating cake and bread, because once I alter a garment to your shape, I do not want to find you've expanded. Besides which, it is very uncomfortable to have a tight middle when you've eaten cake.' He patted his stomach and laughed.

'Monsieur, are you asking me to show your clothes? I mean, not just for tonight?'

'I think I am. I like having you around, Alix, and you are an easy shape to fit. I punished you by sending you back to the benches, now I pluck you away again. You understand couture and you have no boyfriend, which is an excellent thing in a mannequin, as poor Solange's fate will demonstrate.'

'Her fate?'

'She has lost her job, *petite*. Tonight she would have been photographed wearing a dress that in a week's time will be seen by thousands at the World's Fair. Instead, she is . . . *pouff*.' He launched an invisible butterfly into the air. 'Mme Kilpin told me that you had the making of a mannequin.'

'She did?'

'She is a remarkably good judge, both of what suits her and what suits my clothes. She is not the most loyal client, but she is a valued one. Ah –' he raised a finger – 'one last thing: I have heard a whisper that you have a second job.'

'I . . . I do?' At last her copying was to be thrown at her feet.

'I have been told you go to Montmartre, to a studio on Place du Tertre?'

Alix felt a prickle of relief. 'Yes. I sometimes sit for an artist. More of a favour than a job, though he's very talented. His name is Raphael Bonnet.'

'I know of him – a brave painter, and quite famous for his nudes. If he is painting you so . . .' Javier raised a hand to stop her interrupting, 'I do not need to know. But once you show my clothes, such a thing is impermissible. A Javier mannequin is recognised for her style and beauty – her lovely physique, her air of mystery, her cool untouchability. This promotes the Javier legend, whereas a painter's portrait reveals the human truth. The two are not in sympathy. You understand? You will not sit for Bonnet again.'

'Yes, M. Javier. I mean, no.'

'Good. Now, off you go and make friends with Oro.'

*

340

Twenty minutes later, Alix looked at herself in a long mirror and her eyes widened. Another woman had taken her place. She felt two inches taller. Oro showed the curve of her shoulder, and her dresser, by pinning up her hair, had made her neck seem almost as swanlike as Solange's. Nelly, one of the other mannequins, painted her face, giving her theatrical eyebrows and a crimson mouth. 'Let's do eyes like Bette Davis,' she said, holding a saucer over a candle flame. Smoky carbon appeared, which she mixed with baby oil and shadowed into the creases of Alix's eyes. 'There. Smouldering.'

'Oro pleases you?' Javier asked when Alix appeared in the salon. Carried away by the success of the horsehair lace, he had decorated the dupion flounces with gold vermicelli, which gave the dress a light-reflecting magnificence.

'I feel like the Empress Eugénie.'

'Move then, twirl. Let's see that skirt dance.' Javier snapped his fingers for black evening gloves. Alix had to wear gloves because her fingernails were too short.

'Let them grow and don't bite them, *petite*.'

She posed in profile on the stage that Christine de Charembourg had recently vacated, and Rhona's perfume still hung in the air. Javier made her sit on the top step, her elbows bent, her hands raised in an attitude. An assistant arranged the golden skirts. The lights were lowered, and the photographer asked her to stay absolutely still.

Two hours later, Javier was satisfied and she was allowed to go away and change.

Tears slipped down Alix's cheeks as she stepped out on to Rue de la Trémoille. It was eight o'clock, the sun low above the rooftops and she could still feel the imprint of those steps on her buttocks. Marcy walked beside her, wearing the same bloodless mask, but Marcy was going back to a happy home in Batignolles. Alix was off to visit her grandmother. Then back to her room. A glass of sherry with Rosa before bed and, with luck, a few hours' oblivion.

She'd not told the comte that, a week ago, Mémé had been transferred from the Lariboisière hospital to 'Le Cloître', a clinic an hour's train ride from Paris. Doctors had explained that the full extent of Mme Lutzman's brain injury was difficult to assess. Recovery was possible, but Alix must be realistic, they said. In the meantime, the patient would do best in a facility that specialised in head injury. Le Cloître was giving its care for free, but Alix had to cover the cost of bed linen and feeding. By the time she'd paid those bills and her train fares, she was searching the lining of her coat for odd coins to buy food. She knew the comte would have offered her money, and she also knew that at this moment he was the last person in the world from whom she'd take it.

These days she seemed to bounce between grief, worry and humiliation. The humiliation was Verrian's fault. On the night of Mémé's attack, Alix had waited in the hospital all night. And all the following day, expecting Verrian to join her.

When he didn't come, and fearing his injured hand had turned nasty, she'd telephoned the *News Monitor* and learned that Mr Haviland was not there. She got the same answer from the Hôtel Polonaise, so that evening she'd left her grandmother's bedside and gone to their café on the Champs-Elysées, hoping he would come. She'd sat at their table till midnight, and for three evenings afterwards, enduring the pity of the waiters as she checked every man who passed. She'd waited for a letter, inventing reasons when none came. Perhaps Verrian had gone off to Germany again, or been called back to London. There was a family crisis. He'd fallen ill, had an accident. When she called at the *Monitor* building in person, the smart girl at reception told her that Mr Haviland was 'away for the time being'.

'When will he be back?'

'We don't know.' The receptionist gave her a sugary smile. 'And by the way, dear, you *do* know who he is?'

'Of course,' Alix shot back defensively. She'd come in her workbench clothes. In a suit she'd have garnered more respect. 'He's a reporter.'

'What I mean, dear, is that he's the boss's son.'

'The boss?'

'Lord Calford –' the girl raised her voice – 'is chairman and owner of this newspaper, and Mr Haviland is his son. You *do* know he's the Honourable Mr Haviland?'

Alix had stared, baffled more by the girl's need to relate this information than by the information itself. 'So what?' she countered. 'I am the Honourable Alix Gower. Stick that in your pipe and smoke it.'

Rosa had suggested that Verrian might have gone back to his old lodgings near the Gare du Nord, to Laurentin's place. Alix travelled there one evening, finding a garishly lit hotel.

'M. Haviland?' Laurentin had shrugged. 'Sorry, *puce*, not seen him. Paid his tab ages ago, left for the sunny slopes of Montmartre.' Laurentin looked her up and down and something between pity and embarrassment crossed his face. 'Lives a complicated life, does our friend. Used to make international calls. Ah, don't cry, *puce*, plenty more fish in the sea. Stop and have a drink. Pretty little thing like you, I could put some work your way.'

She'd looked around his bar, saw the girls at the tables and slapped his face.

Why was it that everyone she loved went from her life? Changed, died or abandoned her? Or, in the case of Sylvie le Gal, did all at the same time. Marcy, seeing her tears and misinterpreting them, slung an arm round her shoulder and said, 'This business is tough, but hey, Alix, you're a mannequin now. You will be known as the girl who made Oro beautiful.'

'The other girls will hate me.'

Marcy laughed. 'Not all of them – they're too lazy. Nelly certainly—' She broke off as a taxi pulled up ahead of them and a large woman clambered out. It was Mme Markova, who was in charge of Javier's *cabine*, the room where the mannequins dressed for parades and shows.

Recognising them, she waddled towards them, calling, 'Girls, is Monsieur still at work, do you know?' She was carrying a rolled newspaper.

Marcy was sure that Javier would be in his studio, hard at it. He'd be there until Mme Frankel called a taxi and forced him to go home. 'What's happened?'

'This!' Mme Markova tore the paper in her haste to open it. Alix recognised it at once. It was the *New York Fashion Daily*, the American trade paper that was Mabel Godnosc's bible. 'I was meeting a friend at the Ritz and some American girls left this on a seat. I can't read English –' Mme Markova finally opened the centre spread – 'but I can see pictures. I think I'm going to have a heart attack.'

'Alix will read it,' Marcy said.

Alix took the paper; the date showed it was two weeks old. She read, 'The Collection Too Sexy for Paris.' A nasty taste crept on to her tongue as she translated, 'From Paris to Fifth Avenue, from fifty thousand French francs to one hundred dollars in two weeks, Javier storms New York with a collection that's just *too la-la*.'

'Too what?' Marcy wrinkled her nose. 'Javier doesn't sell to New York, except to select buyers, and never at a hundred dollars.'

'He will explode,' Mme Markova predicted.

The article was little more than a grid of photographs, each featuring a girl in a dress above a caption. 'The dress for sexy senoritas in figure-hugging velvet . . . This swirly silk will *ruffle* the man in your customer's life . . . Cara? You bet! Dear? Not at $75.50.'

The dresses were all copies from Javier's cancelled mid-season line. So— not only had Mabel let the dresses go on sale, she'd put time and energy into their promotion. Suicidal.

Marcy thought they'd better show Javier straight away. Alix made a ready excuse – she had to visit Mémé.

'Of course, you poor thing.' Marcy hugged her. 'I'll go with Mme Markova.'

As they separated, Alix heard Mme Markova say bitterly, 'Thieves. Style pirates. I hope there's a hot chair in hell for them.'

It was late to be taking a train, but it was three days since she'd seen Mémé. Alix always worried she might miss some vital change in her grandmother's condition. There never was any, but the nurses said it was good for her to have visitors. Every time Alix went, somebody presented her with a bill for extras. It would be cheaper to buy flowers and paper napkins herself, but she never had time. And the flowers were a waste, benefiting only the nurses and whoever tended the clinic's compost heap. As Alix passed the *News Monitor* building on the way to the métro, a car horn made her jump.

Serge Martel wound down his window and said, 'Good evening, Belle of Maison Javier. I want to take you to dinner.' He had a rose in his buttonhole, reminding her that she'd last seen him standing under a shower of petals.

She edged away as he got out of his car, distracted by recurring images of Javier in his studio throwing the *New York Fashion Daily* across the room. Go out to dinner? Maybe it was what she needed, a few hours in the company of someone new, someone who would amuse and distract her. But she didn't like this man, and anyway, she must visit Mémé. She was preparing to refuse when Serge Martel held out his hand and she saw fingernail tracks on it. Looking up, she saw matching tracks down his cheek.

He nodded, understanding her intake of breath. 'Solange. I came to pick her up today as usual and found myself opening the car door for a spitting wildcat. She'd been sacked. Did you see the blood on the pavement? Mine, I should tell you.' He seemed to enjoy her squeamishness. 'Beneath the surface, we're all animal. So, dinner?'

'Shouldn't you be comforting Solange?'

He shook his head. 'I don't know what she wants but it isn't me. So . . . ?'

'I can't. I have to visit my grandmother. She's in hospital a long distance away and I'm running late.'

'Then get in, I'll take you.' He stepped back. 'D'you need anyone's permission to go out for an evening?'

She thought about it. She'd always had Mémé at home, fretting if she was late, imagining the worst. But now she had nobody. She answered, 'I can do what I like.'

The Le Cloître clinic lay west, which meant driving into the sunset. Alix could hardly see the map Serge handed to her. They were an hour into their journey before she realised that reading a map was not the same as following a dress pattern, where you mentally reverse left and right. She'd sent them way off course, and by the time she noticed they were as far from the clinic as when they'd started. Serge found it hugely funny and knocked on the shuttered window of a farmhouse to ask directions. An hour later, turning into Le Cloître's drive and seeing only dark windows, Alix wanted to cry. Visiting hours were over.

Serge lifted a hand from the wheel and stroked her knee. 'Just watch.'

Half a dozen words at the front desk and the matron who ruled Le Cloître with a rod of disinfected iron was ushering them down corridors as if they were the diplomatic corps. While Alix replaced tired bedside flowers with ones they'd bought on their way out of the city, Serge pulled up a chair and began a one-sided conversation with the patient.

He told Danielle all about his own 'darling granny', who'd practically brought him up. A wonderful cook, famous for her confit of duck leg, made to a secret recipe involving flageolet and haricot beans, smoked garlic, parsley and diced ham seasoned in the best Epernay wine. *A little much for Mémé's diges-tion*, Alix thought privately. Nor would her grandmother be thrilled to find ham on her plate, but the way Serge spoke, as if Mémé were his dearest friend, made anything forgivable.

The hour, which usually passed so bleakly, flew by and Matron escorted them out in person. Alix, bringing up the rear, heard Serge say, 'Do you have patrons, Mme Angèle? I'm talking about money – your running costs. Is there room here for a bad man from Paris to do a little good?'

'There's always room for goodness,' Matron simpered. 'And my name is Sister Marie-Andrée.'

'Angèle to me.'

At the door, Alix watched Serge raise matron's fibrous knuckles to his lips and doubted she'd ever be told off for arriving late again.

He took her to a roadside auberge where the fare was simple and good and she let him talk. She learned he came from the Champagne region, near Epernay. Why he adored drinking it, he said, and why he'd taken over a cousin's nightclub.

'You told me it was your father's.'

'And a cousin's too. Think, Alix, a party every night in your own place, people having fun, forgetting their troubles, all because of you. Shall we drink champagne now?'

'I'd rather not, not with Mémé the way she is.'

'Never say no to champagne.' He clicked his fingers for ser-vice.

She had to ask. 'Where is Solange now?'

'Ah . . . poor Gigi – that's what I call her. On her way back to her people in Corsica.' He touched his wounded cheek. 'With her nails trimmed, I hope.' He raised his glass. 'To you, rising star. Will we stay together tonight?'

She choked on her drink. What happened to slow seduction? 'I'm . . . not . . .' She hurled herself into a safety net. 'I'm not a rising star; I'm just me. I want to be a couturier, not a mannequin. I loved wearing Oro, but tomorrow I mean to tell M. Javier I want to keep learning the business.'

'You won't stay with Javier. He's not famous enough for you.'

'I'm not famous enough for him more like.'

'I mean what I say. You've just landed the job every girl in France would die for.' He leaned forward. 'And we will be the couple everyone in Paris is dying to know.'

Serge seemed sincere in his desire to know her better, fast. The next day, Saturday, which was her day off, he took her to the Bois de Boulogne on the western edge of Paris, where they rode through the trees in a horse-drawn carriage. Alix wanted to be distracted, but not even Serge's chatter, the motion of the carriage, nor the birdsong, could keep her mind off the approaching Monday morning. When Serge kissed her in the shade of a tree, half her mind was on Javier and what might be awaiting her at work on Monday. By now Javier might have figured out who'd sold his designs to America. He might be planning a reception for her at Rue de la Trémoille . . . one involving the police.

She spent Sunday alone, sitting in Place du Tertre filling a sketchbook with portraits and fashion drawings, keeping her hands busy while dreaming up slow deaths for the ladies God-nosc and Kilpin. They had ignored her warnings, allowed Javier's mid-season collection to hit New York *and* publicised it in a mass-circulation paper.

Monday dawned, and she walked to work to burn off her nervous energy. She found Marcy in the second-floor cloakroom, pulling on her smock. In an undertone, her friend told her how Javier had reacted to the *New York Fashion Daily*.

With dead silence apparently. He'd stared at the pictures for half a minute before throwing the paper towards the bin. He'd then called a taxi to take Marcy home, because he was concerned she'd be late for supper.

'That was it – nothing else?' Alix couldn't believe it.

'I don't know what he said to Mme Markova after I'd gone. He wants to see you though. One of his assistants has already been down to find you, so you'd better go up straight away.'

As Alix entered the studio, Javier gave her a bow. 'And how is my new favourite house mannequin?'

Before she could answer, Simon Norbert walked in and snorted, 'She's not my favourite, offending one of our best customers.'

'What my friend means, Alix, is that on Friday, in the salon, you were offered insult for which I apologise.'

Alix checked Javier's face for signs of imminent retribution. Finding nothing alarming in his gaze, she turned her attention to what he'd said. 'Insult . . . yes. By Mme de Charembourg.'

A finger to the lips. 'No names, *petite*. It is not the first time this lady has abused my staff for their religion or origins, or simply because she is in a temper and they are in the way. But it is the last.'

Norbert pointed at Alix. '*She* provoked it. By talking to the lady's husband in a familiar way. I've had a taste of her impudence. She gets a look on her face—'

'I do not!' Alix flared.

'Shush, both,' Javier replied. 'In the world now is great evil, and the prejudices of certain figures in society are a painful reminder of it. Sometimes one must make a stand. On Saturday, when she came here for a fitting, I put on my white gloves.' Javier extended his hands, presumably so there would be no mistake as to where the gloves went. 'I bowed and said, "Mme la Comtesse will oblige me by leaving my establishment." Dear me. She was suddenly all open mouth in purest shock. I explained that all outstanding items would be delivered as promised but that I did not expect to see Madame herself ever again. I offered my arm and escorted her out.'

'And made an enemy for life.'

Javier acknowledged it. 'As I say, M. Norbert, sometimes one must choose between evils. And now I will tell you why I summoned you, Alix. I have been told your grandmother is very ill. Do you wish for time off?'

'Oh, no, Monsieur. I can't afford to. In fact, I want keep working as your assistant, to keep learning.'

'Instead of being a mannequin?'

'As well as, if possible.'

Javier stayed silent a while. 'That would be most unusual, to work as an apprentice in the morning before retiring to the salon to present my clothes.'

'It wouldn't do,' Norbert thrust in. 'It gives the girl too much exposure to the clothes at every stage. Reaped the benefits of that, haven't we?'

'Ah, our New York exposé. "The Collection Too Sexy for Paris."' Javier flashed a hard smile. 'Did the headline writer ever come to Paris?'

'Do you know who might have . . . you know?' said Alix, wishing she were a better actress.

'Stolen my work?' Javier nodded. 'It is a person able to view my designs, who mixes with bad company. A person who we see each day but never suspect. Can you not guess? You shake your head, Alix. You grow pale. Solange, of course.' Javier touched his heart. 'She has too much or too little of this vital organ and a boyfriend who makes her miserable.'

Alix thought, *Can I be getting off so easily?* 'Will you sue?'

Javier gave a broad shrug. 'Sue a trade paper that lies outside

French law? Or the little New York typist who thinks she is wearing Javier for seventy-nine dollars fifty?'

'Makes me sick,' Norbert spat.

'I say good luck to her. So, Alix, you wish to help me with my next collection? The days will be long. You will never grow your fingernails.'

'I'll wear gloves in the salon. I don't mind late nights.'

Javier sighed. 'You will expect me to pay you twice?'

Ignoring Simon Norbert's objection, Alix said, 'A small pay rise would be welcome. I will earn it, I promise.'

Chapter Twenty-Five

A perfect June day. A breeze skimmed off the Seine, making canvas awnings dimple and flap. It filled the air with sparkling droplets from the fountains. The Paris Exposition, the 'World's Fair', whose pavilions and walkways covered hundreds of acres, was in full swing.

The site wasn't finished. But nobody had expected it would be and the crowds were eager to enjoy, not complain. When she looked at the brooding eagle atop the German pavilion and the sickle-wielding man and woman crowning the Russian pavilion opposite, Alix imagined she heard Mémé keening, '*Vey ist mir*.' She also understood something Verrian had told her: 'This fair's a last stab at peace for nations who, in their heads, are already at war.'

Not that she was left to her own thoughts for long. Serge strolled alongside her, arm linked with hers, giving a running commentary on the swarming crowds. He was particularly contemptuous of foreigners, their oddities and babble, though he was fascinated by the huge cameras slung around the Americans' necks. He embarrassed Alix because he never lowered his voice and their twelve days' acquaintance had taught her that Serge voiced every thought in his head. Not for him contemplation or layers of meaning; if he said it, he meant it – though his opinion was likely to change a minute later.

The breeze wrapped Alix's skirt around her legs. She was wearing 'Rose Noire', her own design. Mabel Godnosc had proudly presented a version of the dress to Alix at the Champs-Elysées office a few days ago. Una had been there and it had been their first get-together since Alix had warned Mabel – in vain – to abort production of Javier's pirated mid-season line. Una had brought the offending copy of *New York Fashion Daily* with her, saying with a shaky laugh as she opened it up, 'I didn't expect us to make the centre pages.' Then, as if that closed the matter, told Alix to, 'Go try on that little number Mabel's so kindly rustled up for you.'

The 'little number' turned out to be two inches shorter than Alix had drawn it. It was tight across the back and the collar sagged. And it was synthetic silk, not the crêpe Alix had specified. 'I can't wear it,' was Alix's verdict.

Mabel answered, 'Shoot, at fifteen dollars, whaddya expect? Ginger Rogers's dancing dress?'

And then it was back to business. Back to copying because, in Una's words, they were all still poor and still the Three Musketeers. Four, if you counted Mabel.

Yesterday Una had put a parcel into Alix's arms. 'A peace

offering. Don't open it now – your tears of gratitude will over-whelm me.' The package contained Rose Noire as Alix had intended it; jet crêpe with hand-printed detail – so closely resembling her sketch Una must have scoured fabric warehouses all over Paris and had a gifted seamstress make it up for her.

Alix stared into the diamond mist of a fountain, relishing the spray of water on throat and face. Most of the time she hated Una, despised and resented her. Then Una would make her laugh or do something so generous Alix found herself almost admiring the woman.

Serge tugged her arm. 'Let's go back to the Pavillon d'Elégance. I want to see you next to Oro, see if anyone else recognises you.'

She groaned. 'I don't like people nudging each other and gawping.'

'Well, I do. You're famous. You're wearing Oro in *Marie Claire*, the Expo edition.'

'It's only an illustration.'

'A good one. People still recognise you.'

'It's the dress people want to see, not me.' *Marie Claire* had described Oro as a 'collision between a star and a comet', and Serge was deriving endless pleasure from her resulting minor fame. 'We'll go back for a while,' she bargained, 'if we can go to the Spanish pavilion afterwards.'

'We'll go and have coffee after. I'm not interested in any-thing Spanish.'

'Serge, I want to see the Spanish pavilion. There's a painting there.'

'What painting?'

'By Picasso, part of a set of panels. Bonnet told me about it.'

Serge's mouth buckled in contempt. 'Picasso paints women who look like horses and puts noses on the sides of their faces with both eyes looking out at you at once. I wouldn't feed my dog off one of his paintings. Who's Bonnet anyway? How come he tells you what to look at?'

'Bonnet's a friend. You don't have a dog, and I'm going. Please let go of my arm.'

He backed away from the quarrel, nuzzling her neck. 'All right, but I expect you to be very nice tonight. A bit more than kissing and cuddling, maybe? No more holding out on me?'

'I'm working. I told you.'

'What work?'

Alix drew a breath. 'My other job, at Maison Godnosc.'

'You don't need to work. You're my girl. Or maybe you don't want to be my girl.'

'I'll come to the club afterwards and we'll have dinner. You choose where. Can we go to the Spanish pavilion now?'

'Pavillon d'Elégance first,' he said stubbornly and because he'd already treated her to lunch and bought her a butterfly brooch at an artisan stall, she let him lead her there.

★

The Pavillon d'Elégance was a plastered pink grotto under a tented azure sky, housing the cream of Parisian couture. Alix had supposed there would be daily parades, each house providing a favoured mannequin to exhibit their creations. But no. Gowns were displayed on faceless seven-foot figurines made of lumpy plaster. Elsa Schiaparelli hated them so much, she'd covered her exhibition space with flowers and Alix applauded her for it. Those surreal scarecrows upset her too.

Even so, she was keen to examine the offerings from Chanel, Patou and Lucien Lelong, but Serge kept dragging her back to Oro. So keen to parade 'his girl', he shoved in front of a man and woman quietly discussing the dress's merits. Alix recognised them, premières from a competitor house whom she'd met at one of the Expo's opening parties. She saw their astonishment, their covert examination of Serge's suit. She blushed to hear one of them whisper, 'Chicago chic.'

As she slunk away, a girl she recognised approached her. It was Zinaida, Javier's Greek mannequin, who whispered, 'Isn't that Solange's old flame? What's the story?'

'No story.'

'You know why she went? Solange, I mean.'

Zinaida must have heard rumours that Solange was the couture thief. Alix muttered an affirmative and turned away, then jumped as Serge's arm came around her.

'Any chance of you borrowing that gold dress? We could have

a special night at the club, you and me dancing. Then afterwards I'd make love to you while you wear it.'

She told him, 'Let's go before you get any more mad ideas.'

While the Pavillon d'Elégance was a place of hushed reverence, the Spanish pavilion was a jostle with one focus: a stark monochrome panel. *Guernica* had been painted by Pablo Picasso in the weeks following the bombing and had acted as a magnet for Paris's grieving Spanish and Basque population, as well as for artists of all nationalities, men and women voicing their opinions all at once – arguing over the composition and the politics behind it.

Bonnet had told Alix she must see *Guernica*. Javier had said the same. Alix privately felt she must because, had he been here, Verrian would surely have brought her. One day he might ask her what she thought of it and she must have a ready answer. But wait – why was she behaving as if Verrian would come back to her?

It took some minutes to worm to the front of the crowd. Serge took one look and complained the panel wasn't finished – it was a mess, something a child of two could do in his painting book. Why was it called Guernica. What was Guernica?

'A town, but really an event. A bombing.'

'Doesn't look like a bombing to me. Looks like someone's gone mad in an abattoir. What's that eye doing? I like surrealism when it's funny. That's not funny.'

Alix tried to see the panel through Bonnet's eyes, then Javier's. And, though she tried not to, through Verrian's. And then through the eyes of the bearded men who shoved up close to her and poured out their thoughts — admiration, condemnation, she had no idea — in streams of impenetrable Basque. Serge had a point, Alix thought. It *was* a mess. But a mess inspired by rage. She saw a man's attempt to translate an afternoon's atrocity through simple forms: a bull; a dying horse; a woman with a dying child; a dove; a blazing eye . . . or was it a bomb exploding, or the eye of God? It seemed to her that Picasso had created the moment any hope of peace exploded and humanity perished. She heard Verrian's voice in her head: 'A single German bomber circled over the town at low altitude, then dropped six heavy bombs . . . thenceforward the bombing grew in intensity, ceasing only with the approach of dusk . . .'

Dusky bergamot stole into her nostrils and, as she stared at the panel, she saw a new face. Strong features, bearded, in pain . . . She felt herself sway.

Somebody behind her caught her. A paternal voice said in her ear, 'I think you forgot to breathe. I'm not surprised. Come outside for air.'

'M. Javier. What are you doing here?'

'You think I should be with the dresses?'

'No. You're an artist; you needed to see this painting.'

'*Muy cierto*. I have come ten times now and always, I see something new. But you are pale, Alix. Should I fetch you a glass of water?'

'Leave her.' Serge barged forward. 'We don't need your help. Get lost.'

'Serge!' Alix choked with embarrassment. 'This is M. Javier. *The* M. Javier, Oro's creator and my employer.'

'Oh.' Serge brushed his nose with his palm. 'My apologies – I've been in your salon a dozen times, watching the girls, but I never saw you there.'

Javier regarded him quizzically. 'I too watch my parades, but always from behind a column so as not to distract my young ladies. Haven't I seen you before – escorting Mlle Antonin from the premises?'

'Maybe once or twice. Look, I'll take care of Alix now. She's fine. It got too hot in there. Too many Spaniards. We were admiring her dress a little while back – the gold one? I tell you, M'sieur, you're good.'

'And you are far too kind.' Javier gave his impeccable bow and left.

Alix gasped when Mabel Godnosc showed her photographs of the Mainbocher gown Wallis Simpson had worn for her marriage on 3rd June 1937. She saw a close-fitting dress on a woman without hips. Square shoulders and a buttoned panel under the bust, which drew the eye to the middle. That feature was strikingly similar to her 'Rose Noire'.

'Half New York's wearing the Wally dress already, and you had it on paper before she did,' Mabel enthused. 'You tell me – is the old-fashioned corset about to make a comeback?'

Alix had no idea. But maybe she did possess the designer's muscle, that skill of leapfrogging the obvious, of capturing a bit of the future.

Una brought her back to earth. 'Don't get starry, Alix. Copying's where the money is.'

'I hate it,' Alix retorted. 'Every time I come here I betray a man I respect. If it weren't for my grandmother, I'd walk out.'

Rosa had let her have Verrian's old room at a fair rent, so her living costs ought to be manageable. But a week or so back the St-Sulpice landlord had sent her a bill for 'dilapidations' to his property; damage to the apartment walls from kerosene fumes and 'unauthorised hammering in of picture hooks'. He wanted the equivalent of three months' rent to put things right. That, on top of Mémé's weekly bills . . . Alix now knew why Paul always looked so haggard. You put a little money by, then bam! Fate picks your pocket.

Thanks to the 'Collection Too Sexy', Alix had finally been paid for her copying. After Mabel took her cut and Una hers, there'd been thirty thousand francs each for Alix and Paul. A long way from the riches they'd dreamed of in the Jardin du Luxembourg. Alix's had gone on bills. Paul's boat still leaked and Suzy's speech therapy continued once a month with a lady who did it for charity. Alix picked up the glass by her elbow and knocked back its contents. Una had recently taken to mixing her Gin Alexanders. She'd hated the taste at first, but now she craved the bitterness.

Today Alix sketched the Scottish-inspired suits from Javier's autumn–winter collection, her pencils going so fast, they practically steamed. Funny, the more she hated this game, the better she got at it. After an hour she sat back. 'I'm done for tonight.'

As always, Mabel gathered up the sketches and locked them away. First thing tomorrow they'd be couriered to Cherbourg or Le Havre, where they'd catch the fastest ocean liner to New York. Javier's autumn–winter show was fixed for 29th July, a full seven weeks away, and Mabel had promised on the lives of all her nephews and nieces that no pirate Javiers would appear in New York until mid-August at the earliest.

To help Mabel remember, Alix had circled Sunday, 15th August 1937 on the calendar. 'Not a seam to be stitched before, you understand?'

'Boy scouts' honour.' Mabel had even given the salute.

Onstage at the Rose Noire, Lenice Leflore sang 'Body and Soul' and conversations died away. Cigarette holders stalled on their way to lips. Alix let her eyes drift closed. Serge didn't want to dance tonight. He was keeping her warm for later, he said. First he had to talk with some men about an investment. 'Investment' was code for bootleg absinthe brought in from Spain, Alix had learned.

Serge had picked her up from the Champs-Elysées and taken her to dine at his favourite place, a restaurant in Pigalle. Ardennes pâté, then a slow-cooked chicken casserole. He had ordered for her as he liked to do . . . as Jean-Yves had liked to do. *Jean-Yves*. On the day Christine's wedding photograph had been taken, Alix's parting gift to the comte had been a look of utter scorn. She hadn't let him know her new address, and with his wife now banished from Javier, there'd been no opportunity for them to bump into each other. Come to think of it, the family must all be in Alsace, with Christine's wedding so close.

Alix drank the last inch of champagne in her glass, and looked around for a waiter. After they'd eaten, Serge had driven them back here, his hand on her knee as he flicked in and out of the traffic. He'd wanted to make love to her the moment they got inside the club – he'd have taken her on the foyer carpet had they not been disturbed by staff coming in to work. She'd run upstairs, locking a door behind her, and changed into an evening dress.

Tonight's was a black faux Chanel with a keyhole back that Mabel had sold her cheap because a customer had returned it, used. It was the kind of dress that made you feel magically grown-up. Alix sat alone at Serge's table by the dance floor. This table was never given away, no matter how crowded the Rose Noire became. To sit here made a girl a queen – a lonely queen.

A waiter refilled her glass without a word. None of the staff ever got familiar with Serge's women. Not that she'd exactly chosen to be Serge's woman. He'd simply assumed it, talked it into being and taken her life over. While she had chosen to play along, it was why she hadn't yet succumbed to him sexually – she wanted that to be her choice, not his. But tonight felt different. There was no reason to hold out any more, was there? She watched him greeting his visitors, shaking hands, clapping shoulders. People here liked him. Women loved him. She'd seen them actually shake with passion when he stood close by. Some said it was his reputation for violence that excited them, though she'd seen no evidence of violence. True, he didn't like drunks. He'd have his doormen tip them on to the street, and once a boy who'd snuck in to steal evening purses had been rammed against the bar until his nose ran scarlet. That had been horrible to witness. But Alix had never seen Serge personally hurt anyone.

Would Verrian ever walk in here again? Heavens, where had that thought come from? Well, would he? Approach with that half-smile that never quite delivered its message? She imagined him leading her to the dance floor, explaining what had kept him away for more than a month. A heartbeat of silence as the bandleader paused before swinging his music men into 'My Blue Heaven'. Their tune, their universe. The dance floor would shimmer with silk and lamé, sequins and satin, and she would melt like fondant . . . .

She wrinkled her nose because champagne bubbles had whizzed up. She could feel them in her forehead. Wind back the film. Verrian would get halfway across the floor to find Serge in front of him – *Alix is mine now. I'll take care of her.*

'May I have this dance, Miss?'

She turned in surprise. A fresh-faced young man stood a couple of feet away. American by the sound of him. 'No,' she said, keeping it short because she would slur anything more complex.

He backed away. 'Didn't like seeing you on your own, Miss Muffet. Sorry I bothered.'

Miss Muffet. Sat on a tuffet. There came a big spider . . . Alix drank down her champagne. Today's date was a very special one. Today was 11th June. Today, she turned twenty-one.

She'd dropped hints about her birthday. Obviously not loudly enough. Serge was still with his black-market friends at the bar, not even looking her way. The band began to play 'C'est à Robinson', a lilting tune that tore at her heart. Then the lights went out. Laughter and little screams greeted it, though this was such a regular gimmick, people must surely be used to it by now. When the lights came up again, balloons would fall from the ceiling . . . or petals, or feathers. Alix squirmed irritably. She heard squeaking wheels. Whispers. She saw a wavering candle flame in the dark. Then another flame, then another. Men in white waiter's jackets were coming towards her. Each carrying a candle . . .

They surrounded her. It felt pagan, those candles in the dark. And then, in harmony, they began to sing first in French '*Bon anniversaire, nos vœux les plus sincères –*' and then in hilariously bad

English – '*Happy birthday to you* . . .'

Applause rippled, the lights came up and she saw that a platform had been wheeled into the middle of the dance floor. It supported an edifice of champagne goblets six tiers high. Serge was on a ladder, grinning as he trickled champagne into the topmost glass, which overflowed into the glasses below. And the glasses below . . . and below. Her own birthday champagne cascade. As he emptied each bottle, another was passed up. He poured a seamless plume of champagne. People left their tables to cheer at the spectacle, making a path for Alix, who stood where she was, enthralled.

Finally Serge picked off the top glass and carried it down the ladder. He handed it to Alix, but before she could put the glass to her lips he pulled her to him, kissing her hard. Holding a glass full to its brim, she could do nothing but comply, and then the band was playing 'Rendez-vous sous la Pluie' and people were cheering. As the fashionable crowd clustered around the fountain for their share, she and Serge danced. The band speeded up and, knowing Serge was about to whirl her around, she knocked her champagne back in one. She shouted, 'Catch, Félix!' to the head sommelier and tossed the glass over her shoulder. Félix made a perfect save and a roar of approval greeted her wildness.

Serge began laughing and she caught his mood. They whirled and laughed through 'Rendez-vous', 'St Louis Blues' and 'Sweet Georgia Brown'.

She was drunk by the time they reached his bedroom. So drunk the fancy four-poster bed had no straight lines. And what was that on the side table, next to the lamp? A blue glass bottle-thing with pipes attached . . . it looked awfully like the vaginal douche the nurse at Maison Javier had shown her during her pep talk on the perils of pregnancy. Only this one was terribly pretty. Was she supposed to use it later? Why did it have two pipes?

She heard Serge swear as he tripped over the threshold after her. He turned off the main light and switched on a silk-shaded lamp, turning the room into a rosy chamber. She arched as he stood behind her, threading his arms round her, stroking her stomach, hips and breasts. Why'd she got so worked up about this moment? She was ready. She was . . . wasn't she? Only she wished the room would stay still. One moment she was losing herself to caressing hands, to Serge's lips, which found all the flesh her dress left bare. Next moment the floor sagged and everything started spinning.

A ripping sound brought her back to her senses. Her dress was under attack. Shaking Serge off, she sat on the bed, kicked off her shoes and angled herself so Serge could undo her fastenings. 'Extra, extra careful,' she told him. 'I like this dress.'

He was hauling it over her head, giving her no option but to stick her arms in the air. She mumbled a complaint as it hit the floor. He didn't hear; his breathing was harsh, his hands raking her. This was not the Serge who had laughed them upstairs. The new Serge was pushing her into the middle of the bed, where she had a lapse of consciousness. She came round to find her knickers being pulled off. All she was wearing now was her slip, a waist girdle and stockings and she felt suddenly conscious of her nakedness. 'Careful,' she slurred, meaning, 'Be careful with me.' Shuddery conversations in school locker rooms had warned of this first time, and Alix had also overheard young female shop assistants at Arding & Hobbs whispering about 'giving in' to their admirers, 'going all the way', and the need for special caution. She tried to articulate this, but Serge was on top of her, his mouth covering hers. He was pulling at his trouser buttons, his breath hot against her face. She'd have liked to put her arms around him and to hear words of reassurance, but she couldn't get her arms free from her sides. It was like being trussed.

Panic took her. Last time she'd felt like this, she'd been on the floor at St-Sulpice, a slimy rag in her mouth. She struggled as Serge pushed her legs apart, alternately kissing her and murmuring indistinct words into her neck. Something hard struck between her legs . . . A moment of stunned realisation was followed by the sharpest pain she'd ever felt in her life. She'd have yowled if she'd been able to open her mouth. Every muscle tensed in defence, but he was already inside her, pushing, and his movements became powerfully rhythmic. The pain grew almost unbearable and tears welled up, her fingers closing into fists. She was going to die.

And then, thank God, he shuddered, grinding and roaring incoherent passion into her hair. A second later he collapsed, spent.

Alix lay in shock. Raw pain between her legs, bruised breasts, burning where his chin had rubbed. Worse, a sense of loss. That something had been taken but not valued. This was lovemaking? Weren't you supposed to fly into the outer realms of physical rapture? Be caressed and told you were beautiful? Obviously not. That must be a big lie to make women agree to do it.

Perhaps Serge realised he'd been rough, because he rolled off her. Reaching for her hand, he said, 'First time's always bad, best to get it over with fast. You'll learn what to do, so don't worry and, anyway, it's your fault.'

'Mine?'

He leaned over her and nibbled the tip of her nose. 'That sexy body of yours . . . I couldn't hold back. First time Serge Martel's ever come first, so consider yourself special.'

The mattress creaked as he got up and she heard him removing the rest of his clothes. A double clunk told her he was only just taking his shoes off . . .

Tears still rolling down her cheeks, she told herself he'd been frantic because she'd denied him too long. He got into bed and lifted up the covers so she could get underneath with him. She wanted to go to the bathroom, not liking the sticky sensation between her legs. She'd like to gargle away the taste of the night's champagne. And was she supposed to use that douche-thing?

But Serge was asleep, his arm slung across her stomach, and she was afraid to wake him.

Chapter Twenty-Six

It was done, the civil ceremony, the church ceremony and the party that had lasted two days. Christine was the Duchesse de Brioude and had gone away with her husband to honeymoon by Lake Geneva. That was his gift. Rhona had wanted the newly-weds to go to London. The dowager duchesse wanted them at her château in Haute-Loire. Jean-Yves's intervention had offended both ladies, but Christine's gratitude made it worth-while.

And she was safe. Whatever was pursuing him would not touch his family.

'Papa, wait. I want to come with you.'

Ninette was scrambling to catch him up. He was on the path that led through the castle's outer wall to the river. It was a steep incline, constructed from centuries of broken masonry. He had intended to follow the riverside walk into Kirchwiller town and hadn't imagined anyone might join him. The ladies of his family took their strolls on boulevards and were not known for their solid footwear.

'My dear, you'll turn your ankle. If you want to take the air, have Pépin drive you to the public park. I'm sure your mother would enjoy it. Ferryman will squire you.'

Ninette swayed from side to side like a child. 'Papa, what happened to Grandmother's pearls? Why didn't Christine wear them for her wedding?'

She'd asked the question at breakfast too and he'd ducked it. Well, no more ducking. 'I sold them.'

Ninette looked so appalled he wondered if he should have kept up the diplomatic pretence that the jewellers had lost them. Staring down at the river foaming between iron-red boulders, he murmured lines by the English poet Cowper: 'He is the freeman whom the truth makes free.' Then to Ninette he said, 'The pearls had a fine orient, were well-matched and they paid for Christine's wedding. Otherwise she'd have worn a second-hand dress and gone away on a bicycle. I hope when it's your turn, we can dig out some other precious trinket.'

When Ninette cried, 'They were an heirloom!' he thought, *How like Rhona she's become*. The Ninette who used to be my favourite would have laughed and said, '*Bien*, Papa, let's sell the castle.' In fact, he'd misled her. He'd sold the bulk of his remaining Banque d'Alsace shares to pay for the wedding, while the pearls had repaid the loan he'd taken out to satisfy his black-mailer's most recent demand. If the pig came back for more . . . Well, there was no more. He could sell a tranche of land here, but his steward had put paid to hopes of high returns.

Prices in the region had dropped – people were worried about the German build-up over the border. Local landowners were selling off property and stockpiling gold.

Advising Ninette to watch her footing on her way back to the garden – a polite way of dismissing her – Jean-Yves edged down the path and followed the river to where it flowed beneath a medieval bridge. From there he climbed to Rue du Pont, Kirchwiller's main street. A sustained uphill walk lay before him.

Thirty years ago Rue du Pont had been called Brückenstrasse – Bridge Street – but the cobbles were the same even if the name had changed. So were the timbered shops and houses, though the paintwork was faded. Every roof had its customary stork's nest, busy with hatchlings. Storks brought luck, it was supposed, which suggested Kirchwiller's were not doing their job. One clear change was apparent though – at the dawn of the century his parents had owned the only motor vehicle in town. Now he saw a dozen parked alongside rustic carts.

Jean-Yves turned up Rue des Avocats and into the shadowy Rue des Ecrivains, stopping at an impasse, a dead-end alley just wide enough for two men to walk abreast.

As he walked up it, his leg throbbed. A splinter of shrapnel in his femur made itself known whenever he stood for any length of time, as he had often these last days. He counted the right-hand doors and stopped at one with a rusty spyhole. Fitted a key into the lock.

In the empty attic that had been Alfred Lutzman's studio, he leaned against the stove to get his breath, then twitched violently. Right here, Lutzman had fallen.

The day Lutzman died, 21st December 1903, Jean-Yves had come to collect a portrait he'd commissioned. He was late because heavy snow had fallen, and the chauffeur had been reluctant to let him take the Mercedes out. Jean-Yves had insisted, but it had been so cold that day, it took fifty turns of the crank to get the engine started. Jean-Yves had come shivering up these stairs feeling intense sympathy for Lutzman. How could an artist work in this temperature? His paints must go stiff, and as for sitting for a portrait . . . intolerable. His own portrait had been sketched out at the castle, Jean-Yves posing before a blazing fire. Lutzman had brought it back here to finish.

People said Lutzman was mad because he painted in wild, dancing colours. What you thought was flesh was not one colour, but minuscule flecks of scarlet, green and blue. Some people called it a form of trickery, sinful even, but what did the fat burghers of Kirchwiller know? If a painting didn't look like something they saw in church or on top of a tin of chocolates, they thought it came from the Devil.

He'd commissioned Lutzman *because* of his radicalism. The picture had been intended as a surprise Christmas gift for his mother, his first truly independent act since he'd succeeded to the title of comte a year before. Célie Haupmann had done her best to spoil the surprise of course. She'd always got between

Jean-Yves and his mother, disturbing their quiet moments, telling tales. That afternoon had been no different. As he'd waited in the great hall for the chauffeur to finish battling with the crank handle, she'd sidled up to him, smirking. 'Off to pick up your secret picture? I think your mother knows already what her Christmas present is going to be.'

'Because you've told her.'

'We could play a game, try to guess who the painting is meant to show. The one your friend Lutzman did of the mayor looked like a squashed monkey.'

'Because the mayor looks like a squashed monkey.'

She'd followed him out into the snow, angry at his refusal to be riled. 'She'll hate it. Madame la Comtesse hates modern painting.'

He'd told her that, on the contrary, if she cared to step into her mistress's writing room, she'd see several Lutzman landscapes on the wall. After that, he'd ignored her, crunching to the garage where the chauffeur had finally got the Mercedes engine to catch. Haupmann's voice chasing him –

'Doesn't your fine painter have a servant who can bring the wretched thing over? Have you turned into an errand-boy, saving a Jew the trouble of a walk in the snow?'

Actually Lutzman did have an assistant, a cheerful, stocky young man who'd proved himself handy for lugging easels and paintboxes up to the castle. Young Raphael Bonnet would watch his master at work, mix his paints and wipe his brushes and was occasionally allowed to fill in a detail or two. And yes, Bonnet was supposed to have delivered the finished painting several days ago, but he hadn't. It was Christmas Eve in three days and Jean-Yves had run out of patience.

In Lutzman's studio, Célie Haupmann's scorn ringing in his ears, he'd found the artist at work on a landscape. His own portrait stood on another easel, unframed and unfinished. So sticky, paint came off on his fingers. Not a chance of its being ready in time. Disappointment had slammed him and he'd turned on the artist. 'Are you not capable of a simple commission, man?'

Lutzman had blinked, then said in a voice without inflection, 'It is a portrait, *mein herr*, not a cake. It is complete when it is complete.' Was that triumph in his raven eyes? They seemed to say, *I have what you need, so for once I have power over you.*

A cord had snapped in Jean-Yves. 'Have you never heard of Christmas, damn Jew?'

Wicked words. Bitter words, because he knew that Haupmann would taunt him when he arrived home empty-handed. He hadn't planned what happened next.

Thirty-five years on and he was finally going to make his confession. He knelt under the skylight, the sun hard upon him. 'I killed a man and have tried to make amends. I have given my life to make good. Let me be forgiven.' He kept his eyes shut, reaching into the silence for an answer. For absolution. 'End my punishment.'

Downstairs, a door clashed. Footsteps, then a high voice: 'Papa? It's me. Are you there?'

His heart pitched violently. He lurched to his feet and staggered to the wall for support.

'Papa?'

A child rushing upstairs to see her father. She would find a corpse. He must stop her . . . His vision fractured, every muscle in his chest twisting. He fell to his knees again.

'Papa? Oh God . . .' Ninette was beside him. 'Papa, are you ill?'

He heard a male voice and realised that Ferryman was coming up after her. He rasped at his secretary to fetch water from the kitchen. When Ferryman came back with an old tin mug the cramp finally lessened. The water tasted foul.

'Lucky we found you, monsieur,' Ferryman said as he helped Jean-Yves downstairs. 'A neighbour saw you go in. Thing is, there's an emergency at the castle.'

Ninette took over. 'Mme Haupmann tried to get out of bed and fell. The nurse couldn't lift her, so had to call for the doctor. Haupmann's burbling on about you being –' his daughter began to laugh – 'a murderer.' She gasped as the laughter caught in her throat, doubtless from shock. 'Sorry, I'm so sorry, but you should have seen their faces.'

The doctor doubted Haupmann would last the night and offered to take her to hospital. 'For convenience's sake. Mme de Charembourg wishes it.'

'You spoke to my wife?' Rhona had been nowhere near Haupmann since they'd arrived for the wedding.

The doctor looked a little uncomfortable. 'I have, Monsieur. Madame sent for me, while you were being fetched. Understandably your lady doesn't wish for a death to take place here so soon after your daughter's wedding. She feels it would be . . .'

'Inconvenient? I think it would be cruel to move Haupmann now and surround her with strangers. Let her pass quietly here, tended by her nurse.' Jean-Yves ushered the doctor out. He told the nurse to get some rest, saying he would sit with the invalid for an hour or so. At the bedside he held a glass of water to the yellowish lips and said conversationally, 'I went to Lutzman's studio today, Mme Haupmann. I owned up to my crime, spoke the words out loud and asked God's pardon.'

The nurse had put a rosary into Haupmann's hand. The beads ticked restlessly as the housekeeper absorbed his words. She muttered, 'They were behind with their rent. His wife reckoned if you liked your picture, you'd let them off. That's how Jews think – money and what they can get.'

He stood and walked to the other side of the room, her poisonous words testing the limits of his charity. He stopped to look at a framed print of the Virgin and child, which aggravated his mood further. Mary looked more like a Swiss milkmaid than a girl of Nazareth. Straightening it he said, 'I have lived three decades torn from the company of God for a crime I committed.

Your spiteful words sent me to Lutzman's house with my pride stirred. You must admit the part you played.'

The silence, broken only by the stubborn click of beads, unseated something in him. He strode back to the bed and grabbed the string. It broke and beads bounced to the floor. 'You've never killed a man, have you, Madame? But your hatred and bitter prejudice have incited others to act. All your adult life you've pulled people's emotional strings and stood back with a smile on your face, enjoying the consequences. Confess it.'

'No reason to.'

'My mother gave you money to bribe the local chief inspector – Kern. You asked him to erase all trace of my visit to Lutzman's studio. He was diligent – he had Danielle Lutzman arrested, kept in a solitary cell so she couldn't incriminate me. She nearly went mad, separated from her child. Later Kern filed a report saying itinerant thieves did the killing. Neat, but there is always a reckoning. Kern took hundreds of thousands of francs from us, and bought himself a fast car. He crashed it into a tree on a bend by the river.'

'Didn't know Kern.'

'He and his wife came here for dinner once a month, right up until war broke out. Drop the pretence, Madame. Make your confession.'

Haupmann's lips cracked with the effort of speaking. 'Your mother loved you so much.'

'I know. She helped wash away my crime, but I wish I'd had

the guts to face it –' a movement made him look up. 'Rhona? How long have you been there?'

'Long enough. Is it over?'

'We should send for the priest.'

Rhona raised an eyebrow. 'And give the Abbé a taste of her rambling goodbyes? I can't think that's wise.' She came to stand beside him. 'What you were saying just now––'

'Not here,' he interrupted.

'Actually this is probably the safest place. Am I to take it you're guilty of a mortal sin?' She might have been asking about the weather, or what he'd like for lunch.

Not trusting himself to speak, he crouched down and picked up Haupmann's scattered rosary beads. A moment later he heard the gentle creak of the rocking chair beside the fireplace. Rhona was rocking, her eyes half closed. In the country, she threw off Parisian chic. Out came the tweed, the cable-knit cardigans. She was less brittle here.

She yawned. 'Is guilt why you make such a fuss of the little tart who works for Javier? I know she's something to do with this place and what went on here.'

'I don't want to discuss it, and I certainly don't want a quarrel. Not with poor Haupmann forced to listen.'

'I doubt she'll be telling tales, Jean-Yves.' The chair creaked back and forth. 'Very well,' Rhona sighed. 'Since you won't talk to me, I'll tell you what I know. A year or so after the war finished, I had our London chauffeur follow you on one of your trips out. You were always so secretive, pretending you were going to your club in town, but you always headed off in the wrong direction. So I had you followed. I thought you had a mistress, you see. Well, we'd been ten years married. It seemed possible.

'The chauffeur tailed you to Wandsworth, to a squalid road. I went there a few days later. I knocked at a narrow little house and said I was the health visitor. The stupid woman who lived there invited me in, even though I had no bag and no badge. She gave her name as Lutzman. I asked if she was related to an artist of that name, as we had some paintings by him in our home. I must have a sympathetic manner because, after a few false starts, I got her life story. She said she'd never told anybody so much about herself. Your name came up – she admitted she'd sometimes taken money from you.' Rhona imitated a high, Germanic voice; '"I tell him always Mathilda and I need nothing, but when he is gone away there is money in a drawer or on the table. He is the reverse of a thief." I've never forgotten that phrase – *reverse of a thief*. You're a do-gooder by stealth, my noble husband.'

Rhona fell silent and Jean-Yves suspected she was seeing herself back in Danielle's dingy London parlour. He knew it when she said reflectively, 'There was a brat in the room and I remember it watching me, sucking its thumb, and all I wanted to know was where its mother was and was it yours. I asked the woman about Mathilda and she started crying. Mathilda,

I deduced, had died giving birth . . . that brat is yours, isn't it? You paid for its schooling.'

'Yes, I paid for Alix's schooling. Who told you?'

'Now then . . .' Rhona closed her eyes, pretending to think. 'Receipts in your desk drawer, I seem to recall. Thirty pounds a term to Kingswood Place, Hampshire. Imagine my feelings, my husband paying for a beggar's education while refusing his own daughters their chances.'

He stared at her, prepared to believe that last comment was a joke. No, she seemed utterly in earnest. It had always baffled him, her ability to fashion the universe to suit herself. 'I never refused Christine or Ninette anything – the best schools, horse-riding, music tuition, Italian lessons, deportment, finishing school. And now driving lessons. What did I deny them?'

But Rhona wasn't listening. 'So, is Alix yours?'

He considered his reply. 'She is not your concern.'

'Is that the classically educated way of saying "she's my bastard"? I intend to know, Jean-Yves.'

'There is only one person entitled to ask that question: Alix. And until she asks, I will say nothing.'

An annoyed shrug answered him. Rhona had stopped rocking. 'You and the girl's mother . . . you were lovers? For how long? Where did you meet?'

He sighed. His instinct was always to close down these conversations, but now he thought, *Why go on denying it?* 'I'd known Mathilda since she was a child. I met her in her father's studio in Kirchwiller.' Over the corpse of her father, but that was a detail he would not share. 'I helped her and her mother move to London, and kept in touch with them. Yes, I helped support them. Mathilda charmed me, but I assure you my feelings were entirely brotherly and I saw relatively little of her during her childhood. Then war broke out. Unknown to me, she enrolled as a nurse and we met in France, behind the lines, when she was assigned to the casualty station near Arras where I was recovering. She was twenty-two.'

'This was all by chance, I suppose?'

'You don't imagine anyone could plan assignations amid that chaos? I emerged one day from a blur of sleep and morphine to find her smiling down at me.'

'And smiled back, even though you were married to me? Even though I was waiting at home, terrified for you every minute?'

Jean-Yves felt a wave of pity. Rhona, rocking again in her chair, hands clasped so tightly the bones showed, had once been the entirety of his desires. The sum of his dreams. 'I smiled back and we met again, after I was sent home to that sanatorium in south London. She'd been sent back too and was working there.'

'Happy coincidence. You had an affair?'

'A brief one. She married someone else that same year and then she died. That's all there is to say.'

'All?' Rhona got up so fast her chair skidded backwards. 'You betrayed me and all you have to say is "that's all?"' She slammed both hands against his chest, her nails piercing through his clothes. For the second time he dropped Célie Haupmann's beads.

Rhona clawed at his neck. 'How could such a woman eclipse me? A pauper . . . a foreigner! Was she so beautiful, or just a clever slattern?'

'She was beautiful, and she was no slattern.'

'No? Bedding you when you were already married?'

'You'll never understand, but I loved Mathilda from the first moment I saw her. She was in terrible need, and I was the only person in the world who could help. I had no idea how deeply I felt until years later when I opened my eyes in a hospital near Arras. I realised—'

'What?'

Realised I should have waited and married her. Backing away from the raking fingernails, he felt his legs collide with Célie Haupmann's bed. He shoved Rhona away and the fight seemed to go out of her.

He said, 'Let's remember where we are.'

A moment later he was reeling from a vicious slap.

'It all began here, didn't it?' Rhona forced herself past him and stood over Haupmann, whose eyelids fluttered. 'I heard what you said to this old witch. You killed Lutzman and she knew it. It's why you've kept her here all these years on full salary. Keeping her sweet. Keeping her quiet. Isn't that right, Haupmann?'

For a hideous moment Jean-Yves thought Rhona was going

to strip the bed cover off the old woman. He grabbed her elbow. 'Control yourself. Show some decency.'

'She knew you were a killer. It's why you've stayed away from here most of your life. Well, I could go to the police. I heard enough to have you arrested.'

'You won't,' he said, pulling her away from the bed, steering her towards the door. 'You've got more to lose than I have. Now get out. Send in the nurse and have the priest fetched.'

She defied him. 'Our marriage is over, Jean-Yves. Oh, we'll stay together. Don't think I'll set you free. But understand, from now on, I shall have my freedom too. As for that girl, Mathilda's brat—'

'Leave Alix alone. She's utterly blameless.'

Rhona laughed. 'No, she's a grubby little seamstress who has already learned the cost of crossing my path and meddling with my family. She'll pay hard. Someone has to, for what you've done to me.'

Chapter Twenty-Seven

❦

Paris, 3rd July

Alix opened her eyes, realising her bathwater was cold. Somebody was knocking on the door.

'You all right in there, ducks? Not whooshed yourself down the plughole?'

She proved that she was fine by climbing out, grabbing a towel and unlocking the door. 'Went to sleep,' she grinned at Rosa.

'That's a habit to get out of. As I see it, you can be an owl or a lark but not both. Tea on the table, five minutes.'

Alix buffed herself dry, then rubbed paraffin cream into her nails. After that she massaged her skin with coconut oil, jasmine and glycerine. It was Saturday, and Saturday night at the Rose Noire always attracted a glamorous crowd. Alix felt better sitting at her solitary table if she was impeccably groomed. Rosa was right though; she was burning the candle at both ends and the middle. Couture, copying, being a mannequin, her duties as Serge's girl . . . any one of those jobs would have kept a normal person busy. Smoothing the oil into her legs, she felt a tentative ripple of erotic response. Serge had been right – after that first horrible time on her birthday, the pain had lessened. Three weeks on, she felt no pain, but not much pleasure either. Apparently it was because she didn't relax. She tried to, but certain parts of her body had a mind of their own. Certain parts locked up.

Serge had sent roses after that first night, twenty-one red-black blooms. Rosa, who'd taken the delivery, had passed them over with one eyebrow raised and commented, 'I shan't ask, but in my experience roses usually have a lot to do with pricks. I hope he's looking after you.'

When Alix muttered, 'Of course,' Rosa elucidated –

'I mean *looking after* you. Either he's the marrying kind or he'll play the gentleman. He'll use French letters – condoms – or jump off at Fratton.'

'Where? What? I beg your pardon?'

'Pull out one stop from the terminal. Oh, look at that innocent face. Way you're going, it's married with babies by twenty-two or a backstreet abortion. Get some rubbers.'

Blushing and stammering, she mentioned the matter to Serge, who showed anger for the first time. 'I don't wear those things, I don't have the pox and I'm not a fruit.'

'Serge, I'm not suggesting . . . just, I don't want to get pregnant. You need to . . . I mean *we* . . . We need to be careful.'

They'd been on their way to see Mémé. Alix kept checking the rigid profile, thinking, *Any minute he's going to remind me how much fuel he's spending on me. Or he'll smile and stroke my knee.* Serge's moods were like a billiard ball flicked with a bent cue. You couldn't predict their direction. What he did was slam on the brakes. Alix shot forward, smacking her head against the car's dashboard.

Serge watched her struggle back onto her seat before saying, 'Your problem is, you're a bag of worries. It makes you tense. Tight is one thing, but I'm getting tired of knocking at the cathedral door.'

A few kilometres on came a pat on the knee. 'I can see I'm going to have to procure you some medicine. Sorry about the bang. A deer shot out in front of me – didn't you see it?'

Saturday evening . . . Alix checked the time. Six hours before she was due at the Rose Noire. She'd do her hair, she decided, and slouch around in an old dress until it was time to change. Serge had been away the last few days, meeting business associates at Le Havre on the Normandy coast. The separation had softened her anger at his behaviour. He was right; she *was* a bag of worries, because half the time her mind was at Mémé's bedside. Tonight, when he returned, she'd ease up, she decided. Smile and show Serge how much she liked being at his table, dancing with him. Drinking champagne. Three days without bubbles, she felt twitchy.

Pouring out tea in the lounge, Rosa took in Alix's pin curls, kept in place with kirby grips and a knotted scarf. 'Time was, I used to make that sort of effort. I know the man you should have hung on to.'

'He left me, Rosa.'

'He was a gent, Mr Haviland. Didn't have to pretend – in the blood. What d'you reckon, Toinette?'

Rosa's housemaid, watching the summer evening crowds through the open window, said, 'Alix, isn't that your nice friend coming across the square? The boy who helped you move your stuff here? The one with the little girls?'

'Paul's here?' Alix joined Toinette at the window and her heart sank. It *was* Paul coming, Lala and Suzy skipping alongside him. She hadn't seen much of him since starting her affair with Serge. In the beginning it had been fine because Paul hadn't known about them. Then, somehow, he'd found out. Maybe through Bonnet, who'd bumped into her and Serge on Place Pigalle. It had been the early hours and they'd been on their way to sound out a new jazz club. Leaving Serge to park the car, Alix had gone ahead, night air soft on her shoulders. She'd seen a figure coming out of a subterranean cabaret she knew to be a gambling club. Bonnet. He'd spotted her and come over, arms outstretched, looking rougher than ever, and as if he'd lost all interest in washing. Knowing Serge would take him for a vagrant, she'd smiled and tried to walk on. Bonnet hadn't taken the hint, grasping her arm and burbling something about 'losing his next month's rent, and if Alix was a true friend . . .'

Serge had sped up to them, roaring threats, and Bonnet had stumbled away. Since then, everyone seemed to know she was Serge Martel's latest. At their last meeting Paul had been distant, and they'd quarrelled after he referred to Alix as 'Serge's moll' . . .

This time he was polite, just. Alix made a fuss of Lala and Suzy to cover her awkwardness, but when Toinette brought in cake and fresh tea she left the room, making the excuse of needing to finish her hair. Paul followed her upstairs.

He said from the doorway of her room, 'Una says you're slowing down with the sketches. Too much on your plate. You can't shoot five ducks with one gun, she says.'

Alix, pulling the scarf off her head of curls, retorted, 'You can, if they stay still. Look, I'm giving her a steady stream and I can't do more. I don't want to do more. How often do I have to explain?'

'We won't get paid again until the autumn–winter line is in production and, Alix, I'm in a fix. I got fined again for mooring illegally. And my propeller driveshaft is going – that's funny?'

She hadn't meant to laugh. She was picking up bad habits from Serge. 'It's not funny, but listen, I'm not a machine.' She loosened a pin curl to see if it was dry. 'New York won't go into production until the middle of August and it's only just July.'

Paul usually accepted her reasoning, but this time, seeing his eyes burning holes in the mirror, she snapped, 'What?'

'It's you. Since becoming a mannequin and going out with that hoodlum, your nose has got stuck in the air. You haven't time for your friends.'

'How dare you?'

'It's true! You've dumped Bonnet, and I suppose I'm next.'

A twinge of truth . . . Bonnet that night had repelled her. She still cared for Paul, but his affair with Una and the unremitting pressure to copy had robbed their friendship of its casual innocence. What she was doing to Javier was breaking her heart, and Paul didn't seem to understand. It made her want to be cruel to him. 'Yes, you're right, I'm more choosy now. I mean . . . Serge doesn't leave chalky footprints on the floor.' She threw a meaningful glance at the floorboards. 'I ride in a car these days, drink champagne and sleep on satin sheets –' She stopped, seeing the alteration in Paul's expression.

He said quietly, 'Is that what you always wanted? Cars? Tables in flashy bars? Why didn't you say? Then I wouldn't have spent all this time waiting and hoping. When I knew you'd been with Martel . . .' he swallowed, 'I thought, Why him, not me? Why, with all the love I sent to Alix, the way I held her but never forced myself on her . . . why go with a hog like Serge Martel?'

She grabbed her hairbrush and hurled it at him, purposely missing, because even in her spite she didn't want to hurt him more. 'He's not a hog!'

'No, hogs are honest.' He strode up to her and grabbed the hand reaching for a powder compact. 'Why not me?' he

392

said into her hair. 'How about, because you only get rough wine at my table, which is only a cable drum. Because I give you lifts on a bicycle not in a Peugeot? Oh, Alix, I'd have loved you like a king. You would never have been ashamed of me in bed.'

A dry cough stopped him. From the top of the stairs Rosa said, 'Come down, if you want any of that cake. And kindly stop throwing things at my walls.'

Paul went out, pausing to say to Alix, 'It's gypsum, not chalk – on my boots. I'm still doing shifts at the exhibition site. It won't be finished till the day before it closes. I'm the muscle who mixes the plaster.'

'Right, what's up?' Rosa said, soon as the door closed on Paul and the girls. A few well-aimed questions had Alix crying into a napkin.

'I don't understand him,' she sobbed. 'He has Una, who probably knows more about sex than . . . than . . .'

'What? A tomcat? A tart?'

'No.' It didn't matter. 'He has her, so why is he blaming me for having someone?'

'Because he's a man and not rational,' Rosa told her. 'Not when it comes down to trouser basics. When a man wants a woman so badly it hurts, you could swap his brain for a cabbage and not notice the difference.'

'I was cruel.'

'It was always going to happen, dear, sooner or later. The being-cruel bit, I mean.'

29th July 1937

The heat in the mannequins' *cabine* was stupefying. Not just because twelve young women and their dressers were crammed in, but because the ironing women were at work. No electrical flexes allowed in here. The women kept their irons at the right heat by continually returning them to a special oven. Their faces glowed with perspiration.

'Five minutes, girls,' cried Mme Markova. As *chef de cabine*, she would marshal every girl in and out of the salon. 'Stand by for Waverley, Falcon, Lomond and Wild Heather.'

Sounds like the stations on a Scottish railway, Alix thought, dusting her underarms with talcum powder. In her nervousness, she tipped some on to her feet, adding the scent of gardenia to the florals and musks. Oh, for a cool breeze. Her mind sped to the banks of the Seine and those fountains and to the woods near Versailles where she and Serge had strolled one evening after sitting with her grandmother.

She stepped into a skirt. Tweed lined with silk, while outside Paris sweated, thunder nestling in the clouds. Today was Javier's autumn–winter launch, her first collection as a professional mannequin. She was no longer Alix, the girl Javier had plucked from the sewing room. She'd become 'Aliki', choosing Mémé's pet name for her because she felt different now and wanted the world to know it. She was the silent, aspen-slim girl whose enigmatic air added something extra to the dresses she wore.

She had the double distinction of wearing clothes she'd helped put together. One day, maybe a year or two from now, she could be showing dresses she'd helped design.

She reached out to her dressing table. *Touch wood*. Checked her accessories and made sure her schedule was pinned to her mirror frame. Noise was building on the other side of the curtains as buyers, clients, trendsetters and journalists found their seats.

Two things missing – Serge and Mémé. If she could have seen either of them craning their necks out there it would have soothed her. Serge was at the Rose Noire auditioning a new jazz band. Mémé still lay deep in a coma.

Alix buttoned up her blouse, then put her arms into the jacket of specially commissioned tartan her dresser held out for her. Finally she pinned a tam-o'-shanter at a rakish angle. Suede gloves and a sprig of white heather at her cuff completed 'Lomond'. She had a few minutes to feel sick before Mme Markova put motherly hands on her shoulders and told her, 'Enjoy yourself, and don't fall over.'

Alix followed Zinaida, Nelly and Claudette into an amphi-theatre of faces.

She was supposed to promenade along a raised platform, pose at the far end, turn and amble back as if smelling the roses. But it seemed to take about three breaths. All she took in was the rustle of programmes, the odd cough. Una Kilpin's wink. Then it was over – she was being disrobed by lightning hands and thinking, *Thank God I didn't fall*.

Marcy mouthed, 'Well done,' as Alix stepped into an afternoon dress, one of Javier's 'Duenna' line. Javier joked that his autumn–winter collection was inspired by the Moors, Spanish ones and Scottish ones. This dress took the swirling flamenco theme of the mid-season collection and tamed it for winter wear. It was velvet. *I'm going to suffocate*, Alix thought. Change of shoes, wriggle into tight elbow-length gloves. Hair in a chignon. Earrings and a marcasite hair comb, a pat of face powder.

By the time she was parading a satin evening dress called L'Arabie, she was enjoying herself. Really, people were looking at the clothes, not at her. So long as she counted steps and didn't bump any of the other girls, it was easy. She was striking her pose at the end of the catwalk when, above the whispering and rustling, came a strident voice . . .

'I've had enough. Not one of the models you've shown today, M. Javier, is your own original work. I declare this collection is nothing more than a heist!'

A silence, then a single gasp left a hundred mouths. A rabid bustle as people tried to identify the speaker. Alix could see her from her vantage point, but the woman was unknown to her. Middle-aged, in a black hat and white cotton suit.

Mlle Lilliane manifested onstage, those belligerent eyebrows promising violence.

The speaker faced the directrice calmly. 'I am happy to repeat what I just said, if you wish me to.' The accent was North American.

Alix sought out Una Kilpin, but Una was whispering to her neighbour. Then Javier was among them. In the mildest of tones he addressed the heckler. 'Madame? You will perhaps oblige me by explaining your words and, I trust, withdrawing them. I, Javier, have received many slights in my life, but the charge of plagiarism has never before been pointed at me.'

'I'm sincerely sorry to be the first. I'm Gladys Fisk-Castelman and I'm a fashion journalist.' The woman named a leading New York paper. 'I saw this collection in New York on July 16th, the day before I sailed.'

Alix and Una made eye contact, reading each other's disquiet.

'Madame,' Javier gave his infinitely respectful bow, 'this work has been created in my ateliers and cannot also be in New York.'

'Uh-huh?' Mrs Fisk-Castelman, unabashed at being the sole focus of attention, squeezed along her row, issuing 'pardon me's' and 'mind your knees' as she went. She stepped on to the platform inches from Alix. There she unbuttoned her jacket, let it fall.

She wore a fitted blouse in camel-coloured silk, with mother-of-pearl buttons, a neat collar and a tie neck. It was, Alix conceded, twin to the one she herself had worn with 'Lomond'.

Then again, the blouse was as simple as a blouse could be. Javier clearly thought the same.

'I agree, Madame, your blouse could be the one I designed for my Scottish *tailleurs*. Or indeed, one I made for my spring collection in 1935. You might find similar blouses this season in three or four other houses. Sometimes a blouse is intended simply to lie quietly beneath a jacket.'

Someone in the audience began to clap. Someone else shouted, 'Get on with the show. We don't want to see an old prune undressing.'

Mrs Fisk-Castelman cricked her jaw. 'I am sorry, ladies and gentlemen, but I saw every item of this collection already, at a show put on by a friend of mine.' Her finger sketched the outline of Alix's dress in the air. 'L'Arabie? Seen it. Tried it on. Go ask Yetta Flatmeyer, or better still, visit her boutique on East 49th Street, which specialises in high-end ready-to-wear. I know which wholesaler she got that dress from and I know she paid a shave under ninety dollars for it. You couldn't get a candy wrapper between hers and the one this young lady is wearing.'

'No. This is not possible.' For the first time in Alix's presence, Javier surrendered his famous composure. 'It cannot be!'

'How about an experiment, Monsieur? How about I draw you the climax of your show today? The big dress that's going to knock the ball out of the park.'

Javier looked like a man dragged across stones and left for

dead. Alix could have wept for him as he beckoned Mlle Lilliane. 'Oblige this lady, if you please.'

With a dignity Alix couldn't help but admire, Lilliane handed over her seating plan, complete with clipboard and pencil. Against a background of hostile whispers, Mrs Fisk-Castelman peeled off a page and began to sketch, Alix willing with every fibre of her being for that pencil to break.

But, actually Alix was as mystified as everyone else by Mrs Fisk-Castelman's claims, or nearly so. Javier had completed L'Arabie during the first weekend of July and Alix had drawn it for Mabel Godnosc around the seventh or eighth of the month. If the woman was sketching the show's climax, a ball gown called Duquesa de la Noche, well, that hadn't been finished until 9th July. She'd handed over the sketch of Duquesa the following week, on the 14th, *quatorze juillet*, a date fixed in her mind as she'd pushed her way along the Champs-Elysées through swarms of holiday revellers. Given that even the *Normandie*, the fastest boat plying between France and the United States, spent five days on the Atlantic, Mrs Fisk-Castelman couldn't have seen that dress in New York on the sixteenth. Not unless Mabel Godnosc had made a pact with the Devil.

The journalist presented her sketch to Javier, who regarded it as if it were his death warrant. 'This is the very dress, the climax to my show. How can this be?'

Alix couldn't look any more. All she wanted was to pull Una

Kilpin off her chair and make her somehow explain how this horrible thing had happened.

For two days afterwards, Alix avoided the muttering huddles that filled every room and corridor of Maison Javier. So jumpy was she, Mme Frankel sent her once more down to the sanatorium. The nurse assumed she was coming down with summer flu and sent her home. Alix closed her shutters and lay in bed, very frightened.

Three days in to her supposed flu, Marcy called with a box of marzipan sweets and the news that Javier had called in the police. As soon as she left, Alix finally got up, going to the Abbesses post office, where she called Una Kilpin's residential number, trying repeatedly when she couldn't connect. But either the telephone rang out or the maid fobbed her off, claiming 'Madame' was unwell.

At least Serge filled her nights. Champagne, music and his earthy preoccupation with her body occupied her sleepless hours. He found it hilarious that, a few nights before, she'd unknowingly smoked a hashish joint at the jazz club they went to on Pigalle. 'Mezz is a Saint,' he crowed, referring to the club's maitre d'. 'He doesn't like to see a lady looking sorrowful and will always provide the medicine.' After that he'd made sure that the dealers who padded around the Rose Noire's tables kept her supplied. Alix stayed in a blessed half-haze for several days until she woke one afternoon fully dressed on Serge's bed with a pounding head, a fly buzzing in a fold of window net. Heading to the bathroom, she muttered, 'Damn this. If I'm for prison, so is Una.'

An hour later she was on the Champs-Elysées, hammering at the street door of Maison Godnosc.

At a table strewn with samples stood Mabel and Una. They looked to be in the silent stage of an argument which had hit the buffer. Mabel was holding a dress up to the light, pretending to examine it. It was one Alix had designed, kept on hand for customers Mabel didn't trust. Even the dress looked forlorn. Green was difficult. Green so often wanted to be poison. No gin cocktails tonight, Alix noted, before accusing Una of hiding from her.

'No, I really was ill.' She looked it. Mabel also looked positively gaunt. Even so, Alix launched an attack.

'The stupidity of what you've done! Javier is talking to a police department that puts couture thieves in prison.'

Una nodded. 'I took Gladys Fisk-Castelman to lunch, one ex-patriot to another, and she says autumn–winter Javiers are flooding New York and the great man will sue if he's got anything resembling balls.' Those last words were aimed at Mabel, who buried her face in the green dress.

Alix snatched the garment away and threw it on to the table, yelling, 'Again! You gave a collection to New York before it was presented in Paris.'

Mabel made a 'whaddya expect?' gesture. 'I'm the middle woman. Can I go to a wholesaler like Samuels or Weinstock and say, "Start manufacturing, but keep schtum until this date or that date"?'

'We agreed we'd wait till mid-August. You only had to hold off a couple of weeks, so instead of one suspect – me – there'd be five hundred.'

'They use us because we give them designs fresh out the egg. It's our selling proposition. Our risk.'

'Well, we're dead.' Alix swung round to include Una. 'You're nothing but a pair of cardsharps.' The advantage of keeping a lid on your anger was that, when you let it out, it had the power to turn pistons. 'What's more, I know you have somebody else working for you at Javier; you must do. You couldn't have got my last sketches to New York in time to have them made up and beat Javier to his own show.'

Una denied it. 'You're our one true love, honour bright.'

That did it, that little stab at humour. Alix picked up a chair, walked with it to the window. 'I'm going to hurl this on to the Champs-Elysées. Then I'll hurl out every fake dress, and scream until the police arrive. You have until the count of three to tell me the truth.' She lined the chair up with the middle of the window.

'OK, kiddo. Put down the weapon. Sit on it and I'll tell you.'

So Alix sat and Una folded her hands and Mabel clacked her bangles.

'Belinograph,' said Una.

'Bell-what?' Alix demanded.

'Mr Kilpin's latest toy. It's a radio wire that transmits pictures. Instead of days at sea on a boat they whoosh across the Atlantic in minutes. It's a miracle of technology.'

Alix narrowed her eyes. Was Una gulling her? 'If there was a wire over the sea, ships would get caught in it.'

'Bless you, it goes by cable laid on the seabed. Just like a telegraph message, only this time it's your drawings reduced to a series of beeps . . . never mind, take it from me: nobody has to send pictures by boat so long as they have a Mr Kilpin. He bought the machine for sending weather charts and marine maps around the world. I use it some evenings; his secretary turns a blind eye.'

'You sent my sketches on this Bell-thing? Mme Godnosc, you knew?'

Mabel made a grinching face. 'If technology's there, you use it. We don't wear twigs or cook dinner in a pit any more. That's progress.'

Alix swung back to Una. 'All for one and one for all?'

Una twitched. 'I told Mabel to wait, but controlling Big Apple entrepreneurs, that's hard.' She reached out and patted Alix's cheek. 'Chin up, kiddo, we'll pull through.'

Alix yelled, 'You can be calm because nothing will happen to you.'

'Oh? When my husband finds out we wired from his office, he may divorce me. And did you get paid? Well, did you?'

'A lick and a promise and it all went to my grandmother's clinic.'

'I'm sorry for your trouble, but like Mabel said—' Una stopped. They heard men's voices, a protest from the receptionist. After that, footsteps coming closer.

Three men entered dressed in smart civilian suits. The eldest said courteously, 'Mme Godnosc?'

'No.' Una gestured faintly to Mabel, who cleared her throat and bleated, 'Oh, God.'

'Madame, we are following up evidence presented by the couturier Javier to the effect that you are involved in the illegal copying and transmitting of fashion designs. He has proof that designs were stolen from his premises and sent abroad for copying. We are also investigating his claim that you pirate the work of other leading couturiers. We intend to conduct a search of this office and confiscate any items that implicate you.' He spoke French, of course, and when Mabel returned mute incomprehension, he turned to Una. 'We are also looking for a Mme Kilpin in connection with the offence.'

'Look no further, honey.' Una attempted an invincible smile.

'Mademoiselle?' One of the other men looked at Alix, who stared back, mouth opening and closing without sound.

'Her?' Una snatched a sheet of brown pattern paper from the table. She created a travesty of a parcel around the green dress and flung it at Alix, who caught it. 'English, not a word of French, but the poor idiot strives to be chic so we do our best with what she's got.' She hustled Alix to the door. '*Au revoir,* Mademoiselle. . . er . . . Garland.' Shoving Alix into the corridor, she hissed, 'Bring me grapes in jail.'

Entering Maison Javier next morning, Alix knew by the texture of the air that something had changed. She'd just put down the valise-style bag that contained her mannequin's accessories and make-up when Mme Markova came to her and said, 'Monsieur wishes to see you in his studio.'

Simon Norbert and Mlle Lilliane stood either side of Javier. Like a bodyguard, blank-faced. In a further office, telephones were ringing. Somebody was answering them, but clearly could not cope. Javier invited Alix to sit. His sketchbooks were piled at either elbow, walling him in. One was open, a paperweight keeping the page.

For some time he said nothing, so that when he did speak her overstrained pulse leaped. 'I believe this is the blackest time of my life, Alix. The damage done to my reputation . . .' He shook his head. 'A second collection ruined. Journalists' sneers proved right. Twenty years' work thrown in my face. You know Mme Kilpin has been arrested for pirating?'

Alix cleared her throat. 'I – er – heard.'

'Whether they will charge her . . .' He shrugged. 'Her husband is so rich and influential. I mention this because she is in a way your patroness. You are here because of her recommendation.'

Hope surged. Maybe Una's quick thinking had saved her. Alix knew she didn't deserve to get off, but keeping Javier's affection suddenly felt all-consuming. That, and keeping her job. She knew precisely on which day this month the money to pay Mémé's bills would run out.

'Tell me your opinion of this.' Javier turned a sketchbook towards her, removing the paperweight. It was a sketch of a woman in medieval dress and Alix recognised its inspiration. One of the 'Lady with the Unicorn' tapestries which hung in the Cluny museum. Its sleeves were similar to those of Christine de Charembourg's wedding dress. The neckline too, the one originally designed to show off the family pearls. Why was Javier showing her this?

The dress was in the middle of the page, with small details reproduced in each corner. Each subsidiary sketch had another detail, or fabric idea, drawn at its corner, giving the page the symmetry of a Moorish tile. Javier always presented his ideas this way. Alix considered his sketchbooks miniature works of art.

'I don't recall your ever making this, Monsieur.'

'No,' he acknowledged. 'The medieval motif is too "Arts and Crafts", too recently out of fashion to risk in these more stringent times.' He picked up a sheet of art paper and placed it on the scrapbook.

Alix stuttered, 'Oh, I – oh.'

406

It was her sketch of Rose Noire, the dress she'd thrown out for Mabel Godnosc on a night when her head ached and she'd been longing to meet Verrian.

'It interests me, Alix, how you absorbed my way of laying out ideas. You are a good pupil. Now let me explain what I know of this dress. It was created for Mme Kilpin who wanted to sell it to an American wholesaler as part of a summer line. That is nothing to me – she is entitled to be a dress dealer if she wishes. But also she wished for some samples to be made here in Paris, for herself and friends. She approached –' Simon Norbert came forward – 'a friend of my good lieutenant here to procure the fabric. You were a little suspicious, *mon ami*, when your friend showed you this drawing?'

Simon Norbert's mouth puckered, but for the first time he looked happy in Alix's presence.

'Most suspicious. First I thought it was one of your drawings, Monsieur, but on closer inspection I realised it was a rake-together of lots of your ideas. The collar with the contrast revere, well, that was spring–summer 1934, and that lozenge insert defining the waist, we discussed that last winter before *she* –' he aimed a toxic glance at Alix – 'arrived here. But we produced a fair few drawings trying it out. She must have leafed through your sketchbooks and seen it.'

'No!' Alix cried. 'I did no such thing!'

'Thank you.' Javier's gaze was pure sorrow. 'Did you think, Alix, you had come up with something strikingly original?' He shook his head. 'Little in this world is truly original, but I commend you. The idea is fresh, it has verve and I had the pleasure of seeing the dress itself in the Spanish pavilion at the World's Fair. I remember thinking, *Even when evil stalks the world, the simple pleasure of a beautiful girl never wanes.* Please come forward, Mlle Lilliane.'

Alix thought she was going to faint. Anything to escape the humiliation that was coming.

'You warned me not to employ this young woman,' Javier said.

'I did, Monsieur.'

'I rejected your advice and now formally beg your pardon. It is a lesson to me, that the instincts I have learned to rely upon may lead me wrong.'

'Your intentions were good,' Mlle Lilliane said. 'I'm just sorry they were wasted. Just as I'm sorry that we ever thought Solange was a thief.'

'Poor Solange indeed. Go now, if you please. Both.' The two assistants left the studio, but Alix knew they hadn't gone far. She could hear them in the corridor outside.

'So . . .' Javier raised his hands. 'I know now that you were Mme Kilpin's beetle, gnawing inside this great tree of mine, digesting the goodness and turning it over to her. You do not deny it?'

'No.'

His silence was agony. At last he said, 'It is because your grandmother is so ill that you did this?'

Alix could hardly see through her tears. In a moment she'd be weeping in that unstoppable way, like whooping cough. A handkerchief was held out and she snatched it. She tried to tell him something of her shame; how copying had started out as a sideline, almost a game, that allowed her to buy clothes and make up the shortfall in hers and her grandmother's income. How she was then pressured into stealing collections. His collections. How it had sickened her from the start, how she'd tried to stop. 'But then my grandmother was attacked, and I'm all she has because my mother died when I was born, and I had to pay hospital bills and I couldn't see my way out.'

Javier spoke gently. 'Specialist care is so expensive and you have no father or family to help. You take it all on yourself, Alix. You steal because others –' his voice grew hard – 'see they can use you. They offer you money. You cannot turn it down. In a way, you steal for love.'

'For love?' She met his eyes and, through tears, saw a match for her own misery. Javier needed to believe in her innate goodness and she wished she could say something to restore his faith. What could she say when the consequences of her behaviour were clear in his face? In the destruction of his life's work? 'Don't be kind to me,' she sobbed. 'Don't try to see the best in me. But please believe that I respect you and care about you and am so ashamed I would work for you for the rest of my life for nothing.'

'Ah.' He spread his hands in helpless regret. 'I think that would be illegal and quite rightly so. Come, I will take you downstairs.'

M. Javier conducted her to the pavement as if she were a valued customer. He sent a subordinate for her bag, handing it to her as she climbed into the rear of a taxi. The taxi had appeared from nowhere. Someone must have ordered it. So everyone knew. Marcy, Pauline Frankel, Mme Albert with her bobbin drawers, kind Mme Markova . . .

As the taxi inched through clogged streets, bumper grazing until they reached the artery of Boulevard de Magenta, Alix felt a lifetime's misery swelling inside her. All she could think was, *Now I know how Sylvie le Gal felt. I hate my life and I want to die.*

Chapter Twenty-Eight

One month earlier – July 1937. Villanueva del Pardillo, west of Madrid

He lay stretched out on a hillside. Raised his head and a bullet sang over his scalp. An instant later a shell exploded above the shallow dip where he was sheltering. Missiles spattered his back and, thinking he'd been hit, he pressed his knuckles against his jacket, testing for blood. Only stones and dry soil, he realised. He was still being lucky. Further down in the dip where he'd crawled for shelter, two comrades lay dead.

They'd been at this assault over six hours, and he was still unsure what his commanders were trying to achieve. Not that he was sure of much. The incessant slam of shells and remorseless rifle fire from nearby Villanueva had liquefied his brains. Flies wouldn't stay off him, crawling into his collar, over the backs of his hands. A hundred degrees of heat, no water to drink. Every now and then a whistle would blow and his unit would move forward, crawling in the dust on their bellies, firing as they went. They'd get a little nearer the enemy and the street fighting they'd been promised – then they'd be pushed back by the shelling. Those streets were never less than five hundred yards away.

With each advance, more men would fall. The hillside was a garner-floor of bodies. Another shell exploded and more dust rained on Verrian's neck. As the shock of it died away, he heard the fresh crack of rifle fire, men shouting to each other in English. A new advance was imminent, and he must be part of it. He'd taken shelter while his gun cooled because the barrel had been in danger of exploding from continuous fire. Then a comrade had been hit and he'd tried, in vain, to help. A second man had fallen nearby. A Welshman, who'd survived long enough for them to have an intriguing conversation.

Hearing Verrian's voice beside him, the man had rasped, 'You sound too posh to be on our side. What are you, a sodding Tory?'

'I have no politics. I was a newspaperman,' Verrian had answered. 'I see politics with its trousers down, which makes it hard to belong to any party.'

'A reporter? *Duw*, you should have kept to it. Like I should have kept to delivering the *Socialist Worker* around Merthyr. What made you join up?'

'Guilt.'

'About what?'

'A man I helped kill, and a girl.'

'Now you're talking. Pretty, was she?'

'Very. Her name was Maria-Pilar.'

'Spanish?'

'From Guernica originally, though we met in Madrid. Are you married?'

'I am. She's a Mary too. Four children and she'll kill me when I get home.' The Welshman tried to laugh and it turned into a hideous gargling. 'In my pocket – a letter. Will you –'

'I'll get it into the mail. And I'll write to your Mary, tell her what happened.'

Verrian had searched the man's pockets, found a letter addressed to Queen's Road, Merthyr, and identity documents which he also slipped into his own pocket. When it came time to leave this mangled country, he might find it easier to travel as a Welshman than as Miguel Rojas Ibarra, a Basque. If he didn't first fall victim to a shell or a bullet or die of thirst. He'd give his soul right now for a pint glass of iced water. *His soul*. Had war turned him religious?

'You have no religion, no prayer. You are unmoved by the sacrament of marriage. What hope have you if there is no God in your life?' Maria-Pilar's words a few days after their wedding when she'd finally realised that he wasn't going to embrace her Catholicism.

He did have hope. Though God was not much in vogue among the International Brigades, every man here believed in an ideal as powerful as religion: the right of men and women to live free from oppression. He'd put that in the letter he'd asked Ron Phipps to ensure reached Alix, and had felt the irony as he wrote it. He believed in freedom and was asking a girl he hardly knew to keep herself for him on the off-chance he might make it back to her. One day he hoped to tell Alix that the thought of seeing her again had been his salvation in this hell on earth.

A whistle blew. He pushed his rifle over the top of the hollow and clambered out. Wishing himself continued good luck, he zigzagged towards occupied Villanueva.

PART THREE

PART THREE

Chapter Twenty-Nine

The world of Paris couture first noticed the English girl at the mid-season shows in November 1937. She went from house to house viewing the collections and her card stated that she was a buyer for an exclusive department store in Manchester, England. As the winter closed in, she disappeared. When the spring–summer shows opened in February 1938, she popped up again. Saleswomen nudged each other and whispered, 'How could such a girl end up working in fashion?'

Dorothy M. Sprat was broad-hipped and bosomy. Thick-lensed spectacles gave her a piggy stare, and her hair was plaited unbecomingly over her ears. Her eyebrows were shaggy and a few stray hairs sprouted from her upper lip. A vendeuse at the house of Lanvin had been heard to mutter, 'One look at her and I run for a razor and shaving soap.'

On this February day, a day of wet shoulders and umbrellas blown inside out, Dorothy M. Sprat squeezed into the House of Chanel, using her handbag to beat a path through the crowd all shoving through the same door. She thanked the vendeuse who handed her a programme listing the models being shown that day.

As the show progressed, her pencil touched the programme a few times. Those behind might see an underlining, a question mark. Miss Sprat never attempted to sketch a design, or scribble notes as to cut or fabric. When she purchased, which was not often, she paid in cash.

The show over, she left Rue Cambon, taking the Métro to Pont Neuf. Crossed the river and walked to Rue Jacob on the Left Bank. Halfway along Jacob, she turned into a cobbled courtyard, so hidden away that morning frost still lingered. She spent a moment appreciating the crystal mopheads on a hydrangea bush, then unlocked a yellow door, having rubbed mist off its name plaque.

The plate read 'Modes Lutzman'.

She shouted to the accounts clerk who doubled as the door-keeper, 'Only me, Hubert. Any callers?' Answered by a snore from the depths of an armchair, she rapped the point of her umbrella on the floor. 'Monsieur Hubert, wake up. You're meant to be guarding the place.'

A voice muttered something about being perfectly awake. Mademoiselle didn't need to be quite so military; he was only taking the weight off his ankles.

Miss Sprat handed him a roll of receipts. 'Enter these into the books and please tidy yourself. You resemble a basking blancmange in mixed tweeds. Remember, you're the first person customers see.'

'You don't pay me enough to look lovely.'

'But I pay you and I give you a two-hour lunch break.' Miss Sprat went upstairs. The door at the top of the stairs opened before she reached it, indicating that Hubert had found sufficient vigour to press the electric bell by his chair four times, which meant 'bona fide caller.'

'How was it?' the receptionist asked.

'Sublime. Have we visitors?'

'An English lady, new client. She's having a fitting.'

Miss Sprat proceeded down a corridor and knocked four times on the door at its end. This was unlocked by an older woman whose eyebrows were obsidian black and whose grey hair was done in a chignon.

'Ah, Mlle Sprat.' She spoke English with BBC modulation, as if she practised saying, 'How now, brown cow,' fifty times a day. She indicated a large lady, undressed to her slip and stockings. 'May I introduce Mrs Hawkesley? She is from Manchester, England, and was kindly directed here by Mme Kilpin.'

Greetings were exchanged. Mrs Hawkesley, whose dimensions were being noted down by a fitter, observed that she would never have known this place existed had not 'Dear Mrs K.' given her directions and drawn a map. 'Rue Jacob is a teeny bit off the beaten path.'

'Indeed, but Mme Kilpin sends many clients this way,' said

the lady with the chignon. 'Marguerite will complete your measurements, Mrs Hawkesley. After which, our new season's collection will be shown by our house mannequin. Would Madam care for tea and biscuits?'

The courtesies done, she and Miss Sprat went along a network of passages and let themselves out on to an iron walkway that linked the main building – owned in former times by a rich merchant – to a block that had housed the merchant's servants and his stables. The smaller building had a derelict air, though, with its creeping vine tinged with frost, a romantic one. Neither woman spoke until they were inside the stable block, the door clanking behind them.

'Gawd-a-hell, we needed two tape measures for her arse – and would she stop talking? If she told me once her husband's Mayor of bloody Salford, she told me ten times. You look as though you could drown in a cup of tea, Miss Sprat.' Rosa Konstantiva went to the stove and turned on the gas. 'How was it?'

'Chanel's collection? Beautiful, but I can't help feeling she's letting off all her fireworks at once. Does she know something we don't? Afterwards it was a cattle market for screaming harpies. Some of those buyers would eat human flesh to get hold of the models they want.'

'Was it useful?'

'Yes. I have to see these shows, Rosa, to remind myself why I'm in this world at all.' Miss Sprat sat down at a dressing table and arranged porcelain dishes and a wooden wig stand.

She removed her spectacles and said to her reflection, 'Do it, Spratty.' Holding the corner of one bushy eyebrow, she pulled it off with a sharp, 'Ow.' Same again on the other side. 'Ow.'

Behind her Rosa said, 'Takes me back to when I danced the Firebird – red feathers stuck on with gum arabic. Getting them off was liked being plucked. Nobody recognised you?'

'I don't recognise myself.' Kirby grips clinked into a china bowl. Miss Sprat tipped her head forward, and a moment later the rustic plaits were on the wig stand. Alix pushed her fingers through her own newly cut waves, lifting them at the roots. This was the shortest she'd had her hair since childhood. She wasn't sure she liked it, but long hair itched under the wig. She smoothed her natural brows into a neat line and, while Rosa brewed tea, hurled off her dowdy suit, removing the padding to breasts, belly and hips. Finally, she rolled off her thick English stockings. 'I'll be glad when the shows are over. Miss Sprat is becoming a bore.'

'You'll be able to visit the collections as yourself one of these days.'

'Perhaps. If I tried it now, I'd be given a leg-and-a-wing in to the gutter.' Alix sat down and massaged her sore feet. 'Do I really have to show clothes to Mrs Hawkesley?'

'I can't do it, love.' Rosa put a steaming cup on the dressing table and picked up tweezers. 'Close your eyes and think of England.' Fast as bee's wings, Rosa plucked the twenty or so bristles that created Dorothy M. Sprat's moustache.

The Dress Thief

'Wish I'd never started with those,' Alix said. 'They give me a rash. Lucky the Rose Noire has subdued light.'

'You're going there tonight?'

'Mmm.' Alix savoured her tea. 'It's Serge's life, that place.'

'Love, I wish you'd leave him. You've changed this last year. I've watched you lose weight, and you don't laugh so much.'

That was because she was running her own business, Alix reflected as she belted a silk wrap. Out of the devastation of her removal from Javier had come something that had saved her life: Modes Lutzman. She was proud of her business, but running it alongside nights at the Rose Noire sapped her strength.

Following the raid on the premises in the Champs-Elysées, Una and Mabel had spent several days in police custody. In the end, charges had been dropped because nothing incriminating had been found. Mabel had been careful never to leave sketches in the office overnight, and no pirate Javier models were there at the time, either. The police raid had uncovered a few fake Chanels and Lanvins, but without proof they'd been made on the premises, there was nothing on which to base a prosecution. Una's husband had pulled strings. Una had confirmed later – 'One of the things that makes Gregory so boring is that he knows everyone in government.'

Mabel, having feared deportation, found herself released without a stain. But the experience had rocked her and she'd sailed home in the autumn of 1937, bobbing up as a valuable customer as Alix went into business on her own. Through Mabel,

422

Modes Lutzman supplied Paris originals to the boutiques of New York. Not copies. Never again would Alix pirate. But because she couldn't yet survive on her own original work, she turned out clothes 'in the style of' leading couturiers. Nothing wrong in that, because everything that left her workrooms had a Modes Lutzman label sewn into it. The charade of Dorothy M. Sprat was necessary for now because, in the first week of opening, somebody had tried to sabotage Alix. The word 'salope' – 'slut' – had been painted on her building. Dog excrement had been put through her letter box. Walking down Rue du Faubourg St-Honoré, she'd been hit by a bag of flour hurled from a passing car. She never knew who was behind these attacks and if she'd seen the people involved, she'd probably have been none the wiser. They'd be in the pay of others who wished her ill.

Una had also suffered the discomfort of stares and whispers. Feeling that Paris needed a break to appreciate her better, she'd followed her husband to England. 'Manchester, would you believe, on the grounds that it is halfway between hell and Glasgow.'

Una sent customers to Alix and took a commission. After that dreadful day at Javier's when she'd been escorted out in disgrace, Alix had vowed never to speak to the woman again. The new business she was planning would be hers alone – no Una to goad her into betraying her principles. But just before the Kilpins left Paris, Una had sent a car to fetch Alix to Avenue Foch. The driver had given Alix a note: 'Just get in, kiddo. Let's part as buddies.'

Alix had paled at the sight of Gregory Kilpin in the flat, seated on a white sofa, a tumbler of whisky in his hand. She braced herself to be blamed for his wife's disgrace and his first words were not encouraging.

'So, lassie, I hear you lost your job, but you're having another go at it. You're either brave or crazy. Whisky on the rocks?'

'No, thank you.' She'd gazed about, awed despite her determination to be coldly polite. The walls of the Kilpins' living room were sheer beige. A closer look showed them to be covered with suede . . . suede on walls? It explained the lack of pictures. The only ornaments were sculptures of blistered bronze on the floor. Stunningly avant-garde. Alix said, 'I'd like gin, please.'

'Oh, would you? Una had better do the honours then.'

On cue, Una appeared and mixed Gin Alexanders. 'Take the weight off, kiddo. I'm happy you came.'

Sitting on the sofa, Alix found herself captured by such deep cushions she couldn't keep her feet on the floor. Nor could she lean forward to put her glass on the coffee table. Mind you, with its deer-hide top, it probably wasn't designed to hold drinks.

'See this.' Before her astonished eyes, Gregory Kilpin flipped the tabletop, which must be on some kind of hydraulic hinge. It revealed an underside of polished copper with a cigarette box and lighter welded to the metal. And a third shiny object – a gold ingot, which Alix realised was the gold-plated tenement brick that reminded Kilpin how far he'd come in life.

'I despise clutter,' he said, lighting cigarettes for them all. 'So – does this copying malarkey make money?'

Una nervously lifted the pearls at her neck, letting them fall with a clatter. 'In the right hands, yes.'

Instantly suspicious, Alix cut in, 'It's not a hobby for society women, and it ruins lives.'

'So how will you make money now?' Kilpin asked her, blowing smoke at the ceiling.

'I intend to build a legitimate business, selling clothes to speciality shops in London and New York . . . if I can find the contacts. I'll licence my designs to wholesalers. They may as well pay a small sum for them as go to the trouble of stealing them.'

'Irony in one so young,' Kilpin said. 'Una said you were smart. Go on.'

She faltered. Gregory Kilpin, admirer, was not an easy concept to swallow. 'I, er, think there's a business making made-to-measure without the price tag of the big couturiers.'

'How do you get quality without cost?'

'By staying small and doing a lot myself. By having premises in a cheap part of town. But it has to be done well, and that means employing expert sewing women, taking a building and opening accounts with the fabric houses.'

Gregory Kilpin grunted. 'It means capital.'

'Money up front,' Una translated.

Alix nodded. 'Fabric manufacturers won't extend credit to me. And a lease anywhere means six months' rent in advance.'

Gregory Kilpin underwrote her lease in Rue Jacob and loaned her the seed capital to fund Modes Lutzman for one year. It was not a gift. He was charging interest and he expected the capital back. He would watch Alix's progress closely.

Alix guessed that Una was behind this uncharacteristic generosity. She'd persuaded her husband to fund Alix as a way of saying sorry.

At Rue Jacob, Alix had found premises that not only housed her enterprise – salon on floor one, design studio and sewing ateliers above – but also gave rudimentary living accommodation in the shape of the stable block. Rosa had agreed to work for her as a saleswoman 'for a week or two' because Alix couldn't afford both a fitter and a vendeuse. Two weeks became three, by which time Rosa had discovered that selling clothes was more fun than sitting at home giving desultory orders to her maid. Now a fixture at Modes Lutzman, Rosa's only regret was putting on a posh voice which she now had to keep up. In just six months, Modes Lutzman had grown to a staff of ten, including a fitter, receptionist and première.

An application of lipstick completed Alix's transformation from Sprat to Gower. She gulped her tea and said, 'Aliki rises from the rubble.' Taking the walkway back to the main building, she paused to smell the air. Tobacco smoke. Another unexpected development – Bonnet lived here with them. Thrown out of his studio for not paying his rent, he'd moved into the old carriage lodge beneath Alix's flat promising that it was only 'for a week or two'. Four months on, he showed no sign of moving out. But Alix liked having a man about the place. And so did . . .

You would never write life as a play, she thought. Nobody would believe it. Two days after she'd left Javier, a letter had come from Le Cloître, summoning Alix urgently. Serge had driven like a madman, silent for once because Alix was crying so hard. She'd known in her bones she was on her way to say goodbye to her grandmother.

The matron had met them at the door and said gravely, 'I thought you should know at once – Mme Lutzman is sitting up in bed, accusing my nurses of having stolen her spectacles.'

Mémé liked having Bonnet around. Her old disapproval had melted. Bonnet was once again the amiable young man who'd mixed her husband's paints. She often mistook him for her dead Alfred, which was not surprising as Bonnet painted with a new intensity and talked of Kirchwiller while Mémé dozed beside him in an armchair.

In a dressing room, Alix put on silk stockings and a slip, after which Rosa buttoned her into a dress of toffee-coloured cashmere. This model was called No. 1. No fancy names for Modes Lutzman. It was mid-calf in length, fitted into the waist with a narrow belt of the same fabric, its only drama an embroidered neckline inspired by a tribal necklace Alix had seen at the newly opened Museum of Mankind. This, her first collection, numbered thirty models, stylish 'safe sellers', because whenever she considered anything more daring, Gregory Kilpin's face appeared before her.

She paraded No. 1 to Mrs Hawkesley, then more day dresses, then suits and evening gowns.

'It's all tip-top,' Mrs Hawkesley declared as Alix made her final turn in a floor-length coat of écru lace over an evening dress of watered silk. 'Dear Mrs Kilpin – ever so generous, sending me here. I could wear that lovely dress at our next mayoral do. Did I mention that my husband's Mayor of Salford? Only –' with a glance at Alix's whip-slim figure – 'I shall never fit into it.'

Rosa stepped forward and said in her best elocution, 'Modes Lutzman will make a version to flatter Modom's figure to perfection, and knock the mayor's socks off, while we're at it.'

Summer 1938 arrived with heavy heat. At the Rose Noire, 'Tiptoe Through the Tulips' had all the finesse of a stampede of bullocks. Frazer Hoskins had left after Serge sacked his Creole singer without consulting him. His Smooth Envoys had gone with him. Their replacement, Roistering Rex's Regents of Rhythm, didn't know which end to blow their instruments.

The young Englishman beside Alix issued a cloud of cigarette smoke and said, 'Save your agonies for the true low point, when Miss Dulcie L'Amour steps up to sing. The Rose Noire is sliding.'

'Then find another club that gives you free champagne.' A crushing glance accompanied her words. She knew why Jolyan

Ferryman came here—and it wasn't just because Serge supplied him with champagne and cigarettes. He came as Rhona de Charembourg's escort and, she suspected, her spy. The Comtesse de Charembourg had been a regular visitor here for some months. Though Paris was thinning out as wealthy people left for their summer holidays, she continued to come. Always with the same group of friends, which included a Swiss businessman named Maurice Ralsberg. And she never passed Alix's table without delivering a scorching glance.

From the way Rhona and Ralsberg danced, bodies locked, Alix deduced that the friends were camouflage and that Jolyan's role was that of smokescreen. As he was known to be the Comte de Charembourg's secretary, his presence implied that Rhona was on the town with her husband's consent.

Tonight, under the pink-frosted lights, Rhona's dress shimmered like a metallic rainbow. Ten thousand *paillettes* stitched on to tulle . . . fabulously expensive as every disk would have been sewn by hand. Alix gave a shudder. It was snakelike, that dress. Ralsberg couldn't keep his hands still, so he must like stroking scales. 'Must like paying her account too,' she murmured. That was a dress to be worn for a lover, not a husband.

In spite of Roistering Rex's murdering of the jazz repertoire, the Rose Noire was still the 'in' venue. Still *the* place to dance in a sexually charged environment. But not really the sort of place you'd expect a dull dog like Jolyan Ferryman to wash up.

He'd planted himself at her solitary table some weeks ago,

ignoring her scowl and offering her a cigarette. 'Black Russian. You won't have tried one, I'm sure.'

'Actually I have. My landlady smokes them.'

He lit hers, then his. 'I'm told you're Miss Gower and that you're English. Do let's chat . . . in English. I'm starting to dream in French which, I assure you, is alarming for a boy from Tunbridge Wells.'

'I don't speak English here,' she'd said curtly, checking to see if Serge had noticed this stranger at her side. Serge had different tactics when it came to rivals, depending on his mood and the status of the interloper. He might sit down at the table, drawing the stranger into conversation, only to floor him with some humiliating comment. Or he might stand beside Alix, exuding threat. If he felt lazy, he'd send a henchman to do the business. Yes, Serge had seen them. Goosebumps rose on Alix's arms as she saw him beckon a burly waiter. A minute later, champagne arrived at their table.

Serge had explained later. 'The kid may be the comtesse's bag-carrier for now, but I've watched him, chiselling his way into Maurice Ralsberg's favour. Give him time, he'll be Ralsberg's right-hand man. Grovellers like that are useful. Particularly when they have secrets.'

Studying Ferryman covertly, Alix acknowledged that the Englishman had at least one secret – his source of income. His evening suit was new. Those gold-tipped Sobranies were smoked from an inlaid ebony holder. He smelled of cologne way out of the price range of a humble secretary. Clearly it paid to chaperone the Comtesse de Charembourg.

It was Ferryman's hair that most repelled her, she decided. So slickly oiled, move one strand, the whole lot would shift.

He caught her staring and gave her a razor-sharp smile. 'Want the name of my barber, Miss Gower?'

'Stop calling me Miss Gower. Alix or Mademoiselle. "Miss" is pretentious.'

'Why? But speaking of "pretentious" –' he plucked their champagne from its ice and topped up their glasses – 'what do we make of Serge and the family château at Epernay? He talks about it all the time, its unique *terroire*, its lovingly tended slopes and yet . . . and yet . . .'

'He talks of it. Why not?'

'"The champagne acres of Cuvée Martel . . ."' He tipped the bottle to the light to read its label. 'And yet he serves Lanson. Been to visit?'

'Not yet, it's too far. We're always busy. Shut up and let me listen to the band.'

'You want to listen? I'd say those poor tulips have been flattened to a pulp.'

'Rex and his band are new. Give them a chance to settle in – or go and lower the tone in some other club.' Alix was in no mood for banter. She and Serge had quarrelled that evening. She'd arrived with her dress sticking to her in the July heat, and one glance at the sweating press on the dance floor had made

431

her long for a cool bath and a muslin sheet. Serge had gripped her arm and walked her unceremoniously to their table, fuming because he'd sent a car to Rue Jacob and she'd kept it waiting for two hours.

She'd tried to explain that customers had arrived to see her collection just as she was closing, and she'd had to call her staff back. The visitors had made her show everything twice, then departed without buying. When Serge shrugged, she'd yelled that she didn't run to a timetable like a Paris bus. He could be pleasant, or she'd go home. She'd walk; she didn't need his precious car.

He'd told her she was getting shrewish, like Solange.

Bloody men. But she knew how to blot them out. Pot cut with tobacco, rolled and smoked from her own twenty-two-carat gold holder. Turning away from Ferryman, she sank into a creative trance, fixed on an attractive woman on the dance floor and mentally dressed her in a Lutzman original. She started with the finished dress, stripping back to the basics of construction, drawing on everything she'd learned from Javier and Mme Frankel.

Tonight she saw fresh evidence of a trend – 'Return to Romance'. The willow-wand anatomy was giving way to draped lines. Skirts were getting fuller. Waists more defined. Sleeves, puffed and fluted. Javier had seen it a good year ago in '37. She, curse her caution, had failed to reflect it in her 1938 spring—summer collection because she'd argued that the world was not getting lovelier, or wealthier. Would people want romance when the newspapers were full of riots, shortages and military build-up? The answer, it seemed, was yes.

She'd once asked Javier, 'Why does fashion change so slowly, then change overnight?' He'd laughed and said, 'I quote the Sun King: "Fashion is the mirror of history." We will look back at this era and say, "Aha, that is what killed the Puritan chimney pot and brought back the crinoline." But don't ask me what will trigger it, for by definition history needs distance.'

You couldn't predict fashion, Alix thought. It was an inter-action of art, technology, dreams and caprice. To know what might come next year, you needed what Rosa called the 'div-vy's nose'. The autumn–winter collection Alix was planning for this next month – August – was a risky departure. She'd dug deep into her loan from Gregory Kilpin, ordering hundreds of metres of Jacquard silk and silk velvet, stiffening fabric and – yes – horsehair lace. Too poor to commission her own textiles, she'd bought everything in plain colours. She would add surface embroidery and trimmings, but the risk was in the shapes she was creating. Not a chimney pot to be seen.

'Scent of drains?' Ferryman murmured in her ear, jolting her from her reverie. He smirked. 'You were frowning. We both know we're slumming it here.' His gesture encompassed the dance floor, the pink globe ceiling lights, black lacquer tables and chairs, the long bar with its art deco brass. 'The Rose Noire is a harlot, silk and fur on the surface, all slut underneath.'

'Jolyan, why do you come here? Is it just to use this table to impress your very few friends?'

After a flicker of antipathy he couldn't hide, he said, 'I'm drawn here by the thrilling Dulcie L'Amour.' He pointed his cigarette holder towards the stage. 'What she lacks in tunefulness, she makes up for in stamina. I admire a girl who can gyrate all night after an athletic afternoon stint with Serge and the boys.'

'A what?'

'Rehearsing her set, dear. What did you think I meant?'

Alix drew on her hashish cigarette, inviting stupor into her system. She'd seen the looks Serge gave Dulcie, an American blonde who wiggled and shimmied so you didn't notice she couldn't sing. Didn't notice if you were a man, anyway. Alix didn't need Ferryman to point out that Serge's interest was straying. He was drawing people around him that he could control, who flattered him. Getting rid of those who stood up to him. How much longer would he want her? She was no longer a glamorous mannequin. Nor was she an inexperienced girl unseated by his masculine confidence. These days, she was a career woman who worried about cash flow and fell asleep in the bath. For all that, the thought of losing Serge rocked her. Like hashish, he took the sharp edge off daily living. She didn't always love him . . . in fact, she didn't always like him. Sometimes he frightened her, and it was a rare day that she wasn't exasperated by him. He was vain and manipulative, but the fact that he wanted her was immeasurably important. To feel needed was everything. It eased the pain of Verrian's rejection, Javier's disgust, Jean-Yves's dishonesty. When a plate of oysters arranged in a heart shape arrived at their table, the waiters setting down dipping-bowls of *Mignonette* sauce and lemon, Alix didn't know whether to laugh or grind her teeth.

This was Serge saying sorry for his temper. But why couldn't he come and sit by her instead? Take her hand? Dance with her?

Jolyan misunderstood the shake of her head. 'Can pride come before an oyster, Miss Gower? Freshly torn from the Ile de Ré, voluptuously raw. I dare you to resist. Are you going to share?'

'Have them all.'

'You don't like oysters?'

'I don't like to be bribed, with seafood or francs. I leave that to you.'

'Nasty.'

A short while later, a bouquet of dark-crimson roses added to the clutter on their table. No note attached. Their brooding colour was their calling card.

'Why are red roses the universal apology?' Jolyan downed an oyster in one, his throat convulsing. 'Or indeed the universal thank-you?' He peered around the display. 'Is it the association with scarlet boudoirs . . . or a nod to deflowering? They say Serge has corrupted you beautifully. Oh dear, you're scowling again. Has love grown stale? Have your petals started to curl?'

Alix turned her head away but Jolyan was set on having the last word.

'You've shackled yourself to a man with cheap taste in flowers, who hasn't the courage to care for you. Men like Serge Martel never understand the value of what they have. They acquire what other people seek and they cradle it as a miser cradles gold. Then they grow tired of it, destroy it and pursue the fantasy of the next possession. What I admire in you, Miss Gower, is your peasant mulishness. You're a sticker. Unfortunately for you, you're stuck with Martel.'

'You think I should leave him?'

'Lord no.' Jolyan pretended to choke on his oyster. 'No saying what our friend would do to you if he thought you were casting him off. You're in for the long run, his favourite doormat until he tires of you.'

Alix closed her eyes as Roistering Rex swung his men into a wince-inducing rendition of 'Take the "A" Train'.

In the early hours, she undressed slowly, Serge in bed watching and waiting. The room smelled of shisha tobacco and, from the strength of the vapour, she guessed Serge had added nubs of resin to 'liven the mix' as he put it, though it usually had the opposite effect. He would smoke it from the hookah next to his bed. That blue glass bottle with its snakeskin hose she'd once mistaken for a vaginal douche. God, that had made him howl the first time he'd invited her to join him in using it.

'Here?' she'd asked, blushing to the roots. 'With you watching? Shouldn't I go to the bathroom?' When he'd unravelled her confusion, he'd fallen out of bed laughing and she knew he'd passed the story around because next time they went to the Pigalle jazz club, his friend Mezz had rolled a joint for her and said, 'You want lessons on just where to put this, sugar?'

She undressed to her underwear, the way Serge liked. A satin corselet, lightly boned, silk stockings. As she got in beside him, he reached for her and pulled her on top of him. He had that lost look which meant he'd be slow and languorous, but not really there. He offered her the hookah hose but she refused.

'No more. I drank too much. I wanted to blot out Ferryman.'

'I told you to be nice to him, get in his good books.'

'He hasn't any good books – no, I don't want to smoke.' Serge was trying to angle the hose between her lips.

'Yes, you do. You're all elbows tonight. Loosen the screws, Alix.' He covered the hookah's bowl with the base of a champagne glass to let the smoke build. 'Come on, nice and slow. Don't waste it.'

Soon she too had that slumberous feeling, as if the ceiling were an inch above her head and made of rubbery atoms. Then Serge was pinning her down – though not like a wrestler as he sometimes did – just smothering her, the way that excited him.

He entered her and thrust fast and furiously, to the point where she pushed him away, saying, 'Serge, let me catch up.'

But he wasn't listening. Before he came, he rolled off her with a sigh and said, 'You take over.'

Knotted with frustrated need, she knelt beside him and, closing her eyes, put her lips around his erect penis. He groaned, while she kept her hand braced against his stomach, because once he'd gripped the back of her head so hard she'd nearly suffocated. With her free hand, she caressed him intimately until he was writhing under her. Then, raising her head, she brought him to climax with her hand. She'd learned some tricks with Serge . . . Was that what Ferryman meant about scarlet boudoirs?

While Serge recovered, Alix got pins and needles. Her mind sticky, her heart heavy, she tested an idea: Alix Gower, doormat.

Doormat? When she had the table of honour by the dance floor, and all the champagne and hashish she wanted? Serge must feel something for her. All those car rides to Le Cloître when she'd needed him . . . he'd been kind that way. He'd bought her the gold cigarette holder and numerous bits of jewellery.

Alix Gower, mistress.

Getting out of bed, she studied herself for a long time in a vertical mirror. Rosa was right, she'd got too thin. *Alix Gower, last year's fashion.* She walked to the bed, and stared down at Serge, who had already slid into thoughtless sleep. She could almost feel Jolyan Ferryman beside her, chuckling, 'Shackled, dear, until he decides it's over.'

438

Quickly she put on her dress and shoes, staggering as she balanced on one heel. She fell heavily and swore, but Serge didn't stir. Damn him, leaving her halfway up the flagpole, frustrated, unloved like . . . like Mme Rey's mop. Yes. That's what she was, a mop Serge took out of the cupboard when he needed it. He'd left her alone all evening, thrown himself into bed, smoked himself witless, then expected her to perform on him like a –

'To hell with it.' She strode to his bedside, seized the hookah with the notion of cracking it over his head, but then turned and flung it against the wall. Blue glass shattered.

Using her lipstick, she wrote, 'It's over, goodbye', on the dressing-table mirror and left. Serge slept on.

July 1938 dragged itself to a close, sultry and airless. Alix, who had feared that Serge would come calling on her, demanding explanations, was perplexed as one week, then two, passed without word. Maybe he was too self-absorbed to be vengeful? When August arrived with no communication, she decided this must be true.

The abrupt change to her nightly routine took some getting used to. All those spare hours . . . but she adjusted and filled them by working on her upcoming collection.

Alix spent the morning of the 10th August with her première, testing different lining fabrics to go with the cloth she'd selected for her tailor-mades. Having stitched a sample to prove that her choice of rayon silk would work best, she instructed Mme

LeVert to order a bale and get cutting, then went up to her flat and ate a lunch of lettuce leaves and cucumber. Her autumn-winter show was in eight days and she already felt sick with nerves.

That afternoon, she assumed her role as a mannequin, parading to some Englishwomen who spent the time fanning themselves and asking if windows could be opened wider. By the time they'd left, she was ready to drop and said to Rosa, 'We should have siestas like the Spaniards do. Sleep in the afternoon and come back to work at night.'

Rosa told her to go and have a lie-down. 'We won't miss you for an hour.'

Alix was listing all the reasons why she couldn't take a rest when three long rings of the bell made her gasp. Rosa breathed, 'Oh, my giddy aunt.' Three rings was M. Hubert's code for a police raid. They'd agreed on the signal in the early days of the business, when Alix was convinced the couture police would come after her because of who she was.

The fitter, Marguerite, came running in and they all stared at each other.

'Right,' Alix said. 'No point waiting for them to find me.' She went downstairs, Rosa and Marguerite behind her. From the ground-floor office came a drizzling sound – M. Hubert asleep in his chair, toupée awry, head pressed against the bell.

They joked about it in the end, but Alix was still jittery at the close of the day. With a new collection almost complete, she felt vulnerable. There were people in the jealous world of couture who wanted to see her fail. She knew for a fact that Simon Norbert and Mlle Lilliane had played a part in blackening her name. Marcy Stein, whom she'd met one day buying buttons in Rue St-Denis, had told her so.

As Alix was slicing bread in her flat that evening, Hubert knocked, contrition on his face and his arms full of roses. 'These came as I was locking up.'

Sighing, Alix took them and put them in the sink. Twenty-four stems, boudoir red. Tomorrow she'd distribute them among her sewing girls. Bonnet, who ate with Alix and Mémé several times a week, put one to his nose and said, 'He obviously wants you back, for all he was furious when you left.'

'How do you know Serge was furious?'

'Because I still visit my old Montmartre haunts, and the saga of Serge Martel's feral rage was the talk of the cafés. Everyone wanted to know my opinion because they know I'm your special friend.' Snapping the head off a rose and tucking it into a ragged button hole of his overalls, he described how Serge had hurled a shoe at the mirror where Alix had written her lipstick 'goodbye'. The glass had shattered and Serge had cut himself badly. The cleaning woman who'd witnessed the outburst had been sacked on the spot. 'And later he flung a bottle of wine at a waiter who didn't fetch him a glass quickly enough, though I'm told he often does that. A few days on –'

Bonnet shrugged – 'the storm had passed. Things end and he knows it.'

It was Dulcie L'Amour who now sat at the special table, sipping Lanson champagne and eating oysters arranged in a heart shape – when she wasn't on stage wiggling and cooing.

Serge had cared enough about her to hurt himself and lash out, Alix told herself. But then he'd replaced her so quickly. So then why the roses? His way of telling her she could have him back, if she wanted?

A thunderstorm that night gave little respite. The next morning Alix went up to her atelier and found her girls stripped down to their petticoats. Una had told her once that American department stores had a thing called 'air conditioning' that sucked out heat and moisture, leaving the atmosphere pleasantly cool even in the grip of summer. One day, she promised herself. One day.

'Mlle Gower?' Marguerite poked her head into the atelier. 'A visitor. I've put her in the salon.'

Alix said she'd be right down. She turned to her première, who was holding out a muslin toile. Inspecting it, Alix nodded. 'Very well, Mme LeVert, cut the fabric. We've fitted this toile a thousand times and we can't waste the time we have left.' Always frightening, the moment the scissors bit into costly cloth. She always put it off far too long, but then, so had Javier.

Alix went down to meet her guest, feeling guilty relief. You could sense the temperature decreasing with every step. The salon's walls were painted ice grey. Unable to afford carpet, she'd painted the floorboards white. She'd had the eighteenth-century mouldings and ceiling roses lime-washed and the effect was ghostly, like Javier's salon through the voile drapes. Her only extravagances had been table lamps and elegant sofas. Her clients might come upstairs wondering what sort of backstreet oddity they'd stumbled into, but the moment they sat down, they were at home.

A leggy girl got up as Alix came in. Alix immediately knew her to be a mannequin, from the way she moved. It took her a moment to recognise Javier's Nelly under a pale straw hat. Last time she'd seen her had been at Javier's ruined show last July. She stiffened, but Nelly embraced her and, with a gesture for the salon, said, 'Room to swing a cat?'

Alix fixed them iced lemon water and sat back to learn why Nelly had called. It took a while because Nelly wanted to tell about her engagement to a theatrical entrepreneur and her September wedding, for which Javier was making her a gown. But eventually she pouted and said, 'I've been meaning to call for some days. I saw Serge Martel a little while ago in a club. He came over and mentioned you.'

'We aren't together now,' Alix said quickly.

'Hmm. That's not quite what he said. He thinks you'll go back when you've had your sulk out.'

So Bonnet was wrong. Serge hadn't accepted the end of the affair. 'A long sulk, Nelly.'

'I'm glad. You ought to know what happened to Solange. I don't want the same thing to happen to you.' Nelly's face lost its humour. 'That time Solange was so impossible? Kept storming out? Only a couple of us knew . . . she was pregnant.'

Alix whispered, 'I had no idea. Was it . . . ?'

'Serge's. Solange thought he was going to marry her. He said he would, then –' Nelly wrinkled her nose – 'he met you.'

'He left her for me?'

'Worse than that. He got some tablets.' Nelly glanced around, though nobody could have entered the salon without them seeing. 'They brought on a miscarriage. It went wrong and she nearly died. She had to go to her parents'.'

'To Corsica?'

'Corsica? No. Her family live in Le Havre. Anyway, when I saw her she looked awful. She was wearing a hat, the sort little schoolchildren wear. She said she was staying away, getting over what happened, only . . . Alix, in the end she showed me. She's . . . disfigured.'

Alix frowned. 'From having a miscarriage?'

'No. Because of Serge. Solange's parents were threatening to go to the police about the pills. Serge agreed to pay compensation to Solange, only they had an argument and he bit her.'

'Bit? How?'

'Sank his teeth into the side of her face and tore her ear.' Nelly gathered up her things. 'Look, I have to rush. I'm meeting my fiancé at the Crillon. Alix, you had to know.'

'Wait. Serge isn't violent, not to women.' Alix followed Nelly to the door. 'He's selfish, but he never hurt me.'

'Don't give him the chance. Don't end up like Solange.'

Alix couldn't let her go without asking after Javier. Nelly was quiet for a moment. 'You obviously don't hear much these days. He's closed his doors. After last summer's fiasco he tried to keep going. He brought out a fabulous collection in February.'

'I know. I saw pictures—'

Nelly gave her such a look she fell silent. 'Then all the fabric companies demanded payment at once. There's a foreign businessman called Maurice Ralsberg who has bought out all the smaller companies. He foreclosed. Javier tried to get financiers to help, but the debts were too big. One afternoon when he and Mme Frankel were sitting down to discuss ideas for July, he threw down his pen and said it was over. Go down Rue de la Trémoille, you'll see boarding on the windows.'

After Nelly left, Alix sat, numb, until Rosa came to find her.

'Look at you. Hubert hasn't been ringing his bells again?'

'Oh, Rosa, I've just heard the two most dreadful things.'

'Two, eh? Means number three's on its way. May we shut? Everyone's wilting and it's gone seven.'

Number three came an hour later.

Alix always took a couple of hours off for dinner. Mémé no longer cooked. Her injury had affected her balance, and though she was lucid some of the time, the powders she took to ease a persistent headache inhibited her memory and concentration. Much of her life in London and Paris before the attack was a blur, yet she still recalled her youth with absolute clarity.

Putting together a potato salad with cold salt beef, Alix laid the table and filled water jugs. It was this time of night she got the champagne twitch, a gnawing need to see the bubbles rise, the bloom appear on the glass. Drinking water helped, so did keeping busy. Going down the steps to Bonnet's studio, she smelled the inevitable strong coffee and something else. That putrid tang that announced her friend was priming a canvas.

'Rabbit size,' she said. 'You're still buying the cheap stuff.'

'No,' Bonnet said without breaking stroke. 'I buy expensive stuff and the bastard who makes it swaps it for the cheap stuff.'

'Take it back.'

'The factory's out in La Villette, too far. Your grandmother's in the garden. Pick your way around the clutter.'

Mémé came in before Alix reached the door. Taking her granddaughter's arm and leaning against her, she watched Bonnet's paintbrush moving up and down, apparently fascinated.

'Horrible smell, Raphael Bonnet, and I smelled it before. I smelled it when I was bashed on the head.'

Bonnet stopped. Turned slowly.

Mémé went on, 'I had no idea until now why my head hurt and why I had to leave my flat in St-Sulpice. Now I remember.'

'Grandmère, are you telling us you know who hit you?'

'The man who smells like Bonnet's paintbrush.'

Alix stared at Bonnet, who made a flummoxed face back.

'I got home from playing cards. It was dark. The front door was open and I thought you were home. I called "Aliki?" No answer, so I supposed you were in bed. I went to the kitchen to make my hot milk. I heard a door open and I shouted, "You call this a time to come home?" I turned, but instead of you, there he was.'

'Who, Mémé?'

'The man who smelled like Bonnet's paintbrush,' Danielle Lutzman repeated with great patience. 'I couldn't see his face. When he said, "You're back too early," I picked up the iron skillet but I couldn't hold its weight.' Mémé held up her hands, displaying frail wrists. 'He took it and hit me very hard.' She patted the place. 'I fell and I remember his stink as he knelt beside me.'

Alix remembered being sent flying in the dark. She remembered a foul rag in her mouth, a man's face covered by a mesh of oily wool. She picked up Bonnet's tin of rabbit size and sniffed. 'It's the same odour, you're right.'

Her grandmother gazed back at her with childlike eyes. 'Shall we tell the police that I remember how the bad man stank?'

Alix thought – a smell as evidence? They'd be laughed out of the police station. Besides, she didn't want to go anywhere near the police.

At supper, Bonnet agreed wholeheartedly. 'Stay away from

those police bastards. They'd make Danielle go over and over her attack until she was more confused than she is now.' He helped himself to seconds of meat. 'Best thing you ever did, moving out of St-Sulpice. I meet Fernand Rey every now and again – the concierge's son? He keeps a stall at Mouffetard market. He has ideas who the culprit might have been. He saw your friend de Charembourg at the flat that night.'

'That's not possible. The comte would have said something. I mean, surely he would?'

'Maybe.' Bonnet glanced at Mémé, who was eating the beef Alix had cut into small squares. 'Perhaps he thought it indelicate to mention it. But this is more to the point. Do you remember the gypsies who lived in the courtyard?'

'Course I do. You don't suspect them?'

'Fernand Rey does and, you know, it's not so far-fetched. Not after what your grandmother said. The stink? Those gypsies make their money catching rabbits in Bois de Boulogne. They sell the meat and cure the skins in urine. It's why your courtyard reeked of it.'

Chapter Thirty

Bonnet's words were on Alix's mind next day. Fernand Rey might be right; one of those gypsies might have broken into the flat and tried to silence Mémé when she discovered him. But it didn't *feel* true. Alix had been wary of the refugees, but never afraid of them. On the other hand, she clearly recalled Fernand Rey coming into the flat with his mother. He'd watched her rehang her grandfather's pictures and Alix had felt he was pricing them up.

As she thought about Fernand Rey and his reasons for deflecting suspicion on to outsiders, she watched the fitter Marguerite and the première take a new client's dimensions. They were making suggestions as to the style of suit that would best complement the lady's neat figure, and as Alix liked their ideas she said nothing. Gradually Fernand Rey became secondary to the business of waist darts, false pockets and a scoop neck.

Seeing Alix in the doorway, the client smiled and gave her name as Adèle Charboneau. 'Mme Kilpin mentioned your name. We used to be neighbours on Avenue Foch. I'm hoping

449

you'll make me a lovely cranberry-red suit. I know exactly what I want.' She sketched a shape with her hands. 'With lace at the cuff and neck.'

As the conversation went on, Alix realised the new client was asking for a direct copy of a suit that Chanel had recently shown. She politely explained that Modes Lutzman did not produce copies. 'We'll be glad to show you our original designs.'

Abruptly the woman began to cry, explaining in broken sentences that her fiancé, who worked abroad for the government, had sent her money to buy a Chanel to wear when she sailed out to join him. But – 'I took my mother to Deauville for a holiday, spent it on her. She's had so little happiness in her life . . . our last weeks together. Now I have to confess. My fiancé doesn't like my mother. Oh, he'll be so angry.' Swimming eyes pleaded. 'I was hoping you'd make a copy so he needn't know.' She gave Alix a business card with an Avenue Foch address on it. 'This isn't my flat. I'm just a housekeeper. I couldn't afford a real Chanel if I saved for ten years.'

Alix felt sorry for the woman but held her ground. 'Would your fiancé know the difference if we made you a fabulous made-to-measure suit?'

'Would you sew a Chanel label in it?'

'Certainly not.'

Adèle Charboneau bit her lip, but when Alix suggested that few men would know a Chanel suit if it came up and hugged them, she brightened. 'You're right. Make me one of yours.'

Alix thought no more about Mlle Charboneau that day or the next, which was a Sunday but definitely not a day of rest. Her autumn–winter show was now just four days away and her mind was buzzing like a hive. This season's clothes had been built around herself and four hired mannequins and were, dare she say it? . . . Breathtaking. Well, they took her breath.

Her evening dresses had overskirts of embroidered net and chiffon. Her suits, by contrast, were plain to the point of military, and her day dresses were ultra-simple, plain silk. She *knew* people would come to this collection, from curiosity if nothing else. She'd hired a publicity agent renowned for her 'little black book' full of names of ladies who spent heavily on couture clothes. The agent had sent invitations to the cream of them, and also to department-store buyers, boutique owners and fashion journalists. Alix had booked a stylist to decorate the salon, and yesterday she'd taken delivery of two hundred programmes which read '*18th August 1938, Modes Lutzman presents* . . .'

She and the mannequins would show the clothes. The star dress, which Alix would wear herself, was of gold silk velvet with a satin waistband; lustrous, supple fabrics costly enough for a queen. Its skirt, as big as anything Javier had produced last summer, was decorated with flying birds. A quick glance suggested they were woven into the cloth, but a closer one proved that the velvet's pile had been shaved away. Alix had chalked round stencils, razoring away the pile inside the lines to reveal the lighter base. Only she knew how many evenings she'd worked through, sneezing as silk fibres flew up her nose. She'd given this one dress a name: Ma Fuite. 'My escape.'

Not every idea had succeeded. There was the doomed No. 10 for instance. Alix had bought a roll of coffee-coloured rayon, a modern fabric ideal for draped dresses, and conceived a clinging evening gown with a V-neck back. Bands of silk fringe were to spiral down its length, moving with the body, calling attention to the figure beneath. Alix had experimented, weighting the fringe at the rear of the dress with glass beads to accentuate the low back. The back looked gorgeous, but the front was all bunched up. A technical step too far? Javier would have made up a dozen toiles and trialled the dress in rayon until he had perfection. Alix didn't have the time or the staff for that. Nor did she have Mme Frankel's skills to hand. How she missed that calm voice taking control of a fractious studio: *'It will work, so long as we do it like this –'* Her own Mme LeVert saw more problems than solutions, and in the end No. 10 had been wrapped up and put into storage, in pieces. When her collection was over and her nerves relaxed, Alix would have another go.

It was as she took a last, sad look at No. 10 on the Monday morning that she saw a cranberry-red jacket and skirt being passed to a seamstress for finishing. If that was Adèle Charboneau's suit, the lady ought to be impressed at the speed with which her order had been fulfilled. A closer look suggested the suit was dangerously close to Chanel's original, and a look at the lining showed a 'Chanel, Paris' label. 'Lock this away in a cupboard!' Alix barked at the workroom supervisor. 'On no account is it to be delivered. Who authorised that label?'

'Mme LeVert,' the supervisor told her. 'The customer gave it to her, asking for it to be sewn in. I was surprised, I admit.'

Alix went off in search of her première, but Mme LeVert had gone home with a sore throat. It wasn't long before the demands of staging her collection took over and Alix forgot about Adèle Charboneau and the fake Chanel.

On the morning of 18th August, Alix awoke feeling dizzy with nerves. In the salon, she counted the rows of chairs twelve times but the result always came out different. Then she passed between them, straightening them, though they were straight already.

She sat down, feeling pure terror at what would take place in just a few hours. Fourteen models would whizz past like an express train and people would say they'd been sold short. If they came at all. But afterwards they would be served Alsace wine and canapés. Those who wished could mingle and see the girls walking about in the clothes. She, Alix, would be available to discuss her models woman to woman. It was more of an afternoon party than a collection, in the end. Violette, Alix's upstairs receptionist, and Rosa would take orders – if anybody liked her designs enough to order them.

By midday the air was so humid the windows beaded. Thank

heavens there was none of the frantic bustle that had charac-
terised Javier's shows. Everything was ironed, hung, brushed,
ready. The four mannequins sat in their robes, waiting for the
signal to dress. Paying the florist gave Alix a brief diversion,
and then it was back to that minute-before-the-curtain panic,
in which it freshly dawned on her that she'd done everything
wrong. Her clothes were a disaster and she was a failure. Rosa,
catching her mood, said, 'I'd forgotten how bloody awful stage
fright is. Hour from now, you'll be laughing.'

They heard three long rings of the doorbell and stared at
each other. Hubert's 'police raid' warning signal. Rosa muttered,
'You'd think he'd get it right today, silly sod.'

Alix said, 'If he's gone to sleep on that damn chair . . .' But
then she heard footsteps down below, a door clunked and her
heart did a cartwheel. People were arriving for her show. There
were always those who'd come early to get a front-row seat.

Rosa called, 'Violette, stand by for action.' She poked Alix.
'You'd better get out of sight.'

Alix slipped into the office that had been turned into a *cabine*.
Every spare mirror and table had been brought in and lamps
glowed, making the clothes shimmer in unexpected colours.
Alix fanned herself and checked the window was open. It was.

The mannequins, professional young women who had
brought their own underpinnings and makeup, stared at her
expectantly. 'Do I hear an audience?' one of them asked.

'Might as well get into our first clothes,' Alix answered,

nodding at Marguerite who was acting as *chef de cabine*. Alix wished she could conjure up Mme Markova, though, mind you, Madame was too rotund for such a tiny space. She slipped off her robe and reached for a tailor-made of russet wool. 'Oh, why do winter collections have to be in July and August?'

Which was when she heard, 'Now just one moment, hold your horses!' and realised Rosa was speaking English and sounding rattled.

Before Alix could react, three men were at the *cabine* door. The mannequins in their undergarments screamed. Alix pulled the russet skirt against herself. 'What is this? Who are you?'

'Mlle Lutzman?'

'I'm Gower, Alix Gower.'

'Is there a Mlle Lutzman?' The speaker was a middle-aged man, smartly dressed. He had the decency to stare at the ceiling as he demanded to see the proprietress.

'That's me. I own Modes Lutzman.'

He looked at her and they recognised each other at the same moment. A year ago this man had finished the Paris career of Mabel Godnosc. For a hideous moment, Alix thought her bowels were going to give way and she pulled every muscle tight.

'Mademoiselle, we have a warrant to search these premises as we believe counterfeit items are produced here for sale.'

'That's rubbish. You can't search!' Two other men were eyeing the room eagerly and Alix heard her five-year-old self make a bid for clemency. 'Please – I'm showing a collection in just a few minutes. People are coming. Don't do this.'

But they were already doing it. The girls scrambled into their robes as men began emptying the rails of Alix's precious collection.

The men in suits were the advance party. There were others behind, wearing bland laboratory coats that gave them the air of museum curators. Alix watched her collection being fed into wooden crates on wheels. Her collection, her future . . . She was in such shock she hardly heard when Rosa hissed in her ear, 'I'm going to drop the keys to your own wardrobe into the lavatory cistern. If those buggers want to see your private stuff, they'll have to get their arms wet.'

Alix made no reply because a man was pulling Ma Fuite off its hanger. She pleaded, 'It's velvet, you'll crush it.'

A policeman asked her to stand aside. When she heard cupboards being opened elsewhere in the building, she knew they were raiding their way up to the ateliers. They'd find couture items, all her own legitimate property. No copies except . . . oh, God. They'd find the black Chanel evening gown she'd bought off Mabel Godnosc, and the caramel-coloured Lucien Lelong she'd borrowed from Una all those months ago, which Una had given her before going to England. And the almost-Schiaparelli coat with its embroidered collar. Would those three items constitute piracy? She was persuading herself not when she remembered the cranberry-red suit. A suit with a Chanel label sewn inside.

She tried to sit down, missed the chair. One of the girls ran to help her and put a robe around her. She saw their shock, their pity. Nice girls, but this humiliation would garnish every tea plate in Paris. They wouldn't be able to stop themselves. *'You'll never guess . . .'*

It got worse. At 1 p.m. she heard the raiding party retreating down the stairs, colliding with the fashion *cognoscenti* coming up. A seasoned torturer couldn't have designed it better. Who had she to thank for this? Whoever it was, many in the fashion world would agree that Alix Gower was reaping her just reward.

A pair of arms. She needed a pair of arms around her. The flesh-and-blood reality was Rosa, who let her cry on her bosom, then set her aside so she could announce, in her poshest voice, the regrettable cancellation of today's show.

Chapter Thirty-One

Rosa watched her maid pour tea and, as it was nudging four o'clock, she broke the waxed seal over the contents of a tartan tin. 'All the way from Edinburgh, Scotland. Go on, Toinette, take one. Lucky for me the franc's so low. My annuity with the Prudential buys more shortbread here than it would in London. Only way I can afford you, dear.'

A knock at the door. Rosa said, 'Answer it, but I'm not in unless he's tall, dark and handsome.'

With the maid's departure, her cheerful expression faded. Losing her job with Alix back in August still hurt. She'd stayed with Alix for seven days and nights following the police raid. Then Alix, who was inconsolable and, Rosa suspected, a little deranged from shock, had asked her to go. She needed to be alone to think. Rosa had waited for a word, for the invitation to return to work. Not a squeak. Now it was the last Sunday in October and Rosa had no more illusions. She'd lost a job and a friend.

She didn't blame Alix. After the raid, it had been panic. Half

458

the sewing girls had walked out and any number of customers had rung, cancelling their orders. The police hadn't arrested Alix in the end. The lawyer she'd been forced to hire reckoned there were insufficient grounds for a prosecution. But Alix had lost so much money, she'd only have kept her business going by cutting staff to a skeleton and doing fifty jobs herself.

'Bloody world,' Rosa sighed, biting into her biscuit. 'Knocks us down, watches us stagger up, knocks us down again.' Hearing voices in the hall, she swore pithily. She didn't want visitors. 'What happened to tall, dark and handsome?' she demanded as Toinette opened the door and stepped aside. 'Blimey O'Riley,' she exclaimed as she saw who stood there. 'Where've you been and what the hell happened?

He'd only come for information, but there was something about Rosa that got you talking. Within an hour he'd unveiled more than he knew he was hiding. The war – that part played by the International Brigades – was over, he told her. They were disbanded. Well, obviously, or he wouldn't be here. They were all, officially, Heroes of Democracy.

After parading through Barcelona, three or four hundred Britons had embarked for home, but he'd crossed into France instead. He told Rosa that nothing in his life as a reporter had prepared him for the reality of infantry warfare. 'You become a machine. It's the only way to survive.'

Rosa had Toinette fill the biggest teapot. She told him she'd had four brothers who'd fought in the last rotten war, so nothing shocked her. So he told her about the women and children driven out of their villages by the Fascists and used as shields. 'Mown down. Boys called up to fight for the government side, and shot for running away. That's when it struck me – soldiers have to fight for something. I don't mean politics. What every soldier needs is salvation. His girl.'

Rosa pushed the tartan tin at him, followed by the sugar bowl, though she knew he didn't take sugar. 'I hope you've got one in reserve.'

'Do I need a reserve, Rosa?' He looked around for signs of Alix, but saw only Rosa's possessions.

She topped up his cup. 'So – when you disappeared so suddenly, it was to fight the Fascists? Why d'you have to fight other buggers' wars?'

'Blood payment.' The tea was stewed but Verrian didn't mind. He doubted he'd ever quench his thirst. 'I caused the deaths of two people in Spain. Of my wife, Maria-Pilar, and a friend, Miguel. I don't expect you to understand, but I couldn't rest until I offered my blood in return for theirs.'

'How does the tab stand?'

'I'm alive, so perhaps I'm forgiven. Rosa, is Alix still here?'

'No. Went ages ago. I've let her room to a Polish chap.'

What he'd feared. Call it survivor's sensitivity, but he'd looked at the upstairs front window as he crossed the square and known there was no Alix behind it. 'Where is she?'

'I'd rather not say.'

'Is Bonnet still next door? He'll tell me.'

'He's gone too. Law unto himself, Bonnet. Word to the wise: things changed for Alix after you left.'

The word 'things' felt like a drum roll, building to a climax he dreaded. 'Where is she?'

'She'll be at work in her fashion house, cutting clothes or swanning around in them, or nagging her sewing girls. Those she's got left.'

'I see.' Though he didn't at all. 'Is there a man . . . anyone I should know about?'

'Sort of.' Rosa gave an uneasy shrug. 'She got mixed up with this fellow after you left. I warned her . . . bad lot. She left him in the end but I'm told she's since gone back. She had a horrible upset, see, and sort of lost the will. She pruned off all her friends and let nobody near her. Except *him*. No – don't ask.'

'That's rather a tall order.'

Rosa peeled the knitted cosy off the teapot and peered inside. She muttered about 'making fresh' but Verrian stopped her from getting up.

'Where can I find her?' He kept his gaze on her until she broke.

'All right. I'm fond of both of you and don't see nothing but trouble. But all right . . . If she asks, I didn't tell you.'

And then she told him.

*

'Wake up, Miss Gower.' Jolyan Ferryman pitched his voice over the mesh of laughter and scraping chairs. 'Glaze over any more, somebody will call for a window cleaner.'

Alix realised that everyone was getting up to dance. Serge had sacked Roistering Rex and secured a mellifluous six-piece from New Orleans with a lead trumpeter who, in his own words, could swing a cat just by looking at it. Dulcie L'Amour's baby voice was so overwhelmed by a tight brass section, she was more stage decoration than singer. Nobody noticed. People came for the swing, they came for the chef Serge had tempted away from a top restaurant. They came because the Rose Noire was the place to be seen even on a damp Monday night.

A waiter served champagne and she watched its mist climb her glass. Watched the warring bubbles, felt them enter her nose as a brut flow hit the back of her mouth.

Jolyan spoke right into her ear. 'Why did you come back to Serge, Miss Gower?'

She answered without thinking. 'I needed to look at something worse than failure.'

'*She* didn't cheer.' Jolyan bucked his cigarette holder in the direction of Dulcie L'Amour, who was singing 'Chick, Chick, Chick, Chick, Chicken'. 'Yours was the last face she wanted to see back again. God, she'll lay an egg if she pushes any harder.'

'Serge tells me he likes blondes, that I'm too dark and thin.'

Jolyan snorted. 'Doesn't mean he doesn't want you. There's a rumour flying around that you're starving him of affection.'

'Don't listen to rumours.'

'Actually he told me himself. He confides in me, you see. After you walked out on him, he picked me out as his new best friend. He would unburden himself – "himself" being his favourite subject – and because I don't speak French fast enough to interrupt him, he had a silent audience. An unhappy Serge is rotten company, so any chance of loosening the screws – as he so charmingly puts it – tonight?'

'No. Not until he confesses what he did to Solange. I need him to tell me he didn't hurt her.'

'Ah, feminine logic. Naturally, his silence cannot imply innocence, because you've already convicted him in your mind.'

'I know he isn't innocent.'

'Then why wait all these weeks for an answer you have already?' Jolyan rolled his eyes in mock exasperation. 'Let me put you out of your misery. Men like Serge always hurt their women when they feel out of control. Of course he hurt what's-her-name. He'll go for you 'ere long.'

She waited for a break in the music, then said harshly, 'Why don't you go and annoy Rhona de Charembourg? You're in her pay, or her lover's. Why should I be saddled with you?'

'I'm Rhona's social eyes and ears, not her companion. I ring ahead and reserve her the best tables. I check her furs into cloakrooms, ensure the same ones are given back. I order her taxis. That's all.'

'Does the Comte de Charembourg know what you do?'

'Naturally. He approves. These days he's rarely away from his place of business. He's taken over as Chairman of FTM, which involves travel to Alsace. He likes being busy. When he's at home, he prefers to work or read in his study.'

'Does he know you sit and chat with me?'

Jolyan eyed her in amusement. 'Do we chat? I sit here because it's a good table for people-watching. Also, Mme de Charembourg likes me to keep an eye on you. We often have breakfast together, she and I, where I report everything I've heard you say . . . every gauche confession, every acid remark. She laps up your naiveties, but I doubt she bores her husband by repeating them.'

'You are a fox. No, a polecat. Light me a cigarette.'

'Hashish joint or ordinary?' Jolyan asked, opening his cigarette case.

'Ordinary. You do it so well.'

He laughed. 'Touché. I like you better since you got raided. It kicked your smug little rear.'

'What do you know about that?' Alix flashed back.

'Not a lot and care less. Oh, look, Rhona and Maurice are dancing. Admit it – they are a superb couple. What colour would you call Madame's dress?'

'Mud,' Alix grunted, though privately 'coffee-cream' came to mind. Hard to judge its precise colour under artificial light. It was slinky, made of synthetic fibre, judging from its sheen, and rimmed with silk fringe. As Rhona turned in Ralsberg's arms,

Alix got a full view of the back and her mouth dropped. It was her own failed No. 10. She staggered to her feet, yelping, 'That's my dress! The one I couldn't . . . good God. How on earth—'

Jolyan grabbed her hand. 'Come on, let's dance.' A song, 'Tipi Tipi Tin', had burned like a brush fire all that summer and the band had just struck up the opening bars. Alix let herself be pulled on to the dance floor because she wanted a proper look at Rhona and the back of that dress.

'Tipi Tipi Tin' went like a train. No chance of manoeuvring Jolyan, who seemed to guess her motives and was steering her ever further from Rhona and Ralsberg, a sly smile on his lips. Then the band slewed into 'Glad Rag Doll'. The tempo slowed, dancers moving like whipped cream. Damn – Rhona and her partner were leaving the floor, heading for their table in one of the club's niches. Alix almost throttled Jolyan as she lunged sideways to get a last glimpse of Rhona. Frustratingly, Maurice Ralsberg placed his hand in the small of Rhona's back, and Alix gave up. It could be No. 10. Or it could be somebody else's creation entirely. As Javier had once pointed out, 'Very little in this world is truly original.'

And now she was stuck with Jolyan Ferryman, which felt like one of those dreams where you find yourself slow-dancing with your old chemistry teacher or a toad-faced bellboy. Jolyan obviously felt the same as he said, 'Don't loll. I don't like breathing somebody else's air.'

'Maybe you're not interested in girls, Jolyan.'

'I'm not interested in girls, correct. I like women. Your milksop gropings for a sexual identity don't hit the spot.'

'I'll ask you to sleep with me when I'm as old as Rhona de Charembourg. Is she going to divorce the comte, or is Ralsberg simply amusing himself while he's in Paris?'

She expected Ferryman to show some offence, but he replied placidly, 'Ralsberg is head over heels. In love with love. Nobody falls harder than a mature man whose life is money, money and money. It's like watching a native tribesman coming into contact with European smallpox. Straighten up.' He tapped the exposed skin of Alix's back with his knuckle. 'I know it's "Glad Rag Doll", but don't flop at the knees. Ah – the Relief of Mafeking, Serge is coming. He can prop you up.'

Serge took Alix in his arms. 'You'll come upstairs with me tonight? I'm still waiting for you to sweep up that blue glass.'

She stared deep into Serge's eyes and thought, *At least with Jolyan you feel there's a personality inside, even if it's horrid. Here I am, gazing into a void. Serge has no character. He's a manufacture of my fantasies and his lies*. 'I don't like stairs any more, Serge. Why did you tell me Solange lived on Corsica when she lives at Le Havre?'

'I don't know where she lives.'

'Liar. You went to her and hurt her. I know it.'

'What is it with you women, always peering into your souls? What was Jolyan Ferryman telling you?'

'That you'd hurt me badly in time, but I don't think you

have the guts. Once you tried – braking so hard I slammed into the dashboard? There wasn't a stray deer on the road that night. I'd asked you to behave like a man, so you behaved like a brat.'

Serge's pupils flickered a warning, which she ignored. She'd come back to him because she'd been in despair, imagining the world was riddled with enemies hunting her to death. Serge, alcohol and hashish had offered a refuge and she'd stumbled back into the trap. Now that she was clear-headed again, she'd just have to climb out.

As if he heard her thoughts, Serge pulled her against him and dug his thumb into the curve of her neck. She shifted but the pressure moved with her.

'Serge, that hurts!'

He didn't reply, nor did he ease off. The band segued into a new tune. Their leader held his trumpet against his leg and began to croon, 'Vous, qui passez sans me voir' – a song about a man seeing the love of his life walk by without a glance.

Serge's spittle hit her cheek. 'Think I can't behave like a man? Come upstairs and I'll show you.'

'Serge, I'm tired of your games, your lies.'

'What lies?'

'You buying this club off your cousin? There was no cousin. You bought it off an Italian who went bankrupt. One of your staff told me.' Because the pressure of his thumb was growing unbearable, she owned up to another long-held doubt. 'You don't come from champagne people. The Epernay estate? Jolyan thinks it's all make-believe and I agree. Your accent slips. You come from Paris, not from the banks of the Marne. You've lied from the first hour we met.'

'Why would you say that, Alix?'

'You let me believe that you and Solange separated by consent, but the truth is you abandoned her. She was pregnant with your child—'

'So she says.'

'And you wouldn't help her. All you did was injure her so badly she can't work. You *bit* her, like a dog—'

At the word 'dog', his thumb dug deeper into her neck, pressing so hard on her collarbone her vision started to swim. 'You're staying tonight, Alix. We're back together, yes?'

'I'm walking out, after this dance.'

The singer ended his sad song, '*Adieu, bonsoir,*' but Serge shouted, 'Play something loud. Get Dulcie on.'

A minute later, 'I've Found a New Baby' blasted out. A fast tune, but Serge stood immobile, keeping Alix in an excruciating embrace while other couples twirled around them. 'You'll black out when your collarbone snaps,' he said. 'I'll carry you upstairs and show you what I did to Solange.' With a quiver that might have been laughter, he kissed her face and took her ear into his mouth. 'Yes, I bite.' His tongue stippled the groove where her ear joined her head. 'Then I bite harder—'

She gasped as he nipped her, but nobody heard over the

applause as Dulcie L'Amour walked up to the mike and began singing, 'Everybody look at me . . .'

'I bite harder . . . harder . . . one jerk and, rip, off it comes. That's when you start screaming.' Serge's lips were moving, as if searching for the place to sink his teeth in.

In desperation, Alix looked to where Jolyan was sitting. She raised her eyebrows in a silent appeal, but Jolyan misunderstood, lifting his champagne glass in response. She went rigid as Serge's teeth encircled her ear. She'd been told about this side of him, hadn't she? Even Paul had warned her.

Dulcie sang about her new baby's way of loving. Happy shrieks drowned her out as a net of balloons was released. Red and black, they floated down. Alix stepped on one and it burst. Serge's teeth were breaking her skin. She'd black out in a minute . . . he'd carry her away and everyone would say what a perfect gentleman he was, how she didn't deserve him. She could hear balloons bursting around her, like the advance of rifle fire. A man was walking towards them, bursting balloons in his path with the flame of a cigarette lighter.

Above her head, somebody said, 'My dance, would you mind?' The question was without inflection and in English. Serge's answer was short and obscene.

Alix saw a burst of flame, felt a lick of heat, then yelped in pain as Serge tore away from her. He was shrieking like an animal, clutching at his mouth. A tall man in evening clothes dropped the hinge on a cigarette lighter. He had dark hair cropped short and the face of someone who has suffered under the sun. Blue, blue eyes. Impossible – she was hallucinating.

Nothing hallucinatory in the way Serge hunched low, eyes filming over as a terrifying entity seemed to take him over. Alix waited for her rescuer to run.

He didn't. He moved in close so that Serge's punch cracked the side of his jaw. The next blow was his, a piston below the ribs.

Serge Martel doubled over. As he recovered, an upward punch flung his head backwards. He went down, clasping his nose, blood pumping through his fingers. Music stopped amid screams. Staff hurried forward.

'Shall we dance?' her rescuer asked. 'Or go? Go, I think.' He steered her across the floor, in no particular hurry, which was a good thing. Her legs had forgotten how to walk straight.

'What have you done?' she moaned.

'Moved the hands of the clock to midnight. Come on. I've a car waiting.'

She thought he meant a taxi, but a long-bodied vehicle stood at the kerb, engine idling, cabriolet top folded back. He opened the passenger door and she fell onto a seat of glove-soft leather. Then he was beside her and the car was moving away with a baritone throb.

He reached behind for a tartan travel rug, which he dropped on her lap. 'Where to?'

'Rue Jacob.'

He threw her a look. 'Am I to meet another rival?'

'Don't you dare ask questions after the way you treated me, Verrian Haviland. Just drive.'

Chapter Thirty-Two

She changed her mind about Rue Jacob. Mémé would be asleep in the flat, Bonnet snoring in the studio below. She didn't want to wake either of them. 'Just drive around.'

'Until I run out of petrol?' He parked close to Pont Marie and they walked on to Île St-Louis, Alix still wearing the tartan blanket like a shawl. On the tip of the island they sat in the shadows of the foliage, the Seine at their feet. The loudest sound was the creak of mooring lines and the bumping of craft along the wharf.

'You left me,' she accused. 'After what happened to Mémé – left me with nowhere to turn.' This was her moment. She'd waited eighteen months to pour this out. 'I don't want you any more.'

'You needed my help just now.' He put his arm around her. She was too exhausted and shocked to move away. 'What the hell was happening back there?'

'Serge was going to rip my ear off because I wouldn't go back to him.'

Verrian swore viciously. 'Go back? That means you were with him. A man famous even in Pigalle for violence . . . how much were you "with him?"'

He'd never spoken to her in such a voice before and she swiped back, 'You can talk. You flicked your lighter in his mouth.'

'Not "in"; that wouldn't have worked. Against. For which nasty technique, derived from Fascist mercenaries, you continue to have the benefit of both your ears.'

Neither spoke until Verrian said, 'I gave a letter to someone I trusted, to pass to you.'

'I got no letter,' Alix said coldly. 'I don't believe you wrote one.' She felt his arm stiffen but thought, *If we're to quarrel, let's do it*. 'What sort of man writes a letter? You come and you go. You have a wife, you don't have a wife. You lie about your name and your family. Every man I know does that. Yes, I know who your father is,' she snapped, feeling him turn towards her, 'and I don't care. I can take my pick of better men than you.' She pulled away, but he pulled her back.

'I didn't come back to find myself in a queue behind Serge Martel.'

She heard the anger, the raw disbelief. Male jealousy was a monster, she was discovering. It made even the sanest man dangerous. 'If you hurt me, I'll scream,' she warned him. 'I'll swim across the river. I don't care if I drown.'

'Alix, what happened while I was away?'

'I grew up.' Another silence, filled with the patient sounds

473

of the water. This time Alix broke it. 'You can tell me where you disappeared to, if you want.'

He told her, 'Spain.' He told her a little more, then a little more. Marseille first, then the Spanish border at Perpignan. Endless waiting in reception camps. International Brigades, a British Battalion. Uniform. Training and, finally, action. Her head sank on to his shoulder. When she awoke, the sky was milky and Verrian suggested they find breakfast.

Their evening clothes caused a stir at Laurentin's. The patron let out a roar, 'Ehhh, *mon ami*. You went so suddenly we thought you'd got a girl pregnant.' He noticed Alix and whistled. Her evening dress was her own design – a successful version of No. 10. A step on from the version she'd seen on Rhona in blue chiffon velvet with a plunging back and a sweeping skirt.

'Quick, quick, put a cloth on a table, Marie,' Laurentin shouted to his waitress. 'Wipe two chairs.'

Bread, crisp from the oven, butter, Auvergne ham and pâté were placed in front of them. An enamel jug of coffee followed, with hot milk and two bowls. Alix slipped marcasite combs out of her hair and let her curls, now grown to nearly the length they had been before, fall loose. Laurentin happened to look her way. Something about her must have ignited a memory because he shouted, 'You came looking for him, sweetheart! Slapped my face because I couldn't help you find him.' He laughed in delight. 'All forgiven, eh?'

Stealing a look over the rim of her coffee bowl, Alix caught a glimpse of the old Verrian. A slight thaw, a smile.

'You came searching for me?' he asked.

'I wanted to break things off with you.'

'Break off what? We weren't a couple.'

'Then why write me a letter?' She reached for bread, buttered it lavishly, rolled ham into cigars and balanced it on the bread.

'Maybe I was breaking things off with you.'

'Why bother, as you were about to leave? Here –' she passed the pâté – 'get going or I shall eat it all.' She made a face. Marie was passing with trenchers of steaming *andouillettes*, strongly flavoured sausage derived from the inner organs of pig and veal. 'You'd need to have done a long night's work to want that.'

'D'you know, I had my first conversation with you from that lobby?' Verrian pointed to the gap in the curtains. 'You were my lady telephonist. My "Hello Girl". I adored your voice.'

'You asked me to marry you. You should be ashamed.'

'Even then, I knew you weren't just anybody. You look exquisite, by the way.'

'Serge liked me to look like a mannequin.' She touched her ear, which brought to mind Solange, swan neck bloodied . . . If Verrian hadn't come when he had . . . she wanted to throw her arms around him, but he looked so forbidding she didn't dare.

'Was Serge your lover all the time I was away?'

She parried. 'The night Mémé was attacked, did you know you were leaving?'

'No. I got a call in the early hours.'

She nodded. The sunburned skin and new scars filled out the story he'd told her earlier. A white scar lay between the fingers of his left hand, bright as Shellac against his tan, but that wasn't a battle wound. That was a blade in a dark hallway. 'Why so suddenly?'

'I explained in my letter: I answered a cry for help from a Spanish friend who was stranded in Marseille.'

'So you could have come back within a day.' It flooded back, all that waiting. A tear rolled on to her cheek. 'I thought you'd left me because I was always getting into trouble. I *was* in trouble. What was their plight to mine, these Spanish friends?'

He reached for her hand, and when she withdrew hers coldly, took out cigarettes instead. Finding the packet empty, he flung it down on the table. 'You live in a country at peace. You had Rosa, Paul, Bonnet, the Comte de Charembourg. In Marseille I realised I had to go back to Spain and pick up a gun or never again look in the mirror and see a man I liked and trusted. It mattered.'

'More than me?'

'More than you. I was under arms for fifteen months. Afterwards I could have gone to England, but I came here.' This time he grabbed her hand and kept it. '*For you.*'

'And what about your wife, the one whose ring you used to wear?'

'That's over.' He paid the bill and they got up to leave, fending off Laurentin's enthusiastic reassurances that Verrian's old room was empty, if he wanted it.

Walking out into daylight, Alix discovered that the car with the baritone throb was a new model Hispano-Suiza J12 Torpedo in cigar brown with gold trim. 'This isn't yours,' she accused.

'Actually it is. I had it shipped over some time ago. It's garaged at the Hôtel Polonaise, where my father retains permanent suites. I'm staying there. Would you like to come back with me?'

She wavered, the thought of a hot bath, a soft bed utterly beguiling. But Mémé would be waking soon, calling for her. And she had Modes Lutzman to run – mauled and semi-bankrupt as it was, it needed daily attention. And, from now on, she was going to be picky over her bedfellows. 'No,' she answered curtly.

Verrian dropped Alix off in Rue Jacob. He'd have liked to see inside her building, but she hadn't invited him in. A big, rickety place she must struggle to maintain, he thought.

As she unlocked her door, he stared into the courtyard. His gaze hardened as he saw a bearded man smoking beside an overgrown shrub. Bonnet – still painting? Verrian had enjoyed endless thinking time in Spain, and a lot of it had centred on Bonnet, his undoubted talent and his love of gambling dens. He'd thought about the Comte de Charembourg too. Yesterday Rosa had given him a letter which had arrived months ago. She'd kept it, assuming Verrian would eventually return. He wished she hadn't, because now he had the burden of passing on its contents.

The letter laid bare a cruel deception. From his suite at the Polonaise, while a valet set a bath running and brought him his shaving brushes and soap, he telephoned Alix's workplace, inviting her to join him at five that afternoon for a tour of the *News Monitor*. Having just left him, she was suspicious, and so she should be. Verrian knew he was going to hurt her, but it was a surgical decision. Like cutting off an infected limb to save a life.

The receptionist at the *News Monitor* was the one Alix had crossed swords with before. Back then she'd been in shock *and* badly dressed. This time, in high heels, an hourglass suit and a stingingly chic hat, she was better prepared.

However, the girl made Verrian her focus. Peering at the colourful bruising on his jaw, she fluttered her eyelashes. 'May I help, sir?'

Verrian peered back at her. 'I don't recognise you. Are you new?'

'I've been here for over a year.'

'Mmm. Well, I've been away longer than that . . . I'm Verrian Haviland and this is Miss Gower. I hope Miss Theakston's still with us?'

'Goodness, yes! She's in her office. Mr Haviland, did you say?' The receptionist slowly made the connection. 'I'm sorry, sir, I didn't realise—'

'Call Beryl, would you?' Verrian steered Alix towards the lift. 'Tell her we're on our way up.'

In the lift Alix hissed, 'I still think it was rotten of you not to tell me your father was Lord Calford.'

'Does it matter?'

'Yes. I made a fool of myself by not knowing.'

'When was that?'

'When I came here.'

'You came here?'

'No. Well, only to check you were all right. When you vanished, I thought you might have had an accident.'

The lift gave a rattling shrug as it reached its floor. Verrian unhitched the door, ushering Alix over the metal sill. 'When you discovered that instead of the out-at-elbows hack you thought me I was the boss's son, did it change anything?'

'Of course. I'm a republican.'

'Are you?' He grinned. 'You'd sweep away wealth and privilege, and the couture houses with them?'

'What I mean is, aristocratic titles are a . . . a . . . they're old-fashioned. Americans get by without them.'

'My title is a courtesy, and I never use it.'

Through the windows of a glass-walled office Alix saw a woman bending over the open drawer of a filing cabinet. Verrian tapped on the door, pushed it open. 'Beryl?'

The woman gave a cry and whatever she'd dug out of her drawer flew sideways as she rushed towards them. 'Mr Haviland, you're back! Have you any idea how anxious we were? Goodness, what have you done to your face?'

'I walked into the protruding foot of an equestrian statue.'

'Really? Your pilot friend . . . what was his name?'

'Ron Phipps?'

'Came here, said he'd flown into Le Bourget without you because you'd gone to fight in Spain. We couldn't trace you and feared the worst. The casualty lists were dreadful in the summer of 'thirty-seven. Then the man who replaced you as Spanish correspondent said he'd seen you near Madrid and you seemed to be in one piece – but that was before last summer's bloodshed . . . oh, but you're back. Does Mr Chelsey know?'

'Not yet. Give him a few more minutes' untrammelled happiness. Beryl, may I introduce Miss Alix Gower?' He drew Alix forward. 'Alix, Miss Theakston runs the Paris edition of the *Monitor* – Oh, you do, Beryl, and you know it.'

Alix was aware of being closely investigated. Aware, too, of proprietary feelings rising from a well-buttoned-up breast. But Miss Theakston shook her hand cordially.

Verrian said, 'Beryl, did Phipps bring a letter for Miss Gower? Because she didn't receive it.'

'Yes.' Miss Theakston drew her brows together. 'I delivered it next day, as directed.' She turned to Alix. 'We met outside the entrance of Javier's couture house. I introduced myself, asked your name and handed you the letter.'

'Madame, I've never seen you before in my life.'

Verrian leaned against the desk. 'Beryl, which door? Tradesman's or main?'

'Door?' Beryl Theakston raided her memory. 'Erm, the grandiose one. I didn't know there was a tradesman's door. Though I suppose there must be. I assure you, I gave you the letter, Miss Gower. I would not mistake you.' She indicated Alix's ensemble. 'I'm rather in awe of you girls. Never a hair out of place.'

'Alix wouldn't have been wearing anything like this suit then. True?' Verrian consulted Alix.

'No. Back then I wore a brown smock. Nor did I come or go by the main door.'

'I don't understand.'

Alix did. 'The girl you gave the letter to, Madame, she was very tall? As dark as me?'

'I'm sure it was you.'

'Like this –' Alix lifted her nose as high as it would go.

'Yes, exactly that.'

'*Voilà*. You gave it to Solange Antonin.'

'But I asked her if she was you. She said yes.'

'She would.' Alix shrugged. 'Poor Solange hated me. But, Madame, it's only a letter.'

Cruelty felt good sometimes, she thought to herself. At the words 'only a letter', Verrian had flinched as if acid had been flicked at him. But there – men lied; women flicked acid; the world kept turning.

Verrian told Miss Theakston he was taking Alix upstairs. 'Is old Sturridge in?'

'No, out on assignment.'

'Even better,' said Verrian.

Alix had no idea why Verrian had asked her to his former workplace, nor why she was to bring along a wartime photograph of her father. She watched suspiciously as he adjusted the wing nuts on a piece of equipment that looked as though it belonged in a science lab.

'It's a magnifier,' he explained. 'Put your photo on the plate – here, face up.' He angled the viewer to her height. 'Now look through there.'

She did and saw her father in his unremarkable uniform. John Gower looked so very young. For the first time the insignia on his hat and tunic were visible.

'Tell me again what regiment he served in.'

She didn't like the terrier note in Verrian's voice so she said nothing.

He answered for her; 'London Rifle Brigade – you told me at our café on the Champs-Elysées.'

'You have a good memory.'

'Where you're concerned I do. Your father served in the same battalion as the Comte de Charembourg, yes?'

'You make it sound like a crime.'

'Before I left Paris, I had a friend in London do some research.

He works in the government department dealing with war widows' pensions and wrote to tell me what he'd found out. The comte certainly served in the Rifles, 5th battalion, known as the City of London Brigade. Recruits were mainly stockbrokers and bank employees, which makes sense as the he worked at the Banque d'Alsace on Threadneedle Street. Your father doesn't show up in the brigade's list, though.' Verrian nudged her aside so he could inspect the image of John Gower. 'Alix, there's no kind way to say it: Jean-Yves de Charembourg and your father were never comrades in arms. Gower served in the Royal Army Medical Corps.'

'He was a doctor?'

'A driver, with a Field Ambulance unit. He was deployed two years into the war, in 1916. I haven't yet found out where he was sent, but I can tell you he rose to lance corporal and was injured shortly before Armistice, when his ambulance was struck by shellfire.' Verrian straightened up. 'You have every reason to be proud of your father, but de Charembourg lied to you.' He invited her to look again. 'See for yourself – the badge on your father's sleeve bears a red cross and there's an RAMC insignia on his cap.'

She was crying, so it was pointless to look again. 'You're trying to tell me that my father wasn't a proper soldier.'

'What on earth makes you think that? Ambulance crew were as brave as any of the men who fought at the front. Alix, I am not belittling your father.'

But she wouldn't be comforted. 'I know what you're doing. Punishing me for preferring other men to you.'

Was he punishing her? He wanted to help Alix clear the fog of her childhood so she could see the present. He wanted her free of sorrow, free to concentrate on him . . . so yes, he was being selfish. But enjoying the process? Far from.

And he must see it to the end. When she retired to the ladies' room to rinse her face, he asked Beryl to find him a Paris telephone number, quickly. The secretary wrote it for him on a card.

He dialled, and when a young man answered he announced, 'Verrian Haviland, wishing to speak with the Comte de Charembourg.'

Chapter Thirty-Three

The patterns, drawings, toiles and garments that had been taken away from Rue Jacob by the police that devastating August day were returned as suddenly on 2nd November, the day after Alix's visit to the *News Monitor*. They arrived in boxes like the turnout of a lost-property cupboard. The silk velvet was ruined and Alix wept over Ma Fuite, which had cigarette burns on the skirt, then searched in vain for the pieces of coffee-coloured No. 10. Nevertheless, this was the final welcome confirmation that she would not be prosecuted. Once again, she'd escaped through some quick thinking.

Rosa had been good as her word, dropping the keys to Alix's private wardrobe into the water tank. She'd invited the police to retrieve them and, while they'd dithered, had climbed another flight of stairs to the atelier and tossed Adèle Charboneau's cranberry suit out of the window. While every shelf, drawer and rail in the upper workrooms was cleared, the cranberry suit had dangled, unseen, on a hydrangea bush in the courtyard below. That had saved Alix.

She was convinced it was that suit that had triggered the raid. Mme LeVert had fallen for Adèle Charboneau's tears and privately agreed to make a suit 'as near Chanel as possible' and had then been cajoled into adding a counterfeit Chanel label. Alix had visited the address on Adèle Charboneau's card and learned that nobody of that name had ever lived in the flat on Avenue Foch. A fake client, a good actress. The real question – who had wheeled in that tearful Trojan horse? Alix was forming a strong suspicion, but doubted she'd ever be able to prove it.

Though the raid had taken place two-and-a-half months ago, business was still shaky. The clientele she'd begun to build up beforehand, moneyed Parisians intrigued by an ingénue designer, still mostly cold-shouldered her these days. Loyal Una continued to send English customers, and one or two of her old clients had given her the benefit of the doubt. Orders trickled in still, but never enough to clear the debts arising from her ruined collection. It was a struggle to pay her reduced staff each week. The rent fell due at Christmas, and she didn't have the cash to buy fabric in for the next season either. If Gregory Kilpin ever guessed how dire her circumstances were, he'd foreclose on her. And a new affliction had struck: the horror of the blank page. She ought to be working on her spring–summer line for February 1939, but her creative spark had died.

A cry – 'Aliki, where are you?' – brought her into the salon. Mémé sat by the window, a paraffin stove a safe distance away, a pool of crochet work at her feet. A skill she'd learned as a child, which her fingers could still perform. 'I couldn't hear you. Will you help me to the lavatory?'

'Take my arm.' They walked across the room, Mémé's stick tapping a slow dirge.

'At breakfast you were going out to buy silk velvet, but you didn't come to show me.'

Alix thought, *She's back in last summer.* 'Not silk velvet this time, Mémé, plain shantung. I'll show you when it's delivered.'

'How many models have you finished?'

'Oh, twenty.' *None.*

'Shall you parade them to me?'

Alix couldn't help smiling. Mémé's mellowing had extended to Alix's profession. Their arguments on the evils of a seamstress's life had slipped from her memory. And she'd totally forgotten about the telephone exchange.

Verrian arrived from his office, and they retired to the flat for lunch. Alix knocked vegetables around her plate and listened to Verrian engaging Mémé in conversation. *How patient he is*, she thought. *Not angered by human frailty. Except by mine.*

As Mémé settled for her afternoon nap, Verrian said, 'You can't run a business and look after your grandmother. You need a companion-nurse.'

'I can't afford one.'

He gave her the considering look she was familiar with. Since hustling her out of the Rose Noire, he'd hardly touched her.

He was impeccably restrained, but she longed for him to take her in his arms and just kiss her, as he had before.

'Will you let me help?' he asked.

'It's not your business, Verrian.'

'You are my business, Alix. Get used to it.'

He presented his solution the next morning. Alix was in her office. A telephone call from Mr Pusey, Gregory Kilpin's financial controller who was in Paris overseeing his master's French interests, had interrupted an equally tense conversation with Mme LeVert. Banging the receiver down, Alix ran her tongue over her teeth, expecting to find a layer of enamel ground off. Pusey had gone through her quarter's costs, invoice by invoice, right down to her purchase of tacking thread. God, if this was what Una had put up with, no wonder the woman tried to dig an escape route. Now Mme LeVert was insisting that the synthetic silk they used to line tailored garments was a false economy.

'Because it needs a larger needle, Mlle Gower.'

'Then use larger needles.'

'The girls get used to a size and weight. Larger ones feel clumsy and quality decreases. More times than I like, I have to persuade them to unpick their work and start again. Then we have ructions.'

Alix scanned today's page in her diary. English clients mid-morning, so she must put flowers in the salon and change.

Why had she let Rosa go? Why hadn't she sacked Mme LeVert instead? Rosa would never have fallen for Adèle Charboneau's tears. She remembered Javier saying, 'A good première is worthless. Anyone can cut and measure. A *great* première brings that supreme ingredient – the fruits of her passions.' He'd added wickedly, 'Passion for cloth, passion for life and love.'

Alix went to the window to investigate a *thrubbing* noise filling the courtyard. Verrian's Hispano slid into view. Her brow creased as she saw him open the passenger door for a woman wearing a dark coat and headscarf. A little boy scrambled out. Verrian then reached into the car and brought out a shallow box, the sort that contains a fruit tart.

Mme LeVert said, 'And another thing—'

'Madame –' Alix turned – 'you are called première for a reason. Please go upstairs and assert your authority.'

Two things struck Alix about Pepe Rojas García. Firstly, that he was an extraordinarily beautiful child, with lashes that cast long shadows on his cheeks. Secondly, that he called Verrian 'Señor' in a heartbreakingly grown-up way. And yet his mother, introduced to Alix as Celestia García y Rojas, interacted with Verrian in a way that suggested an emotional reliance. Or something deeper. It made Alix wonder – had Verrian flown down to Marseille to rescue this woman out of disinterested chivalry?

'This is your work here? You are dressmaker?' Celestia asked in broken French. Alix had invited them all into the salon. Pepe was thundering up and down its length, displaying the energy of a child confined too long.

'Until rent day,' Alix said stiffly.

Verrian said, 'I've brought Señora García y Rojas along because I think she'd be perfect to look after your grandmother. The arrangement could help you both.'

Alix said, 'I see.'

He raised an eyebrow, implying, *Why else did you think I brought her?* He explained something of the life Celestia had led in Spain and her reasons for fleeing. 'She has leave to remain in France, and has been working as a housekeeper. However, the lady of the house has started objecting to Pepe. It's become rather fraught. You wouldn't mind having a child around?'

I haven't agreed to have either of them, Alix thought resentfully. 'A little boy might be too much for Mémé.' She didn't want this woman, with her secret sadness and her links to Verrian's Spanish identity. 'And, forgive me, being a housekeeper doesn't equip a person to care for an old lady.'

'Forgive me – as she's intelligent, needs a job and I will pay half her salary, I suggest you stop looking for problems and smile. Or have you forgotten how?'

'If I had something to smile about, I expect I would remember.'

'Please, you speak too fast.' Celestia looked from Alix to Verrian. 'If I offend, you have my apology. I care for my own grandmother. I am kind with old ladies. All I ask is Pepe is welcome.'

'A modest ambition, wouldn't you say?' Verrian was unpicking the twine that secured the cake box.

Why not just say I'm mean-spirited? Alix fumed as she went to ask a member of staff to make tea. *I might not be able to read Celestia's expressions, but, boy, can I translate his.* Returning some time later with Mémé, she found Verrian pouring tea while Pepe stood in watchful anticipation of an apple custard tart.

'*Tarte alsacienne,*' Verrian said, rising to shake Mémé's hand. 'Alix says yours were the best, but it's shop-bought just for today.'

Pepe's table manners were impeccable, Alix discovered. He passed plates to the ladies and offered the sugar bowl. Then he positioned himself beside Mémé and watched her hands, clearly fascinated by the raised knuckles and bent joints. He asked something in Spanish which contained the word '*dedos*' – fingers.

His mother reproved him.

Mémé made claws and wiggled them and the boy laughed.

His mother looked embarassed. 'I so regret, Madame. Your pardon.'

Danielle Lutzman said gravely, 'The Pobble who has no toes, had once as many as we. When they said, "Some day, you may lose them all," he replied, "Fish diddle-de-dee!"'

Pepe scrunched into giggles.

'She learned that from me years ago,' Alix said in astonishment. 'Edward Lear – I had to say it at a school recital.'

Mémé continued: 'And she made him a feast at his earnest wish of eggs and buttercups fried with fish. And she said, "It's a fact the whole world knows, that Pobbles are happier without their toes."'

Pepe clapped. Even Celestia laughed. She'd taken off her headscarf revealing mahogany curls. Alix was shocked at the difference it made. The woman was thirty, no more, and very pretty. Rising, she held out her hand. 'The Pobble didn't have three suits under construction in his workroom. Thank you for coming, Madame.'

As she left, she heard Celestia say, 'It is necessary to practice, no? In the way of a child, to love and to laugh.'

Alix took off the last dress she'd shown, hung it on a rail and peeled off her underwear. The latest English ladies – Manchester matrons sent by Una – had gone. Alix had paraded her autumn–winter range, ten or so models salvaged from summer's wreckage. The ladies had promised to come back later when they'd looked around some other shops. Alix groaned softly. Rosa – where was Rosa, who could cajole stuffy or nervous women into buying one of everything because she made the process such fun?

Alix hooked on a waist girdle and put powder-blue camiknickers over the top, not bothering with a brassière. She was contemplating which of two jersey dresses to put on – black or olive – when she heard her name called. 'In here,' she replied, and before she had time to add, 'but don't come in,' the door opened.

Verrian took in the blue silk, the bare arms and legs and stopped as if he'd walked into a glass wall.

Alix grabbed the nearest dress, the black one, and held it against herself. 'You were taking your Spanish friend home,' she accused.

'I did.'

'That was quick. Isn't it your habit to see a lady indoors? You used to think I couldn't get my door open without your help. Or did life on the battlefield obliterate your manners?'

He came right into the room, tilting her chin, then kissed her with the controlled hunger of a man who has given up on waiting. When he broke off he said with his lips taut against hers, 'Do you mean to provoke me into proof of it? No? Then don't ever look at me in that snooty way again.' He reached for the olive jersey dress and thrust it into her shocked arms. 'I'm fed up of women in black. Let's go to your office and work out terms for Celestia.'

'I haven't agreed yet.'

'Your grandmother has. After you flounced out, she and Pepe danced together in the salon. They're inseparable already.' He went to the door. 'I want to be able to take you out, and much as I like Mémé, I don't want her making a third at every restaurant table. Can you take a little time off now?'

493

She toyed with saying no, but it was such hard work, being up in arms all the time. And that kiss had woken an impatience to confront the real reason she was keeping Verrian at a distance; the revulsion she felt for her time as 'Serge's moll' and that rough, hashish-fuelled education she'd received at his hands. 'Maybe. In a minute. I have to make a couple of telephone calls to suppliers.' As they approached her office, Alix stopped dead. Her door was slightly ajar and she heard a muffled voice growling, 'Another five hundred thousand francs, same drop-off, six o'clock tomorrow evening, Friday . . .'

Somebody was using her telephone. It was the only one in the building and nobody used it without first asking her. And it wasn't the well-spoken Violette or Mme LeVert. It was a man's voice. A drunkard making threats through a mouthful of dust. She stepped forward but Verrian caught her, his breath against the back of her head. They heard –

'You won't pay? Then I'll tell the world what I know.' Coarse laughter made Alix shudder. 'Oh, I agree, M. le Comte, Lutzman's killing is history but I have a new hold on you. You beat Mme Lutzman in her flat and I have a witness. Somebody saw you. You left the door open. You went back. A witness will testify.'

Verrian clamped his arms around Alix to stop her running forward. He whispered, 'We're backing off. Not a sound.'

He drew her on to the walkway that led to hers and Mémé's living quarters. There he held her, their hearts beating in confederacy. After a minute or two, the downstairs door clashed. They saw a figure in overalls squeeze past Verrian's car and stump towards the coach house, swearing as he went. Verrian pulled Alix back inside.

'You heard –' she sputtered. 'Oh God – Bonnet. He's—'

'Blackmailing the Comte de Charembourg.'

She tried to get free. 'Mémé's in the flat. I have to be with her.'

'She's in no more danger now than she was yesterday. But yes, go to her. Try to act normally. I'll be back shortly.'

'Where are you going?'

'To see the comte. I rang him from the *News Monitor* office the other day and arranged a meeting between us all – including his wife.'

'Are you mad?'

Verrian gave a 'possibly' shrug. 'It's a chance for the comte to explain his lies to you. You won't be happy till you've heard his side of the story. His wife's coming because . . . well, I thought she might like to be included. I mean, all this secrecy must have affected her too, don't you think? It'll be good to clear the air.'

'It'll be unbearable.'

'Actually, Alix, very few things are, once you face up to them. Go to your flat, sit with Mémé. I'm going to Boulevard Racan, to bring this meeting forward. I won't be long.'

But Alix clung. 'Don't go! You heard Bonnet making those

accusations. That voice . . . it's the same as the man who attacked me, at Place du Tertre and at St-Sulpice. Bonnet – oh, Verrian, it can't be!'

Verrian pulled her towards him. 'I'll take you to your grand-mother and make sure you're locked in.'

'You'll spend the night with us?'

'No. I'll spend it with Bonnet. If he goes anywhere near your stairs, I'll break his neck.'

Alix went back into her office to fetch her handbag and house keys. A smell tainted the air, redolent of old animal skins. 'Rabbit-skin glue. He always buys the cheap stuff. Pretends it's the supplier cheating him.'

Verrian was close behind her. 'There are levels to Bonnet. A hint of the sublime, but mostly base notes.'

Sunday, 6ᵗʰ November

Her sleeve felt kid-soft under his hand, and because this was Alix, it was more than just a grey town suit. It had a green cross-thread which caught the light every few paces, just enough to intrigue. And she wasn't wearing the suit, she was dipped in it. How could wool be so sexy? Her hat was emerald green, slanted to cover one eye. His knowledge of women told him she was dressed for combat. He wasn't taking chances either. As they passed the telephone exchange on Rue du Louvre, he felt in his pocket for the *navaja* – the hunting knife he'd taken off a dead Fascist. He didn't expect to use it – but he liked to be prepared.

On Rue du Sentier, evening sun glazed the cobbles. 'Do you know which building?' he asked. They were meeting at the comte's place of business. 'I know it's an upstairs office and I think it's –'

Alix pointed. 'By the fabric warehouse. Who else are we meeting?'

'Be patient.'

As they entered the unremarkable premises of Fabrication Textile Mulhouse, a woman stepped out of a side office, saying, in a voice of relief, 'Mr Haviland, thank goodness. I don't mind being hired as a temporary receptionist, but I do like at least some instruction.' It was Beryl Theakston. Seeing Alix's confusion, she explained, 'Mr Haviland telephoned me yesterday, saying he needed an unflappable presence at the door.'

'Are we the first, Beryl?' Verrian asked.

'A gentleman and lady have already gone upstairs.'

'The comte and comtesse?'

'Erm, yes.' Beryl Theakston was peering at Alix's jacket. She bit her lip. 'Mme de Charembourg is wearing a very similar outfit to yours, Miss Gower. *Very* similar.'

'Impossible,' Alix said. 'This is my own design and I made only one sample, this one.' She tugged Verrian's arm. 'I don't want to see the comtesse. She insults me.'

'The comte is looking forward to seeing you though. Go

on up.' Verrian stepped aside to let Alix go ahead of him. He said quietly to Beryl, 'I'm expecting three more visitors. One may give trouble, so shout if you—' He was going to say, 'need me,' but a banshee scream from above made him take to the stairs. Fearing Alix was being attacked, he flung himself into the small boardroom and got in front of her, only to hear her threatening to pull Rhona de Charembourg's suit off head first.

Beryl had tried to warn them, he realised. The Comtesse de Charembourg was tailored identically to Alix, even to the green hat crowning her blonde hair. Alix fully intended to follow through with her threat, Verrian could see, so he seized her, swearing as he took kicks to his shins. Rage lent Alix primitive strength. Had she been wearing something she could actually move in, she'd have been lethal. She vented frustration by throwing whatever she could reach – her bag, an ashtray. The comte, roused from static astonishment, came over and put his hand to Alix's cheek.

'Child, I don't understand what I'm seeing, but you will have explanations. As for you, Madame –' he turned to his shaking wife – 'at least take off the hat.'

Alix shouted, 'She stole that design – from my autumn–winter collection.'

Rhona, who was clearly fearful of Alix breaking loose again, said with a stab at disdain, 'You habitually stole what was not yours, Alix Gower. Now you know how it feels. I confess, I hadn't imagined we'd be wearing the same ensemble. So very droll.'

'You stole an evening gown too,' Alix hurled at her. 'You were behind the police raid. You're in bed with Adèle Charboneau as well.'

'Charboneau?' The comte frowned. 'Didn't somebody of that name come to Boulevard Racan?' He waited for Rhona to answer, and when she rolled her eyes in theatrical boredom, said through his teeth, 'Didn't you employ an unemployed actress called Charboneau to write out the invitations for Christine's wedding?'

'Possibly. I don't remember.'

When he persisted, 'Did you send the police to Alix's atelier?' she merely raised her brows. 'No,' he frowned as if the truth were an inch away, ready to fall into his palm with the right question. 'You don't wield that kind of influence. But you know those who do . . .' Comprehension flooded him. 'Maurice Ralsberg – a man wealthy enough to buy favours anywhere. He bought you a police raid, and that's how you got hold of Alix's designs. I wouldn't call it droll; rather, unprincipled.'

Rhona looked away, flushing.

The comte turned to Verrian. 'Mr Haviland, it's good to meet you again. One day I hope we can sit and talk man to man. Your despatches from Spain were among the few that treated readers as adults. When you called on me yesterday, you promised an end to my troubles. An end to blackmail and deception. Deliver, and I will be in your debt.'

'What can this man possibly know of your affairs?' Rhona had recovered her voice if not her poise. 'If he has any opinion at all, it will be an impudence.'

'Undoubtedly, but then Mr Haviland is a journalist,' her husband agreed. 'Do sit down, Rhona. Alix –' he drew a chair forward – 'you sit this side of me.'

Verrian judged it safe to go down and check that Beryl was all right. He threw Alix a warning. *Stay calm.* Her chest still heaved as though she'd run two furlongs. He was downstairs in time to see Beryl opening the door to Celestia and Danielle, who was in her best coat and hat. The old lady looked about in pleasure. 'So long since I went shopping. What sort of shop is this?' She peered at Verrian. 'Ah, Mr Haviland, how do you do?'

Verrian told Celestia to come back in an hour and asked Beryl to take Mme Lutzman upstairs. He felt his first qualms. No escape from that windowless boardroom. He hoped he wasn't throwing rabbits in with dogs.

He checked his watch. Two minutes to six. He went out on to the street and looked both ways . . . one person still to come. And here he came, dressed in his usual overalls, boots streaked with cigarette ash, beret pulled low.

As Raphael Bonnet hesitated on the threshold of Fabrication Textile Mulhouse, scanning the doorway as if he expected to find something, Verrian pushed him inside. He'd shut the door before the other man knew what was happening.

'Walk straight up, my friend. Not the smallest chance of getting away, so you may like to hang on to your dignity.'

Mémé was the most relaxed of them, Alix realised. That Mémé could sit among strangers without showing any of her former fretful responses showed how her injuries had changed her. For her part, when Verrian pitched a sweating Bonnet into the room, she'd wanted to be sick.

Verrian pushed Bonnet down on a chair and stood against the door. He shot Alix a look saying, *I'm here. Don't worry*. Silence fell.

Verrian broke it. 'Monsieur le Comte, I promised to present your blackmailer to you, and here he is. Say what you want.'

The comte said nothing for a long while. Just stared across the table at Bonnet, his hands clasping and unclasping. At last he sighed. 'I am very sorry. Sorry that my tormentor should be a man of my own soil, whom I knew and liked. An artist . . . yes, that's a shock. One expects artists to be above such vices as extortion, though I can't think why. Perhaps because we assume they're closer to the angels. *Raphael* –' he reached under the table for a satchel, which he slid across – 'you hoped I would fill this with thousand-franc notes. Even though I assured you I was at the end of my resources you came back for one last try. As an artist, you are inspiring. As a blackmailer, you have neither mercy nor intelligence. I cannot forgive you for carrying out your threat to hurt this girl.'

He reached and squeezed Alix's hand.

Alix smelled the fear seeping through the yarn of Bonnet's sweater. That scratchy jersey had a roll neck which could be pulled up over the beard, over the mouth. She'd felt that wool against her face, against the back of her neck as its owner cut her hair. Her eyes sought Verrian's, searching for his reassuring nod.

Bonnet pushed the satchel aside. 'Don't know what you mean.'

The comte said affably, 'I think, my dear fellow, we'll leap over the bluster and denials. The room is growing a little airless. You first telephoned me at home in March 1937 threatening to harm those I loved. I assumed you meant somebody in my household. How could I know you meant Alix?' He turned to her. 'Whatever else I'm guilty of, I never ignored the threat to you once I understood it. I made two substantial payments to this man, to buy him off.'

Bonnet said furiously, 'I got a note through my door this morning promising something valuable would be left for me outside this building. I was to come at six.' He turned angrily to Verrian. 'Did you write it? Did you get me here on false pretences?'

Verrian shrugged. 'I merely implied that somebody would leave a bagful of francs in the doorway. It was your greed that brought you here.'

The comte spoke over Bonnet's explosion of outrage. 'The sad irony is that I admire you, Bonnet. Had you asked me for help, I'd have been delighted to become your patron. As for your latest threats to brand me a violent felon . . .' he glanced at Mémé, who was occupied with a swatch of silk samples, seemingly oblivious to the tension in the room, 'the sort that beats old ladies, that smacks of such desperation I presume you've run through the money I gave you.'

Trapped in a small room, ringed by accusing faces, Bonnet abruptly dropped his charade. His voice was sullen as he said, 'You did beat Mme Lutzman. I can prove it.'

'My shortcomings are many,' said the comte, 'but attacking females, no.'

'Fernand Rey saw you go into her flat –' Bonnet responded to Alix's protest with a sour smile, then peered at Danielle, who remained oblivious. 'I run into Rey all the time on Rue Mouffetard. He has a stall, selling game. He was visiting St-Sulpice the night Mme Lutzman was attacked and swears he saw you going up the stairs.'

The comte nodded, adding, 'In the evening, not at night. I visited Mme Lutzman briefly, escorted her downstairs and left.'

'He'll make a sworn statement you went back later. You waited for her to return.'

'Untrue,' said the comte. 'If he says such a thing to the police, he'll be making false statements.'

'Fernand used to steal the light bulbs on our landing.'

Everyone stared at Danielle, who laid down the swatch of silks. 'He would put them in when the landlord was there, then take them out and sell them. He stole our coal too. Fernand Rey won't go anywhere near the police. And he did not see anybody that night. He was in his mother's rooms filling his cheeks with ragout of hare.'

'You don't remember, Danielle,' Bonnet said contemptuously. 'You told me your mind was blank.'

'I told you much, Raphael. But just as much I didn't tell you.'

'Monsieur le Comte,' Verrian said from the doorway, 'I suggest you go back to the beginning of this evil. Blackmail is a symptom. We need to know the cause.'

'Need?'

'Alix needs to know. She was terrorised by this man.' Verrian jerked a thumb at Bonnet.

Alix stared down at her hands. When she'd sat naked for Bonnet, trusting him, confiding, he'd been planning to attack her. Her darling, lawless Bonnet was a beast who – and this was the hardest part – had nearly killed Mémé.

'I will tell my story,' said the comte, 'on the understanding that nobody attaches the word "confession" to it. Confession is between me and the Almighty. To my fellow man and woman, I will give an explanation. And yes, I'll start at the beginning which means a trek into the last century.'

Rhona spoke for the first time since Bonnet had stumbled into the room. 'Shall you wash our linen in public?'

'*My* linen, Rhona. I shall leave yours out of it. Alix –' he turned an earnest gaze on her – 'it's time you knew the facts.'

'It was the year 1890. I was nine, home from school and acutely attuned to the state of affairs between my mother and father. They did not enjoy a happy marriage. One day, after a particularly tense quarrel, I saw my father strike my mother to the floor. I was behind a curtain, afraid to move. My father saw me and sent a look which said, *You next. I can do this. This is my right.* It made me grow up fast. But, strangely, when I got to the age and size where I might have fought back and defended my mother, my father took care never to hurt her in my presence. He died shortly before my twenty-first birthday. I felt no sorrow. At last, my mother and I could live without fear.

'Let us jump to Christmas 1903. I took it into my head to surprise my mother with a portrait of myself, choosing a local artist who worked in the loose, modern style my father had considered degenerate. I chose Alfred Lutzman. There was power in this choice, because it was *my* choice.'

Alix fancied the comte was looking for water, usually always supplied in this room. Verrian was keeping them dry. Turning up the temperature.

The comte cleared his throat. 'At our last sitting, I extracted a promise from Alfred Lutzman that the painting would be finished for Christmas. My plan was to hang it in the dining room. There it would be on Christmas Eve to delight my mother. Our symbol of freedom. Three days beforehand, I went to the artist's house, driving as far as I could in the snow, walking the rest through the Jewish quarter.'

Danielle glanced up. 'You came to see my husband.'

'Exactly, Madame.'

'I let you in. You thought I was the maid.'

'My belated apologies.'

'Ah, well, I was an untidy schlump. You went upstairs and I hoped you had money to pay for the painting. We had no food. Our rent was due and I thought, *He'll get the money back in rent anyway.*'

'Only Alfred Lutzman had a shock waiting,' Verrian said.

'Stop it,' Alix shot at him. 'You don't know everything.'

Verrian said straight back, 'I know that, like Bonnet here, Lutzman wouldn't finish his work.'

'Finishing isn't the point.' Bonnet turned a sneer on Verrian. 'It takes an artist to understand that.'

'And a wife to despair of it,' said Danielle. 'All very well being an artist, as I tell you often enough, Bonnet. But when your house is so cold the coffee pot freezes, and your child goes to school in the snow without breakfast, then "being an artist" is as much use as farting in the coal shed.'

A moment of shock met this remark. Danielle continued, 'I was hit over the head. Now I say the things I used only to think.'

'You were angry with Lutzman that evening?' Verrian asked the comte.

'Naturally. He'd sabotaged a moment I had been planning for weeks. Actually for years because – did I say this? – commissioning the portrait was my first real adult decision. He ruined it and didn't grasp it.'

'No, he wouldn't,' agreed Danielle.

'He blinked at me as if I were a species of fool he could not hope to enlighten. I saw a gloating in his expression that I couldn't stomach . . . I went for him.'

'Attacked him?' Alix gasped.

The comte patted her arm. 'Verbally. I told him he was a letdown, a charlatan and worse. Much worse, I'm ashamed to say. He simply blinked. I would have gone then, but Mme Lutzman came into the studio. She brought in the coal scuttle.'

'Always letting his stove go out,' Mémé sighed. 'He would blame me. In front of my girl, Mathilda, calling me a bad wife. I was coming upstairs when I heard the comte shouting and I knew again my husband had failed. Anger bled to the soles of my feet and I don't remember what I said.'

The comte did. 'You told Lutzman he was afraid of finishing a painting because by so doing, he would see that he was nothing but a copyist. A man who absorbed the genius of others and excreted sluggish homage.'

'I said that?' Danielle stared. 'How cruel.'

'And untrue,' Bonnet told her.

Danielle murmured some words of Yiddish, then explained, 'I was days from begging our neighbours for a scrap of bread;

I'm supposed to mind my manners?' She turned back to the comte. 'I must have knelt down to fill the stove.'

'You did,' he agreed. 'You raked out the ashes.'

Danielle moved her gnarled hands as if remembering a sequence. 'The door had a handle you put on and off, to open when the stove was hot.'

'A metal bar, with a claw on the end. You held it up, Madame,' the comte said, 'and suggested you would beat your daughter over the head with it when she came back from school, to save her from starving.'

'A quick blow instead of the pain of hunger.' Danielle touched her temple. '*Vey ist mir*. I told Alfred, "You paint another landscape nobody wants and break your promise to a man who comes all this way in the snow?" And Alfred shouted—'

'"Get down to your kitchen and your cabbages." And then he kicked you and you struck your face against the side of the stove.'

Alix stared at the comte, then at her grandmother. 'Mémé, no!'

Danielle Lutzman touched the white scar beside her eye.

The comte said quietly, 'Kept kicking the way a madman kicks a dog. Your grandmother crawled away, whimpering, and I felt something go inside me. I took the bar from her hand and struck. Alfred fell forward, cracking his forehead on the body of the stove. I stood over him, and for a moment it wasn't that poor, overburdened wretch I saw, it was my father, beating my mother. I realised he was dead and that moment is ingrained in my soul.'

Alix looked at the hand holding hers. '*You* killed him?'

The comte nodded. 'He was kicking his wife's ribs to kindling. I struck to protect her. Damned myself to help her.' A sigh moved him. 'I could have knocked him senseless, but I killed him. And you need to hear the ending. My wife has already asked me why I pursued Danielle and her child to England. Why I kept abreast of their lives and took on your education, Alix. Why I lied even about my war service to explain my persistent presence.'

'Never a great idea to lie about a regiment,' Verrian said. 'Too many records.'

The comte acknowledged it. 'Alix, I met your mother the day I killed your grandfather. She came running upstairs to his studio, no idea what she was about to see. I was too slow to stop her entering the room, but I stopped her throwing herself down beside his corpse, treading in his blood. It was I who told her he was dead. Danielle was conveniently accused of the murder, which drew the attention from me. Through manipulations and bribes, my mother got her released. By the same methods, I was washed clean of my deed. But I knew little Mathilda would never get over the horror inflicted on her. So I provided for her, and later I provided for you.'

Alix whispered, 'You watched my mother grow up?'

'I did. And if you wish it, I'll tell you all about her. All about us.'

'But you never knew my father at all?'

'Never met him.'

Alix struggled to her feet. 'You're worse than a liar. You're a cheat. You could have told me everything I most wanted to know – no, I don't want your stories now. How would I know if you were telling the truth?'

'I lied to protect you. As today proves, knowledge can be dangerous.'

'So can ignorance.' Verrian said it quietly and nobody responded.

Alix walked over to Verrian, who pulled himself straight as if he thought she was going to hit him. She felt a tremor pass through him as she put her arms around him and laid her head on his chest. 'You saw through him. You made me come here and listen. I don't know if I hate you or love you.'

Verrian seemed in no hurry to ask which, or to break the embrace. After a while he said, 'Monsieur le Comte, tell me if I'm wrong, but everyone who might bear witness to Alfred Lutzman's death is either dead or in this room. True?'

'True,' Jean-Yves confirmed.

'Then if everyone agrees the matter is closed, everybody can walk away from here free.'

'Why should he?' Alix tore herself from Verrian and pointed at Bonnet. 'He's tried to push the blame on to others, but I know he attacked me – twice – and left Mémé for dead. I know he broke into the flat . . . he had a key.' She bared her teeth at Bonnet. 'You stole my key at Mother Richelieu's café! I thought it was a pickpocket but it was you, grubbing around in my bag!'

Bonnet got up fast but Verrian moved faster and his blade crossed the painter's neck. He said softly, 'You're a parasite, Bonnet, and you could spend the rest of your life in prison being kicked by bigger parasites. D'you want that, Madame?' he asked Danielle, but she was fiddling with her gloves so he put the question to Alix.

Alix pictured the endless sequence of police interviews and court hearings if they made this official. 'No. I want him to leave Rue Jacob, go away for ever. I never want to see him again. But I need to know why he hurt Mémé. Why he . . . ? Just tell me, Bonnet.'

Bonnet looked down and said in a low, thick voice, 'I never meant to hurt anyone. I came to St-Sulpice that night, you're right, and let myself in with your key. I supposed you'd both be in bed, asleep. I didn't expect Danielle to come home so late and make herself hot milk, or you to be out on the town with your man.' He sent Alix a look that was almost resentful.

She stared stonily back.

'I needed money.' He made a helpless gesture. 'That is all. I needed money.'

'But you nearly throttled me! You split Mémé's scalp open.'

'It was a mistake. Things sometimes get out of hand.'

'Did you break in to steal?' Alix asked. 'Was it really only about money?'

'You'd told me your rent was going up, and I guessed you'd be stowing francs away. Like me, you never had a bank account. I searched your living room, your bedrooms, all the places people put money. I turned Danielle's workbox upside down. Even pulled the pictures off the wall. All I found were a few lousy centimes. You were poorer than I was!'

'You searched while my grandmother lay bleeding.'

'I was desperate!' Bonnet made a plea with his hands. 'All the money I ever got went to pay those robbers who own the gambling clubs on the Butte. You've no idea how it feels to be a slave to the roulette wheel, to owe people everywhere –'

'Spare us.' Verrian pulled Bonnet up off his seat and turned him towards the door. Alix thought he was about to hurl the man down the stairs. But he checked himself and turned Bonnet back to face the comte. 'Make your peace with this gentleman. Never again to blackmail or speak ill of him. Say it.'

Bonnet muttered a response. Verrian opened the door and shoved him out. 'Two hours to clear out of Rue Jacob. Hope we never come after you.'

Verrian left the door open and cool air rushed into the room.

The comte waited until the click of the street door told them that Bonnet was gone. 'And so the soul of a blackmailer is laid bare.' To Danielle he said gently, 'One last time, Madame: did you tell that man the facts of your husband's death?'

Danielle gave Verrian a twinkle. 'He asked me that before.'

'Perhaps you need to answer him.'

Danielle obediently wriggled in her chair so she was facing de Charembourg. 'Yes, I told Bonnet.'

The comte closed his eyes. 'Why did you not say so?'

Danielle considered a moment. 'Because when I told him, we were on the boat crossing the English sea. *Ach*, the waves, the rolling side to side. I was so sick he gave me schnapps to cure my stomach. That is when I told him. I had drunk too much and we were in bed and, what was it, your business?'

Chapter Thirty-Four

'When we sat by the river, the night I found you again, I told you what I did in Spain. Now I want to know what you got up to in Paris.'

They were in the Apricot Suite, the larger of Lord Calford's two suites at the Polonaise, in a drawing room decorated like a country-house conservatory. Bowls of peach-pink roses bled their fragrance. They sat either side of a table, Verrian watchful, Alix trying to digest the last few hours. The meeting on Rue du Sentier had not ended politely.

Rhona de Charembourg had sought her husband's arm, though there was nothing wifely in her grip. 'This has been enlightening, my dear husband,' she said with false amusement, 'but one question remains. We're all gasping to know —' she gestured to Alix — 'is this your daughter?'

Alix tried to shout, 'No!' but all that came out was a distorted squeak.

'Do you wish me to say, Alix?' the comte asked her.

She shook her head. She wouldn't let him replace John

514

Gower. Nobody was going to reduce John Gower to a foot-note in her life.

'In that case,' the comte continued in a flat voice, 'I shall say nothing.'

Rhona made a noise of disgust. 'Whatever she is, your atten-tions have done her no favours. Education without breeding – she's Serge Martel's prostitute.'

The comte had bundled his wife away. Verrian had flagged down taxis to take Mémé and Celestia back to Rue Jacob, and Beryl Theakston home. He secured a separate taxi for himself and Alix. They'd said nothing much since. Rhona de Charem-bourg's words sat in the room with them.

Alix muttered, 'I need a bath.'

Verrian got up. 'I'll show you where.'

She'd never before seen a bathtub with gold-plated taps. When Verrian turned on the hot water, it gushed a steaming jet.

'You have first go,' he said. 'Unless you'd like to share. I'm still waiting to hear if you love or hate me.'

She escaped into the bedroom adjoining the bathroom. In front of the dressing table mirror, she unpinned her hat and used the hotel's hairbrush set. Verrian watched her. She knew he wanted her, knew how much he wanted her, but Rhona's comment must surely have torpedoed his respect for her. 'Pros-titute' was not a word to brush under the carpet. Not to a man. She'd learned a lot about male nature in the last year.

Male desire had the hunter's gaze. It fixed on the object. A woman could tell how much she was wanted by checking if the flame guttered or burned steady. Alix took off her jacket then sat down at the dressing table. Pushing her skirt to mid-thigh, she unhooked a stocking.

She knew Verrian was transfixed. Why was she doing this . . . a game, to punish him for manipulating her? Or to prove Rhona's horrible words were true? Or escape a conversation she dreaded . . . her year with Serge?

She rolled off her stocking, unhooked the second and rolled it down, taking her time. She heard Verrian's breathing change and glanced through her lashes. He hadn't moved from the doorway. He took her look as an invitation and came to her chair, taking the stocking out of her hand. He put it to his face. 'Jasmine.'

'I always massage in jasmine oil after a bath.'

A groan escaped him. 'Every day in Spain, I thought of you. Your voice. And your legs.' He knelt to run his lips along her calf, over her knee to the tender flesh each side. 'Thoughts of loving you were my escape. You, waiting in Paris, took the place of water, sleep, food and reason.'

'How could you remember my legs? You never saw them.'

'Well . . .' Amusement glimmered, though it didn't dilute desire. How could it when his lips were moving by degrees to the inside of her thigh? 'Occasionally you came out in something slinky and legs were implied.'

All she wanted to do was wind her arms around his neck, but that word 'prostitute' wouldn't shift. He mustn't think her a pushover, or they'd never get rid of it. She stood and presented her back. 'Unbutton my waistband.' He made a poor job of it and she teased, 'You haven't had much practice.'

'The buttons are too large for the loops.'

'No, they're not. They're designed not to gape.'

'Then they're working.'

When he'd undone them, she slithered out of the skirt, out of her slip, shivering as Verrian's lips made butterfly touches to her spine and shoulder blades. For twenty heartbeats she stood in satin and lace, leaning into him as he caressed the back of her neck.

'Thank God I found you again. Thank you for waiting.'

It took every particle of resolution to pull away and say, 'I'm sorry to disappoint you, Verrian. Perhaps you would like to make love to your rifle, or your Spanish friends. I'm going to have my bath.'

Ignoring the harrowed protest that fell from his lips, she stalked to the bathroom and locked the door. Testing the temperature of the water, she gave herself marks out of ten. If her aim was to strip all the love from her life, then ten.

Chapter Thirty-Five

They were coming to the end of a long lunch at a restaurant on Place Pigalle. Alix was nervous. They'd invited Rosa to join them, and let her choose the venue, and by ill luck she'd picked Serge Martel's favourite eating place.

Blissfully unaware of Alix's discomfort, Rosa raised her brandy glass and told Alix how much better she was looking. 'Last time I saw you, you were bleary-eyed from too much you-know-who.' Not noticing that Verrian's expression iced over, she winked. 'Up all hours, then comes home smelling like a Turkish harem.'

'Leave Alix her dignity.' Verrian lit cigarettes for them and ordered coffee. The glitter in his eye told Alix this was her last chance. He showed it by saying, 'Alix, I heard you tell Celestia that you might not keep your business going much longer. I may need to go home to London and don't want to leave her and Pepe in the lurch.'

Alix inhaled cigarette smoke. 'I'm trying to stay open until Christmas. Then who knows?'

'Aw, no, ducks.' Rosa raised her cigarette holder in protest. 'You can scrape through, surely?'

'Not on the clientele I have. If I'm to survive, I need to plan a spring–summer show that erases all memory of last summer's disaster, but I have no money to fund it. You can't be in this business with no cash.'

'I'm on, if you want me.'

Alix blew out smoke. 'I can't design any more, Rosa. I look at blank paper and it laughs back at me.'

'Know what you need? Bit of fun.'

No doubt Rosa meant 'a sex life'. Alix agreed – if only she could get over her terrors. She hadn't realised until Verrian's lips were touching her thigh how deeply Serge Martel had scarred her. She wanted Verrian, and there was Serge, etched in her brain. The more she pushed Verrian away, the more Serge invaded and the more rigid she became. The power games were over. She was just frightened.

Rosa was looking at her narrowly. 'You need a holiday – a few days with no customers, no grandma, no pins and needles.' She left them after that, saying, 'I need a strong cuppa and a lie-down. You two want to talk.'

'Just the two of them' felt like pillars either side of a cold doorway. Alix said, 'Any moment, Verrian, you'll look at your watch.'

He took her cigarette and stubbed it out along with his own. With a soft knuckle, he brushed her bottom lip, spreading tingling heat that made her open her mouth slightly. 'Do you know how it grinds me up to think of you with Martel?'

'Then don't think of it.'

A flash of anger. 'How – when I see him in your eyes all the time? Was it so damn good with him?'

'Don't.'

An accordionist outside began playing 'Vous, qui passez sans me voir'. Verrian gave a painful smile. '"You walk by . . ." Give me the truth.'

All right, she thought. 'What Rosa said about me living half-drugged in a harem . . .' his gaze shot up to meet hers, 'I did. I did things I didn't want to do with someone I didn't always like. But you had left, everything had fallen apart and living like that dulled reality.'

'Weren't there other ways . . . country walks or something?'

'This is Paris, not a Hampshire girls' school. Maybe you don't want to go on seeing me – Verrian? Don't look away.'

But something had taken his attention. Waiters were scuttling. The doorway filled with a wide-shouldered silhouette. Alix's heart tripped a beat. Oh God, not him.

Serge Martel sauntered up to them. Verrian stood. Alix felt the atmosphere electrify and guessed she wasn't the only one calculating the odds of Serge producing a knife. That was a glint of metal in his hand, wasn't it?

Serge said in a grazing whisper, 'Alix, I've come to ask

this bastard to give you back.' There was a shiny scar under his lip.

'Alix is free to leave,' Verrian said.

She read the warning signs. Serge's slowed-down voice, the flat gaze. But did Verrian see it? She breathed, 'Take care.'

Verrian had the advantage of height. Serge had meat-market shoulders. And a knuckleduster on his punching fist. Alix saw it the second before Serge drove it into Verrian's ribs. So hard Verrian collapsed. She tried to get to him but was trapped by the table, which his fall had pushed towards the wall. All she could do was dash her coffee in Serge's face. Serge grabbed her hair, twisting it until she thought her scalp would tear off.

'You bring another man on to my patch?'

She screamed so piercingly he let go. He yanked the table aside to get at her, his voice strangely gentle as he said, 'He's dead if you aren't back with me –' he lifted her hand and put her finger into his mouth in the most suggestive of moves – 'by nightfall. You were getting so good at pleasing me, why waste it?'

'Serge –' she went very still because he was holding her finger between his teeth – 'I won't come back to you.'

He let her pull her finger free. 'Alix, Alix. Big baby eyes one moment, then cold as a fishmonger's gloves. You're punishing me for going with Dulcie. Hey – she can't do any of the things you can do, and the Rose Noire misses you . . .'

A light thud interrupted him. A short knife had been driven

blade-down into the tabletop. Verrian was on his feet, a trickle of blood at the corner of his mouth. He said through painful breaths, 'I like a fair fight. Take the knife.'

Serge laughed. 'What are you going to do, read me the rules of cricket? Or roast me with your cigarette lighter?' He grinned at Alix and reached for the knife.

As his fingers closed around it, Verrian's elbow came down on Serge's arm, clubbing his funny bone against the table. Serge crumpled in shock. Verrian smashed Serge's forearm downwards, at the same time snapping the wrist backwards. Alix cried out at the brutal crack. Serge gave an animal howl and fell.

Verrian slumped on to a chair. 'Your taste in men stinks,' he said. 'Ask for the bill. My wallet's in my top pocket. You can drive us.'

'I can't drive.'

'And I thought you had all the talents.'

Alix returned to Rue Jacob feeling as if she'd run through fire crackers. Every muscle quaked. Verrian had driven them through Paris and she'd feared he might collapse against the wheel. She'd wanted to pull him into her arms and cry over him, but he wouldn't let her touch him. When they reached Place Vendôme, the staff of the Polonaise had taken over. He hadn't wanted her. Hadn't wanted a doctor. If he needed a nurse, he'd told her harshly, he'd ask for Celestia.

Instructing her receptionist, Violette, to make her double-strength coffee, Alix checked her diary. God help her, Una's Manchester matrons were booked in again. Parade required. She didn't think she could walk in a straight line, let alone turn and pose. There was a letter beside her telephone and she tore it open, shaking out a picture postcard of an English seafront. The Queen's Hotel, Hastings. Hastings was on the south coast of England. Who the hell was on holiday there at this time of year . . . ? She sought the name at the bottom and groaned.

Greetings from the front, kiddo. I've escaped to the bracing briny, where I am to be joined by Paul. Yes, that Paul. Be a sweetheart and look after his sisters, will you, so we can have some together time?

'No!' Alix howled, 'you have to be joking –'

I won't demean myself by suggesting you owe me. A dig inside the envelope will reveal my practical gratitude –

Ten five-thousand-franc notes.

Keep the change. I shall keep Paul till Mr Kilpin turns up to spoil things. See you February for your collection. Make it stupendous. Last week some butt-blister from the War Office called on Mr K

*to discuss turning his ships into troop carriers. It's coming, the big
dark one. One more party, then we all put on our raincoats.*

Una

Alix read the card again. No hint as to when childminding duties
would begin.

The Manchester matrons – an industrialist's wife, her married
daughters and two country cousins – complained they'd given
themselves bunions window-shopping on Rue de Rivoli and
Faubourg St-Honoré. The prices had shocked them, so they'd
come back to Modes Lutzman. 'High style at sensitive prices,
dear Mrs Kilpin assured us.'

Dear Mrs Kilpin needed a good shake, Alix fumed as the
women asked her to turn this way and that, throwing interminable
questions about her 'modes'. Who did her sewing? Were
these really the latest styles? All of them calling her 'Marm'zel'.
They didn't seem to like anything.

Alix thought, *I couldn't sell a carrot to a rabbit today*. She'd close
early and take to her bed like a diva. But as she made an entrance
in a little black dress set off with gold metal necklaces and slave
bracelets, hopes of a lie-down dissolved. Cries of, 'Alix, we're
here!' told her that the rest of the day was spoken for. The rest
of the month.

Paul came in, preventing his sisters from running forward by
holding the belts of their coats. The Manchester ladies tutted and

Alix made frantic motions to Paul to go away. Either he didn't notice or was still angry with her. Her ornaments clanking, she threw aside formality and hugged the girls. 'Two other ladies to see the collection,' she said brightly. 'Find your own chairs.'

Lala and Suzy had been well trained by their Aunt Gilberte. They gave little curtsies to the English guests and said, '*Enchantée*, Madame,' to each one. Manchester jaws relaxed. Smiles appeared. 'Couldn't you just eat them?' said one of the women. Paul took the window seat and lit a cigarette.

'No smoking in the salon,' Alix told him.

'We don't mind,' one of the country cousins tittered. 'We like a man to be a man.'

So Paul, wearing a ribbed black sweater that caressed his muscles, watched the parade in a haze of moody smoke. Alix soldiered on, thinking, *I need a new name for what I'm doing. You can't have a parade of one.*

She came back in an evening gown to find Verrian sitting on a sofa arm. Pale, but clearly in no need of tender nursing. The ladies were enjoying something he'd just said, and, Alix thought crossly, he was supposed to be dying.

'So, dear,' the industrialist's wife blared as Alix came out in her final model, 'that sweet dress is not a real Chanel, but quite alike and costs eight thousand francs.' She counted on her fingers. 'I make that about forty pounds. Will people think it's Chanel? That's the question.'

'I'd prefer they thought it was a real Lutzman,' Alix said

through gritted teeth. She caught Verrian's eye and read sardonic amusement, which, along with his presence, was a positive sign.

'Celestia is extraordinary.' Verrian turned the Hispano into Boulevard St-Germain, accelerating to get into the stream of night-time traffic.

'She's a godsend,' Alix agreed, giving him a cautious smile. 'You were right, I admit it.' She'd closed the office early today, in celebration. After yesterday's parade, she'd taken eighteen orders from the Manchester ladies, fifty per cent paid up front. So relieved that her barren period was over, she was not only prepared to like Celestia, she was letting Verrian whisk her away for the night, just the two of them. 'She might have refused to look after two extra children at such short notice, as well as caring for Mémé. But she seemed pleased. I hope they all behave.'

'I'm not sure I care –' Verrian braked to let a taxi cut in front of him – 'having got you to myself at last. But it was inspired, taking the children into Bon— to the downstairs studio and getting them painting. Big sticky mess, perfect icebreaker. Oh, look, that's where you first flirted with me.' The smile he gave her was an open invitation. 'Could we carry on where we left off, d'you think? Then move on from flirtation to seduction?'

Alix glanced where Verrian pointed and saw the Deux Magots café, lit up like a dinner party. 'Celestia yearns for family,' she said to mask the flutter of panic his words provoked, 'and it's good for Pepe to have playmates. I'm paying her extra,' she threw in. 'Una sent money. Actually enough for me to plan a spring–summer collection.'

Verrian's reply was cool. 'You should send the money back. While Una Kilpin pulls your strings, you aren't free. Anyway, what's the point of keeping your business going? You told me that every time you try to sketch something, your mind goes blank.'

'A moment ago you were flirting and now you're bullying. We're meant to be having a holiday.'

'That doesn't start until we've crossed the river. My point is—'

'I know what your point is, Verrian. Please, just drive.'

He had booked a table in the Polonaise's restaurant for eight. 'Which gives you an hour to change,' he told Alix as he held open the door of the Lilac Suite for her. 'Don't go to sleep in the bath.'

They would stay here tonight. A suite each, no forced togetherness, though there was a connecting door. The axe of 'last chance' still hung over her head. If, tonight, she took a new lover, it had to be without the mask of intoxicants or music. If she couldn't . . . well, that was it. She never would.

After her bath, she dried herself and rubbed jasmine into her skin. She'd brought Javier's Eirène with her, a perfume he'd created to go with Oro, inspired by the World Fair's theme of peace, and he'd given her a flask of it days before dismissing her.

The top unscrewed to provide a thin gold stick to apply the fragrance. Coco Chanel said that a girl should apply perfume where she wanted to be kissed. Alix brushed the insides of her wrists, behind her ears, the hollow of her throat.

So far, so Sunday-school teacher. Consulting her wide eyes in the mirror, she ran the stick between her breasts and across her stomach. Then she thought, *If I don't get dressed, he'll think I've fallen asleep.*

Walking into his suite, she met Verrian in the connecting doorway.

Both stopped still. Alix was wearing a cherry silk evening dress, slippery as mayonnaise, with an overskirt of shadow-worked chiffon. It left one shoulder bare and the chiffon caught every air current. The dress was intolerant of underwear, so that was pretty much it, apart from a stole of black gauze she trailed from her hand.

He wore the uniform of his class. Black tie, tuxedo, the only colour topaz cufflinks in gold settings. He recovered first. 'I have Bollinger on ice.'

A fire crackled in a marble fireplace in the lounge of his suite. They stood before it and he poured. She accepted a glass and they touched rims. Those bubbles always gave her courage. She'd decided in the bath that she was not going to play the penitent. He had some explaining to do as well. Tonight she'd ask him once again about the wedding ring that had disappeared.

He laid a hand on her bare shoulder, giving her the chance to shy away. When she didn't, he put his lips to hers. Just a touch. Alix swayed towards him.

A knock at the door, a waiter, informing 'Monsieur' that his table was ready downstairs. Verrian put their glasses on the mantelpiece, fetched her stole and laid it across her shoulders. 'This is the best restaurant in Paris, give or take. Not many places would drag me away just now.'

It was a wonderful restaurant, the best food, service, surroundings she'd ever encountered. And so old-fashioned, her youth and dress drew eyes. Her escort was definitely worth a second glance too.

Perhaps it was the pearlescent lighting, but Verrian seemed to have shed the fatigue he'd brought back from war. He'd recovered from his winding by Serge. Paris magic, she thought, reaching for her glass. She'd already drunk white wine with her hors d'oeuvre and with her filet of sole. Now she was drinking red with roast grouse and potatoes à la Hollandaise.

Verrian said, 'Get drunk if you want to, but not because you have to. There's no ordeal awaiting you.'

'It is an ordeal. After what the comtesse said, I mean, I can understand –' A waiter topped up their glasses. By the time he went, Alix had lost her thread.

Verrian laid his hand over hers. 'No man is very imaginative when it comes to his woman being with another man, but I know what hardship does. I realise the need to snatch at comfort.'

'I did not snatch and there was no comfort, only a form of madness. If you don't care for me any more, I'd rather know.' *Actually*, she thought, *I wouldn't.*

He didn't answer at once, and when he did he sounded distant. 'Nothing hurts more than the death of love.'

She looked down at her plate. 'I see.'

'I don't think you do. When I left England in 'thirty-five, I was engaged to be married to a neighbour's daughter. I loved Moira, but when I told her my intention to go to North Africa to cover what looked like a short-lived conflict, she showed a side I hadn't seen before. Her attitude was "to hell with dying foreigners". She wanted to spend that season toting me around house parties and hunt balls, showing off her engagement ring. I went anyway, and she began seeing my brother. The death of love.'

'She can't have loved you.'

'The point is, my love for her died.'

Alix raked a piece of potato through the sauce and put it into her mouth because whatever emotional carnage was on its way, you should always eat. Mémé's philosophy.

'In Spain I met a girl, Maria-Pilar, and understood what love was. It's not just physical attraction, or "doing the right thing". It's not even working out how much you've got to live on and where you might set up house. Nor about stealing kisses in taxis, though I'm fond of that.' He smiled, pulling her back into his net. 'It's finding someone who fits around you and inside you, who you would die for because you want them to exist more than you want your own life to go on. There's independence in that kind of love. It makes you both strong, so long as it's mutual.'

A topaz cufflink kicked out a spark as Verrian drank, his hand moving close to the candle flame. The phantom wedding ring had vanished, his skin uniform brown. 'You stopped loving Maria-Pilar?' Alix asked, dreading the answer. If that could die, any love could. Some men could not sustain it. They left tears behind them all their lives.

'It was she who stopped loving me.'

She stared. 'Why?'

'Because –' he leaned forward, his eyes digging into hers – 'though I was too rash to see it, her belief in God underpinned her very breathing. She thought she could convert me, and when she couldn't, she looked upon me with despair. Then with judgement, and finally with disgust.'

'How long were you were married?'

'For about two months.'

'Where is she now?'

'She's dead, Alix. She died on the battlefield.'

'A nurse?'

'A driver. My official driver. Our car was hit by a shell when she took me out to the front one day. I'd seen an Italian tank in a ditch. The crew had been thrown out and I wanted pictures. At the time, the British press was refusing to acknowledge the presence of Italian and German troops on the ground in Spain. I told Maria to drive on a few yards then turn around. I didn't want her to see those dead boys . . . ridiculous. She'd seen more death than I had. I took the pictures; next second I was blasted into the ditch. I crawled out and saw a bonfire where the car ought to have been. I couldn't get close, but I've never forgiven myself for not being in that car with her. I might have got her out.'

Or died with her, more likely. She lifted his hand to her cheek. 'I'm sorry, Verrian, making you tell me this. Where is she buried?'

'In a mass grave, with other soldiers.'

Waiters cleared their plates. Verrian ordered ice-cream parfaits for them which neither of them finished. When they were ready to leave he said, 'I don't think we should invite the brandy bottle upstairs, but shall I order coffee?'

They didn't speak in the lift. In his suite she drank her coffee fast, because whatever he might think, the next minutes *were* going to be an ordeal. Dutch courage wasn't working. 'The Death of Love' was a terrifying vision. What if he was disappointed with her body, or if he turned out to be like Serge, rough and selfish? When Verrian tugged off his tie and said, 'Alix, may I make love to you at last?' she blurted out her fears in the words, 'No – I'm exhausted. Goodnight,' and fled.

*

In her bathroom she undressed, washed, brushed her teeth. Facing herself in the mirror above the sink, she muttered, 'Did I just kill love?' Death was generally something you didn't recover from. Unless – she bit her lip – you made an extra special effort. She reapplied a few dots of perfume. In her bedroom, she pulled something in powder blue silk from the back of a chair. The garment smelled of rose oil from the soap flakes she'd washed it in. She inhaled once, then slipped it on.

The bathroom door leading to Verrian's bedroom stood ajar, light making a spearhead across a satin bedspread. Alix stood between rooms, poised to run. She heard water draining, then the bathroom light switched off. Stay or scuttle? He wouldn't know she'd been here, since he'd killed the only light. Then a man's shape appeared and fragrant steam billowed into the room.

She was astonished he didn't hear her heart beating. Oblivious, he leaned one knee on the bed and switched on the lamp above it. He came to life in the gleam; bronze flesh, damp hair curling against his ears. He was wearing one of the white seersucker robes the hotel provided. It was loosely belted and a hair-sprinkled chest and bands of muscle pulled her gaze. She responded to the unwitting power of his body, putting her hand against her stomach where the feeling was sharpest, touching sensual silk, asking herself why she'd denied them both so long. Her movement must have hit the corner of his eye because he barked – 'Jesus!' He backed off the bed, stood with his feet planted, arms crossed. She waited for the melting smile, the open arms.

'If this is you having fun, showing me how insanely I want you, then you can get out.'

'I – I just wanted to say goodnight.'

'Goodnight.'

She heard the contained rage and knew she should go while she had a thread of self-respect. But seeing him robed like an Olympian held her transfixed.

He covered the space between them and caught her round the waist, bunching the camiknickers she'd put on.

'And I suppose these are just something you threw on?' His hand travelled, exploring her shape, finding a breast, spanning her waist, caressing hip and buttocks, the curve of a thigh and finally invading the lace trim, finding the furrow between thigh and mound. And all the time he kissed her with a confrontational passion that pushed the breath back inside her. She felt him hardening against her and she knew she'd misjudged him. He was a man of many tones but he was a man, and she'd teased and rejected him and beckoned him back too many times. Schooled in Serge's self-absorption, she'd used her body to punish Verrian. Punished the wrong man . . .

She collapsed against him and he swept her up and then she was lying on a lake of satin. 'Don't hurt me,' she pleaded. Yesterday she'd watched him snap a man's wrist like a piece of firewood. 'I can do this . . . I love you. I will. Just don't hurt me.'

He rolled over, pulling her with him so she lay above him. Words broke against her throat, 'You can have anything from me you want, everything I have, except the last shreds of pride. Hurt you? Why would I hurt the thing I love most, the most precious and beautiful thing I have? Don't run, that's all.'

'I won't,' she said huskily. 'But you don't have to grip the back of my head like a dentist about to pull a tooth out.'

He laughed in reply, a sound mixed with a groan. 'I'll trust you.'

'Yes. Let me.' Alert for any signs of shock or revulsion, she knelt beside him, pushing aside his robe, kissing a trail from his throat, moving lower. She adored the texture of flesh and hair, the faint taste of soap, of skin. She found the marks of Serge's knuckles just under his ribs. She kissed each of the lesions and continued downward. Opened her lips and let her soft warmth envelope him. Without the weight of obligation or of pleasing a careless heart, she was able to give herself to the intimate act, this most private token of love. Never doubting she could trust Verrian, she enjoyed herself, tasting and caressing and feeling his arousal grow with her.

'You'd better stop,' he said thickly, running his fingers through her hair.

She kissed her way back upward, drawing her tongue over his belly, gently teasing each nipple. He groaned and the satin bed cover whispered. She pushed his robe off his shoulders and he shrugged it away. She'd thought a lot about his torso, picturing it before she went to sleep every night in those first weeks of meeting him. She'd always imagined it rearing over her, keeping her sweetly trapped, but Serge had given her a horror of being pinned, so maybe it could happen in reverse. Half expecting to be thrown off, she sat astride him.

His shoulders were honed, with hollows just the right depth for lips and tongue. His throat stretched as her tongue drew a line along it. Teasing his mouth with hers, she absorbed the sensation of a body held captive beneath her. How different a man felt when he wasn't trying to control, when he was allowing himself to be seduced, his whole body a sigh, his breath deepening. Moist readiness lay between her legs, betraying her desire. She rolled off him, quietening his protest with two words, and stripped off, throwing the camiknickers into the dark. He reached for her, finding her breasts and caressing her nipples to buds. She cried out as he put his mouth around one then the other. She threaded her legs around him and moved against him, flesh against muscle until his control broke. He entered her first with his fingers, exploring her core, soft as velveteen until she begged, 'Now, inside me now,' and opened for him, crying out as he invaded.

She climaxed fast, the reality of Verrian on her, in her, more erotically potent than she'd believed possible. His rhythm grew frantic, and in the last moments, as he withdrew, a tide of words and kisses broke against her lips.

They shared the shuddering pleasure. Shared heat and lips. She lay in his arms and thought – I am happy.

They woke at some indistinct hour and reprised their joy slowly. Verrian followed the trail she'd laid with her perfume to show her at languorous length her capacity for pleasure. They fell asleep, wrapped about each other, until daylight clapped its hands. The brief holiday, over.

'You're convinced Rhona de Charembourg sabotaged your last collection?'

They were crossing the Seine at Pont Neuf, on foot. Verrian had ordered a taxi to Rue Jacob, explaining the Hispano was leaking oil. At Alix's suggestion, they'd got out on the Right Bank to enjoy the novelty of crossing the river in a blanket of fog. They held hands and murmured 'excuse me's' to other pedestrians.

'Somebody sent that Charboneau woman. And how else would Rhona have got an identical suit to mine? That grey-green cloth was a short run a Manchester manufacturer decided to pull from production, and Una thought I'd like it. I made myself a suit and cut out another which never made it into the collection. It was among the stuff the police confiscated which proves Rhona got access to the boxes they took away. Wearing it was her way of showing that she has more power than I have.'

Verrian put his arm round her. 'Unspeakably vulgar, as my mother would say.' He asked her if she still meant to close Modes Lutzman.

'No – I'll kick it into life somehow. Though it'll be like flying over a desert with no fuel. Oh, and so you don't have to disapprove of me, I'll post those francs back to Una. She's staying at a hotel in Hastings . . . she can change it to pounds and spend it on cocktails and fish-and-chip dinners. I'll scrape by.'

Verrian made a testing noise. 'You could sell your grandfather's paintings for cash. Knowing what you know of Alfred Lutzman, surely you don't want to keep them?'

Alix looked towards the river where fog made ghosts of the boats and wharfs. 'I couldn't without Mémé's consent and she's not really able to give it. Besides, I need time to see if I still admire my grandfather's work, or if I was deluding myself about him. Do I sound mad?'

'No – scarily rational.'

She shot him an appealing look. 'If my business fails, you won't despise me?'

'You'll be flying prayer-born, as my good friend Phipps would say, and I like courage. But you'll succeed. Rhona de Charembourg likes your stuff—' He laughed as Alix elbowed him. 'Theft is the sincerest form of flattery, all the more believable when it comes from one's sworn enemies.'

As they walked down Rue Dauphine, Alix said, 'I don't want enemies. I want friends.'

He stopped to kiss her. 'Well, you always have me.'

11ᵗʰ November 1938

She'd thrown two sketchbooks into the wastebasket and ripped up more metres of muslin than she cared to calculate. She was discarding yet another drawing when Verrian came into her studio, looked at the bin under its avalanche and said, 'I've just had a stand-up row with my brother . . . if one can have such a thing over the telephone. Did you know there's been a shooting at the German embassy?'

She stared at him. 'In Paris?'

'A Jewish lad took it out on a German official. I filed a sympathetic report, pointing out that the boy had just heard his parents had been deported from Germany. My brother refuses to run it, so I've resigned.'

He looked down at Alix's sketchbook, which was covered in desperate hieroglyphs. He was still wearing his overcoat because Alix was economising on paraffin. Fishing an envelope from an inside pocket, he said, 'As you sent Una's money back, I thought this might be useful.'

The wad of money was more than Alix had ever seen in one place. 'Your pay-off from the *Monitor*?'

Verrian gave a sardonic laugh. 'I quit, so no pay-off.' He hugged her. 'The money's from the Hispano. I sold it.'

'Sold . . . Oh, Verrian. I thought it had oil problems.'

'A red herring.'

'You loved that car.'

'No, I liked it. I love you and I want you to bring out a blazing collection in the new year because I agree with Mrs Kilpin in one respect – clouds are gathering. Soon it'll be on with the raincoats and sensible shoes.'

'You mean war? I thought so once, but the Munich Accord gave Hitler what he wanted, didn't it? He has his Sudetenland and his re-militarised zone. Why should he want a war now?'

'He blackmailed France and Britain very deftly and, as we know, blackmailers always come back for more. The Munich agreement is only as good as Hitler's word, and signing it alienated a vital ally, the Soviets.'

'Oh, them.'

'Yes, them. Munich only moved the chess pieces around.' Noting her dispirited expression, he suggested they go and spend time with the children. 'They're painting as only children can. Let them inspire you.'

Chapter Thirty-Six

It snowed on New Year's Day 1939, making the windows shine like frozen milk. White shantung silk lay in swathes across the salon sofas and, because the floor and walls were white too, Alix felt she had walked into her own blank page.

She'd got halfway through a collection in December then abandoned it. Verrian had asked, 'But why? Nice shapes, nice legs . . . am I missing something?'

She listened . . . his typewriter had fallen silent. He was working on a freelance article for an American newspaper, and he'd probably finished it. Verrian chiselled at a job until it was done. Unlike her, he produced results. As he said, 'An editor would rather have the piece that's ninety-five-per-cent good than the hundred-per-cent-perfect piece that never arrives. Now you know why it's called "hack".'

She looked at the clock – nearly eleven – and took a note from her pocket.

Meet me by the lion, Jardin du Luxembourg, 11.03.

11.03 would mean 11.30. Paul must have something important to ask her. Something to do with Una? To do with copying? This time she had a simple word ready. *No*.

Alix couldn't work out why Paul had written when he could easily have spoken to her at Rue Jacob. Since returning from his English holiday, he'd been coming here every day, dropping his sisters off and picking them up. It had been agreed that Suzy and Lala should stay in Celestia's care until Paul got back into some kind of routine with his work.

At the lion statue, Alix tramped through pristine snow until she heard her name called. Paul was striding towards her. They shook hands, an element of constraint still between them. Paul's face was leaner, his mouth harder. Una's lover had grown up.

'Are we freezing for old times' sake?' she teased.

He took her arm and they walked. 'I wanted to tell you somewhere private – Alix, I have news that will shock you.'

She thought instantly, *Bonnet's back in Montmartre*.

'Serge Martel was arrested for an attack on a girl, one of his singers. He hurt her very badly and they're talking about prison. I thought you should know.'

'I see.' What could she say? 'Poor, poor girl.'

'You were lucky to get away when you did.' They walked in silence until Paul said, 'I hope my sisters aren't driving you mad. Did you know, Suzy speaks to me now?'

Alix seized upon this happier subject. 'That's Pepe's doing. Nobody could explain to him that Suzy didn't speak, so he bombarded her till she gave in. You got your speech therapist in the end. Course they aren't driving me mad. Celestia is wonderful with them and Mémé loves having them.'

'Good.' He made an awkward movement. 'Because, Alix, there's something else I have to tell you. Something that will change my life and theirs.'

Una. The name sat between them as he lit one of his pungent cigarettes. Alix predicted his next words – he and Una were going to live together, would Alix care for the girls while they settled themselves?

'I want to join the navy.'

Her mouth dropped and his smoke drifted into it. 'What?' she spluttered.

'I'd rather sign up than get conscripted.'

'You're talking as though we're actually at war.' From a distant corner of the park came children's voices and Alix felt a formless pain. *Please, not war. Not here. Not poor France again.*

Paul put his arm around her. It was snowing – large, lazy flakes. 'When we were staying in Hastings, Una and I hired a car and drove along the south coast of England. We stopped at a place called "Lee-on-Solent" – am I pronouncing it right?'

'It'll do.'

'We saw ships out on the water and there was one, a battle cruiser. Somebody said she was HMS *Hood*. She was magnificent. We bumped into sailors every place we went, and you know how it is when suddenly you know what you want to do with your life?'

She did of course. 'What about the girls? And Una?'

'Una . . .' Paul sizzled a snowflake with the tip of his cigarette. 'She won't leave Kilpin and I won't live in her pocket. The girls will live at Bobigny, with their great-aunt. Gilberte is strict with them, but she loves them in her way and with decent wages, I can pay their keep.' He took a deep breath. 'I've decided to sell the *Katrijn*.'

Alix nodded sadly. So, an era was over. 'Suzy and Lala can come to me any time, Paul. Every holiday.'

'Thank you.'

They said their goodbyes. They kissed cheeks, then lips. A brief, smoky kiss. 'I do love you, Paul.'

'I love you too, Alix.'

'Will you come to my show in February?'

'If you make it a happy one. No black.'

They parted and she walked as fast as the snow would allow, wanting to get back to Verrian. Children's voices grew louder, and as she rounded a corner she saw a group dressed in motley clothes, mufflers and headscarves. They were playing a game with a streamer of scarves. An older child ran with it, the others chasing to catch its end. They were shouting in German . . . goodness, weren't they the gypsy children from St-Sulpice? This must be their playground. Enraptured, Alix's eyes followed the kaleidoscope of colour they made against the snow and the knots in her mind gave way.

Verrian met her on the front stairs. He noticed the snow on her boots but asked no questions. 'The children have been trying to find you. Be prepared to adopt a surprised expression.' He took her to her flat, where she stopped, poleaxed. One entire wall was a vivid mural.

'This is our gallery.' Pepe beetled over to them, pulling her and Verrian towards the vast painting. Lala came up to sell them a ticket. 'Ten francs each.'

It took Alix a moment to realise that one of Bonnet's rolls of blank canvas had been opened out and nailed up in the living room. Verrian must have done it, and the children must have stood on tables to paint. And such painting. Trees and flowers, strange animals, herself, Verrian in his hat, a princess or two, fairies, aeroplanes, houses and cars and more flowers, all in riotous colour. It took her back to Picasso's *Guernica* – she felt the same awe, but this was the antidote to Picasso's monochrome depiction of atrocity.

Verrian mistook her reaction. 'I haven't damaged the wall much.'

'You're good with hammer and nails?' she asked him, reaching up to kiss him. 'Because I've just realised how I'm going to create my next collection.'

*

Her staff thought she was mad. Hand-paint three hundred metres of silk?

Yes, she told them. It would be stretched over frames, like an artist's canvas. She would cut the children's painting into stencils – with their permission of course – and trace them on to silk, outlining each shape in gutta, a rubber resist. After which, let the painting begin. Anybody capable of holding a brush could help.

The children were early recruits, and soon Mémé and the other staff from Modes Lutzman joined in enthusiastically. Celestia and Verrian couldn't escape and M. Hubert, the sleepy accounts clerk who had guarded Alix's front office until his dismissal, was invited back. Even Paul spent his evenings daubing on shantung. Once he'd shed his inhibitions, he began adding his own designs of ships and river boats, which, Alix confided to Verrian, were almost as good as Pepe's.

Designs poured from Alix's pencil. All she needed was to produce clothes that showed off the fabric. 'I'm going to make peacock tails,' she told Verrian.

Chapter Thirty-Seven

'Madame?'

A desk clerk broke Alix's trance. She'd been mentally rehearsing the opening moments of her show, when her mannequins would walk out four in a line, in beach pyjamas – flared pants and halter-neck tops, a casual style first introduced by Coco Chanel and now creeping into daily wear. Alix's version in printed silk was substantial enough for lounging at home – or risqué enough for a night out. This whole collection involved risk, but that felt good . . .

'A telephone call for you in reception.'

She allowed a smile. She was now 'Madame'. Not because she was married – yet – but because she had gained the status of a businesswoman. 'I'll be just a moment.' The girls would walk down a gangway between tables to a roped-off area where they'd turn and pose. A swing quintet playing from the raised area currently dominated by a grand piano would provide the rhythm.

When Verrian had suggested hiring the Polonaise's Alexandra Lounge for her show, she'd thought he'd missed the point.

'People need to *see* the clothes. I can't have my mannequins jostling through tea-drinking dowagers.'

'We'll hire it privately, in the evening. Tell me a better location.'

She couldn't. Place Vendôme was inner-elite Right Bank. She wouldn't have to persuade people to schlep out to Rue Jacob. Wouldn't have to worry about refreshments, flowers, wine. Wouldn't even have to hire chairs.

And the clincher: 'It can go on my father's bill. It can be his wedding present to us.'

'Are you proposing marriage, Mr Haviland?' she'd asked.

He had left that question dangling, telling her he had an article to finish.

Around the same time, the Comte de Charembourg had written to Alix describing a meeting he'd had with Adèle Charboneau, whose true address he'd found in his wife's contact book. '*She was shocked to find me on her doorstep,*' the comte wrote, '*and quickly confessed that my wife paid her to trick you into making an illegal copy. If it helps, Mlle Charboneau is ashamed of herself as you were so kind. I will show contrition in a more practical way –*' His company, he declared, would provide any remaining fabric Alix needed for her new collection, free of charge. '*Things come full circle, dear Alix.*'

Her collection now had a date; 1st March, four days away. Verrian's Hispano money had disappeared on labour, mannequins, accessories and rent. She was back in business. She'd snatched herself one last chance.

In the hotel lobby she was handed a telephone receiver. 'Alix Gower speaking . . . ?'

When she put the receiver down two minutes later, all her hope was gone. Luck and courage were not enough, it seemed. Not when you had enemies hell-bent on bringing you down.

A caramel voice called, 'Knock-knock, may I come in?'

Alix was in her salon, staring at the rails of clothes that, for a second time, would not be shown. She turned to see Una Kilpin. 'What are you doing here?'

'You could manage a frisson of delighted surprise, surely? I need no excuse to come to Paris, but among other things, I wanted to see you. And dare one say it . . . a show?'

She looks how I feel, Alix thought. Una's glow had dimmed. Still chic though. She carried a tiny handbag against the back of her hand, presumably with a strap through which the palm slid. It was the same tan colour as her suit and gloves.

'Oh, kiddo, why the funeral face?'

'My mannequins have quit,' Alix said. 'The agency supplying them rang to say they weren't available after all. Four days' notice.' She gestured to the rails. 'Everything finished, just the last few bits . . . I have to cancel. Again. Una, I don't know why this keeps happening to me.'

'I do.' Una flicked the popper on her handbag and pulled out a letter. 'It was sent me by the fashion editor of the London *Times* – a friend of mine.'

Alix read:

To whom it may concern,

Haute couture is the flower of French culture, a flower cankered by copying and theft. Those of us who patronise the finest fashion houses of Paris pledge to support their integrity. Our first move is against 'mushroom houses' such as Modes Lutzman, whose proprietor Alix Gower was convicted for counterfeiting –

'Reached the part where you could sue?'

Alix ignored Una.

– and whose endeavours to undermine French couture we will resist. Should you receive an invitation to a showing by this house, we beg you tear it up.

'We' was Rhona de Charembourg and other aristocratic leaders of fashion.

'Her ladyship's been sending that letter out for weeks,' Una said. 'It's gone to every fashion editor, buyer and well-dressed female south of the Arctic Circle. Have you had any press interest, editors returning your calls?'

'Not much,' Alix admitted. 'No French press. I have Americans. The *New York Post* is sending someone and—'

'You'll have to tell them it's off.' Una put a hand on her

shoulder. 'I'll break it to Gregory and his bean-counter Pusey. I'm sorry, kiddo, but Gregory will pull the plug.'

Alix studied Una's face and thought, *She cares but she doesn't quite understand.* 'You were always kicking my backside for being afraid. "No reward without risk" – remember?'

'I never prescribed suicide. You'll be mauled if nobody comes.'

'Then how can they maul me?'

'Alix, get real. Rhona de Charembourg has shot your horses and broken your wheels. You've got no audience and no mannequins. What are you going to do? Have the waiters show the dresses while the cleaners applaud? Do the sensible thing – cut your losses.'

'Thank you for bringing this.' Alix meant the letter. 'I'm glad Rhona de Charembourg's malice is out in the open.' She held her hand out to Una. 'I hope to see you in the audience on Wednesday. Mr Kilpin too. Oh, I heard Mrs Fisk-Castelman is in Paris – your fellow American, the one who almost reduced poor Javier to tears? Find her and bring her too.'

'You're mad. How will you pull it off?'

Alix recalled a foggy walk over the Seine with Verrian the morning after they'd first made love. 'Friends. You only need one or two good ones.'

Alix leaned down. 'You will say, in Spanish, "Good evening, Monsieur." You will hand him the invitation and that is all.'

Having given this instruction to a solemn Pepe, she turned to the employee behind the desk. 'Did you get a reply?'

'Yes, Madame. The gentleman will see you, if you would kindly take the lift to the second floor. Suite number six.'

There were mirrors in the lift and Alix turned her back. She regretted wearing her grey-green suit, wished she'd gone for something safer. In the corridor she counted the doors, took a gulp and knocked. She was pushing courtesy to its limit, calling on a Sunday afternoon when most people might expect to be left in peace.

'Alix, your hand is shaking,' Pepe said.

'I know.' Footsteps, a slight cough. She gripped Pepe's small hand harder and his dark gaze rose reproachfully. Then the door opened.

Javier regarded her without emotion.

'Monsieur, I hope you don't mind . . .' Her throat dried. This was a study in pointless humiliation. Why hadn't she listened to Una?

'They telephoned from downstairs to say a pretty, dark-haired woman was on her way up with a child. I did not imagine it was you. This is your son, Alix?'

'Oh, no, a friend's . . . Pepe, give the gentleman the card.'

Pepe thrust a printed invitation towards Javier and said in Spanish, 'Señor, will you please come to Alix's show and see her dresses and my paintings?'

Javier thanked him gravely and studied the invitation. He

stayed silent so long Alix's awkwardness bubbled out – 'I mean to go ahead with it. I don't know if anyone will come. I've been ambushed, you see. I mean, blacklisted.'

Javier narrowed his eyes. 'Nobody will come, you say? You are asking me to be the only person sitting on the golden chairs? Then the world will say, "Ah, poor Javier has dropped so far, he can assure himself of empty seats wherever he goes."'

She blushed. 'Forgive me. I hoped you might like to see what I can do, and this show is my last hope. If I fail—'

'You will owe a great deal of money, no doubt.'

'This will have won.' She gave him Rhona de Charembourg's letter, and before he could speak, took Pepe's hand and walked away.

As they crossed Parc Monceau, Pepe remarked, 'I think the man was very pleased to be asked to see my pictures.'

She waited all the rest of Sunday for a call from Javier. By midnight she was tearful but resigned. It had been a wild dream, the notion of Javier riding to her rescue. Actually it had been a brazen impudence, asking a man of his standing to associate himself with her at all. Locking up her premises, she took a taxi to the Polonaise, where she and Verrian stayed most nights. Alix had only a single bed at Rue Jacob, and with Mémé and Celestia also in the flat, it was not a place for lovers. Verrian was awake in the Apricot Suite, reading. He threw his book down. 'Well?'

'Not a word. I didn't expect anything else.' She got ready

for bed. 'I'm going to have to make the toughest decision of my life.'

'Well, don't make it now.' Verrian pulled down the covers for her. 'Get in here with me.'

She prepared her speech the following morning in the taxi back to Rue Jacob and delivered it to her staff at nine sharp. 'And so, while I am eternally grateful for your work and support and believe this collection to be the best we've produced –' she swallowed the pebble in her throat and checked Verrian's expression. He stood at the rear, giving nothing away '– I could not let today unfold without telling you—' there came the ring of a bell from downstairs. Verrian went to answer it. '—telling you that I have decided—'

'You're not throwing in the towel?' An aggrieved Rosa overpowered Alix's explanations. 'I haven't come back to work to get the boot on day one, surely?'

Alix closed her eyes. This was hard. She didn't need hecklers. 'With enormous regret I will be closing –' She stopped, hearing Verrian's voice in the corridor –

'Keep going, Monsieur, Madame. You'll find everybody in one place.'

Alix stood on tiptoe to see over the heads of her women. She couldn't see who Verrian had brought in, just that it was a man with dark, oiled hair and a woman in a red hat. Her staff turned, parting down the middle and she saw –

'M. Javier!' She stepped forward, then gasped as she recognised the lady in the hat. 'Mme Frankel. You? Here?'

A gabble of excitement drowned their replies. Mme LeVert looked as if she might curtsy. Alix caught Verrian's eye and detected a ghost of a smile.

Javier looked around, nodding in greeting. 'Mesdames, I believe a very great injustice has been perpetrated against this house. I am here, and my former première is here, to reverse that wrong.'

'You're going to help?' Alix stammered in disbelief.

'I offer my talent and influence, Alix, if you wish it.'

She threw her arms around him. 'Oh, yes, please!'

A little later they convened a meeting of four. Alix said, 'It may be too late. That horrible letter has done so much damage.'

Javier closed an eye. 'If a letter can do damage, cannot also a letter do good? We will write one to send to every newspaper for publication tomorrow morning. Can you do that?'

'Leave it to me,' Verrian answered. 'You write it, I'll have it typed and delivered in time for today's deadline.'

Javier gave his elegant bow. 'Good. So, unveil your collection, Alix. I hope it justifies my faith.'

Dear God, she hoped so too. Shaking with nerves, she drew back the covers on the rails and was gratified, not by whoops of delight, but by intense scrutiny. Javier and Mme Frankel looked. Touched. Consulted. Nodded. They admired her suits; Alix had kept her to her signature shape but had opted for vibrant colours – scarlet, sunflower, swimming-pool blue. They would be worn with blouses, hats and shoes that matched each suit precisely. 'You have borrowed from that great couturier M. Worth,' Javier said. 'When he dressed ladies in one colour top to toe, Paris woke up.' He looked at her rail of evening gowns and chuckled. 'The audacity to print your own cloth – such spirit, *petite*.'

Afterwards he said, 'Do you know what inspired me to come here?'

'That hateful letter?'

'Inspired, *petite*. Malice does not inspire, it merely disgusts. Yesterday, when you turned away from my door, I had a moment in which to inspect the back of your suit.' He described it to Mme Frankel – 'A pleat to the centre of the jacket, a "pinch" belt, just so. Two darts in the shoulder seams, perfect sunrays. Many couturiers care only for the front. To care for the back shows the illogical passion that is the stamp of the artist.'

Verrian, who had listened tolerantly so far, interjected. 'Alix, you haven't mentioned your biggest problem. No girls.'

'The mannequins cried off,' she explained. 'I have the collection, but nobody to wear it.'

She had a moment to wonder at Javier's inscrutable smile when she heard a door crashing open and a youthful voice crying, 'Where is everybody? Is this the right place?'

Then another; 'I've been here before. They'll be in the salon.'

Verrian left and came back with an eye-catching haul. Expectant faces beneath a cluster of stylish hats – Heloïse, Zinaida, Claudette, Nelly, Marie-Josèphe and Arlette.

Javier clapped his hands. 'We have brought these ladies from their beds before noon, so let us see who can wear what.'

28th February 1939

> *We the undersigned pledge our allegiance to excellence in Parisian couture, but understand that for this industry to flourish, 'the new' must be allowed to breathe. For this reason, we will be attending the collection to be shown by Modes Lutzman at the Hôtel Polonaise on 1st March at six in the evening.*

This letter, prominent in *Le Figaro* and other daily papers, was undersigned by Javier and Mme Frankel. Other names too. Over the years, Pauline Frankel had advised some of the most powerful females in France how to dress for public display and she had gone above and beyond for Alix, spending much of the previous afternoon in the 16th arrondissment knocking at glossy doors, discreetly requesting a return of favour.

Afterwards she showed Alix the letter, saying, 'Nine

signatures, but ten would be perfect. Do you know anybody of rank who would be prepared to support you?'

Alix was answering 'No' when it dawned on her that she did.

1ˢᵗ March

In four hours these chairs would fill, or not. By the end of the day her future would be decided.

The mannequins were dressing in a makeshift *cabine* created from cloth-draped rails. Rosa was in charge, assisted by Marguerite and Pauline Frankel. Rosa had expelled Alix, telling her, 'Your nerves are as useful here as an elephant in a lifeboat. Go and get a cup of tea.'

Alix didn't know where to take herself. The last three days had merged into formless hours with minimal sleep. She, Pauline Frankel and her staff had remade every garment to fit the new mannequins, a task that had seemed unachievable. They had done it, though, with only one casualty – a mutiny among the exhausted sewing girls had broken the limits of Mme LeVert's authority and she had walked out. Pauline Frankel stepped into the breach, and from that moment Alix knew they would have a collection.

Javier came to stand by Alix as the mannequins began their rehearsal. 'How have you done this?' he asked, as those risqué beach pyjamas sashayed past him. 'Your textiles are a fairy tale born from the madness of an opium den.'

She told him about the day her muse came back. 'Jewel colours on snow. Children laughing. Three little children were invited to paint whatever they wished on a canvas the size of a wall. Every colour at their disposal, no adults to impose their will.'

'You have fixed the dyes, Alix? Else they will run.'

She laughed. 'We steamed every length, Monsieur. In my flat. It was like living in a laundry.'

Pauline Frankel heard the tail end and said, 'How on earth will you meet all your orders, Alix? You can't possibly hand-paint for every client.'

She'd prepared for that, telling them proudly, 'There's an orphanage behind St-Médard and the children there will paint for me. I have technicians to transfer the designs onto silk and the older children will infill by hand. I'm paying them of course.' She enjoyed the look Javier and his première exchanged.

'So every piece will be unique. Clever Alix, but not so clever Alix.' Javier shook his head. 'Your little orphans will delight in their work, but will not meet demand. Believe me, you will have to bring in professionals. Whatever you intend to charge for each dress, you must double it.'

Double it. She'd give the figures to Pusey who would rub his hands and say, 'Most gratifying.'

Three hours to go. A vast bouquet of peonies arrived with a note: 'Everything's crossed, kiddo. I'll take the ball dress in bordello pink with the suggestive orchids.' An identical bouquet was handed to Javier: 'New York loves Monsieur J. If ever you need a fast boat out, call me'

'Never will I trust Mme Kilpin.' Javier dropped the card.

'You don't have to.' Alix picked it up and put it in his pocket. 'But she has a good side, and you must never close off an escape route. And you wouldn't be the first of my friends to go.'

Alix was thinking of Marcy Stein. After their brief meeting in Rue St-Denis, Marcy had written to Alix to say that she and her family were leaving France for a new life in America. No chance of a last meeting as the letter had been posted just hours before her departure. Alix remembered Verrian saying something about war erasing friendship. In this case, the fear of war had been enough. *Would Marcy pine for her beloved Paris,* Alix wondered? No time to ponder, because the show flowers arrived just then. Fragrant lilies and gardenias. She'd chosen white to let her collection shine.

Two hours. The band arrived and tuned up noisily, then ran through the numbers Alix had specified. The mannequins walked out to each tune and Alix noticed how they responded to the music. How the bandsmen responded to them.

One hour. Celestia arrived with the children, dressed in their best. Pepe's hair was oiled, Lala and Suzy's plaits were so tight they squeaked. Alix allotted them seats and then said, 'You won't be able to sit still until it starts. Go and draw at one of the tables.'

Twenty minutes. Verrian arrived, looking, to her eyes, utterly gorgeous in a black tuxedo, bow tie and stiff-fronted dress shirt. She walked into his arms.

He yelped. 'Needles in your jacket! It's like hugging a pin-cushion. Get behind those curtains and turn into a mannequin.'

She dashed away and was told off by Rosa for running.

Noise was building. People were coming. When Verrian pushed a note through the curtains that said, 'Sixty-four and counting,' she let out a breath. She was not to endure the night-mare of empty chairs. The band began to play the sort of music that wafts people to their seats without disrupting the ambience. Another note was handed to her –

'The mouse is arrived. J.' Before Alix could puzzle this out, yet another note came from Verrian. 'The red-faced man in the back row is my father. The lady fanning him with her pro-gramme will be my mother. That dress with the red and pink roses, will you marry me in it? *Je t'aime.*'

'First girls, make ready!' ordered Rosa. 'Alix, you're shaking like a jellied eel on a tractor.'

The band struck up the opening music – 'Let's Call the Whole Thing Off' – and the first four girls swung out between the curtains. Alix heard a sort of snake-hiss and thought, *People hate it.*

Rosa nudged her. 'They just got the joke. "Let's Call the

Whole Thing Off"'? Like you nearly did . . . Isn't that why you chose it?'

'I chose "A-Tisket, A-Tasket",' Alix said, bewildered. 'Wait a minute, I saw Una talking to the bandleader. That woman – always gets the last word.'

Then it was her turn to step out, and all she could see was blur. She felt the heat of the room, the eyes upon her. Programmes tilting as people checked the model number. Saw Celestia, Pepe, Lala and Suzy waving to her. Mémé, in a cyclamen dress and a new hat. Behind them, the Comte de Charembourg. She hadn't seen him in person since the day of Bonnet's confession. Hadn't wanted to . . . but his smile was so tender she returned it, picked up her stride and carried on. Now she understood Javier's note. Mousy Christine de Brioude sat next to her father. They'd both signed the letter supporting her. She thought, *If Christine will let us, Javier and I will make her the most stylish woman in Paris*.

Javier and I? There he was, her dear, forgiving maestro, near the back. He gave her a quiet nod. Good God, was the scowling man a few seats along Verrian's father? The woman beside him had to be Verrian's mother. There was Gladys Fisk-Castelman taking notes, and beside her, Una Kilpin. Beside Una, the reverse of a ray of sunshine, Mr Kilpin. Ah well. Some people had to stay the same. Verrian . . . where was Verrian? She saw him on her walk back, standing beside a window. They locked eyes.

Back in the *cabine*, Violette – promoted today from

receptionist to dresser – pulled her to a gap in the curtain. 'Look, a gatecrasher.'

Alix saw a girl standing behind the last row of chairs, making marks in a notebook wedged between her thigh and the seat in front.

Alix said to Violette, 'As my first pirate, she can stay and have champagne, but take every piece of paper off her, even her bus ticket.'

Rosa tapped Alix. 'I need you.'

Just time to shake talcum powder under her arms and climb into her next model. This time, she felt more relaxed. Relaxed enough to be sorry that Paul hadn't made it. By the time she'd made four appearances, she knew for sure he wasn't there.

She stepped into a ball gown painted with vast pink and red flowers. The band was playing 'There May Be Trouble Ahead'. As she and the other mannequins came out in a thunderclap of billowing silk, applause erupted and people stood. It was in that moment of stunned disbelief that Alix saw Verrian open a window to let a young man scramble inside. A man with red-gold hair. Paul – in naval uniform. The band swung into a fast foxtrot, and Heloïse, Javier's Titian-haired mannequin, shouted to the newcomer, 'Hello, *Royale*. Come and dance with me again!'

Paul had no objection and suddenly all the girls wanted partners. There were plenty of men to oblige. Only Alix refused, until she felt strong arms come around her, smelled the beguiling invitation of bergamot and plain soap. She sighed, 'I think it's all right.'

'Very all right. Are you going to marry me?'

'Of course. Will you tell your parents?'

'Not now. Lord Calford's never at his best in a crowd.'

'Will he like me?'

'No questions – I might step on your hem.' Verrian said no more while the music played fast. But when a saxophonist improvised a drowsy solo riff, he murmured, 'I swear, Alix, nothing will take me from you but war or death.'

Alix swept her peony-pink skirt over her arm and pressed close to her love, her eyes closed. The saxophonist played 'My Blue Heaven'. Their song, their universe.

Acknowledgements

I would like to thank the following people whose input and support have made the publication of *The Dress Thief* not only possible, but huge fun. Firstly, my agent Laura Longrigg whose creative advice and faith in my writing provided the rocket fuel to get this book into shape. Then there is my editor at Quercus, Kathryn Taussig, whose skill and enthusiasm has brought this novel into being. Thank you Jenny Richards for conceiving the beautiful cover artwork and Talya Baker for her copyediting. I'd also like to thank Brigid Irwin for her early proofing of the manuscript, novelist Helen Carey for her unwavering support over the years, Mel Hayman-Brown, Emma Cameron and my sister Anna McKay for supplying encouragement and for reading early drafts with inspired insight. Thanks to my husband Richard who has not only put up with me longer than is reasonable, but who, with his pilot's hat on, helped my research into aviation. Thanks also to Jeremy Blackham for his advice on navy affairs and who, with Candy Blackham, visited the magnificent interior of St-Sulpice and stood in as my 'eyes' on that occasion. In time-honoured vein I state here that any factual mistakes in the retelling are my own. Appreciation is due to my mother who planted the writing seed and took me on my first trip to Paris; and my son, Sam Evans, who dealt with his writer-mother with patience and good humour. I must acknowledge Eileen Kitchen, doyenne of the London garment industry, whose experience of getting shut into her workroom at night inspired a scene in this book. And Chrissie Kitchen deserves mention for being a fabulous friend, cheering me on and always being up for a glass of sauvignon blanc. And finally . . . this book could not have existed without Paris, the city I fell in love with when I was too young to know what I was getting into.

Natalie Meg Evans
Suffolk, 2014

Author's Note

The Dress Thief makes reference to many couturiers, shops, people and events, and it may help to know which existed – indeed, still exist – and which are my inventions.

Of the couturiers mentioned . . . Chanel, Lanvin, Vionnet, Lucien Lelong, Patou, Poiret, Worth, Schiaparelli and Molyneux are real. Hermès, which features in the early pages, is of course real too, and in 1937 launched the printed silk squares so famously associated with them. Jeanne Lanvin was famous for her perfume, Arpège, whose bottle features a design of herself and her little daughter Marguerite holding hands. She also created 'Lanvin blue', which Jean-Yves de Charembourg considers to be the only blue that blends perfectly with yellow. That is strictly his own opinion but he will happily defend it over a glass of chilled Alsace Riesling. Lanvin blue is described as a lavender shade, but in my view it is closer to the petals of a periwinkle flower. M. Javier, who as a couturier is entirely my own invention, agrees with me as he does in most things.

Mabel Godnosc is also a figment of mine, but there were numerous Mabels in Paris at the time the book is set, in London and in New York, shamelessly copying and reproducing haute couture for the masses – entirely in the service of democracy. Modes Lutzman is Alix's invention and, as Alix is my invention, you will not find it however many times you walk up and down Rue Jacob.

The Deux Magots on Boulevard Saint-Germain is real. I have drunk coffee and written a few paragraphs there, as every novelist should. The carved Chinese wise men gazing down from their high perch alone make a visit worthwhile, though the traffic outside is more intrusive than it would have been for Alix and Verrian. Arantxa's restaurant is invented, but based on a real one near the Sorbonne, whose steaks I will never forget even if I can't recall the exact location. The Rose Noire is fictitious, but Bricktop existed in Rue Pigalle, its proprietess Ada 'Bricktop' Smith being an American hot jazz legend and friend of Cole Porter. She kept her venue open throughout the thirties, closing only with the outbreak of war.

Verrian Haviland's employer the *News Monitor* is invented and I borrowed the title from the long-gone *Loughborough Monitor*. Zollinger's, the Swiss chocolatiers that Alix visits on Rue du Faubourg St-Honoré, is an invention, which is a shame as – had they been real – I'm sure they would have sent me a box of hand-wrapped chocolates every Christmas. Lindt and Suchard *are* real, however, and make lovely chocolate (*Well, you gotta try, petal*, as Mabel Godnosc would say!). Speaking of whom, Mabel's bible, the *New York Fashion Daily*, is emphatically not real. Do you think I'm going to accuse a real newspaper of running counterfeit frocks?

All my named Parisian locations are factual with the exception of Boulevard Racan, where the comte de Charembourg resides. I named his street after Seigneur de Racan – an aristocrat, poet and dramatist – who was, most fittingly, disappointed in love and often financially embarrassed. In one of those moments of strange serendipity, I was in the 16th arrondissement, researching locations, when I glanced up at a street sign and discovered I'd wandered into Square Racan. Kirchwiller in Alsace does not exist, but do go to Alsace if you can – drink its wine and visit its medieval towns. I recommend October when the leaves have turned gold. Mesmerising.

Alix lived in Wandsworth in south London before going to Paris, and Wandsworth is every bit as solid as you might wish. Charlotte Road, Alix's drab street, does not exist. Had it done so, it would now be expensively gentrified and a nightmare for parking. Arding & Hobbs department store, where Alix had her first job, is still going strong as part of the Debenhams chain. Grindle & Whiteleather, Lucy Haviland's clothes store of choice, has no existence outside my imagination and, had it existed, would have gone out of business in the 1960s as Mrs Whiteleather would have vetoed short skirts and Mr Grindle would have refused entry to any gentleman not wearing a tie. Heronhurst, home to the Havilands, is offered up as a vocal exercise and tongue-twister, but can't be found on any map of West Sussex.

The town of Durango in the Basque region of Spain was bombed by German and Italian warplanes on 31 March

1937, entering history as the first undefended civilian settlement to suffer aerial attack. The more famous Guernica was bombed by the German Condor Legion and Italian war planes on 26 April 1937. Though these attacks, and the devastating firestorms they caused, caused international shock and revulsion, it is well to remember that Madrid had experienced repeated bombing over many months without other nations doing much to intervene. The Spanish Civil War is often described as the seedbed of aerial conflict, the grim 'practice run' for the slaughter and destruction of the years following. The report on the Guernica bombing, part of which I selectively quote in the novel, appeared in *The Times* newspaper on 27 April 1937 having been cabled to London from Bilbao by the correspondent George Steer.

Pablo Picasso first showed 'Guernica' at the Paris Exposition *Internationale des Arts et Techniques dans la Vie Moderne*, which features in *The Dress Thief*. Having been commissioned to paint a mural for the Spanish pavilion at the Expo, he added this now-iconic panel in response to the bombing of Guernica, doing much to raise awareness of the atrocity. The painting is now on permanent display in Madrid.

ALIX'S SCRAPBOOK

Ah . . . the cloche hat!

One of those images that sum up an age in a single stroke. Cloches had been lurking at the back of every milliner's shop forever. Country girls liked them in fine straw because they could be pulled down to protect the face and ears from the sun. Fastened with a ribbon, they withstood the briskest wind. In the twenties they came of age, complementing the new proportions of fashion for short skirts and dropped waists. They fitted snugly over shingled hair and were tight enough not to fly off in an open-top car. They masked the eyes while making the most of bow lips, pixie jaws and swan necks. The cloche finished the brand new look, the age of the boy-woman. In the 1930s, brims came back. Hair was a little fuller, but hats needed a brim to balance the widening line of the shoulder.

5 lengths of tulle
Lace
Silk – green or blue?

Coco Chanel was raised in a convent, where she first learned to sew. Her first career was as a singer in a music hall cafe in Moulins, Paris. This is where she picked up her nickname 'Coco'.

The 1920s chemise style, which evolved into the straight, body-skimming styles of the 1930s, came principally from the sketchbooks of Madeleine Vionnet and Coco Chanel. What French designer Paul Poiret began at the dawn of the twentieth century by releasing women from corsets and trip-me-up skirts, Chanel and Vionnet continued and refined.

Linen

Needles — what size?

Tartan wool

Lanvin's signature colour 'lanvin blue' is said to be inspired by her visit to Florence, where she first saw the deep blues in the work of Fra Angelico.

The dancer Caryathis started the trend for short bobs and Eton crops, so it seems . . .

Distressed by a lover's rejection, she scissored off her long skein of hair, tied a ribbon round it and draped it over the faithless one's doorknob. That's a gesture you can only make once. Legend has it she hurried off to an evening party, with no time to cover her head with a turban, entered the room – to gasps of shock – and the rest is history.

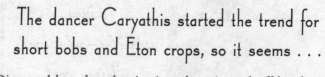

Pour une soupe à l'oignon parfaite, toujours utiliser des oignons blancs – ils ont un goût plus relevé

Soupe à l'oignon
de
Natalie Meg Evans

My favourite recipe for onion soup has a roux base. It starts much like a caramelised onion sauce, but the end result is a creamy soup that works well as an evening meal if you serve it with plenty of Gruyère toast and maybe a side salad. I was always taught to use the mild white onions for this because they have a more delicate flavour. However, when testing this recipe I used the basic ones that come out of Lincolnshire fields and have a coarse, yellowish skin. They were fine. Not sure about red onions, however. Would they make pink soup?

For a generous pan-full, serving 4 people, you'll need:

2oz (50g) butter

1lb (half a kilo) of onions

2 pints (1.2 litres) of bouillon or good stock – chicken, beef, vegetarian . . . whatever you prefer. This soup derives its punch from the stock, so use the one you like the most

1 oz (25 g) plain flour – white or wholemeal

A bay leaf and a stalk of celery

Salt and pepper

A glass of dry white wine

For the Gruyère toast:

1 French baguette loaf
4oz (100g) Gruyère cheese, grated (Cheddar is fine if you can't get Gruyère)
Plan for two slices of toast per person, more if you like
Paprika for sprinkling

First, melt the butter in a large pan over a gentle heat. Careful not to let it burn.

Peel and finely slice the onions, add to the melted butter and sweat them. Check your heat and keep them moving. Cook till *golden and almost caramelised.*

Add the flour and cook it with the buttery onions, stirring until it smells lightly toasted. Now take the pan from the heat, pour in the stock and beat continuously so that it thickens without lumps. A *birch whisk* is ideal for this but my Labrador ate mine, so I just beat it with a wooden spoon. (The soup, I hasten to add, not the dog.)

Return the pan to the heat, turning up the temperature till the onions are simmering in the stock. Adjust the heat. Your soup should be quite *thick and creamy,* but if you boil it too violently, it will stick to the bottom of the pan.

Tip in the white wine, the bay leaf and the celery stalk. Add salt if you need it – but take care if using shop-bought stock because this can be *very salty*. Hold off with the pepper for now.

At a gentle simmer, the soup will be ready in twenty minutes or so, but it's better if you can *slow cook* it for an hour or more.

Start making the toast twenty minutes or so before you want to eat. Get the grill up to a moderate heat. Slice your French bread diagonally into inch-thick (2.5cm) pieces.

You are aiming to toast the bread slowly so that it is *golden brown* and quite dry. Keep an eye on it and turn it.

When the toast is done, turn up the grill. Sprinkle on the grated cheese. Put under the grill and pull them out as the cheese starts to bubble. Shake on a *bit of paprika*.

Taste your soup for seasoning. Remove the bay leaf and celery stalk. *Add your pepper.*

To serve, warm your soup bowls, ladle in the soup and float the cheese toasts on top.

Bon appétit!

Maison Javier

Parc Mo[...]

Les Champ[...]

Bois de Boulogne

Rue de la Trémoille

River Seine

Brd Racan

Alix's
highly
unreliable
map of
Paris

Left bank

Ja[...]

Right bank – Rive droite

Butte

de Montmartre

Bvd Clichy

...ourg St-Honoré

La Rose Noire

Ile St-Louis

Quai d'Anjou

Rue Jacob

Deux Magots

Pont Marie

St-Germain

St Sulpice

Modes Lutzman

Luxembourg

KATRIN

Copyright ©Natalie Meg Evans 2014

Fashion and Femininity in the Thirties

~

Natalie Meg Evans

One of the unexpected side-effects of world war is that it expands opportunities for women. Those inter-war years in Europe and America were often more 'interesting' than comfortable, but they widened female horizons in ways unimaginable to a secure, pre-1914 generation. I think of the English Edwardian age and the French *Belle Epoque* as lush, domestic eras, where feminine culture and manners prevailed, when women were cosseted and corseted. I characterise the 1930s as the hard-nosed 'manly decade' that succeeded the 'boys' own' decade of the 1920s. All highly subjective thinking, I admit, but here are images that spring to mind when I contemplate those inter-war years . . .

Art Deco is the cover-all term for 1930s style, with its cool, unemotional lines. Bold, new industry reflecting a world where machines were to be mankind's saviour. Architects responding with flat-topped, curve- cornered shapes in everything from factories, railway stations and homes to those temples of popular culture – cinemas. Bright, white rendering promising clean, efficient living and wrap-around metal windows gazing inscrutably at a world that is far more chaotic than the inside space.

Painting becomes increasingly abstract: its lines distorted and its forms deconstructed. In art, the principles of machinery are applied to nature, with hardoutlines and geometric shapes predominating. Motor vehicles forget that they evolved from horse-drawn coaches and follow the trend, becoming long and sleek. Furniture joins in, losing its fuss and grandiosity. Fashion is not far behind.

If the thirties were a masculine era, the 1920s scream 'boy' to me. For the first time in recorded history, women leave home with the backs of their necks bare; not because they've rolled their luxuriant locks up in a bun, but because they've left those coils of hair on the hairdresser's floor. This new, elfin look syncs perfectly with post-war reality. Millions of young men have died . . . who wants to be reminded of those golden days of tight waists, indigestion and heavy hair? A legion of serious young women are stepping forward to fill the void left by their dead brothers. The twenties is the era of the working woman, the dawn of the motor age, of bicycles and cheap transport. Cage doors fly open. Hems rise and short hair is jammed under a neat, cloche hat.

America sends jazz to Europe to whip the new freedom into a froth. Dancing becomes intimate and very physical, kicking the waltz rhythm out of the door. I'm sure the time-honoured job of chaperone disappears at this point. How can you keep an eye on your innocent young charge when she's bunny-hopping from one side of the room to the other? Or when the young man holding her so indecently doesn't give a damn for convention, because he's already seen the worst things that life can throw at him?

No doubt many a parent, governess, vicar and politician tried to slam the cage door shut again in the twenties, but the bird had already flown . . . in her mind at least. History shows us that you can change laws but rarely can you change thoughts. Did women embrace the boyish styles of the 1920s because, after four years' indiscriminate slaughter of young men, they secretly rejected motherhood? Or were they kicking off the trappings of fragile femininity that the men had gone to war to protect? Or because they wanted to replace their brothers? Or because they *had* to replace their brothers? What we do know is that there were not enough men to go around any more, and many women lived out their lives as unwilling spinsters. Others discovered the freedom of careers and independent earnings. If fashion seeps from the subconscious . . . what was the female subconscious saying at this point?

On to the 1930s: the decade of *The Dress Thief*, when the boys grew up. The economic crash of 1929 marred the fun anyway, arguably producing the conditions that led to the next war. Fashion reacted.

Hemlines dropped by 1930, as they seem to do in financially stringent times. The waist, one of the markers of female sexual maturity and fertility, returned to its natural level – though on the whole, it wasn't particularly defined. That had to wait for the belt-tightening forties. The thirties silhouette is spare, slender and tall.

Having said that, after studying hundreds of photographs and illustrations of dresses, suits and coats, the 1930s seems to defy stereotype. Just as you tell yourself that skirts are all straight and narrow, you find some that aren't. Just as you decide that the defined waist was shunned, you find a dress with an inset panel showing off a woman's middle with anatomical accuracy. Some of Madeleine Vionnet's evening gowns of the late 1930s have hand-span waists and big, Cinderella skirts. Chanel's farewell collection of 1939 featured red, white and blue gypsy dresses with an hour-glass middle. I have a picture of a 1938 Callot Soeurs dress that is as nipped in as anything that appeared ten years later. But the prevailing mood was not for fairy tale romance, it was for stylish sobriety by day, slinky sexuality by night.

I will say this with conviction, however: shoulders are key in the thirties, whether puffed or padded for daywear or exposed in the evening. They are defined and wider than the hip. Bared shoulders are satin smooth, sexy and strong. Maybe, strung between wars, dealing with economic collapse, women needed a strong pair of shoulders.

So, at the tail-end of the 1930s, Alix builds a business in the most exacting of industries in the least forgiving of cities. She knows it can be done. The boulevards of Paris are dotted with elegant outlets owned and run by women. She has no lack of drive and skill, her experience grows with each season but she knows that funding will be a continued struggle. Couture gowns carry a hefty price tag, then as now, but customers expect credit and are often slow to pay. Borrowing from banks, even having a bank account, is not seen as a natural right for females. Without family money, acquiring capital is almost impossible.

Coco Chanel in 1909 had a wealthy lover to provide the initial funding for workrooms and shop premises. Nothing can take away from Chanel's triumph, rising as she did from peasant poverty to become one of the most successful female self-starters of all time. But that early support allowed her to scale up pretty quickly. For other female couturiers, the only option was to start small, work hard, and capture the imagination of the fashionable elite. Jeanne Lanvin, who struck out at the age of eighteen as a milliner, had only her small savings, the backing of one client, and three hundred francs' worth of credit with suppliers. By 1918, she occupied a whole building in Rue du Faubourg St-Honoré producing the gamut of couture clothes, accessories, lingerie and perfume. After a disappointing start at the couture house Doucet in 1907, Madeleine Vionnet went solo. She began with a modest initial investment. By 1910, she had premises on Rue de Rivoli.

The couture business was – and no doubt still is – money hungry. Every garment that ends up pressed and hung on a rail is the fruit of hours of labour. Of designing and trialling, fitting and finishing. Before the machine age, that pretty much meant hand-sewing, hand embroidering, hand beadwork, hand button-holing etc . . . and all this skilled manual labour was expensive. Individual seamstresses were paid very poorly, but a couture house needed a great many of them. Hundreds, in the case of the bigger houses.

Alix's backer advanced her enough to start up, but survival took tenacity and luck and a loyal workforce willing to work long, weary hours to sustain the dream. What Chanel, Lanvin and Vionnet and most female couturiers had in common, apart from their creative genius and drive, were traditional dressmaking skills. All were taught the fine art of sewing from a young age: Chanel in a convent school, Lanvin with the milliner Madame Felix and Vionnet at Callot Soeurs, a leading Parisian couture house. They knew cloth, they knew how to cut it and put it together. Their designs flowed from technique.

They also shared a devotion to detail and to their art. Paris in the early to mid twentieth century was full of neat-fingered girls who could sew invisible seams. Only a few became queens of their trade. Fashion was a low-paid ghetto for women who, if they didn't have education, family money or qualifications, were starved of choice. For all that, it was one of the few industries where a woman could truly rise on merit and dictate her own terms, and where great wealth was possible. There were sacrifices to be made, of course. It's no coincidence that the leading female couturieres all had a reputation for being remote, even lonely, women who operated strict discipline towards their business, employees and themselves.

From the creator of *The Dress Thief*,
this is wartime Paris like you've never
seen it before . . .

The Milliner's Secret

NATALIE MEG EVANS

. . . a glittering playground of secrets and sin,
where a woman's fate is decided by the
quickness of her wits and the
flexibility of her morals

Spring 2015